THE INSIDE OF THE CUP

27162/29

D0124893

BY

WINSTON CHURCHILL

AUTHOR OF "RICHARD CARVEL," "THE CRISIS,"
"A MODERN CHRONICLE," ETC., ETC.

WITH ILLUSTRATIONS BY HOWARD GILES

(91)

24437

New York
THE MACMILLAN COMPANY
1913

All rights reserved

Copyright, 1912 and 1913,

By HEARST'S MAGAZINE.

Copyright, 1913,

By THE MACMILLAN COMPANY.

———

Set up and electrotyped. Published May, 1913. Reprinted
July, twice, August, three times, September, October, twice,
November, 1913.

PS
1297
I5
1913

Norwood Press
J. S. Cushing Co. — Berwick & Smith Co.
Norwood, Mass., U.S.A.

TABLE OF CONTENTS

CHAPTER | | PAGE

I. THE WARING PROBLEMS 1

II. MR. LANGMAID'S MISSION 15

III. THE PRIMROSE PATH 31

IV. SOME RIDDLES OF THE TWENTIETH CENTURY . 44

V. THE RECTOR HAS MORE FOOD FOR THOUGHT . 57

VI. "WATCHMAN, WHAT OF THE NIGHT?" . . . 80

VII. THE KINGDOMS OF THE WORLD 91

VIII. THE LINE OF LEAST RESISTANCE . . . 103

IX. THE DIVINE DISCONTENT 116

X. THE MESSENGER IN THE CHURCH . . . 136

XI. THE LOST PARISHIONER 157

XII. THE WOMAN OF THE SONG 172

XIII. WINTERBOURNE 184

XIV. A SATURDAY AFTERNOON 198

XV. THE CRUCIBLE 212

XVI. AMID THE ENCIRCLING GLOOM . . . 228

XVII. RECONSTRUCTION 250

XVIII. THE RIDDLE OF CAUSATION 265

XIX. MR. GOODRICH BECOMES A PARTISAN . . 295

XX. THE ARRAIGNMENT 320

XXI. ALISON GOES TO CHURCH 348

XXII. "WHICH SAY TO THE SEERS, SEE NOT!" . . 372

TABLE OF CONTENTS

CHAPTER		PAGE
XXIII.	THE CHOICE	394
XXIV.	THE VESTRY MEETS	411
XXV.	"RISE, CROWNED WITH LIGHT!"	427
XXVI.	THE CURRENT OF LIFE	442
XXVII.	RETRIBUTION	466
XXVIII.	LIGHT	486

LIST OF ILLUSTRATIONS

" 'CAN'T YOU *FEEL* THAT YOU ARE AN INDIVIDUAL, A PER-
SONALITY, A FORCE THAT MIGHT BE PUT TO GREAT
USES?' " . . . . *Frontispiece*

FACING PAGE

" THE TWO SAT GAZING AT EACH OTHER AS FROM MOUNTAIN
PEAKS ACROSS IMPASSABLE VALLEYS " 82

" 'MY GOD, HOW YOU SCARED ME!' " 176

" 'I GUESS I AIN'T HUNGRY AFTER ALL' " 238

" 'YOU'LL WANT MONEY FOR THESE PEOPLE, I SUPPOSE,' HE
ADDED BRUTALLY " 346

" 'WHAT'S YOUR NAME?' SHE ASKED " 350

THE INSIDE OF THE CUP

CHAPTER I

THE WARING PROBLEMS

I

WITH few exceptions, the incidents recorded in these pages take place in one of the largest cities of the United States of America, and of that portion called the Middle West, — a city once conservative and provincial, and rather proud of these qualities; but now outgrown them, and linked by lightning limited trains to other teeming centers of the modern world: a city overtaken, in recent years, by the plague which has swept our country from the Atlantic to the Pacific — Prosperity. Before its advent, the Goodriches and Gores, the Warings, the Prestons and the Atterburys lived leisurely lives in a sleepy quarter of shade trees and spacious yards and muddy macadam streets, now passed away forever. Existence was decorous, marriage an irrevocable step, wives were wives, and the Authorized Version of the Bible was true from cover to cover. So Dr. Gilman preached, and so they believed.

Sunday was then a day essentially different from other days — you could tell it without looking at the calendar. The sun knew it, and changed the quality of his light: the very animals, dogs and cats and horses, knew it: and most of all the children knew it, by Sunday school, by Dr. Gilman's sermon, by a dizzy afternoon connected in some of their minds with ceramics and a lack of exercise,

B   1

by a cold tea, and by church bells. You were not allowed to forget it for one instant. The city suddenly became full of churches, as though they had magically been let down from heaven during Saturday night. They must have been there on week days, but few persons ever thought of them.

Among the many church bells that rang on those bygone Sundays was that of St. John's, of which Dr. Gilman, of beloved memory, was rector. Dr. Gilman was a saint, and if you had had the good luck to be baptized or confirmed or married or buried by him, you were probably fortunate in an earthly as well as heavenly sense. One has to be careful not to deal exclusively in superlatives, and yet it is not an exaggeration to say that St. John's was the most beautiful and churchly edifice in the city, thanks chiefly to several gentlemen of sense, and one gentleman, at least, of taste — Mr. Horace Bentley. The vicissitudes of civil war interrupted its building; but when, in 1868, it stood completed, its stone unsoiled as yet by factory smoke, its spire delicately pointing to untainted skies, its rose window glowing above the porch, citizens on Tower Street often stopped to gaze at it diagonally across the vacant lot set in order by Mr. Thurston Gore, with the intent that the view might be unobstructed.

Little did the Goodriches and Gores, the Warings and Prestons and Atterburys and other prominent people foresee the havoc that prosperity and smoke were to play with their residential plans ! One by one, sooty commerce drove them out, westward, conservative though they were, from the paradise they had created; blacker and blacker grew the gothic façade of St. John's; Thurston Gore departed, but leased his corner first for a goodly sum, his ancestors being from Connecticut; leased also the vacant lot he had beautified, where stores arose and hid the spire from Tower Street. Cable cars moved serenely up the long hill where a panting third horse had been necessary, cable cars resounded in Burton Street, between the new factory and the church where Dr. Gilman still preached of peace and the delights of the New Jerusalem. And before you could draw your breath, the cable cars had become electric. Gray hairs began to appear in the heads of the people Dr. Gilman had married in the '60's and their children were going East to College.

II

In the first decade of the twentieth century, Asa Waring still clung to the imposing, early Victorian mansion in Hamilton Street. It presented an uncompromising and rather scornful front to the sister mansions with which it had hitherto been on intimate terms, now fast degenerating into a shabby gentility, seeking covertly to catch the eye of boarders, but as yet refraining from open solicitation. Their lawns were growing a little ragged, their stone steps and copings revealing cracks.

Asa Waring looked with a stern distaste upon certain aspects of modern life. And though he possessed the means to follow his friends and erstwhile neighbours into the newer paradise five miles westward, he had successfully resisted for several years a formidable campaign to uproot him. His three married daughters lived in that clean and verdant district surrounding the Park (spelled with a capital), while Evelyn and Rex spent most of their time in the West End or at the Country Clubs. Even Mrs. Waring, who resembled a Roman matron, with her wavy white hair parted in the middle and her gentle yet classic features, sighed secretly at times at the unyielding attitude of her husband, although admiring him for it. The grandchildren drew her.

On the occasion of Sunday dinner, when they surrounded her, her heart was filled to overflowing.

The autumn sunlight, reddened somewhat by the slight haze of smoke, poured in at the high windows of the diningroom, glinted on the silver, and was split into bewildering colors by the prisms of the chandelier. Many precious extra leaves were inserted under the white cloth, and Mrs. Waring's eyes were often dimmed with happiness as she glanced along the ranks on either side until they rested on the man with whom she had chosen to pass her life. Her admiration for him had gradually grown into hero-worship. His anger, sometimes roused, had a terrible moral quality that never failed to thrill her, and the Loyal Legion button on his black frock coat seemed to her an epitome of his character. He sat for the most part silent, his remarkable, penetrating eyes, lighting under his grizzled brows, smiling at her, at the children, at the grandchildren. And sometimes he would go to the corner table, where the four littlest sat, and fetch one back to perch on his knee and pull at his white, military mustache.

It was the children's day. Uproar greeted the huge white cylinder of ice-cream borne by Katie, the senior of the elderly maids; uproar greeted the cake; and finally there was a rush for the chocolates, little tablets wrapped in tinfoil and tied with red and blue ribbon. After that, the pandemonium left the dining-room, to spread itself over the spacious house from the basement to the great playroom in the attic, where the dolls and blocks and hobby-horses of the parental generation stoically awaited the new.

Sometimes a visitor was admitted to this sacramental feast, the dearest old gentleman in the world, with a great, high-bridged nose, a slight stoop, a kindling look, and snow-white hair, though the top of his head was bald. He sat on Mrs. Waring's right, and was treated with the greatest deference by the elders, and with none at all by the children, who besieged him. The bigger ones knew that he had had what is called a history; that he had been rich once, with a great mansion of his own, but now he lived on Dalton Street, almost in the slums, and worked among the poor. His name was Mr. Bentley.

He was not there on the particular Sunday when this story opens, otherwise the conversation about to be recorded would not have taken place. For St. John's Church was not often mentioned in Mr. Bentley's presence.

"Well, grandmother," said Phil Goodrich, who was the favourite son-in-law, "how was the new rector to-day?"

"Mr. Hodder is a remarkable young man, Phil," Mrs. Waring declared, "and delivered such a good sermon. I couldn't help wishing that you and Rex and Evelyn and George had been in church."

"Phil couldn't go," explained the unmarried and sun-burned Evelyn, "he had a match on of eighteen holes with me."

Mrs. Waring sighed.

"I can't think what's got into the younger people these days that they seem so indifferent to religion. Your father's a vestryman, Phil, and I believe it has always been his hope that you would succeed him. I'm afraid Rex won't succeed *his* father," she added, with a touch of regret and a glance of pride at her husband. "You never go to church, Rex. Phil does."

"I got enough church at boarding-school to last me a lifetime, mother," her son replied. He was slightly older than Evelyn, and just out of college. "Besides, any heathen can get on the vestry — it's a financial board, and they're due to put Phil on some day. They're always putting him on boards."

His mother looked a little distressed."

"Rex, I wish you wouldn't talk that way about the Church ——"

"I'm sorry, mother," he said, with quick penitence. "Mr. Langmaid's a vestryman, you know, and they've only got him there because he's the best corporation lawyer in the city. He isn't exactly what you'd call orthodox. He never goes."

"We are indebted to Mr. Langmaid for Mr. Hodder." This was one of Mr. Waring's rare remarks.

Eleanor Goodrich caught her husband's eye, and smiled.

"I wonder why it is," she said, "that we are so luke-warm about church in these days? I don't mean you, Lucy, or Laureston," she added to her sister, Mrs. Grey. "You're both exemplary." Lucy bowed ironically. "But most people of our ages with whom we associate. Martha Preston, for instance. We were all brought up like the children of Jonathan Edwards. Do you remember that awful round-and-round feeling on Sunday afternoons, Sally, and only the wabbly Noah's Ark elephant to play with, right in this house ? instead of *that!*" There was a bump in the hall without, and shrieks of laughter. "I'll never forget the first time it occurred to me — when I was reading Darwin—that if the ark were as large as Barnum's Circus and the Natural History Museum put together, it couldn't have held a thousandth of the species on earth. It was a blow."

"I don't know what we're coming to," exclaimed Mrs. Waring gently.

"I didn't mean to be flippant, mother," said Eleanor penitently, "but I do believe the Christian religion has got to be presented in a different way, and a more vital way, to appeal to a new generation. I am merely looking facts in the face."

"What *is* the Christian religion ?" asked Sally's husband, George Bridges, who held a chair of history in the local flourishing university. "I've been trying to find out all my life."

"You couldn't be expected to know, George," said his wife. "You were brought up an Unitarian, and went to Harvard."

"Never mind, professor," said Phil Goodrich, in a quizzical, affectionate tone. "Take the floor and tell us what it isn't."

George Bridges smiled. He was a striking contrast in type to his square-cut and vigorous brother-in-law ; very thin, with slightly protruding eyes the color of the faded blue glaze of ancient pottery, and yet humorous.

"I've had my chance, at any rate. Sally made me go last Sunday and hear Mr. Hodder."

"I can't see why you didn't like him, George," Lucy cried. "I think he's splendid."

"Oh, I like him," said Mr. Bridges.

"That's just it !" exclaimed Eleanor. "I like him. I think he's sincere. And that first Sunday he came, when I saw him get up in the pulpit and wave that long arm of his, all I could think of was a modern Savonarola. He looks one. And then, when he began to preach, it was maddening. I felt all the time that he *could* say something helpful, if he only would. But he didn't. It was all about the sufficiency of grace, — whatever that may be. He didn't explain it. He didn't give me one notion as to how to cope a little better with the frightful complexities of the modern lives we live, or how to stop quarrelling with Phil when he stays at the office and is late for dinner."

"Eleanor, I think you're unjust to him," said Lucy, amid the laughter of the men of the family. "Most people in St. John's think he is a remarkable preacher."

"So were many of the Greek sophists," George Bridges observed.

"Now if it were only dear old Doctor Gilman," Eleanor continued, "I could sink back into a comfortable indifference. But every Sunday this new man stirs me up, not by what he says, but by what he *is*. I hoped we'd get a rector with modern ideas, who would be able to tell me what to teach my children. Little Phil and Harriet come back from Sunday school with all sorts of questions, and I feel like a hypocrite. At any rate, if Mr. Hodder hasn't done anything else, he's made me want to *know*."

"What do you mean by a man of modern ideas, Eleanor?" inquired Mr. Bridges, with evident relish.

Eleanor put down her coffee cup, looked at him help-lessly, and smiled.

"Somebody who will present Christianity to me in such a manner that it will appeal to my reason, and enable me to assimilate it into my life."

"Good for you, Nell," said her husband, approvingly. "Come now, professor, you sit up in the University Club all Sunday morning and discuss recondite philosophy with other learned agnostics, tell us what *is* the matter with Mr. Hodder's theology. That is, if it will not shock grandmother too much."

"I'm afraid I've got used to being shocked, Phil," said Mrs. Waring, with her quiet smile.

"It's unfair," Mr. Bridges protested, "to ask a preju-diced pagan like me to pronounce judgment on an honest parson who is labouring according to his lights."

"Go on, George. You shan't get out of it that way."

"Well," said George, "the trouble is, from the theological point of view, that your parson is preaching what Auguste Sabatier would call a diminished and mitigated orthodoxy."

"Great heavens!" cried Phil. "What's that?"

"It's neither fish, flesh, nor fowl, nor good red herring," the professor declared. "If Mr. Hodder were cornered he couldn't maintain that he, as a priest, has full power to forgive sins, and yet he won't assert that he hasn't. The mediæval conception of the Church, before Luther's day, was consistent, at any rate, if you once grant the premises on which it was based."

"What premises?"

"That the Almighty had given it a charter, like an insurance company, of a monopoly of salvation on this portion of the Universe, and agreed to keep his hands off. Under this conception, the sale of indulgences, masses for the soul, and temporal power are perfectly logical — inevitable. Kings and princes derive their governments from the Church. But if we once begin to doubt the validity of this charter, as the Reformers did, the whole system flies to pieces, like sticking a pin into a soap bubble.

"That is the reason why — to change the figure — the so-called Protestant world has been gradually sliding down hill ever since the Reformation. The great majority of men are not willing to turn good, to renounce the material and sensual rewards under their hands without some definite and concrete guaranty that, if they do so, they are going to be rewarded hereafter. They demand some sort of infallibility. And when we let go of the infallibility of the Church, we began to slide toward what looked like a bottomless pit, and we clutched at the infallibility of the Bible. And now that has begun to roll.

"What I mean by a mitigated orthodoxy is this: I am far from accusing Mr. Hodder of insincerity, but he preaches *as if* every word of the Bible were literally true, and had been dictated by God to the men who held the pen; *as if* he, as a priest, held some supernatural power that could definitely be traced, through what is known as the Apostolic Succession, back to Peter."

"Do you mean to say, George," asked Mrs. Waring, with a note of pain in her voice, "that the Apostolic Succession cannot be historically proved?"

"My dear mother," said George, "I hope you will hold me innocent of beginning this discussion. As a harmless professor of history in our renowned University (of which we think so much that we do not send our sons to it) I have been compelled by the children whom you have brought up to sit in judgment on the theology of your rector."

"They will leave us nothing!" she sighed.

"Nothing, perhaps, that was invented by man to appeal to man's superstition and weakness. Of the remainder — who can say?"

"What," asked Mrs. Waring, "do they say about the Apostolic Succession?"

"Mother is as bad as the rest of us," said Eleanor. "Isn't she, grandfather?"

"If I had a house to rent," said Mr. Bridges, when the laughter had subsided, "I shouldn't advertise five bath-rooms when there were only two, or electricity when there was only gas. I should be afraid my tenants might find it out, and lose a certain amount of confidence in me. But the orthodox churches are running just such a risk to-day, and if any person who contemplates entering these churches doesn't examine the premises first, he refrains at his own cost.

"The situation in the early Christian Church is now a matter of history, and he who runs may read. The first churches, like those of Corinth and Ephesus and Rome, were democracies: no such thing as a priestly line to carry on a hierarchy, an ecclesiastical dynasty, was dreamed of. It may be gathered from the gospels that such an idea was so far from the mind of Christ that his mission was to set at naught just such another hierarchy, which then existed in Israel. The Apostles were no more bishops than was John the Baptist, but preachers who travelled from place to place, like Paul. The congregations, at Rome and elsewhere, elected their own *presbyteri*, *episcopoi* or over-seers. It is, to say the least, doubtful, and it certainly cannot be proved historically, that Peter ever was in Rome."

"The professor ought to have a pulpit of his own," said Phil.

There was a silence. And then Evelyn, who had been eating quantities of hothouse grapes, spoke up.

"So far as I can see, the dilemma in which our generation finds itself is this, — we want to know what there is in Christianity that we can lay hold of. We should like to believe, but, as George says, all our education contradicts the doctrines that are most insisted upon. We don't know where to turn. We have the choice of going to people like George, who know a great deal and don't believe anything, or to clergymen like Mr. Hodder, who demand that we shall violate the reason in us which has been so carefully trained."

"Upon my word, I think you've put it rather well, Evelyn," said Eleanor, admiringly.

"In spite of personalities," added Mr. Bridges.

"I don't see the use of fussing about it," proclaimed Laureston Grey, who was the richest and sprucest of the three sons-in-law. "Why can't we let well enough alone?"

"Because it isn't well enough," Evelyn replied. "I want the real thing or nothing. I go to church once a month, to please mother. It doesn't do me any good. And I don't see what good it does you and Lucy to go every Sunday. You never think of it when you're out at dinners and dances during the week. And besides," she added, with the arrogance of modern youth, "you and Lucy are both intellectually lazy."

"I like that from *you*, Evelyn," her sister flared up. "You never read anything except the sporting columns and the annual rules of tennis and golf and polo."

"Must everything be reduced to terms?" Mrs. Waring gently lamented. "Why can't we, as Laury suggests, just continue to trust?"

"They are the more fortunate, perhaps, who can, mother," George Bridges answered, with more of feeling in his voice than he was wont to show. "Unhappily, truth does not come that way. If Roger Bacon and Galileo and Newton and Darwin and Harvey and the others had 'just trusted,' the world's knowledge would still remain as stationary as it was during the thousand-odd years the hierarchy of the Church was supreme, when theology was history, philosophy, and science rolled into one. If God had not meant man to know something of his origin differing from the account in Genesis, he would not have given us Darwin and his successors. Practically every great discovery since the Revival we owe to men who, by their very desire for truth, were forced into opposition to the tremendous power of the Church, which always insisted that people should 'just trust,' and take the mixture of cosmogony and Greek philosophy, tradition and fable, paganism, Judaic sacerdotalism, and temporal power wrongly called spiritual dealt out by this same Church as the last word on science, philosophy, history, metaphysics, and government."

"Stop!" cried Eleanor. "You make me dizzy."

"Nearly all the pioneers to whom we owe our age of comparative enlightenment were heretics," George persisted. "And if they could have been headed off, or burned, most of us would still be living in mud caves at the foot of the cliff on which stood the nobleman's castle; and kings would still be kings by divine decree, scientists — if there were any — workers in the black art, and every phenomenon we failed to understand, a miracle."

"I choose the United States of America," ejaculated Evelyn.

"I gather, George," said Phil Goodrich, "that you don't believe in miracles."

"Miracles are becoming suspiciously fewer and fewer. Once, an eclipse of the sun was enough to throw men on their knees because they thought it supernatural. If they were logical they'd kneel to-day because it has been found natural. Only the inexplicable phenomena are miracles;

and after a while — if the theologians will only permit us to finish the job — there won't be any inexplicable phenomena. Mystery, as I believe William James puts it, may be called the more-to-be-known."

"In taking that attitude, George, aren't you limiting the power of God?" said Mrs. Waring.

"How does it limit the power of God, mother," her son-in-law asked, "to discover that he chooses to work by laws? The most suicidal tendency in religious bodies today is their mediæval insistence on what they are pleased to call the supernatural. Which is the more marvellous — that God can stop the earth and make the sun appear to stand still, or that he can construct a universe of untold millions of suns with planets and satellites, each moving in its orbit, according to law; a universe wherein every atom is true to a sovereign conception? And yet this marvel of marvels — that makes God in the twentieth century infinitely greater than in the sixteenth — would never have been discovered if the champions of theology had had their way."

Mrs. Waring smiled a little.

"You are too strong for me, George," she said, "but you mustn't expect an old woman to change."

"Mother, dear," cried Eleanor, rising and laying her hand on Mrs. Waring's cheek, "we don't want you to change. It's ourselves we wish to change, we wish for a religious faith like yours, only the same teaching which gave it to you is powerless for us. That's *our* trouble. We have only to look at you," she added, a little wistfully, "to be sure there is something — something vital in Christianity, if we could only get at it, something that does not depend upon what we have been led to believe is indispensable. George, and men like him, can only show the weakness in the old supports. I don't mean that they aren't doing the world a service in revealing errors, but they cannot reconstruct."

"That is the clergyman's business," declared Mr. Bridges. "But he must first acknowledge that the old supports *are* worthless."

"Well," said Phil, "I like your rector, in spite of his anthropomorphism — perhaps, as George would say, because of it. There is something manly about him that appeals to me."

"There," cried Eleanor, triumphantly, "I've always said Mr. Hodder had a spiritual personality. You feel — you feel there is truth shut up inside of him which he cannot communicate. I'll tell you who impresses me in that way more strongly than any one else — Mr. Bentley. And he doesn't come to church any more."

"Mr. Bentley," said her mother, "is a saint. Your father tried to get him to dinner to-day, but he had promised those working girls of his, who live on the upper floors of his house, to dine with them. One of them told me so. Of course he will never speak of his kindnesses."

"Mr. Bentley doesn't bother his head about theology," said Sally. "He just lives."

"There's Eldon Parr," suggested George Bridges, mentioning the name of the city's famous financier; "I'm told he relieved Mr. Bentley of his property some twenty-five years ago. If Mr. Hodder should begin to preach the modern heresy which you desire, Mr. Parr might object. He's very orthodox, I'm told."

"And Mr. Parr," remarked the modern Evelyn, sententiously, "pays the bills at St. John's. Doesn't he, father?"

"I fear he pays a large proportion of them," Mr. Waring admitted, in a serious tone.

"In these days," said Evelyn, "the man who pays the bills is entitled to have his religion as he likes it."

"No matter how he got the money to pay them," added Phil.

"That suggests another little hitch in the modern church which will have to be straightened out," said George Bridges.

"'Woe unto you, scribes and Pharisees, hypocrites! For ye make clean the outside of the cup and of the platter, but within they are full of extortion and excess.'"

" Why, George, you of all people quoting the Bible ! "
Eleanor exclaimed.

" And quoting it aptly, too," said Phil Goodrich.

" I'm afraid if we began on the scribes and Pharisees,
we shouldn't stop with Mr. Parr," Asa Waring observed,
with a touch of sadness.

" In spite of all they say he has done, I can't help feeling
sorry for him," said Mrs. Waring.   " He must be so lonely
in that huge palace of his beside the Park, his wife dead, and
Preston running wild around the world, and Alison no
comfort.   The idea of a girl leaving her father as she did
and going off to New York to become a landscape architect ! "

" But, mother," Evelyn pleaded, " I can't see why a
woman shouldn't lead her own life.   She only has one,
like a man.   And generally she doesn't get that."

Mrs. Waring rose.

" I don't know what we're coming to.   I was taught that
a woman's place was with her husband and children ; or,
if she had none, with her family.   I tried to teach you so,
my dear."

" Well," said Evelyn, " I'm here yet.   I haven't Alison's
excuse.   Cheer up, mother, the world's no worse than it
was."

" I don't know about that," answered Mrs. Waring.

" Listen ! " ejaculated Eleanor.

Mrs. Waring's face brightened.   Sounds of mad revelry
came down from the floor above.

CHAPTER II

MR. LANGMAID'S MISSION

I

LOOKING back over an extraordinary career, it is interesting to attempt to fix the time when a name becomes a talisman, and passes current for power. This is peculiarly difficult in the case of Eldon Parr. Like many notable men before him, nobody but Mr. Parr himself suspected his future greatness, and he kept the secret. But if we are to search what is now ancient history for a turning-point, perhaps we should find it in the sudden acquisition by him of the property of Mr. Bentley.

The transaction was a simple one. Those were the days when gentlemen, as matters of courtesy, put their names on other gentlemen's notes; and modern financiers, while they might be sorry for Mr. Bentley, would probably be unanimous in the opinion that he was foolish to write on the back of Thomas Garrett's. Mr. Parr was then, as now, a business man, and could scarcely be expected to introduce philanthropy into finance. Such had been Mr. Bentley's unfortunate practice. And it had so happened, a few years before, for the accommodation of some young men of his acquaintance that he had invested rather generously in Grantham mining stock at twenty-five cents a share, and had promptly forgotten the transaction. To cut a long story short, in addition to Mr. Bentley's house and other effects, Mr. Parr became the owner of the Grantham stock, which not long after went to one hundred dollars. The reader may do the figuring.

There was some talk at this time, but many things had happened since. For example, Mr. Parr had given away

15

great sums in charity. And it may likewise be added in his favour that Mr. Bentley was glad to be rid of his fortune. He had said so. He deeded his pew back to St. John's, and protesting to his friends that he was not unhappy, he disappeared from the sight of all save a few. The rising waters of Prosperity closed over him. But Eliza Preston, now Mrs. Parr, was one of those who were never to behold him again, — in this world, at least.

She was another conspicuous triumph in that career we are depicting. Gradual indeed had been the ascent from the sweeping out of a store to the marrying of a Preston, but none the less sure — inevitable. For many years after this event, Eldon Parr lived modestly in what was known as a "stone-front" house in Ransome Street, set well above the sidewalk, with a long flight of yellow stone steps leading to it; steps scrubbed with Sapolio twice a week by a negro in rubber boots. There was a stable with a tarred roof in the rear, to be discerned beyond the conventional side lawn that was broken into by the bay window of the dining-room. There, in that house, his two children were born: there, within those inartistic walls, Eliza Preston lived a life that will remain a closed book forever. What she thought, what she dreamed, if anything, will never be revealed. She did not, at least, have neurasthenia, and for all the world knew, she may have loved her exemplary and successful husband, with whom her life was as regular as the Strasburg clock. She breakfasted at eight and dined at seven; she heard her children's lessons and read them Bible stories; and at half past ten every Sunday morning, rain or shine, walked with them and her husband to the cars on Tower Street to attend service at St. John's, for Mr. Parr had scruples in those days about using the carriage on the Sabbath.

She did not live, alas, to enjoy for long the Medicean magnificence of the mansion facing the Park, to be a companion moon in the greater orbit. Eldon Parr's grief was real, and the beautiful English window in the south transept of the church bears witness to it. And yet it cannot be said that he sought solace in religion, so apparently steeped in it had he always been. It was destiny that he should take his place on the vestry; destiny, indeed, that he should ultimately become *the* vestry as well as the first layman of the diocese; unobtrusively, as he had accomplished everything else in life, in spite of Prestons and Warings, Atterburys, Goodriches, and Gores. And he was wont to leave his weighty business affairs to shift for themselves while he attended the diocesan and general conventions of his Church.

He gave judiciously, as becomes one who holds a fortune in trust, yet generously, always permitting others to help, until St. John's was a very gem of finished beauty. And, as the Rothschilds and the Fuggers made money for grateful kings and popes, so in a democratic age, Eldon Parr became the benefactor of an adulatory public. The university, the library, the hospitals, and the parks of his chosen city bear witness.

II

For forty years, Dr. Gilman had been the rector of St. John's. One Sunday morning, he preached his not unfamiliar sermon on the text, "For now we see through a glass, darkly; but then face to face," and when the next Sunday dawned he was in his grave in Winterbourne Cemetery, sincerely mourned within the parish and without. In the nature of mortal things, his death was to be expected: no less real was the crisis to be faced. At the vestry meeting that followed, the problem was tersely set forth by Eldon Parr, his frock coat tightly buttoned about his chest, his glasses in his hand.

"Gentlemen," he said, "we have to fulfil a grave responsibility to the parish, to the city, and to God. The matter of choosing a rector to-day, when clergymen are meddling with all sorts of affairs which do not concern them, is not so simple as it was twenty years ago. We have, at St. John's, always been orthodox and dignified, and I take it to be the sense of this vestry that we remain so. I conceive it our duty to find a man who is neither

c

too old nor too young, who will preach the faith as we received it, who is not sensational, and who does not mistake socialism for Christianity."

By force of habit, undoubtedly, Mr. Parr glanced at Nelson Langmaid as he sat down. Innumerable had been the meetings of financial boards at which Mr. Parr had glanced at Langmaid, who had never failed to respond. He was that *sine qua non* of modern affairs, a corporation lawyer, — although he resembled a big and genial professor of Scandinavian extraction. He wore round, tortoise-shell spectacles, he had a high, dome-like forehead, and an ample light brown beard which he stroked from time to time. It is probable that he did not believe in the immortality of the soul.

His eyes twinkled as he rose.

" I don't pretend to be versed in theology, gentlemen, as you know," he said, and the entire vestry, even Mr. Parr, smiled. For vestries, in spite of black coats and the gravity of demeanour which first citizens are apt to possess, are human after all. " Mr. Parr has stated, I believe, the requirements, and I agree with him that it is not an easy order to fill. You want a parson who will stick to his last, who will not try experiments, who is not too high or too low or too broad or too narrow, who has intellect without too much initiative, who can deliver a good sermon to those who can appreciate one, and yet will not get the church uncomfortably full of strangers and run you out of your pews. In short, you want a level-headed clergyman about thirty-five years old who will mind his own business."

The smiles on the faces of the vestry deepened. The ability to put a matter thus humorously was a part of Nelson Langmaid's power with men and juries.

" I venture to add another qualification," he continued, " and that is virility. We don't want a bandbox rector. Well, I happen to have in mind a young man who errs somewhat on the other side, and who looks a little like a cliff profile I once saw on Lake George of George Washington or an Indian chief, who stands about six feet two.

He's a bachelor — if that's a drawback. But I am not at all sure he can be induced to leave his present parish, where he has been for ten years."

"*I* am," announced Wallis Plimpton, with his hands in his pockets, "provided the right man tackles him."

III

Nelson Langmaid's most notable achievement, before he accomplished the greater one of getting a new rector for St. John's, had been to construct the "water-tight box" whereby the Consolidated Tractions Company had become a law-proof possibility. But his was an esoteric reputation, — the greater fame had been Eldon Parr's. Men's minds had been dazzled by the breadth of the conception of scooping all the street-car lines of the city, long and short, into one big basket, as it were ; and when the stock had been listed in New York, butcher and baker, clerk and proprietor, widow and maid, brought out their hoardings ; the great project was discussed in clubs, cafés, and department stores, and by citizens hanging on the straps of the very cars that were to be consolidated — golden word ! Very little appeared about Nelson Langmaid, who was philosophically content. But to Mr. Parr, who was known to dislike publicity, were devoted pages in the Sunday newspapers, with photographs of the imposing front of his house in Park Street, his altar and window in St. John's, the Parr building, and even of his private car, *Antonia*.

Later on, another kind of publicity had come. The wind had whistled for a time, but it turned out to be only a squall. The Consolidated Tractions Company had made the voyage for which she had been constructed, and thus had fulfilled her usefulness ; and the cleverest of the rats who had mistaken her for a permanent home scurried ashore before she was broken up.

All of which is merely in the nature of a commentary on Mr. Langmaid's genius. His reputation for judgment — which by some is deemed the highest of human qualities — was unimpaired ; and a man who in his time had selected presidents of banks and trust companies could certainly be trusted to choose a parson — particularly if the chief requirements were not of a spiritual nature. . . . A week later he boarded an east-bound limited train, armed with plenary powers.

His destination was the hill town where he had spent the first fifteen years of his life, amid the most striking of New England landscapes, and the sight of the steep yet delicately pastoral slopes never failed to thrill him as the train toiled up the wide valley to Bremerton. The vision of these had remained with him during the years of his toil in the growing Western city, and embodied from the first homesick days an ideal to which he hoped sometime permanently to return. But he never had. His family had shown a perversity of taste in preferring the sea, and he had perforce been content with a visit of a month or so every other summer, accompanied usually by his daughter, Helen. On such occasions, he stayed with his sister, Mrs. Whitely.

The Whitely mills were significant of the new Bremerton, now neither village nor city, but partaking of the characteristics of both. French Canadian might be heard on the main square as well as Yankee; and that revolutionary vehicle, the automobile, had inspired there a great brick edifice with a banner called the Bremerton House. Enterprising Italians had monopolized the corners with fruit stores, and plate glass and asphalt were in evidence. But the hills looked down unchanged, and in the cool, maple-shaded streets, though dotted with modern residences, were the same demure colonial houses he had known in boyhood.

He was met at the station by his sister, a large, matronly woman who invariably set the world whizzing backward for Langmaid; so completely did she typify the contentment, the point of view of an age gone by. For life presented no more complicated problems to the middle-aged Mrs. Whitely than it had to Alice Langmaid.

"I know what you've come for, Nelson," she said re-proachfully, when she greeted him at the station. "Dr. Gilman's dead, and you want our Mr. Hodder. I feel it in my bones. Well, you can't get him. He's had ever so many calls, but he won't leave Bremerton."

She knew perfectly well, however, that Nelson *would* get him, although her brother characteristically did not at once acknowledge his mission. Alice Whitely had vivid memories of a childhood when he had never failed to get what he wanted; a trait of his of which, although it had before now caused her much discomfort, she was secretly inordinately proud. She was, therefore, later in the day not greatly surprised to find herself supplying her brother with arguments. Much as they admired and loved Mr. Hodder, they had always realized that he could not remain buried in Bremerton. His talents demanded a wider field.

"Talents!" exclaimed Langmaid, "I didn't know he had any."

"Oh, Nelson, how can you say such a thing, when you came to get him!" exclaimed his sister.

"I recommended him because I thought he had none," Langmaid declared.

"He'll be a bishop some day—every one says so," said Mrs. Whitely, indignantly.

"That reassures me," said her brother.

"I can't see why they sent you—you hardly ever go to church," she cried. "I don't mind telling you, Nelson, that the confidence men place in you is absurd."

"You've said that before," he replied. "I agree with you. I'm not going on my judgment—but on yours and Gerald's, because I know that you wouldn't put up with anything that wasn't strictly all-wool orthodox."

"I think you're irreverent," said his sister, "and it's a shame that the canons permit such persons to sit on the vestry. . . ."

"Gerald," asked Nelson Langmaid of his brother-in-law that night, after his sister and the girls had gone to bed, "are you sure that this young man's orthodox?"

"He's been here for over ten years, ever since he left he seminary, and he's never done or said anything radical yet," replied the mill owner of Bremerton. "If you don't want him, we'd be delighted to have him stay. We're not forcing him on you, you know. What the deuce has got into you? You've talked to him for two hours, and you've sat looking at him at the dinner table for another two. I thought you were a judge of men."

Nelson Langmaid sat silent.

"I'm only urging Hodder to go for his own good," Mr. Whitely continued. "I can take you to dozens of people to-morrow morning who worship him, — people of all sorts ; the cashier in the bank, men in the mills, the hotel clerk, my private stenographer — he's built up that little church from nothing at all. And you may write the Bishop, if you wish."

"How has he built up the church?" Langmaid demanded.

"How? How does any clergyman build up a church?"

"I don't know," Langmaid confessed. "It strikes me as quite a *tour de force* in these days. Does he manage to arouse enthusiasm for orthodox Christianity?"

"Well," said Gerard Whitely, "I think the service appeals. We've made it as beautiful as possible. And then Mr. Hodder goes to see these people and sits up with them, and they tell him their troubles. He's reformed one or two rather bad cases. I suppose it's the man's personality."

"Ah," Langmaid exclaimed, "now you're talking!"

"I can't see what you're driving at," confessed his brother-in-law. "You're too deep for me, Nelson."

If the truth be told, Langmaid himself did not quite see. On behalf of the vestry, he offered next day to Mr. Hodder the rectorship of St. John's and that offer was taken under consideration ; but there was in the lawyer's mind no doubt of the acceptance, which, in the course of a fortnight after he had returned to the West, followed.

By no means a negligible element in Nelson Langmaid's professional success had been his possession of what may be called a sixth sense, and more than once, on his missions of trust, he had listened to its admonitory promptings.

At times he thought he recognized these in his conversation with the Reverend John Hodder at Bremerton,—especially in that last interview in the pleasant little study of the rectory overlooking Bremerton Lake. But the promptings were faint, and Langmaid out of his medium. He was not choosing the head of a trust company.

He himself felt the pull of the young clergyman's personality, and instinctively strove to resist it : and was more than ever struck by Mr. Hodder's resemblance to the cliff sculpture of which he had spoken at the vestry meeting. He was rough-hewn indeed, with gray-green eyes, and hair the color of golden sand : it would not stay brushed. It was this hair that hinted most strongly of individualism, that was by no means orthodox. Langmaid felt an incongruity, but he was fascinated ; and he had discovered on the rector's shelves evidences of the taste for classical authors that he himself possessed. Thus fate played with him, and the two men ranged from Euripides to Horace, from Horace to Dante and Gibbon. And when Hodder got up to fetch this or that edition, he seemed to tower over the lawyer, who was a big man himself.

Then they discussed business, Langmaid describing the parish, the people, the peculiar situation in St. John's caused by Dr. Gilman's death, while Hodder listened. He was not talkative ; he made no promises ; his reserve on occasions was even a little disconcerting; and it appealed to the lawyer from Hodder as a man, but somehow not as a clergyman. Nor did the rector volunteer any evidences of the soundness of his theological or political principles. He gave Langmaid the impression — though without apparent egotism — that by accepting the call he would be conferring a favour on St. John's ; and this was when he spoke with real feeling of the ties that bound him to Bremerton. Langmaid felt a certain deprecation of the fact that he was not a communicant.

For the rest, if Mr. Hodder were disposed to take himself and his profession seriously, he was by no means lacking in an appreciation of Langmaid's humour. . . .

The tempering of the lawyer's elation as he returned

homeward to report to Mr. Parr and the vestry may be best expressed by his own exclamation, which he made to himself :

" I wonder what that fellow would do if he ever got started ! " A parson was, after all, a parson, and he had done his best.

IV

A high, oozing note of the brakes, and the heavy train came to a stop. Hodder looked out of the window of the sleeper to read the sign *Marcion* against the yellow brick of the station set down in the prairie mud, and flanked by a long row of dun-colored freight cars backed up to a factory.

The factory was flimsy, somewhat resembling a vast greenhouse with its multitudinous windows, and bore the name of a firm whose offices were in the city to which he was bound.

" We 'most in now, sah," the negro porter volunteered. " You kin see the smoke yondah."

Hodder's mood found a figure in this portentous sign whereby the city's presence was betrayed to travellers from afar, — the huge pall seemed an emblem of the weight of the city's sorrows ; or again, a cloud of her own making which shut her in from the sight of heaven. Absorbed in the mad contest for life, for money and pleasure and power, she felt no need to lift her eyes beyond the level of her material endeavours.

He, John Hodder, was to live under that cloud, to labour under it. The mission on which he was bound, like the prophets of old, was somehow to gain the ears of this self-absorbed population, to strike the fear of the eternal into their souls, to convince them that there was Something above and beyond that smoke which they ignored to their own peril.

Yet the task, at this nearer view, took on proportions overwhelming — so dense was that curtain at which he gazed. And to-day the very skies above it were leaden,

as though Nature herself had turned atheist. In spite
of the vigour with which he was endowed, in spite of
the belief in his own soul, doubts assailed him of his ability
to cope with this problem of the modern Nineveh — at the
very moment when he was about to realize his matured
ambition of a great city parish.

Leaning back on the cushioned seat, as the train started
again, he reviewed the years at Bremerton, his first and
only parish. Hitherto (to his surprise, since he had been
prepared for trials) he had found the religious life a primrose path. Clouds had indeed rested on Bremerton's
crests, but beneficent clouds, always scattered by the sun.
And there, amid the dazzling snows, he had on occasions
walked with God.

His success, modest though it were, had been too simple.
He had loved the people, and they him, and the pang of
homesickness he now experienced was the intensest sorrow
he had known since he had been among them. Yes, Bremerton had been for him (he realized now that he had left
it) as near an approach to Arcadia as this life permits,
and the very mountains by which it was encircled had
seemed effectively to shut out those monster problems
which had set the modern world outside to seething.
Gerald Whitely's thousand operatives had never struck;
the New York newspapers, the magazines that discussed
with vivid animus the corporation-political problems in
other states, had found Bremerton interested, but unmoved; and Mrs. Whitely, who was a trustee of the
library, wasted her energy in deploring the recent volumes
on economics, sociology, philosophy, and religion that were
placed on the shelves. If Bremerton read them — and a
portion of Bremerton did — no difference was apparent in
the attendance at Hodder's church. The Woman's Club
discussed them strenuously, but made no attempt to put
their doctrines into practice.

Hodder himself had but glanced at a few of them, and
to do him justice this abstention had not had its root in
cowardice. His life was full — his religion "worked."
And the conditions with which these books dealt simply

did not exist for him. The fact that there were other churches in the town less successful than his own (one or two, indeed, virtually starving) he had found it simple to account for in that their denominations had abandoned the true conception of the Church, and were logically degenerating into atrophy. What better proof of the barrenness of these modern philosophical and religious books did he need than the spectacle of other ministers — who tarried awhile on starvation salaries — reading them and preaching from them?

He, John Hodder, had held fast to the essential efficacy of the word of God as propounded in past ages by the Fathers. It is only fair to add that he did so without pride or bigotry, and with a sense of thankfulness at the simplicity of the solution (ancient, in truth!) which, apparently by special grace, had been vouchsafed him. And to it he attributed the flourishing condition in which he had left the Church of the Ascension at Bremerton.

"We'll never get another rector like you," Alice Whitely had exclaimed, with tears in her eyes, as she bade him good-by. And he had rebuked her. Others had spoken in a similar strain, and it is a certain tribute to his character to record that the underlying hint had been lost on Hodder. His efficacy, he insisted, lay in the Word. . . .

Hodder looked at his watch, only to be reminded poignantly of the chief cause of his heaviness of spirit, for it represented concretely the affections of those whom he had left behind; brought before him vividly the purple haze of the Bremerton valley, and the garden party, in the ample Whitely grounds, which was their tribute to him. And he beheld, moving from the sunlight to shadow, the figure of Rachel Ogden. She might have been with him now, speeding by his side into the larger life!

In his loneliness, he seemed to be gazing into reproachful eyes. Nothing had passed between them. It was he who had held back, a fact that in the retrospect caused him some amazement. For, if wifehood were to be regarded as a profession, Rachel Ogden had every qualification. And Mrs. Whitely's skilful suggestions had on occasions almost brought him to believe in the reality of the mirage, — never quite.

Orthodox though he were, there had been times when his humour had borne him upward toward higher truths, and he had once remarked that promising to love forever was like promising to become President of the United States. One might achieve it, but it was independent of the will. Hodder's ideals — if he had only known — transcended the rubric. His feeling for Rachel Ogden had not been lacking in tenderness, and yet he had recoiled from marriage merely for the sake of getting a wife, albeit one with every qualification. He shrank instinctively from the humdrum, and sought the heights, stormy though these might prove. As yet he had not analyzed this craving.

This he did know — for he had long ago torn from his demon the draperies of disguise — that women were his great temptation. Ordination had not destroyed it, and even during those peaceful years at Bremerton he had been forced to maintain a watchful guard. He had a power over women, and they over him, that threatened to lead him constantly into wayside paths, and often he wondered what those who listened to him from the pulpit would think if they guessed that, at times, he struggled with suggestion even now. Yet, with his hatred of compromises, he had scorned marriage.

The yoke of Augustine! The caldron of unholy loves! Even now, as he sat in the train, his mind took its own flight backward into that remoter past that was still a part of him: to secret acts of his college days the thought of which made him shudder; yes, and to riots and revelries. In youth, his had been one of those boiling, contagious spirits that carry with them, irresistibly, tamer companions. He had been a leader in intermittent raids into forbidden spheres; a leader also in certain more decorous pursuits — if athletics may be so accounted; yet he had been capable of long periods of self-control, for a cause. Through it all a spark had miraculously been kept alive. . . .

Popularity followed him from the small New England college to the Harvard Law School. He had been soberer there, marked as a pleader, and at last the day arrived when he was summoned by a great New York lawyer to discuss his future. Sunday intervened. Obeying a wayward impulse, he had gone to one of the metropolitan churches to hear a preacher renowned for his influence over men. There is, indeed, much that is stirring to the imagination in the spectacle of a mass of human beings thronging into a great church, pouring up the aisles, crowding the galleries, joining with full voices in the hymns. What drew them? He himself was singing words familiar since childhood, and suddenly they were fraught with a startling meaning!

> " Fill me, radiancy divine,
>   Scatter all my unbelief! "

Visions of the Crusades rose before him, of a friar arousing France, of a Maid of Orleans; of masses of soiled, war-worn, sin-worn humanity groping towards the light. Even after all these ages, the belief, the hope would not down.

Outside, a dismal February rain was falling, a rain to wet the soul. The reek of damp clothes pervaded the gallery where he sat surrounded by clerks and shop girls, and he pictured to himself the dreary rooms from which they had emerged, drawn by the mysterious fire on that altar. Was it a will-o'-the-wisp? Below him, in the pews, were the rich. Did they, too, need warmth?

Then came the sermon, "I will arise and go to my father."

After the service, far into the afternoon, he had walked the wet streets heedless of his direction, in an exaltation that he had felt before, but never with such intensity. It seemed as though he had always wished to preach, and marvelled that the perception had not come to him sooner. If the man to whom he had listened could pour the light into the dark corners of other men's souls, he, John

Hodder, felt the same hot spark within him, — despite the dark corners of his own!

At dusk he came to himself, hungry, tired, and wet, in what proved to be the outskirts of Harlem. He could see the place now: the lonely, wooden houses, the ramshackle saloon, the ugly, yellow gleam from the street lamps in a line along the glistening pavement; beside him, a towering hill of granite with a real estate sign, "*This lot for sale.*" And he had stood staring at it, thinking of the rock that would have to be cut away before a man could build there, — and so read his own parable.

How much rock would have to be cut away, how much patient chipping before the edifice of which he had been dreaming could be reared! Could he ever do it? Once removed, he would be building on rock. But could he remove it? . . . To help revive a faith, a dying faith, in a material age, — that indeed were a mission for any man! . . .

He found his way to an elevated train, and as it swept along stared unseeing at the people who pushed and jostled him. Still under the spell, he reached his room and wrote to the lawyer thanking him, but saying that he had reconsidered coming to New York. It was not until he had posted the letter, and was on his way back to Cambridge that he fully realized he had made the decision of his life.

Misgivings, many of them, had come in the months that followed, misgivings and struggles, mocking queries. Would it last? There was the incredulity and amazement of nearest friends, who tried to dissuade him from so extraordinary a proceeding. Nobody, they said, ever became a parson in these days; nobody, at least, with his ability. He was throwing himself away. Ethics had taken the place of religion; intelligent men didn't go to church. And within him went on an endless debate. Public opinion made some allowance for frailties in other professions; in the ministry, none: he would be committing himself to be good the rest of his life, and that seemed too vast an undertaking for any human.

The chief horror that haunted him was not failure, —

for oddly enough he never seriously distrusted his power,— it was disaster. Would God give him the strength to fight his demon? If he were to gain the heights, only to stumble in the sight of all men, to stumble and fall.

Seeming echoes of the hideous mockery of it rang in his ears : where is the God that this man proclaimed? he saw the newspaper headlines, listened in imagination to cynical comments, beheld his name trailed through the soiled places of the cities, the shuttlecock of men and women. " To him that overcometh, to him will I give of the hidden manna, and I will give him a white stone, and upon the stone a new name written, which no one knoweth but he that receiveth it." Might he ever win that new name, eat of the hidden manna of a hidden power, become the possessor of the morning star?

Unless there be in the background a mother, no portrait of a man is complete. She explains him, is his complement. Through good mothers are men conceived of God : and with God they sit, forever yearning, forever reaching out, helpless except for him: with him, they have put a man into the world. Thus, into the Supreme Canvas, came the Virgin.

John Hodder's mother was a widow, and to her, in the white, gabled house which had sheltered stern ancestors, he travelled in the June following his experience. Standing under the fan-light of the elm-shaded doorway, she seemed a vision of the peace wherein are mingled joy and sorrow, faith and tears! A tall, quiet woman, who had learned the lesson of mothers, — how to wait and how to pray, how to be silent with a clamouring heart.

She had lived to see him established at Bremerton, to be with him there awhile. . . .

He awoke from these memories to gaze down through the criss-cross of a trestle to the twisted, turbid waters of the river far below. Beyond was the city. The train skirted for a while the hideous, soot-stained warehouses that faced the water, plunged into a lane between humming factories and clothes-draped tenements, and at last glided into semi-darkness under the high, reverberating roof of the Union Station.

CHAPTER III

THE PRIMROSE PATH

I

NELSON LANGMAID'S extraordinary judgment appeared once more to be vindicated.

There had been, indeed, a critical, anxious moment, emphasized by the agitation of bright feminine plumes and the shifting of masculine backs into the corners of the pews. None got so far as to define to themselves why there should be an apparent incompatibility between ruggedness and orthodoxy — but there were some who hoped and more who feared. Luther had been orthodox once, Savonarola also: in appearance neither was more canonical than the new rector.

His congregation, for the most part, were not analytical. But they felt a certain anomaly in virility proclaiming tradition. It took them several Sundays to get accustomed to it.

To those who had been used for more than a quarter of a century to seeing old Dr. Gilman's gentle face under the familiar and faded dove of the sounding-board, to the deliberation of his walk, and the hesitation of his manner, the first impression of the Reverend John Hodder was somewhat startling. They felt that there should be a leisurely element in religion. He moved across the chancel with incredible swiftness, his white surplice flowing like the draperies of a moving Victory, wasted no time with the pulpit lights, announced his text in a strong and penetrating, but by no means unpleasing voice, and began to speak with the certainty of authority.

Here, in an age when a new rector had ceased to be an

all-absorbing topic in social life, was a new and somewhat exhilarating experience. And it may be privately confessed that there were some who sat in St. John's during those first weeks of his incumbency who would indignantly have repudiated the accusation that they were not good churchmen and churchwomen, and who nevertheless had queer sensations in listening to ancient doctrines set forth with Emersonian conviction. Some were courageous enough to ask themselves, in the light of this forceful presentation, whether they really did believe them as firmly as they supposed they had.

Dear old Dr. Gilman had been milder — much milder as the years gained upon him. And latterly, when he had preached, his voice had sounded like the unavailing protest of one left far behind, who called out faintly with unheeded warnings. They had loved him : but the modern world was a busy world, and Dr. Gilman did not understand it. This man was different. Here was what the Church taught, he said, and they might slight it at their peril!

It is one thing to believe one's self orthodox, and quite another to have that orthodoxy so definitely defined as to be compelled, whether or no, to look it squarely in the face and own or disown it. Some indeed, like Gordon Atterbury, stood the test; responded to the clarion call for which they had been longing. But little Everett Constable, who also sat on the vestry, was a trifle uncomfortable in being reminded that absence from the Communion Table was perilous, although he would have been the last to deny the efficacy of the Sacrament.

The new rector was plainly not a man who might be accused of policy in pandering to the tastes of a wealthy and conservative flock. But if, in the series of sermons which lasted from his advent until well after Christmas, he had deliberately consulted their prejudices, he could not have done better. It is true that he went beyond the majority of them, but into a region which they regarded as preëminently safe, — a region the soil of which was traditional. To wit: St. Paul had left to the world a consistent theology. Historical research was ignored rather than condemned. And it might reasonably have been gathered from these discourses that the main proofs of Christ's divinity lay in his Virgin Birth, his miracles, and in the fact that his body had risen from the grave, had been seen by many, and even touched. Hence unbelief had no excuse. By divine commission there were bishops, priests, and deacons in the new hierarchy, and it was through the Apostolic Succession that he, their rector, derived his sacerdotal powers. There were, no doubt, many obscure passages in the Scripture, but men's minds were finite; a catholic acceptance was imperative, and the evils of the present day — a sufficiently sweeping statement — were wholly due to deplorable lapses from such acceptance. The Apostolic teaching must be preserved, since it transcended all modern wanderings after truth. Hell, though not definitely defined in terms of flames, was no less a state of torture (future, by implication) of which fire was but a faint symbol. And he gave them clearly to understand that an unbaptized person ran no inconsiderable risk. He did not declare unqualifiedly that the Church alone had the power to save, but such was the inference.

II

It was entirely fitting, no doubt, when the felicitations of certain of the older parishioners on his initial sermon were over, that Mr. Hodder should be carried westward to lunch with the first layman of the diocese. But Mr. Parr, as became a person of his responsibility, had been more moderate in his comment. For he had seen, in his day, many men whose promise had been unfulfilled. Tightly buttoned, silk hatted, upright, he sat in the corner of his limousine, the tasselled speaking-tube in his hand, from time to time cautioning his chauffeur.

"Carefully!" he cried. "I've told you not to drive so fast in this part of town. I've never got used to automobiles," he remarked to Hodder, "and I formerly went to

D

church in the street-cars, but the distances have grown so great — and I have occasionally been annoyed in them."

Hodder was not given to trite acquiescence. His homely composure belied the alertness of his faculties; he was striving to adapt himself to the sudden broadening and quickening of the stream of his life, and he felt a certain excitement — although he did not betray it — in the presence of the financier. Much as he resented the thought, it was impossible for him not to realize that the man's pleasure and displeasure were important; for, since his arrival, he had had delicate reminders of this from many sources. Recurrently, it had caused him a vague uneasiness, hinted at a problem new to him. He was jealous of the dignity of the Church, and he seemed already to have detected in Mr. Parr's manner a subtle note of patronage. Nor could Hodder's years of provincialism permit him to forget that this man with whom he was about to enter into personal relations was a capitalist of national importance.

The neighbourhood they traversed was characteristic of our rapidly expanding American cities. There were rows of dwelling houses, once ultra-respectable, now slatternly, and lawns gone grey; some of these houses had been remodelled into third-rate shops, or thrown together to make manufacturing establishments : saloons occupied all the favourable corners. Flaming posters on vacant lots announced, pictorially, dubious attractions at the theatres. It was a wonderful Indian summer day, the sunlight soft and melting; and the smoke which continually harassed this district had lifted a little, as though in deference to the Sabbath.

Hodder read the sign on a lamp post, *Dalton Street*. The name clung in his memory.

"We thought, some twenty years ago, of moving the church westward," said Mr. Parr, "but finally agreed to remain where we were."

The rector had a conviction on this point, and did not hesitate to state it without waiting to be enlightened as to the banker's views.

"It would seem to me a wise decision," he said, looking out of the window, and wholly absorbed in the contemplation of the evidences of misery and vice, "with this poverty at the very doors of the church."

Something in his voice impelled Eldon Parr to shoot a glance at his profile.

"Poverty is inevitable, Mr. Hodder," he declared. "The weak always sink."

Hodder's reply, whatever it might have been, was prevented by the sudden and unceremonious flight of both occupants toward the ceiling of the limousine, caused by a deep pit in the asphalt.

"What are you doing, Gratton?" Mr. Parr called sharply through the tube.

Presently, the lawns began to grow brighter, the houses more cheerful, and the shops were left behind. They crossed the third great transverse artery of the city (not so long ago, Mr. Parr remarked, a quagmire, now lined by hotels and stores with alluring displays in plate glass windows) and entered a wide boulevard that stretched westward straight to the great Park. This boulevard the financier recalled as a country road of clay. It was bordered by a vivid strip of green; a row of tall and graceful lamp posts, like sentinels, marked its course; while the dwellings, set far back on either side, were for the most part large and pretentious, betraying in their many tentative styles of architecture the reaching out of a commercial nation after beauty. Some, indeed, were simple of line and restful to the trained eye.

They came to the wide entrance of the Park, so wisely reserved as a breathing place for future generations. A light haze had gathered over the rolling forests to the westward; but this haze was not smoke. Here, in this enchanting region, the autumn sunlight was undiluted gold, the lawns, emerald, and the red gravel around the statesman's statue glistening. The automobile quickly swung into a street that skirted the Park, — if street it might be called, for it was more like a generous private driveway, — flanked on the right by fences of ornamental ironwork and high shrubbery that concealed the fore-yards of dominating private residences which might, without great exaggeration, have been called palaces.

"That's Ferguson's house," volunteered Mr. Parr, indicating a marble edifice with countless windows. "He's one of your vestrymen, you know. Ferguson's Department Store." The banker's eyes twinkled a little for the first time. "You'll probably find it convenient. Most people do. Clever business man, Ferguson."

But the rector was finding difficulty in tabulating his impressions.

They turned in between two posts of a gateway toward a huge house of rough granite. And Hodder wondered whether, in the swift onward roll of things, the time would come when this, too, would have been deemed ephemeral. With its massive walls and heavy, red-tiled roof that sloped steeply to many points, it seemed firmly planted for ages to come. It was surrounded, yet not hemmed in, by trees of a considerable age. His host explained that these had belonged to the original farm of which all this Park Street property had made a part.

They alighted under a porte-cochère with a glass roof.

"I'm sorry," said Mr. Parr, as the doors swung open and he led the way into the house, "I'm sorry I can't give you a more cheerful welcome, but my son and daughter for their own reasons, see fit to live elsewhere."

Hodder's quick ear detected in the tone another cadence, and he glanced at Eldon Parr with a new interest. . . .

Presently they stood, face to face, across a table reduced to its smallest proportions, in the tempered light of a vast dining-room, an apartment that seemed to symbolize the fortress-like properties of wealth. The odd though struck the clergyman that this man had made his own Tower of London, had built with his own hands the prison in which he was to end his days. The carved oaken ceiling, lofty though it was, had the effect of pressing downward, the heavy furniture matched the heavy walls, and even the silent, quick-moving servants had a watchful air.

Mr. Parr bowed his head while Hodder asked grace. They sat down.

The constraint which had characterized their conversation continued, yet there was a subtle change in the attitude of the clergyman. The financier felt this, though it could not be said that Hodder appeared more at his ease: his previous silences had been by no means awkward. Eldon Parr liked self-contained men. But his perceptions were as keen as Nelson Langmaid's, and like Langmaid, he had gradually become conscious of a certain baffling personality in the new rector of St. John's. From time to time he was aware of the grey-green eyes curiously fixed on him, and at a loss to account for their expression. He had no thought of reading in it an element of pity. Yet pity was nevertheless in the rector's heart, and its advent was emancipating him from the limitations of provincial inexperience.

Suddenly, the financier launched forth on a series of shrewd and searching questions about Bremerton, its church, its people, its industries, and social conditions. All of which Hodder answered to his apparent satisfaction. Coffee was brought. Hodder pushed back his chair, crossed his knees, and sat perfectly still regarding his host, his body suggesting a repose that did not interfere with his perceptive faculties.

"You don't smoke, Mr. Hodder?"

The rector smiled and shook his head. Mr. Parr selected a diminutive, yellow cigar and held it up.

"This," he said, "has been the extent of my indulgence for twenty years. They are made for me in Cuba."

Hodder smiled again, but said nothing.

"I have had a letter from your former bishop, speaking of you in the highest terms," he observed.

"The bishop is very kind."

Mr. Parr cleared his throat.

"I am considerably older than you," he went on, "and have the future of St. John's very much at heart, Mr. Hodder. I trust you will remember this and make allowances for it as I talk to you. I need not remind you that you have a grave responsibility on your shoulders for so young a man, and that St. John's is the oldest parish in the diocese."

"I think I realize it, Mr. Parr," said Hodder, gravely. "It was only the opportunity of a larger work here that induced me to leave Bremerton."

"Exactly," agreed the banker. "The parish, I believe, is in good running order — I do not think you will see the necessity for many — ahem — changes. But we sadly needed an executive head. And, if I may say so, Mr. Hodder, you strike me as a man of that type, who might have made a success in a business career."

The rector smiled again.

"I am sure you could pay me no higher compliment," he answered.

For an instant Eldon Parr, as he stared at the clergyman, tightened his lips, — lips that seemed peculiarly formed for compression. Then they relaxed into what resembled a smile. If it were one, the other returned it.

"Seriously," Mr. Parr declared, "it does me good in these days to hear, from a young man, such sound doctrine as you preach. I am not one of those who believe in making concessions to agnostics and atheists. You were entirely right, in my opinion, when you said that we who belong to the Church — and of course you meant all orthodox Christians — should stand by our faith as delivered by the saints. Of course," he added, smiling "I should not insist upon the sublapsarian view of election which I was taught in the Presbyterian Church as boy."

Hodder laughed, but did not interrupt.

"On the other hand," Mr. Parr continued, "I have little patience with clergymen who would make religio attractive. What does it amount to — luring people int the churches on one pretext or another, sugar-coating th pill? Salvation is a more serious matter. Let th churches stick to their own. We have at St. John's God-fearing, conservative congregation, which does no

believe in taking liberties with sound and established doctrine. And I may confess to you, Mr. Hodder, that we
were naturally not a little anxious about Dr. Gilman's
successor, that we should not get, in spite of every pre-
caution, a man tinged with the new and dangerous ideas
so prevalent, I regret to say, among the clergy. I need
scarcely add that our anxieties have been set at rest."

"That," said Hodder, "must be taken as a compliment to the dean of the theological seminary from
which I graduated."

The financier stared again. But he decided that Mr.
Hodder had not meant to imply that he, Mr. Parr, was
attempting to supersede the dean. The answer had
been modest.

"I take it for granted that you and I and all sensible
men are happily agreed that the Church should remain
where she is. Let the people come to her. She should
be, if I may so express it, the sheet anchor of society, our
bulwark against socialism, in spite of socialists who call
themselves ministers of God. The Church has lost
ground — why? Because she has given ground. The
sanctity of private property is being menaced, demagogues
are crying out from the house-tops and inciting people
against the men who have made this country what it is,
who have risked their fortunes and their careers for the
present prosperity. We have no longer any right, it
seems, to employ whom we will in our factories and our
railroads; we are not allowed to regulate our rates,
though the risks were all ours. Even the women are
meddling, — they are not satisfied to stay in the homes,
where they belong. You agree with me?"

"As to the women," said the rector, "I have to acknowledge that I have never had any experience with the militant type of which you speak."

"I pray God you may never have," exclaimed Mr.
Parr, with more feeling than he had yet shown.

"Woman's suffrage, and what is called feminism in
general, have never penetrated to Bremerton. Indeed, I
must confess to have been wholly out of touch with the

problems to which you refer, although of course I have
been aware of their existence."

"You will meet them here," said the banker, significantly.

"Yes," the rector replied thoughtfully, "I can see that.
I know that the problems here will be more complicated
more modern,—more difficult. And I thoroughly agree
with you that their ultimate solution is dependent on
Christianity. If I did not believe,—in spite of the eviden'
fact which you point out of the Church's lost ground,—
that her future will be greater than her past, I should no
be a clergyman."

The quiet but firm note of faith was not lost on th
financier, and yet was not he quite sure what was to b
made of it? He had a faint and fleeting sense of disquiet
which registered and was gone.

"I hope so," he said vaguely, referring perhaps to th
resuscitation of which the rector spoke. He drummed
on the table. "I'll go so far as to say that I, too, thin
that the structure can be repaired. And I believe it i
the duty of the men of influence—all men of influence –
to assist. I don't say that men of influence are not fa
tors in the Church to-day, but I do say that they are no
using the intelligence in this task which they bring t
bear, for instance, on their business."

"Perhaps the clergy might help," Hodder suggeste
and added more seriously, "I think that many of the
are honestly trying to do so."

"No doubt of it. Why is it," Mr. Parr continued r
flectively, "that ministers as a whole are by no means th
men they were? You will pardon my frankness. Wh
I was a boy, the minister was looked up to as an intelle
tual and moral force to be reckoned with. I have hea
it assigned, as one reason, that in the last thirty yea
other careers have opened up, careers that have prov
much more attractive to young men of ability."

"Business careers?" inquired the rector.

"Precisely."

"In other words," said Hodder, with his curious smi

"the ministry gets the men who can't succeed at anything else."

"Well, that's putting it rather strong," answered Mr. Parr, actually reddening a little. "But come now, most young men would rather be a railroad president than a bishop, wouldn't they?"

"Most young men would," agreed Hodder, quickly, "but they are not the young men who ought to be bishops, you'll admit that."

The financier, be it recorded to his credit, did not lack appreciation of this thrust, and, for the first time, he laughed with something resembling heartiness. This laughter, in which Hodder joined, seemed suddenly to put them on a new footing — a little surprising to both.

"Come," said the financier, rising, "I'm sure you like pictures, and Langmaid tells me you have a fancy for first editions. Would you care to go to the gallery?"

"By all means," the rector assented.

Their footsteps, as they crossed the hardwood floors, echoed in the empty house. After pausing to contemplate a Millet on the stair landing, they came at last to the huge, silent gallery, where the soft but adequate light fell upon many masterpieces, ancient and modern. And it was here, while gazing at the Corots and Bonheurs, Lawrences, Romneys, Copleys, and Halses, that Hodder's sense of their owner's isolation grew almost overpowering. Once, glancing over his shoulder at Mr. Parr, he surprised in his eyes an expression almost of pain.

"These pictures must give you great pleasure," he said.

"Oh," replied the banker, in a queer voice, "I'm always glad when any one appreciates them. I never come in here alone."

Hodder did not reply. They passed along to an upstairs sitting-room, which must, Hodder thought, be directly over the dining-room. Between its windows was a case containing priceless curios.

"My wife liked this room," Mr. Parr explained, as he opened the case. When they had inspected it, the rector stood for a moment gazing out at a formal garden at the

back of the house. The stalks of late flowers lay withering, but here and there the leaves were still vivid, and
clusters of crimson berries gleamed in the autumn sunshine.
A pergola ran down the middle, and through denuded
grape-vines he caught a glimpse, at the far end, of sculptured figures and curving marble benches surrounding a
pool.

"What a wonderful spot!" he exclaimed.

"My daughter Alison designed it."

"She must have great talent," said the rector.

"She's gone to New York and become a landscape architect," said his host with a perceptible dryness. "Women
in these days are apt to be everything except what the
Lord intended them to be."

They went downstairs, and Hodder took his leave,
although he felt an odd reluctance to go. Mr. Parr rang
the bell.

"I'll send you down in the motor," he said.

"I'd like the exercise of walking," said the rector. "I
begin to miss it already, in the city."

"You look as if you had taken a great deal of it," Mr.
Parr declared, following him to the door. "I hope you'll
drop in often. Even if I'm not here, the gallery and the
library are at your disposal."

Their eyes met.

"You're very good," Hodder replied, and went down
the steps and through the open doorway.

Lost in reflection, he walked eastward with long and
rapid strides, striving to reduce to order in his mind the
impressions the visit had given him, only to find them
too complex, too complicated by unlooked-for emotions.
Before its occurrence, he had, in spite of an inherent common sense, felt a little uneasiness over the prospective
meeting with the financier. And Nelson Langmaid had
hinted, good-naturedly, that it was his, Hodder's, business,
to get on good terms with Mr. Parr — otherwise the rectorship of St. John's might not prove a bed of roses. Although
the lawyer had spoken with delicacy, he had once more
misjudged his man — the result being to put Hodder on

his guard. He had been the more determined *not* to cater to the banker.

The outcome of it all had been that the rector left him with a sense of having crossed barriers forbidden to other men, and not understanding how he had crossed them. Whether this incipient intimacy were ominous or propitious, whether there were involved in it a germ (engendered by a radical difference of temperament) capable of developing into future conflict, he could not now decide. If Eldon Parr were Procrustes he, Hodder, had fitted the bed, and to say the least, this was extraordinary, if not a little disquieting. Now and again his thoughts reverted to the garden, and to the woman who had made it. Why had she deserted?

At length, after he had been walking for nearly an hour, he halted and looked about him. He was within a few blocks of the church, a little to one side of Tower Street, the main east and west highway of the city, in the midst of that district in which Mr. Parr had made the remark that poverty was inevitable. Slovenly and depressing at noonday, it seemed now frankly to have flung off its mask. Dusk was gathering, and with it a smoke-stained fog that lent a sickly tinge to the lights. Women slunk by him: the saloons, apparently closed, and many houses with veiled windows betrayed secret and sinister gleams. In the midst of a block rose a tall, pretentious though cheaply constructed building with the words "Hotel Albert" in flaming electric letters above an archway. Once more his eye read *Dalton Street* on a lamp. . . .

Hodder resumed his walk more slowly, and in a few minutes reached his rooms in the parish house.

CHAPTER IV

I

ALTHOUGH he found the complications of a modern city parish somewhat bewildering, the new rector entered into his duties that winter with apostolic zeal. He was aware of limitations and anomalies, but his faith was boundless, his energy the subject of good-natured comment by his vestry and parishioners, whose pressing invitations to dinners he was often compelled to refuse. There was in John Hodder something indefinable that inflamed curiosity and left it unsatisfied.

His excuse for attending these dinners, which indeed were relaxing and enjoyable, he found in the obvious duty of getting to know the most important members of his congregation. But invariably he came away from them with an inner sense of having been baffled in this object. With a few exceptions, these modern people seemed to have no time for friendship in the real meaning of the word, no desire to carry a relationship beyond a certain point. Although he was their spiritual pastor, he knew less about most of them at the end of the winter than their butlers and their maids.

They were kind, they were delightful, they were interested in him — he occasionally thought — as a somewhat anachronistic phenomenon. They petted, respected him, and deferred to him. He represented to them an element in life they recognized, and which had its proper niche. What they failed to acknowledge was his point of view — and this he was wise enough not to press at dinner tables and in drawing-rooms — that religion should have the

44

penetrability of ether; that it should be the absorbent of
life. He did not have to commit the banality of reminding them of this conviction of his at their own tables; he
had sufficient humour and penetration to credit them with
knowing it. Nay, he went farther in his unsuspected
analysis, and perceived that these beliefs made one of his
chief attractions for them. It was pleasant to have authority
in a black coat at one's board; to defer, if not to bend to it.
The traditions of fashion demanded a clergyman in the
milieu, and the more tenaciously he clung to his prerogatives,
the better they liked it.

Although they were conscious of a certain pressure,
which they gently resisted, they did not divine that the
radiating and rugged young man cherished serious designs
upon them. He did not expect to transform the world
in a day, especially the modern world. He was biding
his time, awaiting individual opportunities.

They talked to him of the parish work, congratulated
him on the vigour with which he had attacked it, and
often declared themselves jealous of it because it claimed
too much of him. Dear Dr. Gilman, they said, had had
neither the strength nor the perception of modern needs;
and McCrae, the first assistant clergyman, while a good
man, was a plodder and lacking in imagination. They
talked sympathetically about the problems of the poor.
And some of them — particularly Mrs. Wallis Plimpton —
were inclined to think Hodder's replies a trifle noncommittal. The trouble, although he did not tell them so,
was that he himself had by no means solved the problem.
And he felt a certain reluctance to discuss the riddle of
poverty over champagne and porcelain.

Mrs. Plimpton and Mrs. Constable, Mrs. Ferguson,
Mrs. Langmaid, Mrs. Larrabbee, Mrs. Atterbury, Mrs.
Grey, and many other ladies and their daughters were
honorary members of his guilds and societies, and found
time in their busy lives to decorate the church, adorn the
altar, care for the vestments, and visit the parish house.
Some of them did more: Mrs. Larrabbee, for instance,
when she was in town, often graced the girls' classes with

her presence, which was a little disquieting to the daughters
of immigrants: a little disquieting, too, to John Hodder.
During the three years that had elapsed since Mr. Larrabbee's death, she had, with characteristic grace and ease,
taken up philanthropy ; become, in particular, the feminine patron saint of Galt House, non-sectarian, a rescue
home for the erring of her sex.

There were, too, in this higher realm of wealth in and
out of which Hodder plunged, women like Mrs. Constable
(much older than Mrs. Larrabbee) with whom philanthropy
and what is known as "church work" had become second
nature in a well-ordered life, and who attended with praise-
worthy regularity the meetings of charitable boards and
committees, not infrequently taking an interest in individuals in Mr. Hodder's classes.   With her, on occasions, he
did discuss such matters, only to come away from her with
his bewilderment deepened.

It was only natural that he should have his moods of depression.   But the recurrent flow of his energy swept them
away.   Cynicism had no place in his militant Christianity,
and yet there were times when he wondered whether these
good people really wished achievements from their rector.
They had the air of saying "Bravo!" and then of turning
away.   And he did not conceal from himself that he was
really doing nothing but labour.   The distances were
great ; and between his dinner parties, classes, services,
and visits, he was forced to sit far into the night preparing
his sermons, when his brain was not so keen as it might
have been.   Indeed — and this thought *was* cynical and
out of character — he asked himself on one occasion
whether his principal achievement so far had not consisted
in getting on unusual terms with Eldon Parr.   They were
not lacking who thought so, and who did not hesitate to
imply it.   They evidently regarded his growing intimacy
with the banker with approval, as in some sort a supreme
qualification for a rector of St. John's, and a proof of unusual abilities.   There could be no question, for instance,
that he had advanced perceptibly in the estimation of the
wife of another of his vestrymen, Mrs. Wallis Plimpton.

The daughter of Thurston Gore, with all her astuteness and real estate, was of a naïveté in regard to spiritual matters that Hodder had grown to recognize as impermeable. In an evening gown, with a string of large pearls resting on her firm and glowing neck, she appeared a concrete refutation of the notion of rebirth, the triumph of an unconscious philosophy of material common-sense. However, in parish house affairs, Hodder had found her practical brain of no slight assistance.

"I think it quite wonderful," she remarked, on the occasion at which he was the guest of honour in what was still called the new Gore mansion, "that you have come to know Mr. Parr so well in such a short time. How did you do it, Mr. Hodder? Of course Wallis knows him, and sees a great deal of him in business matters. He relies on Wallis. But they tell me you have grown more intimate with him than any one has been since Alison left him."

There is, in Proverbs or Ecclesiastes, a formula for answering people in accordance with their point of view. The rector modestly disclaimed intimacy. And he curbed his curiosity about Alison for the reason that he preferred to hear her story from another source.

"Oh, but you are intimate!" Mrs. Plimpton protested. "Everybody says so — that Mr. Parr sends for you all the time. What is he like when he's alone, and relaxed? Is he ever relaxed?" The lady had a habit of not waiting for answers to her questions. "Do you know, it stirs my imagination tremendously when I think of all the power that man has. I suppose you know he has become one of a very small group of men who control this country, and naturally he has been cruelly maligned. All he has to do is to say a word to his secretary, and he can make men or ruin them. It isn't that he does ruin them — I don't mean that. He uses his wealth, Wallis says, to maintain the prosperity of the nation! He feels his trusteeship. And he is so generous! He has given a great deal to the church, and now," she added, "I am sure he will give more."

Hodder was appalled. He felt helpless before the weight of this onslaught.

"I dare say he will continue to assist, as he has in the past," he managed to say.

"Of course it's your disinterestedness," she proclaimed, examining him frankly. "He feels that you don't want anything. You always strike me as so splendidly impartial, Mr. Hodder."

Fortunately, he was spared an answer. Mr. Plimpton, who was wont to apply his gifts as a toastmaster to his own festivals, hailed him from the other end of the table.

And Nelson Langmaid, who had fallen into the habit of dropping into Hodder's rooms in the parish house on his way uptown for a chat about books, had been struck by the rector's friendship with the banker.

"I don't understand how you managed it, Hodder, in such a short time," he declared. "Mr. Parr's a difficult man. In all these years, I've been closer to him than any one else, and I don't know him to-day half as well as you do."

"I didn't manage it," said Hodder, briefly.

"Well," replied the lawyer, quizzically, "you needn't eat me up. I'm sure you didn't do it on purpose. If you had, — to use a Hibernian phrase, — you never would have done it. I've seen it tried before. To tell you the truth, after I'd come back from Bremerton, that was the one thing I was afraid of — that you mightn't get along with him."

Hodder himself was at a loss to account for the relationship. It troubled him vaguely, for Mr. Parr was the aggressor; and often at dusk, when Hodder was working under his study lamp, the telephone would ring, and on taking down the receiver he would hear the banker's voice. "I'm alone to-night, Mr. Hodder. Will you come and have dinner with me?"

Had he known it, this was a different method of communication than that which the financier usually employed, one which should have flattered him. If Wallis Plimpton, for instance, had received such a personal message, the fact would not have remained unknown the next day at his club. Sometimes it was impossible for Hodder to go, and he said so; but he always went when he could.

The unwonted note of appeal (which the telephone seemed somehow to enhance) in Mr. Parr's voice, never failed to find a response in the rector's heart, and he would ponder over it as he walked across to Tower Street to take the electric car for the six-mile trip westward.

This note of appeal he inevitably contrasted with the dry, matter-of-fact reserve of his greeting at the great house, which loomed all the greater in the darkness. Unsatisfactory, from many points of view, as these evenings were, they served to keep whetted Hodder's curiosity as to the life of this extraordinary man. All of its vaster significance for the world, its tremendous machinery, was out of his sight.

Mr. Parr seemed indeed to regard the rest of his fellow-creatures with the suspicion at which Langmaid had hinted, to look askance at the amenities people tentatively held out to him. And the private watchman whom Hodder sometimes met in the darkness, and who invariably scrutinized pedestrians on Park Street, seemed symbolic of this attitude. On rare occasions, when in town, the financier dined out, limiting himself to a few houses. Once in a long while he attended what are known as banquets, such as those given by the Chamber of Commerce, though he generally refused to speak. Hodder, through Mr. Parr's intervention, had gone to one of these, ably and breezily presided over by the versatile Mr. Plimpton.

Hodder felt not only curiosity and sympathy, but a vexing sense of the fruitlessness of his visits to Park Street. Mr. Parr seemed to like to have him there. And the very fact that the conversation rarely took any vital turn oddly contributed to the increasing permanence of the lien. To venture on any topic relating to the affairs of the day were merely to summon forth the banker's dogmatism, and Hodder's own opinions on such matters were now in a strange and unsettled state. Mr. Parr liked best to talk of his treasures, and of the circumstances during his trips abroad that had led to their acquirement. Once the banker had asked him about parish house matters.

E

"I'm told you're working very hard — stirring up McCrae. He needs it."

"I'm only trying to study the situation," Hodder replied. "I don't think you quite do justice to McCrae," he added; "he's very faithful, and seems to understand those people thoroughly."

Mr. Parr smiled.

"And what conclusions have you come to? If you think the system should be enlarged and reorganized I am willing at any time to go over it with you, with a view to making an additional contribution. Personally, while I have sympathy for the unfortunate, I'm not at all sure that much of the energy and money put into the institutional work of churches isn't wasted."

"I haven't come to any conclusions — yet," said the rector, with a touch of sadness. "Perhaps I demand too much — expect too much."

The financier, deep in his leather chair under the shaded light, the tips of his fingers pressed together, regarded the younger man thoughtfully, but the smile lingered in his eyes.

"I told you you would meet problems," he said.

II

Hodder's cosmos might have been compared, indeed, to that set forth in the Ptolemaic theory of the ancients. Like a cleverly carved Chinese object of ivory in the banker's collection, it was a system of spheres, touching, concentric, yet separate. In an outer space swung Mr. Parr; then came the scarcely less rarefied atmosphere of the Constables and Atterburys, Fergusons, Plimptons, Langmaids, Prestons, Larrabbees, Greys, and Gores, and then a smaller sphere which claims but a passing mention. There were, in the congregation of St. John's, a few people of moderate means whose houses or apartments the rector visited; people to whom modern life was increasingly perplexing.

In these ranks were certain maiden ladies and widows

who found in church work an outlet to an otherwise circumscribed existence. Hodder met them continually in his daily rounds. There were people like the Bradleys, who rented half a pew and never missed a Sunday ; Mr. Bradley, an elderly man whose children had scattered, was an upper clerk in one of Mr. Parr's trust companies : there were bachelors and young women, married or single, who taught in the Sunday school or helped with the night classes. For the most part, all of these mentioned above belonged to an element that once had had a comfortable and well-recognized place in the community, yet had somehow been displaced. Many of them were connected by blood with more fortunate parishioners, but economic pressure had scattered them throughout new neighbourhoods and suburbs. Tradition still bound them to St. John's.

With no fixed orbit, the rector cut at random through all of these strata, and into a fourth. Not very far into it, for this apparently went down to limitless depths, the very contemplation of which made him dizzy. The parish house seemed to float precariously on its surface.

Owing partly to the old-fashioned ideas of Dr. Gilman, and partly to the conservatism of its vestry, the institutionalism of St. John's was by no means up to date. No settlement house, with day nurseries, was maintained in the slums. The parish house, built in the early nineties, had its gymnasium hall and class and reading rooms, but was not what in these rapidly moving times would be called modern. Presiding over its activities, and seconded by a pale, but earnest young man recently ordained, was Hodder's first assistant, the Reverend Mr. McCrae.

McCrae was another puzzle. He was fifty and gaunt, with a wide flat forehead and thinning, grey hair, and wore steel spectacles. He had a numerous family. His speech, of which he was sparing, bore strong traces of a Caledonian accent. And this, with the addition of the fact that he was painstaking and methodical in his duties, and that his sermons were orthodox in the sense that they

were extremely non-committal, was all that Hodder knew
about him for many months.   He never doubted, however, the man's sincerity and loyalty.

But McCrae had a peculiar effect on him, and as time
went on, his conviction deepened that his assistant was
watching him.   The fact that this tacit criticism did not
seem unkindly did not greatly alleviate the impatience
that he felt from time to time.   He had formed a higher
estimate of McCrae's abilities than that generally prevailing throughout the parish ; and in spite of, perhaps
because of his attitude, was drawn toward the man.
This attitude, as Hodder analyzed it from the expressions
he occasionally surprised on his assistant's face, was one
of tolerance and experience, contemplating, with a faint
amusement and a certain regret, the wasteful expenditure
of youthful vitality.   Yet it involved more.   McCrae
looked as if he *knew* — knew many things that he deemed
it necessary for the new rector to find out by experience.

But he was a difficult man to talk to.

If the truth be told, the more Hodder became absorbed
in these activities of the parish house, the greater grew
his perplexity, the more acute his feeling of incompleteness ; or rather, his sense that the principle was somehow
fundamentally at fault.   Out of the waters of the prole-
tariat they fished, assiduously and benignly, but at random, strange specimens! brought them, as it were, blink-
ing to the light, and held them by sheer struggling.
And sometimes, when they slipped away, dived after
them.   The young curate, Mr. Tompkinson, for the most
part did the diving ; or, in scriptural language, the searching after the lost sheep.

The results accomplished seemed indeed, as Mr. Parr
had remarked, strangely disproportionate to the efforts, —
for they laboured abundantly.   The Italian mothers appeared stolidly appreciative of the altruism of Miss Ramsay, who taught the kindergarten, in taking their charges
off their hands for three hours of a morning, and the
same might be said of the Jews and Germans and Russians.   The newsboys enjoyed the gymnasium and read

ing-rooms : some of them were drafted into the choir, yet the singing of Te Deums failed somehow to accomplish the miracle of regeneration. The boys, as a rule, were happier, no doubt ; the new environments not wholly without results. But the rector was an idealist.

He strove hard to become their friend, and that of the men ; to win their confidence, and with a considerable measure of success. On more than one occasion he threw aside his clerical coat and put on boxing-gloves, and he gave a series of lectures, with lantern slides, collected during the six months he had once spent in Europe. The Irish-Americans and the Germans were the readiest to respond, and these were for the most part young working-men and youths by no means destitute. When they were out of a place, he would often run across them in the reading-room or sitting among the lockers beside the gymnasium, and they would rise and talk to him cordially and even familiarly about their affairs. They liked and trusted him — on a tacit condition. There was a boundary he might not cross. And the existence of that boundary did not seem to trouble McCrae.

One night as he stood with his assistant in the hall after the men had gone, Hodder could contain himself no longer.

"Look here, McCrae," he broke out, "these men never come to church — or only a very few of them."

"No more they do," McCrae agreed.

"Why don't they ? "

"Ye've asked them, perhaps."

"I've spoken to one or two of them," admitted the rector.

"And what do they tell you ? "

Hodder smiled.

"They don't tell me anything. They dodge."

"Precisely," said McCrae.

"We're not making Christians of them," said Hodder, beginning to walk up and down. "Why is it ? "

"It's a big question."

"It *is* a big question. It's the question of all questions, it seems to me. The function of the Church, in my opinion, is to make Christians."

"Try to teach them religion," said McCrae—he almost pronounced it releegion—"and see what happens. Ye'll have no classes at all. They only come, the best of them, because ye let them alone that way, and they get a little decency and society help. It's somewhat to keep them out of the dance-halls and saloons maybe."

"It's not enough," the rector asserted. "You've had a great deal of experience with them. And I want to know why, in your view, more of them don't come into the Church."

"Would ye put Jimmy Flanagan and Otto Bauer and Tony Baldassaro in Mr. Parr's pew?" McCrae inquired, with a slight flavour of irony that was not ill-natured. "Or perhaps Mrs. Larrabbee would make room for them?"

"I've considered that, of course," replied Hodder, thoughtfully, though he was a little surprised that McCrae should have mentioned it. "You think their reasons are social, then,—that they feel the gap. I feel it myself most strongly. And yet none of these men are Socialists. If they were, they wouldn't come here to the parish house."

"They're not Socialists," agreed McCrae.

"But there is room in the back and sides of the church and there is the early service and the Sunday night service, when the pews are free. Why don't they come to these?"

"Religion doesn't appeal to them."

"Why not?"

"Ye've asked me a riddle. All I know is that the minute ye begin to preach, off they go and never come back."

Hodder, with unconscious fixity, looked into his assistant's honest face. He had an exasperating notion that McCrae might have said more, if he would.

"Haven't you a theory?"

"Try yourself," said McCrae. His manner was abrupt yet oddly enough, not ungracious.

"Don't think I'm criticizing," said the rector, quickly.

"I know well ye're not."

"I've been trying to learn. It seems to me that we are only accomplishing half our task, and I know that St. John's is not unique in this respect. I've been talking to Andrews, of Trinity, about their poor."

"Does he give you a remedy?"

"No," Hodder said. "He can't see any more than I can why Christianity doesn't appeal any longer. The fathers and mothers of these people went to church, in the old country and in this. Of course he sees, as you and I do, that society has settled into layers, and that the layers won't mix. And he seems to agree with me that there is a good deal of energy exerted for a comparatively small return."

"I understand that's what Mr. Parr says."

These references to Mr. Parr disturbed Hodder. He had sometimes wondered, when he had been compelled to speak about his visits to the financier, how McCrae regarded them. He was sure that McCrae *did* regard them.

"Mr. Parr is willing to be even more generous than he has been," Hodder said. "The point is, whether it's wise to enlarge our scope on the present plan. What do you think?"

"Ye can reach more," McCrae spoke without enthusiasm.

"What's the use of reaching them, only to touch them? In addition to being helped materially and socially, and kept away from the dance-halls and saloons, they ought to be fired by the Gospels, to be remade. They should be going out into the highways and byways to bring others into the church."

The Scotchman's face changed a little. For an instant his eyes lighted up, whether in sympathy or commiseration or both, Hodder could not tell.

"I'm with ye, Mr. Hodder, if ye'll show me the way. But oughtn't we to begin at both ends?"

"At both ends?" Hodder repeated.

"Surely. With the people in the pews? Oughtn't we to be firing them, too?"

"Yes," said the rector. "You're right."

He turned away, to feel McCrae's hand on his sleeve.

"Maybe it will come, Mr. Hodder," he said. "There's no telling when the light will strike in."

It was the nearest to optimism he had ever known his assistant to approach.

"McCrae," he asked, "have you ever tried to do anything with Dalton Street?"

"Dalton Street?"

The real McCrae, whom he had seemed to see emerging, retired abruptly, presenting his former baffling and noncommittal exterior.

"Yes," Hodder forced himself to go on, and it came to him that he had repeated virtually the same words to Mr. Parr, "it is at our very doors, a continual reproach. There is real poverty in those rooming houses, and I have never seen vice so defiant and shameless."

"It's a shifty place, that," McCrae replied. "They're in it one day and gone the next, a sort of catch-basin for all the rubbish of the city. I can recall when decent people lived there, and now it's all light housekeeping and dives and what not."

"But that doesn't relieve us of responsibility," Hodder observed.

"I'm not denying it. I think ye'll find there's very little to get hold of."

Once more, he had the air of stopping short, of being able to say more. Hodder refrained from pressing him.

Dalton Street continued to haunt him. And often at nightfall, as he hurried back to his bright rooms in the parish house from some of the many errands that absorbed his time, he had a feeling of self-accusation as he avoided women wearily treading the pavements, or girls and children plodding homeward through the wet, wintry streets. Some glanced at him with heavy eyes, others passed sullenly, with bent heads. At such moments his sense of helplessness was overpowering. He could not follow them to the dreary dwellings where they lodged. . . .

Eldon Parr had said that poverty was inevitable.

CHAPTER V

THE RECTOR HAS MORE FOOD FOR THOUGHT

I

SUNDAY after Sunday Hodder looked upon the same picture, the winter light filtering through emblazoned windows, falling athwart stone pillars, and staining with rich colours the marble of the centre aisle. The organ rolled out hymns and anthems, the voices of the white-robed choir echoed among the arches. And Hodder's eye, sweeping over the decorous congregation, grew to recognize certain landmarks: Eldon Parr, rigid at one end of his empty pew; little Everett Constable, comfortably, but always pompously settled at one end of his, his white-haired and distinguished-looking wife at the other. The space between them had once been filled by their children. There was Mr. Ferguson, who occasionally stroked his black whiskers with a prodigious solemnity; Mrs. Ferguson, resplendent and always a little warm, and their daughter Nan, dainty and appealing, her eyes uplifted and questioning.

The Plimptons, with their rubicund and aggressively healthy offspring, were always in evidence. And there was Mrs. Larrabbee. What between wealth and youth, independence and initiative, a widowhood now emerged from a mourning unexceptionable, an elegance so unobtrusive as to border on mystery, she never failed to agitate any atmosphere she entered, even that of prayer. From time to time, Hodder himself was uncomfortably aware of her presence, and he read in her upturned face an interest which, by a little stretch of the imagination, might have been deemed personal. . . .

Another was Gordon Atterbury, still known as "young Gordon," though his father was dead, and he was in the vestry. He was unmarried and forty-five, and Mrs. Larrabbee had said he reminded her of a shrivelling seed set aside from a once fruitful crop. He wore, invariably, checked trousers and a black cutaway coat, eyeglasses that fell off when he squinted, and were saved from destruction by a gold chain. No wedding or funeral was complete without him. And one morning, as he joined Mr. Parr and the other gentlemen who responded to the appeal, "Let your light so shine before men," a strange, ironical question entered the rector's mind — was Gordon Atterbury the logical product of those doctrines which he, Hodder, preached with such feeling and conviction?

None, at least, was so fervent a defender of the faith, so punctilious in all observances, so constant at the altar rail; none so versed in rubrics, ritual, and canon law; none had such a knowledge of the Church fathers. Mr. Atterbury delighted to discuss them with the rector at the dinner parties where they met; none was more zealous for foreign missions. He was the treasurer of St. John's.

It should undoubtedly have been a consolation to any rector to possess Mr. Atterbury's unqualified approval, to listen to his somewhat delphic compliments, — heralded by a clearing of the throat. He represented the faith as delivered to the saints, and he spoke for those in the congregation to whom it was precious. Why was it that, to Hodder, he should gradually have assumed something of the aspect of a Cerberus? Why was it that he incited a perverse desire to utter heresies?

Hodder invariably turned from his contemplation of Gordon Atterbury to the double Waring pew, which went from aisle to aisle. In his heart, he would have preferred the approval of Eleanor Goodrich and her husband, and of Asa Waring. Instinct spoke to him here; he seemed to read in their faces that he failed to strike in them responsive chords. He was drawn to them: the conviction grew upon him that he did not reach them, and it troubled him, as he thought, disproportionately.

He could not expect to reach all. But they were the type to which he most wished to appeal; of all of his flock, this family seemed best to preserve the vitality and ideals of the city and nation. Asa Waring was a splendid, uncompromising survival; his piercing eyes sometimes met Hodder's across the church, and they held for him a question and a riddle. Eleanor Goodrich bore on her features the stamp of true nobility of character, and her husband, Hodder knew, was a man among men. In addition to a respected lineage, he possessed an unusual blending of aggressiveness and personal charm that men found irresistible. . . .

The rector's office in the parish house was a businesslike room on the first floor, fitted up with a desk, a table, straight-backed chairs, and a revolving bookcase. And to it, one windy morning in March, came Eleanor Goodrich. Hodder rose to greet her with an eagerness which, from his kindly yet penetrating glance, she did not suspect.

"Am I interrupting you, Mr. Hodder?" she asked, a little breathlessly.

"Not at all," he said, drawing up a chair. "Won't you sit down?"

She obeyed. There was an awkward pause during which the colour slowly rose to her face.

"I wanted to ask you one or two things," she began, not very steadily. "As perhaps you may know, I was brought up in this church, baptized and confirmed in it. I've come to fear that, when I was confirmed, I wasn't old enough to know what I was doing."

She took a deep breath, amazed at her boldness, for this wasn't in the least how she had meant to begin. And she gazed at the rector anxiously. To her surprise, he did not appear to be inordinately shocked.

"Do you know any better now?" he asked.

"Perhaps not," she admitted. "But the things of which I was sure at that time I am not sure of now. My faith is — is not as complete."

"Faith may be likened to an egg, Mrs. Goodrich," he

said. "It must be kept whole. If the shell is chipped, it is spoiled."

Eleanor plucked up her courage. Eggs, she declared, had been used as illustrations by conservatives before now.

Hodder relieved her by smiling in ready appreciation.

"Columbus had reference to this world," he said. "I was thinking of a more perfect one."

"Oh!" she cried, "I dare say there is a more perfect one. I should hate to think there wasn't — but I can't imagine it. There's nothing in the Bible in the way of description of it to make me really wish to go there. The New Jerusalem is too insipid, too material. I'm sure I'm shocking you, but I must be honest, and say what I feel."

"If some others were as honest," said the rector, "the problems of clergymen would be much easier. And it is precisely because people will not tell us what they feel that we are left in the dark and cannot help them. Of course, the language of St. John about the future is figurative."

"Figurative, — yes," she consented, "but not figurative in a way that helps me, a modern American woman. The figures, to be of any use, ought to appeal to my imagination — oughtn't they? But they don't. I can't see any utility in such a heaven — it seems powerless to enter as a factor into my life."

"It is probable that we are not meant to know anything about the future."

"Then I wish it hadn't been made so explicit. Its very definiteness is somehow — stultifying. And, Mr. Hodder, if we were not meant to know its details, it seems to me that if the hereafter is to have any real value and influence over our lives here, we *should* know something of its conditions, because it must be in some sense a continuation of this. I'm not sure that I make myself clear."

"Admirably clear. But we have our Lord's example of how to live here."

"If we could be sure," said Eleanor, "just what that example meant."

Hodder was silent a moment.

"You mean that you cannot accept what the Church teaches about his life?" he asked.

"No, I can't," she faltered. "You have helped me to say it. I want to have the Church's side better explained, — that's why I'm here." She glanced up at him, hesitatingly, with a puzzled wonder, such a positive, dynamic representative of that teaching did he appear. "And my husband can't, — so many people I know can't, Mr. Hodder. Only, some of them don't mention the fact. They accept it. And you say things with such a certainty — " she paused.

"I know," he replied, "I know. I have felt it since I have come here more than ever before." He did not add that he had felt it particularly about her, about her husband: nor did he give voice to his instinctive conviction that he respected and admired these two more than a hundred others whose professed orthodoxy was without a flaw. "What is it in particular," he asked, troubled, "that you cannot accept? I will do my best to help you."

"Well — " she hesitated again.

"Please continue to be frank," he begged.

"I can't believe in the doctrine of the virgin birth," she responded in a low voice; "it seems to me so — so material. And I feel I am stating a difficulty that many have, Mr. Hodder. Why should it have been thought necessary for God to have departed from what is really a sacred and sublime fact in nature, to resort to a material proof in order to convince a doubting humanity that Jesus was his Son? Oughtn't the proof of Christ's essential Godship to lie in his life, to be discerned by the spiritual; and wasn't he continually rebuking those who demanded material proof? The very acceptance of a material proof, it seems to me, is a denial of faith, since faith ceases to have any worth whatever the moment the demand for such proof is gratified. *Knowledge* puts faith out of the question, for faith to me means a *trusting* on spiritual grounds. And surely the acceptance of scriptural statements like that of the miraculous birth without investi-

gation is not faith — it is mere credulity. If Jesus
had been born in a miraculous way, the disciples must
have known it.   Joseph must have known it when he heard
the answer 'I must be about my father's business,' and
their doubts are unexplained."

"I see *you* have been investigating," said the rector.

"Yes," replied Eleanor, with an unconscious shade of
defiance, " people want to know, Mr. Hodder, — they want
to know the truth.   And if you consider the preponderance of the evidence of the Gospels themselves — my
brother-in-law says — you will find that the miraculous
birth has very little to stand on.   Take out the first two
chapters of Matthew and Luke, and the rest of the four
Gospels practically contradict it.   The genealogies differ,
and they both trace through Joseph."

"I think people suffer in these days from giving too
much weight to the critics of Christianity," said the rector,
" from not pondering more deeply on its underlying truths.
Do not think that I am accusing you of superficiality, Mrs.
Goodrich ; I am sure you wish to go to the bottom, or else
you would be satisfied with what you have already read
and heard."

"I do," she murmured.

"And the more one reflects on the life of our Lord,
the more one is convinced that the doctrine of the virgin
birth is a vital essential; without it Christianity falls to
pieces.   Let us go at the matter the other way round.   If
we attribute to our Lord a natural birth, we come at once
to the dilemma of having to admit that he was merely an
individual human person, — in an unsurpassed relationship
with God, it is true, but still a human person.   That doctrine makes Christ *historical*, some one to go back to, instead of the ever-present, preëxistent Son of God and mankind.   I will go as far as to assert that if the virgin birth
had never been mentioned in the Gospels, it would nevertheless inevitably have become a fundamental doctrine of
the Christian faith.   Such a truth is too vast, too far-
reaching to have been neglected, and it has a much higher
significance than the mere record of a fact.   In spite of

the contradictions of science, it explains as nothing else can the mystery of the divinity as well as the humanity of the Saviour."

Eleanor was unconvinced. She felt, as she listened, the pressure of his sincerity and force, and had to strive to prevent her thoughts from becoming confused.

"No, Mr. Hodder, I simply can't see any reason for resorting to a physical miracle in order to explain a spiritual mystery. I can see why the ancients demanded a *sign* of divinity as it were. But for us it has ceased even to be that. It can't be proved. You ask me, in the face of overwhelming evidence against it, to teach my children that the Incarnation depends on it, but when they grow up and go to college and find it discredited they run the risk of losing everything else with it. And for my part, I fail utterly to see why, if with God all things are possible, it isn't quite as believable, as we gather from St. Mark's Gospel, that he incarnated himself in one naturally born. If you reach the conclusion that Jesus was not a mere individual human person, you reach it through the contemplation of his life and death."

"Then it isn't the physical miracle you object to, especially?" he asked.

"It's the *uselessness* of it, for this age," she exclaimed. "I think clergymen don't understand the harm it is doing in concentrating the attention on such a vulnerable and non-essential point. Those of us who are striving to reorganize our beliefs and make them tenable, do not bother our heads about miracles. They may be true, or may not, or some of them may be. We are beginning to see that the virgin birth does not add anything to Christ. We are beginning to see that perfection and individuality are not incompatible, — one is divine, and the other human. And isn't it by his very individuality that we are able to recognize Jesus to-day?"

"You have evidently thought and read a great deal," Hodder said, genuinely surprised. "Why didn't you come to me earlier?"

Eleanor bit her lip. He smiled a little.

"I think I can answer that for you," he went on; "you believe we are prejudiced, — I've no doubt many of us are. You think we are bound to stand up for certain dogmas, or go down, and that our minds are consequently closed. I am not blaming you," he added quickly, as she gave a sign of protest, "but I assure you that most of us, so far as my observation has gone, are honestly trying to proclaim the truth as we see it."

"Insincerity is the last thing I should have accused you of, Mr. Hodder," she said flushing. "As I told you, you seem so sure."

"I don't pretend to infallibility, except so far as I maintain that the Church is the guardian of certain truths which human experience has verified. Let me ask you if you have thought out the difference your conception of the Incarnation, — the lack of a patently divine commission, as it were, — makes in the doctrine of grace?"

"Yes, I have," she answered, "a little. It gives me more hope. I cannot think I am totally depraved. I do not believe that God wishes me to think so. And while I am still aware of the distance between Christ's perfection and my own imperfection, I feel that the possibility is greater of lessening that distance. It gives me more self-respect, more self-reliance. George Bridges says that the logical conclusion of that old doctrine is what philosophers call determinism — Calvinistic predestination. I can't believe in that. The kind of grace God gives me is the grace to help myself by drawing force from the element of him in my soul. He gives me the satisfaction of developing."

"Of one thing I am assured, Mrs. Goodrich," Hodder replied, "that the logical result of independent thinking is anarchy. Under this modern tendency toward individual creeds, the Church has split and split again until, if it keeps on, we shall have no Church at all to carry on the work of our Lord on earth. History proves that to take anything away from the faith is to atrophy, to destroy it. The answer to your arguments is to be seen on every side, atheism, hypocrisy, vice, misery, insane and

cruel grasping after wealth. There is only one remedy I
can see," he added, inflexibly, yet with a touch of sadness,
"believe."

"What if we can't believe?" she asked.

"You can." He spoke with unshaken conviction.
"You can if you make the effort, and I am sure you will.
My experience is that in the early stages of spiritual development we are impervious to certain truths. Will you
permit me to recommend to you certain books dealing
with these questions in a modern way?"

"I will read them gladly," she said, and rose.

"And then, perhaps, we may have another talk," he
added, looking down at her. "Give my regards to your
husband."

Yet, as he stood in the window looking after her retreat-
ing figure, there gradually grew upon him a vague and
uncomfortable feeling that he had not been satisfactory,
and this was curiously coupled with the realization that
the visit had added a considerable increment to his already
pronounced liking for Eleanor Goodrich. She was, paradoxically, *his kind of a person* — such was the form the
puzzle took. And so ably had she presented her difficulties that, at one point of the discussion, it had ironically
occurred to him to refer her to Gordon Atterbury. Mr.
Atterbury's faith was like an egg, and he took precious
care not to have it broken or chipped.

Hodder found himself smiling. It was perhaps inevitable that he began at once to contrast Mrs. Goodrich with
other feminine parishioners who had sought him out, and
who had surrendered unconditionally. They had evinced
an equally disturbing tendency, — a willingness to be
overborne. For had he not, indeed, overborne them?
He could not help suspecting these other ladies of a craving for the luxury of the confessional. One thing was
certain, — he had much less respect for them than for
Eleanor Goodrich. . . .

That afternoon he sent her the list of books. But the
weeks passed, and she did not come back. Once, when he
met her at a dinner of Mrs. Preston's, both avoided the

F

subject of her visit, both were conscious of a constraint. She did not know how often, unseen by her, his eyes had sought her out from the chancel. For she continued to come to church as frequently as before, and often brought her husband.

II

One bright and boisterous afternoon in March, Hodder alighted from an electric car amid a swirl of dust and stood gazing for a moment at the stone gate-houses of that *rus in urbe*, Waverley Place, and at the gold block-letters written thereon, "No Thoroughfare." Against those gates and their contiguous grill the rude onward rush of the city had beaten in vain, and, baffled, had swept around their serene enclosure, westward.

Within, a silvery sunlight lit up the grass of the island running down the middle, and in the beds the softening earth had already been broken by the crocus sheaves. The bare branches of the trees swayed in the gusts. As Hodder penetrated this hallowed precinct he recognized, on either hand, the residences of several of his parishioners, each in its ample allotted space: Mrs. Larrabbee's; the Laureston Greys'; Thurston Gore's, of which Mr. Wallis Plimpton was now the master, — Mr. Plimpton, before whose pertinacity the walls of Jericho had fallen; and finally the queer, twisted Richardson mansion of the Everett Constables, whither he was bound, with its recessed doorway and tiny windows peeping out from under mediæval penthouses.

He was ushered into a library where the shades were already drawn, where a white-clothed tea-table was set before the fire, the red rays dancing on the silver tea-kettle. On the centre-table he was always sure to find, neatly set in a rack, the books about which the world was talking, or rather would soon begin to talk; and beside them were ranged magazines, French, English, and American, *Punch*, the *Spectator*, the *Nation*, the *Revue des deux Mondes*. Like the able general she was, Mrs. Constable kept her communications open, and her acquaintance was by no means confined to the city of her nativity. And if a celebrity were passing through, it were pretty safe, if in doubt, to address him in her care.

Hodder liked and admired her, but somehow she gave him the impression of having attained her ascendency at a price, an ascendency which had apparently been gained by impressing upon her environment a new note — literary, æsthetic, cosmopolitan. She held herself, and those she carried with her, abreast of the times, and he was at a loss to see how so congenial an effort could have left — despite her sweetness — the little mark of hardness he discerned, of worldliness. For she was as well born as any woman in the city, and her husband was a Constable. He had inherited, so the rector had been informed, one of those modest fortunes that were deemed affluence in the eighties. *His* keeping abreast of the times was the enigma, and Hodder had often wondered how financial genius had contrived to house itself in the well-dressed, gently pompous little man whose lack of force seemed at times so painfully evident. And yet he was rated one of the rich men of the city, and his name Hodder had read on many boards with Mr. Parr's !

A person more versed in the modern world of affairs than the late rector of Bremerton would not have been so long in arriving at the answer to this riddle. Hodder was astute, he saw into people more than they suspected, but he was not sophisticated.

He stood picturing, now, the woman in answer to whose summons he had come. With her finely chiselled features, her abundant white hair, her slim figure and erect carriage she reminded him always of a Vigée Lebrun portrait. He turned at the sound of her voice behind him.

" How good of you to come, Mr. Hodder, when you were so busy," she said, taking his hand as she seated herself behind the tea-kettle. " I wanted the chance to talk to you, and it seemed the best way. What is that you have, Soter's book ? "

" I picked it up on the table," he explained.

"Then you haven't read it? You ought to. As a clergyman, it would interest you. Religion treated from the economic side, you know, the effect of lack of nutrition on character. Very unorthodox, of course."

"I find that I have very little time to read," he said. "I sometimes take a book along in the cars."

"Your profession is not so leisurely as it once was, — I often think it such a pity. But you, too, are paying the penalty of complexity." She smiled at him sympathetically. "How is Mr. Parr? I haven't seen him for several weeks."

"He seemed well when I saw him last," replied Hodder.

"He's a wonderful man ; the amount of work he accomplishes without apparent effort is stupendous." Mrs. Constable cast what seemed a tentative glance at the powerful head, and handed him his tea. "I wanted to talk to you about Gertrude," she said.

He looked unenlightened.

"About my daughter, Mrs. Warren. She lives in New York, you know — on Long Island."

Then he had remembered something he had heard.

"Yes," he said.

"She met you, at the Fergusons', just for a moment, when she was out here last autumn. What really nice and simple people the Fergusons are, with all their money ! "

"Very nice indeed," he agreed, puzzled.

"I have been sorry for them in the past," she went on evenly. "They had rather a hard time — perhaps you may have heard. Nobody appreciated them. They were entombed, so to speak, in a hideous big house over on the South Side, which fortunately burned down, and then they bought in Park Street, and took a pew in St. John's. I suppose the idea of that huge department store *was* rather difficult to get used to. But I made up my mind it was nonsense to draw the line at department stores, — especially since Mr. Ferguson's was such a useful and remarkable one, so I went across and called. Mrs. Ferguson was so grateful, it was almost pathetic. And she's a very

good friend — she came here every day when Genevieve
had appendicitis."

"She's a good woman," the rector said.

"And Nan, — I adore Nan, everybody adores Nan.
She reminds me of one of those exquisite, blue-eyed dolls
her father imports. Now if I were a bachelor, Mr.
Hodder — ! " Mrs. Constable left the rest to his imagination.

He smiled.

"I'm afraid Miss Ferguson has her own ideas." Running through Hodder's mind, a troubled current, were
certain memories connected with Mrs. Warren. Was she
the divorced daughter, or was she not ?

"But I was going to speak to you about Gertrude.
She's had such a hard time, poor dear, my heart has bled
for her." There was a barely perceptible tremor in Mrs.
Constable's voice. "All that publicity, and the inevitable
suffering connected with it ! And no one can know the
misery she went through, she is so sensitive. But now,
at last, she has a chance for happiness — the real thing
has come."

"The real thing ! " he echoed.

"Yes. She's going to marry a splendid man, Eldridge
Sumner. I know the family well. They have always
stood for public spirit, and this Mr. Sumner, although he
is little over thirty, was chairman of that Vice Commission
which made such a stir in New York a year ago. He's a
lawyer, with a fine future, and they're madly in love.
And Gertrude realizes now, after her experience, the true
values in life. She was only a child when she married
Victor Warren."

"But Mr. Warren," Hodder managed to say, "is still
living."

"I sometimes wonder, Mr. Hodder," she went on hurriedly, "whether we *can* realize how different the world is
to-day from what it was twenty years ago, until something
of this kind is actually brought home to us. I shall never
forget how distressed, how overwhelmed Mr. Constable and
I were when Gertrude got her divorce. I know that they

are regarding such things differently in the East, but out here — ! We never dreamed that such a thing could happen to us, and we regarded it as a disgrace. But gradually " — she hesitated, and looked at the motionless clergyman — " gradually I began to see Gertrude's point of view, to understand that she had made a mistake, that she had been too young to comprehend what she was doing. Victor Warren had been ruined by money, he wasn't faithful to her, but an extraordinary thing has happened in his case. He's married again, and Gertrude tells me he's absurdly happy, and has two children."

As he listened, Hodder's dominating feeling was amazement that such a course as her daughter had taken should be condoned by this middle-aged lady, a prominent member of his congregation and the wife of a vestryman, who had been nurtured and steeped in Christianity. And not only that: Mrs. Constable was plainly defending a further step, which in his opinion involved a breach of the Seventh Commandment! To have invaded these precincts, the muddy, turbulent river of individualism had risen higher than he would have thought possible. . . .

" Wait!" she implored, checking his speech, — she had been watching him with what was plainly anxiety, — "don't say anything yet. I have a letter here which she wrote me — at the time. I kept it. Let me read a part of it to you, that you may understand more fully the tragedy of it."

Mrs. Constable thrust her hand into her lap and drew forth a thickly covered sheet.

" It was written just after she left him — it is an answer to my protest," she explained, and began to read : "'I know I promised to love Victor, mother, but how can one promise to do a thing over which one has no control? I loved him after he stopped loving me. He wasn't a bit suited to me — I see that now — he was attracted by the *outside* of me, and I never knew what *he* was like until I married him. His character seemed to change completely; he grew morose and quick-tempered and secretive, and nothing I did pleased him. We led a cat-and-

dog life. I never let you know — and yet I see now we
might have got along in any other relationship. We were
very friendly when we parted, and I'm not a bit jealous
because he cares for another woman who I can see is much
better suited to him.

"'I can't honestly regret leaving him, and I'm not
conscious of having done anything wrong. I don't want
to shock you, and I know how terribly you and father
must feel, but I can see now, somehow, that I had to go
through this experience, terrible as it was, to find myself.
If it were thirty years ago, before people began to be liberal
in such matters, I shudder to think what might have become of me. I should now be one of those terrible women
between fifty and sixty who have tried one frivolity and
excess after another — but I'm not coming to that ! And
my friends have really been awfully kind, and supported
me — even Victor's family. Don't, don't think that I'm
not respectable ! I know how you look at such things.'"
Mrs. Constable closed the letter abruptly.

"I did look at such things in that way," she added,
"but I've changed. That letter helped to change me, and
the fact that it was Gertrude who had been through this.
If you only knew Gertrude, Mr. Hodder, you couldn't
possibly think of her as anything but sweet and pure."

Although the extent of Hodder's acquaintance with
Mrs. Warren had been but five minutes, the letter had
surprisingly retouched to something like brilliancy her
faded portrait, the glow in her cheeks, the iris blue in her
eyes. He recalled the little shock he had experienced
when told that she was divorced, for her appeal had lain
in her very freshness, her frank and confiding manner.
She was one of those women who seem to say, "Here I
am, you can't but like me." And he had responded —
he remembered that — he had liked her. And now her
letter, despite his resistance, had made *its* appeal, so genuinely human was it, so honest, although it expressed a
philosophy he abhorred.

Mrs. Constable was watching him mutely, striving to
read in his grave eyes the effect of her pleadings.

"You are telling me this, Mrs. Constable — why?" he asked.

"Because I wished you to know the exact situation before I asked you, as a great favour to me, to Mr. Constable, to — to marry her in St. John's. Of course," she went on, controlling her rising agitation, and anticipating a sign of protest, "we shouldn't expect to have any people, — and Gertrude wasn't married in St. John's before; that wedding was at Passumset — our seashore place. Oh, Mr. Hodder, before you answer, think of our feelings, Mr. Constable's and mine! If you could see Mr. Constable, you would know how he suffers — this thing has upset him more than the divorce. His family have such pride. I am so worried about him, and he doesn't eat anything and looks so haggard. I told him I would see you and explain and that seemed to comfort him a little. She is, after all, our child, and we don't want to feel, so far as our church is concerned, that she is an Ishmaelite; we don't want to have the spectacle of her having to go around, outside, to find a clergyman — that would be too dreadful! I know how strict, how unflinching you are, and I admire you for it. But this is a special case."

She paused, breathing deeply, and Hodder gazed at her with pity. What he felt was more than pity; he was experiencing, indeed, but with a deeper emotion, something of that same confusion of values into which Eleanor Goodrich's visit had thrown him. At the same time it had not escaped his logical mind that Mrs. Constable had made her final plea on the score of respectability.

"It gives me great pain to have to refuse you," he said gently.

"Oh, don't," she said sharply, "don't say that! I can't have made the case clear. You are too big, too comprehending, Mr. Hodder, to have a hard-and-fast rule. There must be times — extenuating circumstances — and I believe the canons make it optional for a clergyman to marry the innocent person."

"Yes, it is optional, but I do not believe it should be. The question is left to the clergyman's conscience. According to my view, Mrs. Constable, the Church, as the agent of God, effects an indissoluble bond.   And much as I should like to do anything in my power for you and Mr. Constable, you have asked the impossible, — believing as I do, there can be no special case, no extenuating circumstance.   And it is my duty to tell you it is because people to-day are losing their beliefs that we have this lenient attitude toward the sacred things.   If they still held the conviction that marriage is of God, they would labour to make it a success, instead of flying apart at the first sign of what they choose to call incompatibility."

"But surely," she said, "we ought not to be punished for our mistakes!   I cannot believe that Christ himself intended that his religion should be so inelastic, so hard and fast, so cruel as you imply.   Surely there is enough unhappiness without making more.   You speak of incompatibility — but is it in all cases such an insignificant matter?   We are beginning to realize in these days something of the effects of character on character, — deteriorating effects, in many instances.   With certain persons we are lifted up, inspired to face the battle of life and overcome its difficulties.   I have known fine men and women whose lives have been stultified or ruined because they were badly mated.   And I cannot see that the character of my own daughter has deteriorated because she has got a divorce from a man with whom she was profoundly out of sympathy — of harmony.   On the contrary, she seems more of a person than she was; she has clearer, saner views of life; she has made her mistake and profited by it.   Her views changed — Victor Warren's did not.   She began to realize that some other woman might have an influence over his life — she had none, simply because he did not love her.   And love is not a thing we can compel."

"You are making it very hard for me, Mrs. Constable," he said.   "You are now advocating an individualism with which the Church can have no sympathy.   Christianity teaches us that life is probationary, and if we seek to avoid the trials sent us, instead of overcoming them, we find ourselves farther than ever from any solution.   We have to stand by our mistakes. If marriage is to be a mere trial of compatibility, why go through a ceremony than which there is none more binding in human and divine institutions? One either believes in it, or one does not. And, if belief be lacking, the state provides for the legalization of marriages."

"Oh!" she exclaimed.

"If persons wish to be married in church in these days merely because it is respectable, if such be their only reason, they are committing a great wrong. They are taking an oath before God with reservations, knowing that public opinion will release them if the marriage does not fulfil their expectations."

For a moment she gazed at him with parted lips, and pressing her handkerchief to her eyes began silently to cry. The sudden spectacle, in this condition, of a self-controlled woman of the world was infinitely distressing to Hodder, whose sympathies were even more sensitive than (in her attempt to play upon them) she had suspected. . . . She was aware that he had got to his feet, and was standing beside her, speaking with an oddly penetrating tenderness.

"I did not mean to be harsh," he said, "and it is not that I do not understand how you feel. You have made my duty peculiarly difficult."

She raised up to him a face from which the mask had fallen, from which the illusory look of youth had fled. He turned away. . . . And presently she began to speak again, in disconnected sentences.

"I so want her to be happy — I cannot think, I will not think that she has wrecked her life — it would be too unjust, too cruel. You cannot know what it is to be a woman!"

Before this cry he was silent.

"I don't ask anything of God except that she shall have a chance, and it seems to me that he is making the world better — less harsh for women."

He did not reply. And presently she looked up at him again, steadfastly now, searchingly. The barriers of the conventions were down, she had cast her pride to the winds. He seemed to read in her a certain relief.

"I am going to tell you something, Mr. Hodder, which you may think strange, but I have a reason for saying it. You are still a young man, and I feel instinctively that you have an unusual career before you. You interested me the first time you stepped into the pulpit of St. John's — and it will do me good to talk to you, this once, frankly. You have reiterated to-day, in no uncertain terms, doctrines which I once believed, which I was brought up to think infallible. But I have lived since then, and life itself has made me doubt them.

"I recognize in you a humanity, a sympathy and breadth which you are yourself probably not aware of, all of which is greater than the rule which you so confidently apply to fit all cases. It seems to me that Christ did not intend us to have such rules. He went beyond them, into the spirit.

"Under the conditions of society — of civilization to-day, most marriages are merely a matter of chance. Even judgment cannot foresee the development of character brought about by circumstances, by environment. And in many marriages I have known about intimately both the man and the woman have missed the most precious thing that life can give — something I cannot but think — God intends us to have. You see," — she smiled at him sadly — "I am still a little of an idealist.

"I missed — the thing I am talking about, and it has been the great sorrow of my life — not only on my account, but on my husband's. And so far as I am concerned, I am telling you the truth when I say I should have been content to have lived in a log cabin if — if the gift had been mine. Not all the money in the world, nor the intellect, nor the philanthropy — the so-called interests of life, will satisfy me for its denial. I am a disappointed woman, I sometimes think a bitter woman. I can't believe that life is meant to be so. Those energies have gone into ambition which should have been absorbed by — by something more worth while.

"And I can see so plainly now that my husband would

have been far, far happier with another kind of woman. I drew him away from the only work he ever enjoyed — his painting. I do not say he ever could have been a great artist, but he had a little of the divine spark, in his enthusiasm at least — in his assiduity. I shall never forget our first trip abroad, after we were married — he was like a boy in the galleries, in the studios. I could not understand it then. I had no real sympathy with art, but I tried to make sacrifices, what I thought were Christian sacrifices. The motive power was lacking, and no matter how hard I tried, I was only half-hearted, and he realized it instinctively — no amount of feigning could deceive him. Something deep in me, which was a part of my nature, was antagonistic, stultifying to the essentials of his own being. Of course neither of us saw that then, but the results were not long in developing. To him, art was a sacred thing, and it was impossible for me to regard it with equal seriousness. He drew into himself, — closed up, as it were, — no longer discussed it. I was hurt. And when we came home he kept on in business — he still had his father's affairs to look after — but he had a little workroom at the top of the house where he used to go in the afternoon. . . .

"It was a question which one of us should be warped, — which personality should be annihilated, so to speak, and I was the stronger. And as I look back, Mr. Hodder, what occurred seems to me absolutely inevitable, given the ingredients, as inevitable as a chemical process. We were both striving against each other, and I won — at a tremendous cost. The conflict, one might say, was subconscious, instinctive rather than deliberate. My attitude forced him back into business, although we had enough to live on very comfortably, and then the scale of life began to increase, luxuries formerly unthought of seemed to become necessities. And while it was still afar off I saw a great wave rolling toward us, the wave of that new prosperity which threatened to submerge us, and I seized the buoy fate had placed in our hands, — or rather, by suggestion, I induced my husband to seize it, — his name.

"I recognized the genius, the future of Eldon Parr at a time when he was not yet independent and supreme, when association with a Constable meant much to him. Mr. Parr made us, as the saying goes. Needless to say, money has not brought happiness, but a host of hard, false ambitions which culminated in Gertrude's marriage with Victor Warren. I set my heart on the match, helped it in every way, and until now nothing but sorrow has come of it. But my point is this, — I see so clearly, now that it is too late, that two excellent persons may demoralize each other if they are ill-mated. It may be possible that I had the germs of false ambition in me when I was a girl, yet I was conscious only of the ideal which is in most women's hearts. . . .

"You must not think that I have laid my soul bare in the hope of changing your mind in regard to Gertrude. I recognize clearly, now, that that is impossible. Oh, I know you do not so misjudge me," she added, reading his quick protest in his face.

"Indeed, I cannot analyze my reasons for telling you something of which I have never spoken to any one else." Mrs. Constable regarded him fixedly. "*You* are the strongest reason. You have somehow drawn it out of me. . . . And I suppose I wish *some one* to profit by it. *You* can, Mr. Hodder, — I feel sure of that. You may insist now that my argument against your present conviction of the indissolubility of marriage is mere individualism, but I want you to think of what I have told you, not to answer me now. I know your argument by heart, that Christian character develops by submission, by suffering, that it is the woman's place to submit, to efface herself. But the root of the matter goes deeper than that. I am far from deploring sacrifice, yet common-sense tells us that our sacrifice should be guided by *judgment*, that foolish sacrifices are worse than useless. And there are times when the very limitations of our individuality — necessary limitations for us — prevent our sacrifices from counting.

"I was wrong, I grant you, grievously wrong in the course I took, even though it were not consciously deliberate. But if my husband had been an artist I should always have remained separated from his real life by a limitation I had no power to remove. The more I tried, the more apparent my lack of insight became to him, the more irritated he grew. I studied his sketches, I studied masterpieces, but it was all hopeless. The thing wasn't in me, and he knew it wasn't. Every remark made him quiver.

" The Church, I think, will grow more liberal, must grow more liberal, if it wishes to keep in touch with people in an age when they are thinking out these questions for themselves. The law cannot fit all cases, I am sure the Gospel can. And sometimes women have an instinct, a kind of second sight into persons, Mr. Hodder. I cannot explain *why* I feel that you have in you elements of growth which will eventually bring you more into sympathy with the point of view I have set forth, but I do feel it."

Hodder did not attempt to refute her — she had, indeed, made discussion impossible. She knew his arguments, as she had declared, and he had the intelligence to realize that a repetition of them, on his part, would be useless. She brought home to him, as never before, a sense of the anomalistic position of the Church in these modern days, of its appallingly lessened weight even with its own members. As a successor of the Apostles, he had no power over this woman, or very little ; he could neither rebuke her, nor sentence her to penance. She recognized his authority to marry her daughter, to baptize her daughter's children, but not to interfere in any way with her spiritual life. It was as a personality he had moved her — a personality apparently not in harmony with his doctrine. Women had hinted at this before. And while Mrs. Constable had not, as she perceived, shaken his conviction, the very vividness and unexpectedness of a confession from her had stirred him to the marrow, had opened doors, perforce, which he himself had marked forbidden, and given him a glimpse beyond before he could lower his eyes. Was there, after all, something in him that responded in spite of himself ? . . .

He sat gazing at her, his head bent, his strong hands on the arms of the chair.

"We never can foresee how we may change," he answered, a light in his eyes that was like a smile, yet having no suggestion of levity. And his voice—despite his disagreement—maintained the quality of his sympathy. Neither felt the oddity, then, of the absence of a jarring note. "You may be sure, at least, of my confidence, and of my gratitude for what you have told me."

His tone belied the formality of his speech. Mrs. Constable returned his gaze in silence, and before words came again to either, a step sounded on the threshold and Mr. Constable entered.

Hodder looked at him with a new vision. His face was indeed lined and worn, and dark circles were under his eyes. But at Mrs. Constable's "Here's Mr. Hodder, dear," he came forward briskly to welcome the clergyman.

"How do you do?" he said cordially. "We don't see you very often."

"I have been telling Mr. Hodder that modern rectors of big parishes have far too many duties," said his wife.

And after a few minutes of desultory conversation, the rector left.

CHAPTER VI

"WATCHMAN, WHAT OF THE NIGHT?"

It was one of those moist nights of spring when the air
is pungent with the odour of the softened earth, and the
gentle breaths that stirred the curtains in Mr. Parr's big
dining-room wafted, from the garden, the perfumes of a
revived creation,—delicious, hothouse smells. At intervals, showers might be heard pattering on the walk outside. The rector of St. John's was dining with his great
parishioner.

Here indeed were a subject for some modern master, a
chance to picture for generations to come an aspect of a
mighty age, an age that may some day be deemed but a
grotesque and anomalistic survival of a more ancient
logic ; a gargoyle carved out of chaos, that bears on its
features a resemblance to the past and the future.

Our scene might almost be mediæval with its encircling
gloom, through which the heavy tapestries and shadowy
corners of the huge apartment may be dimly made out.
In the center, the soft red glow of the candles, the gleaming silver, the shining cloth, the Church on one side—and
what on the other? No name given it now, no royal
name, but still Power. The two are still in apposition,
not yet in opposition, but the discerning may perchance
read a prophecy in the salient features of the priest.

The Man of Power of the beginning of the twentieth
century demands a subtler analysis, presents an enigma
to which the immortal portraits of forgotten Medicis and
Capets give no clew. Imagine, if you can, a Lorenzo or a
Grand Louis in a tightly-buttoned frock coat ! There
must be some logical connection between the habit and

the age, since crimson velvet and gold brocade would have made Eldon Parr merely ridiculous.

He is by no means ridiculous, yet take him out of the setting and put him in the street, and you might pass him a dozen times without noticing him. Nature, and perhaps unconscious art, have provided him with a protective exterior; he is the colour of his jungle. After he has crippled you — if you survive — you will never forget him. You will remember his eye, — which can be unsheathed like a rapier; you will recall his lips as the expression of a relentless negative. The significance of the slight bridge on the narrow nose is less easy to define. He is neither tall nor short; his face is clean-shaven, save for scanty, unobtrusive reddish tufts high on the cheeks; his hair is thin.

It must be borne in mind, however, that our rector did not see him in his jungle, and perhaps in the traditional nobility of the lion there is a certain truth. An interesting biography of some of the powerful of this earth might be written from the point of view of the confessor or the physician, who find something to love, something to pity, and nothing to fear — thus reversing the sentiments of the public.

Yet the friendship between John Hodder and Eldon Parr defied any definite analysis on the rector's part, and was perhaps the strangest and most disquieting element that had as yet come into Hodder's life. The nature of his intimacy with the banker, if intimacy it might be called, might have surprised his other parishioners if they could have been hidden spectators of one of these dinners. There were long silences when the medium of communication, tenuous at best, seemed to snap, and the two sat gazing at each other as from mountain peaks across impassable valleys. With all the will in the world, their souls lost touch, though the sense in the clergyman of the other's vague yearning for human companionship was never absent. It was this yearning that attracted Hodder, who found in it a deep pathos.

After one of these intervals of silence, Eldon Parr looked up from his claret.

G

"I congratulate you, Hodder, on the stand you took in regard to Constable's daughter," he said.

"I didn't suppose it was known," answered the rector, in surprise.

"Constable told me. I have reason to believe that he doesn't sympathize with his wife in her attitude on this matter. It's pulled him down, — you've noticed that he looks badly?"

"Yes," said the rector. He did not care to discuss the affair; he had hoped it would not become known; and he shunned the congratulations of Gordon Atterbury, which in such case would be inevitable. And in spite of the conviction that he had done his duty, the memory of his talk with Mrs. Constable never failed to make him uncomfortable.

Exasperation crept into Mr. Parr's voice.

"I can't think what's got into women in these times — at Mrs. Constable's age they ought to know better. Nothing restrains them. They have reached a point where they don't even respect the Church. And when that happens, it is serious indeed. The Church is the governor on our social engine, and it is supposed to impose a restraint upon the lawless."

Hodder could not refrain from smiling a little at the banker's conception.

"Doesn't that reduce the Church somewhere to the level of the police force?" he asked.

"Not at all," said Eldon Parr, whose feelings seemed to be rising. "I am sorry for Constable. He feels the shame of this thing keenly, and he ought to go away for a while to one of these quiet resorts. I offered him my car. Sometimes I think that women have no morals. At any rate, this modern notion of giving them their liberty is sheer folly. Look what they have done with it! Instead of remaining at home, where they belong, they are going out into the world and turning it topsy-turvy. And if a man doesn't let them have a free hand, they get a divorce and marry some idiot who will."

Mr. Parr pushed back his chair and rose abruptly, start-

"THE TWO SAT GAZING AT EACH OTHER AS FROM MOUNTAIN PEAKS
ACROSS IMPASSABLE VALLEYS."

ing for the door. The rector followed him, forcibly struck by the unusual bitterness in his tone.

" If I have spoken strongly, it is because I feel strongly," he said in a strange, thickened voice. "Hodder, how would you like to live in this house — alone ? "

The rector looked down upon him with keen, comprehending eyes, and saw Eldon Parr as he only, of all men, had seen him. For he himself did not understand his own strange power of drawing forth the spirit from its shell, of compelling the inner, suffering thing to reveal itself.

" This poison," Eldon Parr went on unevenly, "has eaten into my own family. My daughter, who might have been a comfort and a companion, since she chose not to marry, was carried away by it, and thought it incumbent upon her to have a career of her own. And now I have a choice of thirty rooms, and not a soul to share them with. Sometimes, at night, I make up my mind to sell this house. But I can't do it — something holds me back, hope, superstition, or whatever you've a mind to call it. You've never seen all of the house, have you ? " he asked.

The rector slowly shook his head, and the movement might have been one that he would have used in acquiescence to the odd whim of a child. Mr. Parr led the way up the wide staircase to the corridor above, traversing chamber after chamber, turning on the lights.

" These were my wife's rooms," he said, "they are just as she left them. And these my daughter Alison's, when she chooses to pay me a visit. I didn't realize that I should have to spend the last years of my life alone. And I meant, when I gave my wife a house, to have it the best in the city. I spared nothing on it, as you see, neither care nor money. I had the best architect I could find, and used the best material. And what good is it to me ? Only a reminder — of what might have been. But I've got a boy, Hodder, — I don't know whether I've ever spoken of him to you — Preston. *He's* gone away, too. But I've always had the hope that he might come back and get decently married, and live here. That's why I stay. I'll show you his picture."

They climbed to the third floor, and while Mr. Parr was searching for the electric switch, a lightning flash broke over the forests of the park, prematurely revealing the room. It was a boy's room, hung with photographs of school and college crews and teams and groups of intimates, with deep window seats, and draped pennons of Harvard University over the fireplace. Eldon Parr turned to one of the groups on the wall, the earliest taken at school.

" There he is," he said, pointing out a sunny little face at the bottom, a boy of twelve, bareheaded, with short, crisping yellow hair, smiling lips and laughing eyes. " And here he is again," indicating another group. Thus he traced him through succeeding years until they came to those of college.

" There he is," said the rector. " I think I can pick him out now."

" Yes, that's Preston," said his father, staring hard at the picture. The face had developed, the body had grown almost to man's estate, but the hint of crispness was still in the hair, the mischievous laughter in the eyes. The rector gazed earnestly at the face, remembering his own boyhood, his own youth, his mind dwelling, too, on what he had heard of the original of the portrait. What had happened to the boy, to bring to naught the fair promise of this earlier presentment ?

He was aroused by the voice of Eldon Parr, who had sunk into one of the leather chairs.

" I can see him now," he was saying, " as he used to come running down that long flight of stone steps in Ransome Street to meet me when I came home. Such laughter ! And once, in his eagerness, he fell and cut his forehead. I shall never forget how I felt. And when I picked him up he tried to laugh still, with the tears rolling down his face. You know the way a child's breath catches, Hodder ? He was always laughing. And how he used to cling to me, and beg me to take him out, and show such an interest in everything ! He was a bright boy, a remarkable child, I thought, but I suppose it was my foolishness. He analyzed all he saw, and when he used to go off in my car,

Brennan, the engineer, would always beg to have him in the cab. And such sympathy ! He knew in an instant when I was worried. I had dreams of what that boy would become, but I was too sure of it. I went on doing other things — there were so many things, and I was a slave to them. And before I knew it, he'd gone off to school — that was the year I moved up here, and my wife died. And after that, all seemed to go wrong. Perhaps I was too severe ; perhaps they didn't understand him at boarding-school ; perhaps I didn't pay enough attention to him. At any rate, the first thing I knew his whole nature seemed to have changed. He got into scrape after scrape at Harvard, and later he came within an ace of marrying a woman. . . . He's my weakness to-day. I can say no to everybody in the world but to him, and when I try to remember him as he used to come down those steps on Ransome Street. . . .

"He never knew how much I cared — that what I was doing was all for him, building for him, that he might carry on my work. I had dreams of developing this city, the great Southwest, and after I had gone Preston was to bring them to fruition.

"For some reason I never was able to tell him all this — as I am telling you. The words would not come. We had grown apart. And he seemed to think — God knows why ! — he seemed to think I disliked him. I had Langmaid talk to him, and other men I trusted — tell him what an unparalleled opportunity he had to be of use in the world. Once I thought I had him started straight — and then a woman came along — off the streets, or little better. He insisted on marrying her and wrecking his life, and when I got her out of the way, as any father would have done, he left me. He has never forgiven me. Most of the time I haven't even the satisfaction of knowing where he is — London, Paris, or New York. I try not to think of what he does. I ought to cut him off, — I can't do it — I can't do it, Hodder — he's my one weakness still. I'm afraid — he'd sink out of sight entirely, and it's the one hold I have left on him."

Eldon Parr paused, with a groan that betokened not only a poignant sorrow, but also something of relief — for the tortures of not being able to unburden himself had plainly become intolerable. He glanced up and met the compassionate eyes of the rector, who stood leaning against the mantel.

"With Alison it was different," he said. "I never understood her — even when she was a child — and I used to look at her and wonder that she could be my daughter. She was moody, intense, with a yearning for affection — I've since sometimes thought — she could not express. I did not feel the need of affection in those days, so absorbed was I in building up, — so absorbed and driven, you might say. I suppose I must accept my punishment as just. But the child was always distant with me, and I always remember her in rebellion; a dark little thing with a quivering lip, hair awry, and eyes that flashed through her tears. She would take any amount of punishment rather than admit she had been in the wrong. I recall she had once a fox terrier that never left her, that fought all the dogs in the neighbourhood and destroyed the rugs and cushions in the house. I got rid of it one summer when she was at the sea, and I think she never forgave me. The first question she asked when she came home was for that dog — Mischief, his name was — for Mischief. I told her what I had done. It took more courage than I had thought. She went to her room, locked herself in, and stayed there, and we couldn't get her to come out for two days; she wouldn't even eat.

"Perhaps she was jealous of Preston, but she never acknowledged it. When she was little she used once in a while to come shyly and sit on my lap, and look at me without saying anything. I hadn't the slightest notion what was in the child's mind, and her reserve increased as she grew older. She seemed to have developed a sort of philosophy of her own even before she went away to school, and to have certain strongly defined tastes. She liked, for instance, to listen to music, and for that very reason would never learn to play. We couldn't make her, as a child.

Bad music, she said, offended her. She painted, she was passionately fond of flowers, and her room was always filled with them. When she came back from school to live with me, she built a studio upstairs. After the first winter, she didn't care to go out much. By so pronounced a character, young men in general were not attracted, but there were a few who fell under a sort of spell. I can think of no other words strong enough, and I used to watch them when they came here with a curious interest. I didn't approve of all of them. Alison would dismiss them or ignore them or be kind to them as she happened to feel, yet it didn't seem to make any difference. One I suspect she was in love with — a fellow without a cent.

"Then there was Bedloe Hubbell. I have reason enough to be thankful now that she didn't care for him. They've made him president, you know, of this idiotic Municipal League, as they call it. But in those days he hadn't developed any nonsense, he was making a good start at the bar, and was well off. His father was Elias Hubbell, who gave the Botanical Garden to the city. I wanted her to marry Gordon Atterbury. He hung on longer than any of them — five or six years; but she wouldn't hear of it. That was how the real difference developed between us, although the trouble was deep rooted, for we never really understood each other. I had set my heart on it, and perhaps I was too dictatorial and insistent. I don't know. I meant the best for her, God knows. . . . Gordon never got over it. It dried him up." . . . Irritation was creeping back into the banker's voice.

"Then it came into Alison's head that she wanted to 'make something of her life,' — as she expressed it. She said she was wasting herself, and began going to lectures with a lot of faddish women, became saturated with these nonsensical ideas about her sex that are doing so much harm nowadays. I suppose I was wrong in my treatment from the first. I never knew how to handle her, but we grew like flint and steel. I'll say this for her, she kept quiet enough, but she used to sit opposite me at the table, and I knew all the time what she was thinking of, and then I'd break out. Of course she'd defend herself, but she had her temper under better control than I. She wanted to go away for a year or two and study landscape gardening, and then come back and establish herself in an office here. I wouldn't listen to it. And one morning, when she was late to breakfast, I delivered an ultimatum. I gave her a lecture on a woman's place and a woman's duty, and told her that if she didn't marry she'd have to stay here and live quietly with me, or I'd disinherit her."

Hodder had become absorbed in this portrait of Alison Parr, drawn by her father with such unconscious vividness.

"And then?" he asked.

In spite of the tone of bitterness in which he had spoken, Eldon Parr smiled. It was a reluctant tribute to his daughter.

"I got an ultimatum in return," he said. "Alison should have been a man." His anger mounted quickly as he recalled the scene. "She said she had thought it all out: that our relationship had become impossible; that she had no doubt it was largely her fault, but that was the way she was made, and she couldn't change. She had, naturally, an affection for me as her father, but it was very plain we couldn't get along together: she was convinced that she had a right to individual freedom,— as she spoke of it, — to develop herself. She knew, if she continued to live with me on the terms I demanded, that her character would deteriorate. Certain kinds of sacrifice she was capable of, she thought, but what I asked would be a useless one. Perhaps I didn't realize it, but it was slavery. Slavery!" he repeated, "the kind of slavery her mother had lived. . . ."

He took a turn around the room.

"So far as money was concerned, she was indifferent to it. She had enough from her mother to last until she began to make more. She wouldn't take any from me in any case. I laughed, yet I have never been so angry in my life. Nor was it wholly anger, Hodder, but a queer tangle of feelings I can't describe. There was affection mixed up in it — I realized afterward — but I longed to take her and shake her and lock her up until she should come to her senses. I couldn't. I didn't dare. I was helpless. I told her to go. She didn't say anything more, but there was a determined look in her eyes when she kissed me as I left for the office. I spent a miserable day. More than once I made up my mind to go home, but pride stopped me. I really didn't think she meant what she said. When I got back to the house in the afternoon she had left for New York. . . .

"Then I began to look forward to the time when her money would give out. She went to Paris with another young woman, and studied there, and then to England. She came back to New York, hired an apartment and a studio, and has made a success."

The rector seemed to detect an unwilling note of pride at the magic word.

"It isn't the kind of success I think much of, but it's what she started out to do. She comes out to see me, once in a while, and she designed that garden."

He halted in front of the clergyman.

"I suppose you think it's strange, my telling you this," he said. "It has come to the point," he declared vehemently, "where it relieves me to tell somebody, and you seem to be a man of discretion and common-sense."

Hodder looked down into Mr. Parr's face, and was silent. Perhaps he recognized, as never before, the futility of the traditional words of comfort, of rebuke. He beheld a soul in torture, and realized with sudden sharpness how limited was his knowledge of the conditions of existence of his own time. Everywhere individualism reared its ugly head, everywhere it seemed plausible to plead justification; and once more he encountered that incompatibility of which Mrs. Constable had spoken! He might blame the son, blame the daughter, yet he could not condemn them utterly. . . . One thing he saw clearly, that Eldon Parr had slipped into what was still, for him, a meaningless hell.

The banker's manner suddenly changed, reverted to what it had been. He arose.

"I've tried to do my duty as I saw it, and it comes to this — that we who have spent the best years of our lives in striving to develop this country have no thanks from our children or from any one else."

With his hand on the electric switch, he faced Hodder almost defiantly as he spoke these words, and suddenly snapped off the light, as though the matter admitted of no discussion. In semi-darkness they groped down the upper flight of stairs. . . .

CHAPTER VII

THE KINGDOMS OF THE WORLD

I

When summer arrived, the birds of brilliant plumage of Mr. Hodder's flock arose and flew lightly away, thus reversing the seasons. Only the soberer ones came fluttering into the cool church out of the blinding heat, and settled here and there throughout the nave. The ample Mr. Bradley, perspiring in an alpaca coat, took up the meagre collection on the right of the centre aisle; for Mr. Parr, properly heralded, had gone abroad on one of those periodical, though lonely tours that sent anticipatory shivers of delight down the spines of foreign picture-dealers. The faithful Gordon Atterbury was worshipping at the sea, and even Mr. Constable and Mr. Plimpton, when recalled to the city by financial cares, succumbed to the pagan influence of the sun, and were usually to be found on Sunday mornings on the wide veranda of the country club, with glasses containing liquid and ice beside them, and surrounded by heaps of newspapers.

To judge by St. John's, the city was empty. But on occasions, before he himself somewhat tardily departed, — drawn thither by a morbid though impelling attraction, — Hodder occasionally walked through Dalton Street of an evening. If not in St. John's, summer was the season in Dalton Street. It flung open its doors and windows and moved out on the steps and the pavements, and even on the asphalt; and the music of its cafés and dance-halls throbbed feverishly through the hot nights. Dalton Street resorted neither to country club nor church.

Mr. McCrae, Hodder's assistant, seemed to regard these

annual phenomena with a grim philosophy, — a relic, perhaps, of the Calvinistic determinism of his ancestors. He preached the same indefinite sermons, with the same imperturbability, to the dwindled congregations in summer and the enlarged ones in winter. But Hodder was capable of no such resignation — if resignation it were, for the self-contained assistant continued to be an enigma; and it was not without compunction that he left, about the middle of July, on his own vacation. He was tired, and yet he seemed to have accomplished nothing in this first year of the city parish whereof he had dreamed. And it was, no doubt, for that very reason that he was conscious of a depressing exhaustion as his train rolled eastward over that same high bridge that spanned the hot and muddy waters of the river. He felt a fugitive. In no months since he had left the theological seminary, had he seemingly accomplished so little ; in no months had he had so magnificent an opportunity.

After he had reached the peaceful hills at Bremerton — where he had gone on Mrs. Whitely's invitation — he began to look back upon the spring and winter as a kind of mad nightmare, a period of ceaseless, distracted, and dissipated activity, of rushing hither and thither with no results. He had been aware of invisible barriers, restricting, hemming him in on all sides. There had been no time for reflection; and now that he had a breathing space, he was unable to see how he might reorganize his work in order to make it more efficient.

There were other perplexities, brought about by the glimpses he had had into the lives and beliefs — or rather unbeliefs — of his new parishioners. And sometimes, in an unwonted moment of pessimism, he asked himself why they thought it necessary to keep all that machinery going when it had so little apparent effect on their lives? He sat wistfully in the chancel of the little Bremerton church and looked into the familiar faces of those he had found in it when he came to it, and of those he had brought into it, wondering why he had been foolish enough to think himself endowed for the larger work. Here, he had been a factor, a force in the community, had entered into its life and affections. What was he there?

Nor did it tend to ease his mind that he was treated as one who has passed on to higher things.

" I was afraid you'd work too hard," said Mrs. Whitely, in her motherly way. "I warned you against it, Mr. Hodder. You never spared yourself, but in a big city parish it's different. But you've made such a success, Nelson tells me, and everybody likes you there. I knew they would, of course. That is our only comfort in losing you, that you have gone to the greater work. But we do miss you."

II

The air of Bremerton, and later the air of Bar Harbor had a certain reviving effect. And John Hodder, although he might be cast down, had never once entertained the notion of surrender. He was inclined to attribute the depression through which he had passed, the disappointment he had undergone as a just punishment for an over-abundance of ego, — only Hodder used the theological term for the same sin. Had he not, after all, laboured largely for his own glory, and not God's? Had he ever forgotten himself? Had the idea ever been far from his thoughts that it was he, John Hodder, who would build up the parish of St. John's into a living organization of faith and works? The curious thing was that he *had* the power, and save in moments of weariness he felt it in him. He must try to remember always that this power was from God. But why had he been unable to apply it?

And there remained disturbingly in his memory certain phrases of Mrs. Constable's, such as " elements of growth." He would change, she had said; and he had appeared to her as one with depths. Unsuspected depths — pockets that held the steam, which was increasing in pressure. At Bremerton, it had not gathered in the pockets, he had used it all — all had counted; but in the feverish, cease-less activity of the city parish he had never once felt that intense satisfaction of *emptying himself*, nor the sweet weariness that follows it. His seemed the weariness of futility. And introspection was revealing a crack — after so many years — in that self that he had believed to be so strongly welded. Such was the strain of the pent-up force. He recognized the danger-signal. The same phenomenon had driven him into the Church, where the steam had found an outlet — until now. And yet, so far as his examination went, he had not lost his beliefs, but the power of communicating them to others.

Bremerton, and the sight of another carrying on the work in which he had been happy, weighed upon him, and Bar Harbor offered distraction. Mrs. Larrabbee had not hesitated to remind him of his promise to visit her. If the gallery of portraits of the congregation of St. John's were to be painted, this lady's, at the age of thirty, would not be the least interesting. It would have been out of place in no ancestral hall, and many of her friends were surprised, after her husband's death, that she did not choose one wherein to hang it. She might have. For she was the quintessence of that feminine product of our country at which Europe has never ceased to wonder, and to give her history would no more account for her than the process of manufacture explains the most delicate of scents. Her poise, her quick detection of sham in others not so fortunate, her absolute conviction that all things were as they ought to be ; her charity, her interest in its recipients; her smile, which was kindness itself ; her delicate features, her white skin with its natural bloom; the grace of her movements, and her hair, which had a different color in changing lights — such an *ensemble* is not to be depicted save by a skilled hand.

The late Mr. Larrabbee's name was still printed on millions of bright labels encircling cubes of tobacco, now manufactured by a Trust. However, since the kind that entered Mrs. Larrabbee's house, or houses, was all imported from Egypt or Cuba, what might have been in the nature of an unpleasant reminder was remote from her sight, and she never drove into the northern part of the city, where some hundreds of young women bent all day over the cutting-machines. To enter too definitely into Mrs. Larrabbee's history, therefore, were merely to be crude, for she is not a lady to caricature. Her father had been a steamboat captain — once an honoured calling in the city of her nativity — a devout Presbyterian who believed in the most rigid simplicity. Few who remembered the *gaucheries* of Captain Corington's daughter on her first presentation to his family's friends could recognize her in the cosmopolitan Mrs. Larrabbee. Why, with New York and London at her disposal, she elected to remain in the Middle West, puzzled them, though they found her answer, "that she belonged there," satisfying. Grace Larrabbee's cosmopolitanism was of that apperception that knows the value of *roots*, and during her widowhood she had been thrusting them out. Mrs. Larrabbee followed by "of" was much more important than just Mrs. Larrabbee. And she was, moreover, genuinely attached to her roots.

Her girlhood shyness — rudeness, some called it, mistaking the effect for the cause — had refined into a manner that might be characterized as *difficile*, though Hodder had never found her so. She liked direct men ; to discover no guile on first acquaintance went a long way with her, and not the least of the new rector's social triumphs had been his simple conquest.

Enveloped in white flannel, she met his early train at the Ferry ; an unusual compliment to a guest, had he but known it, but he accepted it as a tribute to the Church.

" I was so afraid you wouldn't come," she said, in a voice that conveyed indeed more than a perfunctory expression. She glanced at him as he sat beside her on the cushions of the flying motor boat, his strange eyes fixed upon the blue mountains of the island whither they were bound, his unruly hair fanned by the wind.

" Why ? " he asked, smiling at the face beneath the flying veil.

" You need the rest. I believe in men taking their work seriously, but not so seriously as you do."

She was so undisguisedly glad to see him that he could scarcely have been human if he had not responded. And she gave him, in that fortnight, a glimpse of a life that was new and distracting : at times made him forget — and he was willing to forget — the lower forms of which it was the quintessence, — the factories that hummed, the forges that flung their fires into the night in order that it might exist; the Dalton Streets that went without. The effluvia from hot asphalt bore no resemblance to the salt-laden air that rattled the Venetian blinds of the big bedroom to which he was assigned. Her villa was set high above the curving shore, facing a sheltered terrace-garden resplendent in its August glory; to seaward, islands danced in the haze; and behind the house, in the sunlight, were massed spruces of a brilliant arsenic green with purple cones. The fluttering awnings were striped cardinal and white.

Nature and man seemed to have conspired to make this place vividly unreal, as a toy village comes painted from the shop. There were no half-tones, no poverty — in sight, at least; no litter. On the streets and roads, at the casino attached to the swimming-pool and at the golf club were to be seen bewildering arrays of well-dressed, well-fed women intent upon pleasure and exercise. Some of them gave him glances that seemed to say, "You belong to us," and almost succeeded in establishing the delusion. The whole effect upon Hodder, in the state of mind in which he found himself, was reacting, stimulating, disquieting. At luncheons and dinners, he was what is known as a " success " — always that magic woi !.

He resisted, and none so quick as women to scent resistance. His very unbending attitude aroused their inherent craving for rigidity in his profession; he was neither plastic, unctuous, nor subservient; his very homeliness, redeemed by the eyes and mouth, compelled their attention. One of them told Mrs. Larrabbee that that rector of hers would " do something."

But what, he asked himself, was he resisting? He was by no means a Puritan; and while he looked upon a reasonable asceticism as having its place in the faith that he professed, it was no asceticism that prevented a more complete acquiescence on his part in the mad carnival that surrounded him.

"I'm afraid you don't wholly approve of Bar Harbor," his hostess remarked, one morning.

"At first sight, it is somewhat staggering to the provincial mind," he replied.

She smiled at him, yet with knitted brows.

"You are always putting me off — I never can tell what you think. And yet I'm sure you have opinions. You think these people frivolous, of course."

"Most of them are so," he answered, "but that is a very superficial criticism. The question is, *why* are they so? The sight of Bar Harbor leads a stranger to the reflection that the carnival mood has become permanent with our countrymen, and especially our countrywomen."

"The carnival mood," she repeated thoughtfully, "yes, that expresses it. We are light, we are always trying to get away from ourselves, and sometimes I wonder whether there are any selves to get away from. *You* ought to stop us," she added, almost accusingly, "to bring us to our senses."

"That's just it," he agreed, "why don't we? Why can't we?"

"If more clergymen were like you, I think perhaps you might."

His tone, his expression, were revelations.

"I —!" he exclaimed sharply, and controlled himself. But in that moment Grace Larrabbee had a glimpse of the man who had come to arouse in her an intense curiosity. For an instant a tongue of the fires of Vulcan had shot forth, fires that she had suspected.

"Aren't you too ambitious?" she asked gently. And again, although she did not often blunder, she saw him wince. "I don't mean ambitious for yourself. But surely you have made a remarkable beginning at St. John's. Everybody admires and respects you, has confidence in you. You are so sure of yourself," she hesitated

H

a moment, for she had never ventured to discuss religion with him, "of your faith. Clergymen ought not to be apologetic, and your conviction cannot fail, in the long run, to have its effect."

"Its effect, — on what?" he asked.

Mrs. Larrabee was suddenly at sea. And she prided herself on a lack of that vagueness generally attributed to her sex.

"On — on everything. On what we were talking about, — the carnival feeling, the levity, on the unbelief of the age. Isn't it because the control has been taken off?"

He saw an opportunity to slip into smoother waters.

"The engine has lost its governor?"

"Exactly!" cried Mrs. Larrabee. "What a clever simile!"

"It is Mr. Parr's," said Hodder. "Only he was speaking of other symptoms, Socialism, and its opposite, individualism, — not carnivalism."

"Poor man," said Mrs. Larrabee, accepting the new ground as safer, yet with a baffled feeling that Hodder had evaded her once more, "he has had his share of individualism and carnivalism. His son Preston was here last month, and was taken out to the yacht every night in an unspeakable state. And Alison hasn't been what might be called a blessing."

"She must be unusual," said the rector, musingly.

"Oh, Alison is a Person. She has become quite the fashion, and has more work than she can possibly attend to. Very few women with her good looks could have done what she has without severe criticism, and something worse, perhaps. The most extraordinary thing about her is her contempt for what her father has gained, and for conventionalities. It always amuses me when I think that she might have been the wife of Gordon Atterbury. The Goddess of Liberty linked to — what?"

Hodder thought instinctively of the Church. But he remained silent.

"As a rule, men are such fools about the women they

wish to marry," she continued. "She would have led him a dance for a year or two, and then calmly and inexorably left him. And there was her father, with all his ability and genius, couldn't see it either, but fondly imagined that Alison as Gordon Atterbury's wife, would magically become an Atterbury and a bourgeoise, see that the corners were dusted in the big house, sew underwear for the poor, and fast in Lent."

"And she is happy — where she is ? " he inquired somewhat naively.

"She is self-sufficient," said Mrs. Larrabbee, with unusual feeling, "and that is just what most women are not, in these days. Oh, why has life become such a problem ? Sometimes I think, with all that I have, I'm not so well off as one of those salesgirls in Ferguson's, at home. I'm always searching for things to do — nothing is *thrust* on me. There are the charities — Galt House, and all that, but I never seem to *get at* anything, at the people I'd like to help. It's like sending money to China. There is no direct touch any more. It's like seeing one's opportunities through an iron grating."

Hodder started at the phrase, so exactly had she expressed his own case.

"Ah," he said, "the iron grating bars the path of the Church, too."

And just what was the iron grating ?

They had many moments of intimacy during that fortnight, though none in which the plumb of their conversation descended to such a depth. For he was, as she had said, always "putting her off." Was it because he couldn't satisfy her craving ? give her the solution for which — he began to see — she thirsted ? Why didn't that religion that she seemed outwardly to profess and accept without qualification — the religion he taught — set her at rest ? show her the path ?

Down in his heart he knew that he feared to ask.

That Mrs. Larrabbee was still another revelation, that she was not at rest, was gradually revealed to him as the

days passed. Her spirit, too, like his own, like Mrs.
Constable's, like Eldon Parr's, like Eleanor Goodrich's,
was divided against itself; and this phenomenon in Mrs.
Larrabbee was perhaps a greater shock to him, since he had
always regarded her as essentially in equilibrium. One
of his reasons, indeed, — in addition to the friendship that
had grown up between them, — for coming to visit her
had been to gain the effect of her poise on his own. Poise
in a modern woman, leading a modern life. It was thus
she attracted him. It was not that he ignored her
frivolous side; it was nicely balanced by the other, and
that other seemed growing. The social, she accepted at
what appeared to be its own worth. Unlike Mrs.
Plimpton, for instance, she was so innately a lady that she
had met with no resistance in the Eastern watering places,
and her sense of values had remained the truer for it.

He did not admire her the less now he had discovered
that the poise was not so adjusted as he had thought it,
but his feeling about her changed, grew more personal,
more complicated. She was showing an alarming tendency to lean on him at a time when he was examining
with some concern his own supports. She possessed
intelligence and fascination, she was a woman whose
attentions would have flattered and disturbed any man
with a spark of virility, and Hodder had constantly before
his eyes the spectacle of others paying her court. Here
were danger-signals again !

Mrs. Plaice, a middle-aged English lady staying in the
house, never appeared until noon. Breakfast was set out
in the tiled and sheltered loggia, where they were fanned
by the cool airs of a softly breathing ocean. The world,
on these mornings, had a sparkling unreality, the cold,
cobalt sea stretching to sun-lit isles, and beyond, the
vividly painted shore, — the setting of luxury had never
been so complete. And the woman who sat opposite him
seemed, like one of her own nectarines, to be the fruit
that crowned it all.

Why not yield to the enchantment ? Why rebel,
when nobody else complained ? Were it not more simple

to accept what life sent in its orderly course instead of striving for an impossible and shadowy ideal? Very shadowy indeed ! And to what end were his labours in that smoky, western city, with its heedless Dalton Streets which went their inevitable ways? For he had the choice.

To do him justice, he was slow in arriving at a realization that seemed to him so incredible, so preposterous. He was her rector ! And he had accepted, all unconsciously, the worldly point of view as to Mrs. Larrabbee, — that she was reserved for a worldly match. A clergyman's wife ! What would become of the clergyman ? And yet other clergymen had married rich women, despite the warning of the needle's eye.

She drove him in her buckboard to Jordan's Pond, set like a jewel in the hills, and even to the deep, cliff-bordered inlet beyond North East, which reminded her, she said, of a Norway fiord. And sometimes they walked together through wooded paths that led them to beetling shores, and sat listening to the waves crashing far below. Silences and commonplaces became the rule instead of the eager discussions with which they had begun, — on such safer topics as the problem of the social work of modern churches. Her aromatic presence, and in this setting, continually disturbed him : nature's perfumes, more definable, — exhalations of the sea and spruce, — mingled with hers, anæsthetics compelling lethargy. He felt himself drowning, even wished to drown, — and yet strangely resisted.

" I must go to-morrow," he said.

" To-morrow — why ? There is a dinner, you know, and Mrs. Waterman wished so particularly to meet you."

He did not look at her. The undisguised note of pain found an echo within him. And this was Mrs. Larrabbee !

" I am sorry, but I must," he told her, and she may not have suspected the extent to which the firmness was feigned.

" You have promised to make other visits ? The Fergusons, — they said they expected you."

"I'm going west — home," he said, and the word sounded odd.

"At this season! But there is nobody in church, at least only a few, and Mr. McCrae can take care of those — he always does. He likes it."

Hodder smiled in spite of himself. He might have told her that those *outside* the church were troubling him. But he did not, since he had small confidence in being able to bring them in.

"I have been away too long, I am getting spoiled," he replied, with an attempt at lightness. He forced his eyes to meet hers, and she read in them an unalterable resolution.

"It is my opinion you are too conscientious, even for a clergyman," she said, and now it was her lightness that hurt. She protested no more. And as she led the way homeward through the narrow forest path, her head erect, still maintaining this lighter tone, he wondered how deeply she had read him; how far her intuition had carried her below the surface; whether she guessed the presence of that stifled thing in him which was crying feebly for life; whether it was *that* she had discovered, or something else? He must give it the chance it craved. He must get away — he must think. To surrender now would mean destruction. . . .

Early the next morning, as he left the pier in the motor boat, he saw a pink scarf waving high above him from the loggia. And he flung up his hand in return. Mingled with a faint sense of freedom was intense sadness.

CHAPTER VIII

THE LINE OF LEAST RESISTANCE

From the vantage point of his rooms in the parish house, Hodder reviewed the situation. And despite the desires thronging after him in his flight he had the feeling of one who, in the dark, has been very near to annihilation. What had shaken him most was the revelation of an old enemy which, watching its chance, had beset him at the first opportunity ; and at a time when the scheme of life, which he flattered himself to have solved forever, was threatening once more to resolve itself into fragments. He had, as if by a miracle, escaped destruction in some insidious form.

He shrank instinctively from an analysis of the woman in regard to whom his feelings were so complicated, and yet by no means lacking in tenderness. But as time went on, he recognized more and more that she had come into his life at a moment when he was peculiarly vulnerable. She had taken him off his guard. That the brilliant Mrs. Larrabbee should have desired him — or what she believed was him — was food enough for thought, was an indication of an idealism in her nature that he would not have suspected. From a worldly point of view, the marriage would have commended itself to none of her friends. Yet Hodder perceived clearly that he could not have given her what she desired, since the marriage *would have killed it* in *him*. She offered him the other thing. Once again he had managed somehow to cling to his dream of what the relationship between man and woman should be, and he saw more and more distinctly that he had coveted not only the jewel, but its setting. He could not see her out of it — she faded. Nor could he see himself in it.

Luxury, — of course, — that was what he had spurned.
Luxury in contrast to Dalton Street, to the whirring
factories near the church which discharged, at nightfall,
their quotas of wan women and stunted children. And
yet here he was catering to luxury, providing religion for
it! Religion!

Early in November he heard that Mrs. Larrabbee
had suddenly decided to go abroad without returning
home. . . .

That winter Hodder might have been likened to a Niagara for energy ; an unharnessed Niagara — such would have
been his own comment. He seemed to turn no wheels, or
only a few at least, and feebly. And while the spectacle
of their rector's zeal was no doubt an edifying one to his
parishioners, they gave him to understand that they would
have been satisfied with less. They admired, but chided
him gently ; and in February Mr. Parr offered to take him
to Florida. He was tired, and it was largely because he
dreaded the reflection inevitable in a period of rest, that he
refused. . . . And throughout these months, the feeling
recurred, with increased strength, that McCrae was still
watching him, — the notion persisted that his assistant
held to a theory of his own, if he could but be induced to
reveal it. Hodder refrained from making the appeal.
Sometimes he was on the point of losing patience with
this enigmatic person.

Congratulations on the fact that his congregation was
increasing brought him little comfort, since a cold analysis
of the newcomers who were renting pews was in itself an
indication of the lack of that thing he so vainly sought.
The decorous families who were now allying themselves
with St. John's did so at the expense of other churches
either more radical or less fashionable. What was it he
sought? What did he wish? To fill the church to overflowing with the poor and needy as well as the rich, and
to enter into the lives of all. Yet at a certain point he met
a resistance that was no less firm because it was baffling.
The Word, on his lips at least, seemed to have lost it efficacy. The poor heeded it not, and he preached to the

rich as from behind a glass. They went on with their carnival. Why this insatiate ambition on his part in an age of unbelief? Other clergymen, not half so fortunate, were apparently satisfied; or else—from his conversation with them—either oddly optimistic or resigned. Why not he?

It was strange, in spite of everything, that hope sprang up within him, a recurrent geyser.

Gradually, almost imperceptibly, he found himself turning more and more towards that line of least resistance which other churches were following, as the one Modern Solution, — institutional work. After all, in the rescuing of bodies some method might yet be discovered to revive the souls. And there were the children! Hodder might have been likened to an explorer, seeking a direct path when there was none—a royal road. And if this were oblique it offered, at least, a definite outlet for his energy.

Such was, approximately, the state of his mind early in March when Gordon Atterbury came back from a conference in New York on institutional work, and filled with enthusiasm. St. John's was incredibly behind the times, so he told Hodder, and later the vestry. Now that they had, in Mr. Hodder, a man of action and ability—ahem!— there was no excuse for a parish as wealthy as St. John's, a parish with their opportunities, considering the proximity of Dalton Street neighbourhood, not enlarging and modernizing the parish house, not building a settlement house with kindergartens, schools, workshops, libraries, a dispensary and day nurseries. It would undoubtedly be an expense—and Mr. Atterbury looked at Mr. Parr, who drummed on the vestry table. They would need extra assistants, deaconesses, trained nurses, and all that. But there were other churches in the city that were ahead of St. John's—a reproach—ahem!

Mr. Parr replied that he had told the rector that he stood ready to contribute to such a scheme when he, the rector, should be ready to approve it. And he looked at Mr. Hodder.

Mr. Hodder said he had been considering the matter

ever since his arrival.   He had only one criticism of institutional work, that in his observation it did not bring the people whom it reached into the Church in any great numbers.   Perhaps that were too much to ask, in these days. For his part he would willingly assume the extra burden, and he was far from denying the positive good such work accomplished through association and by the raising of standards.

Mr. Ferguson declared his readiness to help.   Many of his salesgirls, he said, lived in this part of the city, and he would be glad to do anything in his power towards keeping them out of the dance-halls and such places.

A committee was finally appointed consisting of Mr. Parr, Mr. Atterbury, and the rector, to consult architects and to decide upon a site.

Hodder began a correspondence with experts in other cities, collected plans, pamphlets, statistics; spent hours with the great child-specialist, Dr. Jarvis, and with certain clergymen who believed in institutionalism as the hope of the future.

But McCrae was provokingly non-committal.

"Oh, they may try it," he assented somewhat grudgingly, one day when the rector had laid out for his inspection the architects' sketch for the settlement house.   "No doubt it will help many poor bodies along."

"Is there anything else?" the rector asked, looking searchingly at his assistant.

"It may as well be that," replied McCrae.

The suspicion began to dawn on Hodder that the Scotchman's ideals were as high as his own.   Both of them, secretly, regarded the new scheme as a compromise, a yielding to the inevitable. . . .

Mr. Ferguson's remark that an enlarged parish house and a new settlement house might help to keep some of the young women employed in his department store out of the dance-halls interested Hodder, who conceived the idea of a dance-hall of their own.   For the rector, in the course of his bachelor shopping, often resorted to the emporium of his vestryman, to stand on the stairway which

carried him upward without lifting his feet ; to roam, fascinated, through the mazes of its aisles, where he invariably
got lost, and was rescued by suave floor-walkers or pert
young women in black gowns and white collars and cuffs.
But they were not all pert — there were many characters,
many types. And he often wondered whether they did
not get tired standing on their feet all day long, hesitating
to ask them; speculated on their lives — flung as most of
them were on a heedless city, and left to shift for themselves. Why was it that the Church which cared for
Mr. Ferguson's soul was unable to get in touch with, or
make an appeal to, those of his thousand employees?

It might indeed have been said that Francis Ferguson
cared for his own soul, as he cared for the rest of his property, and kept it carefully insured, — somewhat, perhaps,
on the principle of Pascal's wager. That he had been a
benefactor to his city no one would deny who had seen
the façade that covered a whole block in the business district from Tower to Vine, surmounted by a red standard
with the familiar motto, "When in doubt, go to Ferguson's." At Ferguson's you could buy anything from a
penwiper to a piano or a Paris gown; sit in a cool restaurant in summer or in a palm garden in winter ; leave your
baby — if you had one — in charge of the most capable
trained nurses; if your taste were literary, mull over the
novels in the Book Department; if you were stout, you
might be reduced in the Hygiene Department, unknown
to your husband and intimate friends. In short, if there
were any virtuous human wish in the power of genius to
gratify, Ferguson's was the place. They even taught you
how to cook. It was a modern Aladdin's palace: and,
like everything else modern, much more wonderful than
the original. And the soda might be likened to the
waters of Trevi, — to partake of which is to return.

"When in doubt, go to Ferguson!" Thus Mrs. Larrabbee and other ladies interested in good works had altered
his motto. He was one of the supporters of Galt House,
into which some of his own young saleswomen had occasionally strayed; and none, save Mr. Parr alone, had been

so liberal in his gifts. Hodder invariably found it difficult to reconcile the unassuming man, whose conversation was so commonplace, with the titanic genius who
had created Ferguson's; nor indeed with the owner of
the imposing marble mansion at Number 5, Park Street.

The rector occasionally dined there. He had acquired
a real affection for Mrs. Ferguson, who resembled a burgo-
master's wife in her evening gowns and jewels, and whose
simple social ambitions had been gratified beyond her
dreams. Her heart had not shrunken in the process, nor
had she forgotten her somewhat heterogeneous acquaint-
ances in the southern part of the city. And it was true
that when Gertrude Constable had nearly died of appendicitis, it was on this lady's broad bosom that Mrs. Constable
had wept. Mrs. Ferguson had haunted the house, regard-
less of criticism, and actually quivering with sympathy.
Her more important dinner parties might have been
likened to ill-matched fours-in-hand, and Hodder had sometimes felt more of pity than of amusement as she sat with
an expression of terror on her face, helplessly watching
certain unruly individuals taking their bits in their teeth
and galloping madly downhill. On one occasion, when he
sat beside her, a young man, who shall be nameless, was
suddenly heard to remark in the midst of an accidental
lull:

"I never go to church. What's the use? I'm afraid
most of us don't believe in hell any more."

A silence followed: of the sort that chills. And the
young man, glancing down the long board at the clergyman, became as red as the carnation in his buttonhole,
and in his extremity gulped down more champagne.

"Things are in a dreadful state nowadays!" Mrs.
Ferguson gasped to a paralyzed company, and turned an
agonized face to Hodder. "I'm so sorry," she said, "I
don't know why I asked him to-night, except that I have
to have a young man for Nan, and he's just come to the
city, and I was sorry for him. He's very promising in
a business way; he's in Mr. Plimpton's trust company."

"Please don't let it trouble you." Hodder turned

and smiled a little, and added whimsically : " We may as well face the truth."

" Oh, I should expect you to be good about it, but it was unpardonable," she cried. . . .

In the intervals when he gained her attention he strove, by talking lightly of other things, to take her mind off the incident, but somehow it had left him strangely and — he felt — disproportionately depressed, — although he had believed himself capable of facing more or less philosophically that condition which the speaker had so frankly expressed. Yet the remark, somehow, had had an illuminating effect like a flashlight, revealing to him the isolation of the Church as never before. And after dinner, as they were going to the smoking room, the offender accosted him shamefacedly.

" I'm awfully sorry, Mr. Hodder," he stammered.

That the tall rector's regard was kindly did not relieve his discomfort. Hodder laid a hand on his shoulder.

" Don't worry about it," he answered, " I have only one regret as to what you said — that it is true."

The other looked at him curiously.

" It's mighty decent of you to take it this way," he said. Further speech failed him.

He was a nice-looking young man, with firm white teeth, and honesty was written all over his boyish face. And the palpable fact that his regret was more on the clergyman's account than for the social *faux pas* drew Hodder the more, since it bespoke a genuineness of character. He did not see the yearning in the rector's eyes as he turned away. . . . Why was it they could not be standing side by side, fighting the same fight? The Church had lost him, and thousands like him, and she needed them; could not, indeed, do without them.

Where, indeed, were the young men? They did not bother their heads about spiritual matters any more. But were they not, he asked himself, franker than many of these others, the so-called pillars of the spiritual structure?

Mr. Plimpton accosted him. " I congratulate you upon

the new plans, Mr. Hodder, — they're great," he said. "Mr. Parr and our host are coming down handsomely, eh? When we get the new settlement house we'll have a plant as up-to-date as any church in the country. When do you break ground?"

"Not until autumn, I believe," Hodder replied. "There are a good many details to decide upon yet."

"Well, I congratulate you."

Mr. Plimpton was forever congratulating.

"Up-to-date" — "plant"! *More* illuminating words, eloquent of Mr. Plimpton's ideals. St. John's down at the heels, to be brought up to the state of efficiency of Mr. Plimpton's trust company! It was by no means the first time he had heard modern attributes on Mr. Plimpton's lips applied to a sacred institution, but to-night they had a profoundly disquieting effect. To-night, a certain clair-voyance had been vouchsafed him, and he beheld these men, his associates and supporters, with a detachment never before achieved.

They settled in groups about the room, which was square and high, and panelled in Italian walnut, with fluted pilasters, — the capitals of which were elaborately carved. And Hodder found himself on a deep leather sofa in a corner engaged in a desultory and automatic conversation with Everett Constable. Mr. Plimpton, with a large cigar between his lips, was the radiating centre of one of the liveliest groups, and of him the rector had fallen into a consideration, piecing together bits of information that hitherto had floated meaninglessly in his mind. It was Mrs. Larrabbee who had given character to the career of the still comparatively youthful and unquestionably energetic president of the Chamber of Commerce by likening it to a great spiral, starting somewhere in outer regions of twi-light, and gradually drawing nearer to the centre, from which he had never taken his eyes. At the centre were Eldon Parr and Charlotte Gore. Wallis Plimpton had made himself indispensable to both.

His campaign for the daughter of Thurston Gore had been comparable to one of the great sieges of history, for

Mr. Plimpton was a laughing-stock when he sat down before that fortress. At the end of ten years, Charlotte had capitulated, with a sigh of relief, realizing at last her destiny. She had become slightly stout, revealing, as time went on, no wrinkles — a proof that the union was founded on something more enduring than poetry. Statesmanship — that was the secret! Step by step, slowly but surely, the memoranda in that matrimonial portfolio were growing into accomplished facts; all events, such as displacements of power, were foreseen; and the Plimptons, like Bismarck, had only to indicate, in case of sudden news, the pigeon-hole where the plan of any particular campaign was filed.

Mrs. Larrabbee's temptation to be witty at the expense of those for whom she had no liking had led Hodder to discount the sketch. He had not disliked Mr. Plimpton, who had done him many little kindnesses. He was good-natured, never ruffled, widely tolerant, hail-fellow-well-met with everybody, and he had enlivened many a vestry meeting with his stories. It were hypercritical to accuse him of a lack of originality. And if by taking thought, he had arrived, from nowhere, at his present position of ease and eminence, success had not turned to ashes in his mouth. He fairly exhaled well-being, happiness, and good cheer. Life had gone well with him, he wished the same to others.

But to-night, from his corner, Hodder seemed to see Mr. Plimpton with new eyes. Not that he stood revealed a villain, which he was far from being; it was the air of sophistication, of good-natured if cynical acceptance of things as they were — and plenty good enough, too! — that jarred upon the rector in his new mood, and it was made manifest to him as never before why his appeals from the pulpit had lacked efficacy. Mr. Plimpton didn't want the world changed! And in this desire he represented the men in that room, and the majority of the congregation of St. John's. The rector had felt something of this before, and it seemed to him astonishing that the revelation had not come to him sooner. Did any one of them, in his heart, care anything for the ideals and aspirations of the Church?

As he gazed at them through the gathering smoke they had become strangers, receded all at once to a great distance. . . . Across the room he caught the name, Bedloe Hubbell, pronounced with peculiar bitterness by Mr. Ferguson. At his side Everett Constable was alert, listening.

"Ten years ago," said a stout Mr. Varnum, the President of the Third National Bank, "if you'd told me that that man was to become a demagogue and a reformer, I wouldn't have believed you. Why, his company used to take rebates from the L. & G., and the Southern—I know it." He emphasized the statement with a blow on the table that made the liqueur glasses dance. "And now, with his Municipal League, he's going to clean up the city, is he? Put in a reform mayor. Show up what he calls the Consolidated Tractions Company scandal. Pooh!"

"You got out all right, Varnum. You won't be locked up," said Mr. Plimpton, banteringly.

"So did you," retorted Varnum.

"So did Ferguson, so did Constable."

"So did Eldon Parr," remarked another man, amidst a climax of laughter.

"Langmaid handled that pretty well."

Hodder felt Everett Constable fidget.

"Bedloe's all right, but he's a dreamer," Mr. Plimpton volunteered.

"Then I wish he'd stop dreaming," said Mr. Ferguson, and there was more laughter, although he had spoken savagely.

"That's what he is, a dreamer," Varnum ejaculated. "Say, he told George Carter the other day that prostitution wasn't necessary, that in fifty years we'd have largely done away with it. Think of that, and it's as old as Sodom and Gomorrah!"

"If Hubbell had his way, he'd make this town look like a Connecticut hill village — he'd drive all the prosperity out of it. All the railroads would have to abandon their terminals — there'd be no more traffic, and you'd have to walk across the bridge to get a drink."

"Well," said Mr. Plimpton, "Tom Beatty's good enough for me, for a while."

Beatty, Hodder knew, was the "boss," of the city, with headquarters in a downtown saloon.

"Beatty's been maligned," Mr. Varnum declared. "I don't say he's a saint, but he's run the town pretty well, on the whole, and kept the vice where it belongs, out of sight. He's made his pile, but he's entitled to something — we all are. You always know where you stand with Beatty. But say, if Hubbell and his crowd —— "

"Don't worry about Bedloe, — he'll get called in, he'll come home to roost like the rest of them," said Mr. Plimpton, cheerfully. " The people can't govern themselves, — only Bedloe doesn't know it. Some day he'll find it out." . . .

The French window beside him was open, and Hodder slipped out, unnoticed, into the warm night and stood staring at the darkness. His one desire had been to get away, out of hearing, and he pressed forward over the tiled pavement until he stumbled against a stone balustrade that guarded a drop of five feet or so to the lawn below. At the same time he heard his name called.

"Is that you, Mr. Hodder?"

He started. The voice had a wistful tremulousness and might almost have been the echo of the leaves stirring in the night air. Then he perceived, in a shaft of light from one of the drawing-room windows near by, a girl standing beside the balustrade; and as she came towards him, with tentative steps, the light played conjurer, catching the silvery gauze of her dress and striking an aura through the film of her hair.

"It's Nan Ferguson," she said.

"Of course," he exclaimed, collecting himself. "How stupid of me not to have recognized you!"

"I'm so glad you came out," she went on impulsively, yet shyly, "I wanted to tell you how sorry I was that — that thing happened at the table."

"I like that young man," he said.

"Do you?" she exclaimed, with unexpected gratitude. "So do I. He really isn't — so bad as he must seem."

I

"I'm sure of it," said the rector, laughing.

"I was afraid you'd think him wicked," said Nan. "He works awfully hard, and he's sending a brother through college. He isn't a bit like — some others I know. He wants to make something of himself. And I feel responsible, because I had mother ask him to-night."

He read her secret. No doubt she meant him to do so.

"You know we're going away next week, for the summer — that is, mother and I," she continued. "Father comes later. And I do hope you'll make us a visit, Mr. Hodder — we were disappointed you couldn't come last year." Nan hesitated, and thrusting her hand into her gown drew forth an envelope and held it out to him. "I intended to give you this to-night, to use — for anything you thought best."

He took it gravely. She looked up at him.

"It seems so little — such a selfish way of discharging one's obligations, just to write out a cheque, when there is so much trouble in the world that demands human kindness as well as material help. I drove up Dalton Street yesterday, from downtown. You know how hot it was! And I couldn't help thinking how terrible it is that we who have everything are so heedless of all that misery. The thought of it took away all my pleasure. . . . I'd do something more, something personal, if I could. Perhaps I shall be able to, next winter. Why is it so difficult for all of us to know what to do?"

"We have taken a step forward, at any rate, when we *know* that it is difficult," he said.

She gazed up at him fixedly, her attention caught by an indefinable something in his voice, in his smile, that thrilled and vaguely disturbed her. She remembered it long afterwards. It suddenly made her shy again; as if, in faring forth into the darkness, she had come to the threshold of a mystery, of a revelation withheld; and it brought back the sense of adventure, of the palpitating fear and daring with which she had come to meet him.

"It *is* something to know," she repeated, half comprehending. The scraping of chairs within alarmed her, and she stood ready to fly.

"But I haven't thanked you for this," he said, holding up the envelope. "It may be that I shall find some one in Dalton Street —— "

"Oh, I hope so," she faltered, breathlessly, hesitating a moment. And then she was gone, into the house.

CHAPTER IX

THE DIVINE DISCONTENT

I

It was the last Sunday in May, and in another week the annual flight to the seashore and the mountains would have begun again. The breezes stealing into the church through the open casements wafted hither and thither the odours of the chancel flowers, and mingled with those fainter and subtler perfumes set free by the rustling of summer gowns.

As on this day he surveyed his decorous and fashionable congregation, Hodder had something of that sense of extremity which the great apostle to the Gentiles himself must have felt when he stood in the midst of the Areopagus and made his vain yet sublime appeal to Athenian indifference and luxury. "And the times of this ignorance God winked at; but now commandeth all men everywhere to repent." . . . Some, indeed, stirred uneasily as the rector paused, lowering their eyes before the intensity of his glance, vaguely realizing that the man had flung the whole passion of his being into the appeal.

Heedlessness — that was God's accusation against them, against the age. Materialism, individualism! So absorbed were they in the pursuit of wealth, of distraction, so satisfied with the current philosophy, so intent on surrounding themselves with beautiful things and thus shutting out the sterner view, that they had grown heedless of the divine message. How few of them availed themselves of their spiritual birthright to renew their lives at the altar rail! And they had permitted their own children to wander away. . . . Repent!

116

There was a note of desperation in his appeal, like that
of the hermit who stands on a mountain crag and warns the
gay and thoughtless of the valley of the coming avalanche.
Had they heard him at last? There were a few moments
of tense silence, during which he stood gazing at them.
Then he raised his arm in benediction, gathered up his
surplice, descended the pulpit steps, and crossed swiftly
the chancel. . . .

He had, as it were, turned on all the power in a supreme
effort to reach them.   What if he had failed again? Such
was the misgiving that beset him, after the service, as he
got out of his surplice, communicated by some occult telep-
athy. . . . Mr. Parr was awaiting him, and summoning
his courage, hope battling against intuition, he opened the
door into the now empty church and made his way toward
the porch, where the sound of voices warned him that
several persons were lingering.   The nature of their congratulations confirmed his doubts.   Mrs. Plimpton, resplendent and looking less robust than usual in one of her
summer Paris gowns, greeted him effusively.

"Oh, Mr. Hodder, what a wonderful sermon!" she
cried.   "I can't express how it made me feel — so delinquent! Of course that is exactly the effect you wished.
And I was just telling Wallis I was so glad I waited until
Tuesday to go East, or I should have missed it. You
surely must come on to Hampton and visit us, and preach
it over again in our little stone church there, by the sea.
Good-by — and don't forget! I'll write you, setting the
date, only we'd be glad to have you any time."

"One of the finest I ever heard — if not *the* finest,"
Mr. Plimpton declared, with a kind of serious *empressement*,
squeezing his hand.

Others stopped him; Everett Constable, for one, and
the austere Mrs. Atterbury.   Hodder would have avoided
the ever familiar figure of her son, Gordon, in the invariable
black cutaway and checked trousers, but he was standing
beside Mr. Parr.

"Ahem! Why, Mr. Hodder," he exclaimed, squinting
off his glasses, "that was a magnificent effort. I was

saying to Mr. Parr that it isn't often one hears a sermon
nowadays as able as that, and as sound.   Many clergymen
refrain from preaching them, I sometimes think, because
they are afraid people won't like them."

"I scarcely think it's that," the rector replied, a little
shortly.   " We're afraid people won't heed them."

He became aware, as he spoke, of a tall young woman,
who had cast an enigmatic glance first at Gordon Atterbury,
and then at himself.

" It was a good sermon," said Mr. Parr.   " You're coming to lunch, Hodder ? "

The rector nodded.   " I'm ready when you are," he
answered.

"The motor's waiting," said the banker, leading the
way down the steps to the sidewalk, where he turned.
"Alison, let me introduce Mr. Hodder.   This is my
daughter," he added simply.

This sudden disclosure of the young woman's identity
had upon Hodder a certain electric effect, and with it came
a realization of the extent to which — from behind the
scenes, so to speak — she had gradually aroused him to a
lively speculation.   She seemed to have influenced, to a
greater or less degree, so many lives with which he had
come into touch !   Compelled persons to make up their
minds about her !   And while he sympathized with Eldon
Parr in his abandonment, he had never achieved the full
condemnation which — he felt — an impartial Christian
morality would have meted out.

As he uttered the conventional phrase and took her
hand, he asked himself whether her personality justified
his interest.   Her glance at Gordon Atterbury in the
midst of that gentleman's felicitations on the sermon had
been expressive, Hodder thought, of veiled amusement
slightly tinctured with contempt ; and he, Hodder, felt
himself to have grown warm over it.   He could not be
sure that Alison Parr had not included, in her inner comment, the sermon likewise, on which he had so spent himself.   What was she doing at church ?   As her eyes met
his own, he seemed to read a challenge.   He had never

encountered a woman — he decided — who so successfully concealed her thought, and at the same time so incited curiosity about it.

The effect of her reappearance on Gordon Atterbury was painfully apparent, and Mrs. Larrabbee's remark, " that he had never got over it," recurred to Hodder. He possessed the virtue of being faithful, at least, in spite of the lady's apostasy, and he seemed to be galvanized into a tenfold nervousness as he hustled after them and handed her, with the elaborate attention little men are apt to bestow upon women, into the motor.

" Er — how long shall you be here, Alison ? " he asked.

" I don't know," she answered, not unkindly, but with a touch of indifference.

" You treat us shamefully," he informed her, " upon my word ! But I'm coming to call."

" Do," said Alison. Hodder caught her eye again, and this time he was sure that she surprised in *him* a certain disdain of Mr. Atterbury's zeal. Her smile was faint, yet unmistakable.

He resented it. Indeed, it was with a well-defined feeling of antagonism that he took his seat, and this was enhanced as they flew westward, Mr. Parr wholly absorbed with the speaking trumpet, energetically rebuking at every bounce. In the back of the rector's mind lay a weight which he identified, at intervals, with what he was now convinced was the failure of his sermon. . . . Alison took no part in the casual conversation that began when they reached the boulevard and Mr. Parr abandoned the trumpet, but lay back in silence and apparently with entire comfort in a corner of the limousine.

At the lunch-table Mr. Parr plunged into a discussion of some of the still undecided details of the new settlement house, in which, as the plans developed, he had become more and more interested. He had made himself responsible, from time to time, for additional sums, until the original estimate had been almost doubled. Most of his suggestions had come from Hodder, who had mastered the subject with a thoroughness that appealed to the financier:

and he had gradually accepted the rector's idea of concentrating on the children. Thus he had purchased an adjoining piece of land that was to be a model playground, in connection with the gymnasium and swimming-pool. The hygienic department was to be all that modern science could desire.

"If we are going to do the thing," the banker would remark, "we may as well do it thoroughly; we may as well be leaders and not followers."

So, little by little, the scheme had grown to proportions that sometimes appalled the rector when he realized how largely he had been responsible for the additions, — in spite of the lukewarmness with which he had begun. And yet it had occasionally been Mr. Parr who, with a sweep of his hand, had added thousands to a particular feature: thus the dance-hall had become, in prospect, a huge sun-parlour at the top of the building, where the children were to have their kindergartens and games in winter; and which might be shaded and opened up to the breezes in summer. What had reconciled Hodder to the enterprise most of all, however, was the chapel — in the plan a beautiful Gothic church — whereby he hoped to make the religious progress keep pace with the social. Mr. Parr was decidedly in sympathy with this intention, and referred to it now.

"I was much impressed by what you said in your sermon to-day as to the need of insisting upon authority in religious matters," he declared, "and I quite agree that we should have a chapel of some size at the settlement house for that reason. Those people need spiritual control. It's what the age needs. And when I think of some of the sermons printed in the newspapers to-day, and which are served up as Christianity, there is only one term to apply to them — they are criminally incendiary."

"But isn't true Christianity incendiary, in your meaning of the word?"

It was Alison who spoke, in a quiet and musical voice that was in striking contrast to the tone of Mr. Parr, which the rector had thought unusually emphatic. It

was the first time she had shown an inclination to contribute to the talk. But since Hodder had sat down at
the table her presence had disturbed him, and he had
never been wholly free from an uncomfortable sense that
he was being measured and weighed.

Once or twice he had stolen a glance at her as she
sat, perfectly at ease, and asked himself whether she had
beauty, and it dawned upon him little by little that the
very proportion she possessed made for physical unobtru-
siveness. She was really very tall for a woman. At first
he would have said her nose was straight, when he perceived that it had a delicate hidden curve; her eyes
were curiously set, her dark hair parted in the middle,
brought down low on each side of the forehead and tied
in a Grecian knot. Thus, in truth, he observed, were
seemingly all the elements of the classic, even to the firm
yet slender column of the neck. How had it eluded him?

Her remark, if it astonished Hodder, had a dynamic
effect on Eldon Parr. And suddenly the rector comprehended that the banker had not so much been talking *to*
him as *through* him; had been, as it were, courting opposition.

"What do you mean by Christianity being incendiary?" he demanded.

"Incendiary, from your point of view — I made the
qualification," Alison replied, apparently unmoved by his
obvious irritation. "I don't pretend to be a Christian, as
you know, but if there is one element in Christianity that
distinguishes it, it is the brotherhood of man. That's
pure nitroglycerin, though it's been mixed with so much
sawdust. Incendiary is a mild epithet. I never read
the sermons you refer to, I dare say they're crude, but
they're probably attempts to release an explosive which
would blow your comfortable social system and its authority into atoms."

Hodder, who had listened in amazement, glanced at the
banker. He had never before heard him opposed, or seen
him really angry.

"I've heard that doctrine," cried Mr. Parr. "Those

who are dissatisfied with things as they are because they
have been too stupid or too weak or self-indulgent to rise,
find it easy to twist the principles of Christianity into
revolutionary propaganda. It's a case of the devil quoting Scripture. The brotherhood of man! There has never
been an age when philanthropy and organized charity were
on such a scale as to-day."

A certain gallant, indomitable ring crept into Alison's
voice; she did not seem in the least dismayed or overborne.

"But isn't that just where most so-called Christians
make their mistake?" she asked. "Philanthropy and
organized charity, as they exist to-day, have very little
to do with the brotherhood of man. Mightn't it be you
who are fooling yourselves instead of the incendiaries
fooling *themselves?* So long as you can make yourselves
believe that this kind of charity is a logical carrying out
of the Christian principles, so long are your consciences
satisfied with the social system which your class, very
naturally, finds so comfortable and edifying. The weak
and idiotic ought to be absurdly grateful for what is
flung to them, and heaven is gained in the throwing. In
this way the rich inevitably become the elect, both here
and hereafter, and the needle's eye is widened into a
gap."

There was on Mr. Parr's lips a smile not wholly
pleasant to see. Indeed, in the last few minutes there
had been revealed to Hodder a side of the banker's
character which had escaped him in the two years of
their acquaintance.

"I suppose," said Mr. Parr, slowly, drumming on the
table, "you would say that of the new settlement house
of St. John's, whereby we hope to raise a whole neighbourhood."

"Yes, I should," replied Alison, with spirit. "The
social system by which you thrive, and which politically
and financially you strive to maintain, is diametrically opposed to your creed, which is supposed to be the brotherhood of man. But if that were really your creed, you

would work for it politically and financially. You would
see that your Church is trying to do infinitesimally what
the government, but for your opposition, might do uni-
versally. Your true creed is the survival of the fittest.
You grind these people down into what is really an economic slavery and dependence, and then you insult and
degrade them by inviting them to exercise and read books
and sing hymns in your settlement house, and give their
children crackers and milk and kindergartens and sunlight! I don't blame them for not becoming Christians
on that basis. Why, the very day I left New York a
man over eighty, who had been swindled out of all he
had, rather than go to one of those Christian institutions
deliberately forged a check and demanded to be sent to
the penitentiary. He said he could live and die there
with some self-respect."

"I might have anticipated that you would ultimately
become a Socialist, Alison," Mr. Parr remarked — but his
voice trembled.

"I don't know whether I'm a Socialist or an Anar-
chist," she answered. Hodder thought he detected a note
of hopelessness in her voice, and the spirit in it ebbed a
little. Not only did she seem indifferent to her father's
feeling — which incidentally added fuel to it — but her
splendid disregard of him, as a clergyman, had made an
oddly powerful appeal. And her argument! His feelings, as he listened to this tremendous arraignment of
Eldon Parr by his daughter, are not easily to be described.
To say that she had compelled him, the rector of St. John's,
at last to look in the face many conditions which he had
refused to recognize would be too definite a statement.
Nevertheless, some such thing had occurred. Refutations
sprang to his lips, and died there, though he had no notion
of uttering them. He saw that to admit her contentions
would be to behold crumble into ruins the structure that
he had spent a life in rearing; and yet something within
him responded to her words — they had the passionate,
convincing ring of truth.

By no means the least of their disturbing effects was

due to the fact that they came as a climax to, as a fulfilment of the revelation he had had at the Fergusons',
when something of the true nature of Mr. Plimpton and
others of his congregation had suddenly been laid bare.
And now Hodder looked at Eldon Parr to behold another
man from the one he had known, and in that moment
realized that their relationship could never again be the
same. . . . Were his sympathies with the daughter?

"I don't know what I believe," said Alison, after a
pause. "I've ceased trying to find out. What's the
use!" She appeared now to be addressing no one in
particular.

A servant entered with a card, and the banker's hand
shook perceptibly as he put down his claret and adjusted
his glasses.

"Show him into my office upstairs, and tell him I'll see
him at once," he said, and glanced at the rector. But it
was Alison whom he addressed. "I must leave Mr. Hodder
to answer your arguments," he added, with an attempt at
lightness; and then to the rector: "Perhaps you can convince her that the Church is more sinned against than sin-
ning, and that Christians are not such terrible monsters
after all. You'll excuse me?"

"Certainly." Hodder had risen.

II

"Shall we have coffee in the garden?" Alison asked.
"It's much nicer outside this time of year."

For an instant he was at a loss to decide whether to accede,
or to make an excuse and leave the house. Wisdom seemed
to point to flight. But when he glanced at her he saw to
his surprise that the mood of abstraction into which she had
fallen still held her; that the discussion which had aroused
Eldon Parr to such dramatic anger had left her serious
and thoughtful. She betrayed no sense of triumph at having audaciously and successfully combated him, and she
appeared now only partially to be aware of Hodder's presence. His interest, his curiosity mounted suddenly again,

overwhelming once more the antagonism which he had felt
come and go in waves ; and once more his attempted classi-
fication of her was swept away. She had relapsed into an
enigma.

"I like the open air," he answered, "and I have always
wished to see the garden. I have admired it from the
windows."

"It's been on my mind for some years," she replied, as she
led the way down a flight of steps into the vine-covered
pergola. "And I intend to change parts of it while I am
out here. It was one of my first attempts, and I've learned
more since."

"You must forgive my ignorant praise," he said, and
smiled. "I have always thought it beautiful. But I can
understand that an artist is never satisfied."

She turned to him, and suddenly their eyes met and held
in a momentary, electric intensity that left him warm and
agitated. There was nothing coquettish in the glance, —
but it was the first distinct manifestation that he was of
consequence. She returned his smile, without levity.

"Is a clergyman ever satisfied ? " she asked.

"He ought not to be," replied Hodder, wondering
whether she had read him.

"Although you were so considerate, I suppose you must
have thought it presumptuous of me to criticize your
profession, which is religion."

"Religion, I think, should be everybody's," he answered
quietly.

She made no reply. And he entered, as into another
world, the circular arbour in which the pergola ended, so
complete in contrast was its atmosphere to that of the
house. The mansion he had long since grown to recognize
as an expression of the personality of its owner, but this
classic bower was as remote from it as though it were in
Greece. He was sensitive to beauty, yet the beauty of the
place had a perplexing quality, which he felt in the perfect
curves of the marble bench, in the marble basin brimming
to the tip with clear water, — the surface of which, flecked
with pink petals, mirrored the azure sky through the leafy

network of the roof.   In one green recess a slender Mercury hastily adjusted his sandal.

Was this, her art, the true expression of *her* baffling personality?   As she had leaned back in the corner of the automobile she had given him the impression of a languor almost Oriental, but this had been startlingly dispelled at the lunch-table by the revelation of an animation and a vitality which had magically transformed her.   But now, as under the spell of a new encompassment of her own weaving, she seemed to revert to her former self, sinking, relaxed, into a wicker lounge beside the basin, one long and shapely hand in the water, the other idle in her lap. Her eyes, he remarked, were the contradiction in her face. Had they been larger, and almond-shaped, the illusion might have been complete.   They were neither opaque nor smouldering, — but Western eyes, amber-coloured, with delicately stencilled rays and long lashes.   And as they gazed up at him now they seemed to reflect, without disclosing the flitting thoughts behind them.   He felt antagonism and attraction in almost equal degree — the situation transcended his experience.

"You don't intend to change *this?*" he asked, with an expressive sweep of his hand.

"No," she said, "I've always liked it.   Tell me what you feel about it."

He hesitated.

"You resent it," she declared.

"Why do you say that?" he demanded quickly.

"I feel it," she answered calmly, but with a smile.

"'Resent' would scarcely be the proper word," he contended, returning her smile, yet hesitating again.

"You think it pagan," she told him.

"Perhaps I do," he answered simply, as though impressed by her felicitous discovery of the adjective.

Alison laughed.

"It's pagan because I'm pagan, I suppose."

"It's very beautiful — you have managed to get an extraordinary atmosphere," he continued, bent on doing himself an exact justice.   "But I should say, if you pressed me, that it represents to me the deification of beauty to the exclusion of all else. You have made beauty the Alpha and Omega."

"There is nothing else for me," she said.

The coffee-tray arrived and was deposited on a wicker table beside her. She raised herself on an elbow, filled his cup and handed it to him.

"And yet," he persisted, "from the manner in which you spoke at the table ——"

"Oh, don't imagine I haven't thought! But thinking isn't — believing."

"No," he admitted, with a touch of sadness, "you are right. There were certain comments you made on the Christian religion ——"

She interrupted him again.

"As to the political side of it, which is Socialism, — so far as I can see. If there is any other side, I have never been able to discover it. It seems to me that if Christians were logical, they should be Socialists. The brotherhood of man, coöperation — all that is Socialism, isn't it? It's opposed to the principle of the survival of the fittest, which so many of these so-called Christians practise. I used to think, when I came back from Paris, that I was a Socialist, and I went to a lot of their meetings in New York, and to lectures. But after a while I saw there was something in Socialism that didn't appeal to me, something smothering, — a forced coöperation that did not leave one *free*. I wanted to be free, I've been striving all my life to be free," she exclaimed passionately, and was silent an instant, inspecting him. "Perhaps I owe you an apology for speaking as I did before a clergyman — especially before an honest one."

He passed over the qualification with a characteristic smile.

"Oh, if we are going to shut our ears to criticism we'd better give up being clergymen," he answered. "I'm afraid there is a great deal of truth in what you said."

"That's generous of you!" she exclaimed, and thrilled him with the tribute. Nor was the tribute wholly in the words: there had come spontaneously into her voice an exquisite, modulated note that haunted him long after it had died away. . . .

"I had to say what I thought," she continued earnestly; "I stood it as long as I could. Perhaps you didn't realize it, but my father was striking at *me* when he referred to your sermon, and spiritual control — and in other things he said when you were talking about the settlement-house. He reserves for himself the right to do as he pleases, but insists that those who surround him shall adopt the subserviency which he thinks proper for the rest of the world. If he were a Christian himself, I shouldn't mind it so much."

Hodder was silent. The thought struck him with the force of a great wind.

"He's a Pharisee," Alison went on, following the train of her thought. "I remember the first time I discovered that — it was when I was reading the New Testament carefully, in the hope of finding something in Christianity I might take hold of. And I was impressed particularly by the scorn with which Christ treated the Pharisees. My father, too, if he had lived in those days, would have thought Christ a seditious person, an impractical, fanatical idealist, and would have tried to trip him up with literal questions concerning the law. His real and primary interest is in a social system that benefits himself and his kind, and because this is so, he, and men like him, would have it appear that Christianity is on the side of what they term law and order. I do not say that they are hypocritical, that they reason this out. They are elemental; and they feel intuitively that Christianity contains a vital spark which, if allowed to fly, would start a conflagration beyond their control. The theologians have helped them to cover the spark with ashes, and naturally they won't allow the ashes to be touched, if they can help it."

She lay very still.

The rector had listened to her, at first with amazement, then with more complicated sensations as she thus dispassionately discussed the foremost member of his congregation and the first layman of the diocese, who was incidentally her own father. In her masterly analysis of Eldon Parr, she had brought Hodder face to face with the naked truth, and compelled him to recognize it. How could he attempt to refute it, with honesty?

He remembered Mr. Parr's criticism of Alison. There had been hardness in that, though it were the cry of a lacerated paternal affection. In that, too, a lack of comprehension, an impotent anger at a visitation not understood, a punishment apparently unmerited. Hodder had pitied him then—he still pitied him. In the daughter's voice was no trace of resentment. . . . No one, seemingly, could be farther removed from him (the rector of St. John's) in her opinions and views of life, than Alison Parr; and yet he felt in her an undercurrent, deep and strong, which moved him strangely, strongly, irresistibly; he recognized a passionate desire for the truth, and the courage to face it at any cost, and a capacity for tenderness, revealed in flashes.

"I have hurt you," she exclaimed. "I am sorry."

He collected himself.

"It is not you who have hurt me," he replied. "Reflections on the contradictions and imperfections of life are always painful. And since I have been here, I have seen a great deal of your father."

"You are fond of him ! "

He hesitated. It was not an ordinary conversation — they were dealing with realities, and he had a sense that vital issues were at stake. He had, in that moment, to make a revaluation of his sentiments for the financier — to weigh the effect of her indictment.

"Yes," he answered slowly, "I am fond of him. He has shown me a side of himself, perhaps, that other men have not seen,—and he is very lonely."

"You pity him." He started at her word. "I guessed that from an expression that crossed your face when we were at the table. But surely you must have observed the incongruity of *his* relationship with your Church !

K

Surely, in preaching as you did this morning against materialism, individualism, absorption in the pursuit of wealth, you must have had my father in mind as the supreme example! And yet he listened to you as serenely as though he had never practised any of these things!

"Clergymen wonder why Christianity doesn't make more progress to-day; well, what strikes the impartial observer who thinks about the subject at all, as one reason, is the paralyzing inconsistency of an alliance between those who preach the brotherhood of man and those who are opposed to it. I've often wondered what clergymen would say about it, if they were frank—only I never see any clergymen."

He was strongly agitated. He did not stop — strangely enough — to reflect how far they had gone, to demand by what right she brought him to the bar, challenged the consistency of his life. For she had struck, with a ruthless precision, at the very core of his trouble, revealed it for what it was.

"Yes," he said, " I can see how we may be accused of inconsistency, and with much justice."

His refusal to excuse and vindicate himself impressed her as no attempt at extenuation could have done. Perhaps, in that moment, her quick instinct divined something of his case, something of the mental suffering he strove to conceal. Contrition shone in her eyes.

"I ought not to have said that," she exclaimed gently. "It is so easy for outsiders to criticize those who are sincere—and I am sure you are. We cannot know all the perplexities. But when we look at the Church, we are puzzled by that—which I have mentioned—and by other things."

"What other things?" he demanded.

She hesitated in her turn.

"I suppose you think it odd, my having gone to church, feeling as I do," she said. "But St. John's is now the only place vividly associated with my mother. She was never at home here, in this house. I always go at least once when I am out here. And I listened to your sermon intently."

"Yes."

"I wanted to tell you this: you interested me as I had not been interested since I was twenty, when I made a desperate attempt to become a Christian—and failed. Do you know how you struck me? It was as a man who actually had a great truth which he was desperately trying to impart, and could not. I have not been in a church more than a dozen times in the last eight years, but you impressed me as a man who *felt* something—whatever it is."

He did not speak.

"But why," she cried, "do you insist on what you call authority? As a modern woman who has learned to use her own mind, I simply can't believe, if the God of the universe is the moral God you assert him to be, that he has established on earth an agency of the kind you infer, and delegated to it the power of life and death over human souls. Perhaps you do not go so far, but if you make the claim at all you must make it in its entirety. There is an idea of commercialism, of monopoly in that conception which is utterly repugnant to any one who tries to approach the subject with a fresh mind, and from an ideal point of view. And religion must be idealism — mustn't it?

"Your ancient monks and saints weren't satisfied until they had settled every detail of the invisible world, of the past and future. They mapped it out as if it were a region they had actually explored, like geographers. They used *their* reason, and what science they had, to make theories about it which the churches still proclaim as the catholic and final truth. You forbid us to use *our* reason. You declare, in order to become Christians, that we have to accept authoritative statements. Oh, can't you see that an authoritative statement is just what an ethical person *doesn't* want? Belief—faith doesn't consist in the mere acceptance of a statement, but in something much higher—if we can achieve it. Acceptance of authority is not faith, it is mere credulity, it is to shirk the real issue. We must believe, if we believe at all, *without* authority. If we *knew*, there would be no virtue in striving. If I choose a God," she added, after a pause, " I cannot take a consensus of opinion about him, — he must be *my* God."

Hodder did not speak immediately. Strange as it may seem, he had never heard the argument, and the strength of it, reënforced by the extraordinary vitality and earnestness of the woman who had uttered it, had a momentary stunning effect. He sat contemplating her as she lay back among the cushions, and suddenly he seemed to see in her the rebellious child of which her father had spoken. No wonder Eldon Parr had misunderstood her, had sought to crush her spirit! She was to be dealt with in no common way, nor was the consuming yearning he discerned in her to be lightly satisfied.

" The God of the individualist," he said at length — musingly, not accusingly.

" I am an individualist," she admitted simply. " But I am at least logical in that philosophy, and the individualists who attend the churches to-day are not. The inconsistency of their lives is what makes those of us who do not go to church doubt the efficacy of their creed, which seems to have no power to change them. The majority of people in St. John's are no more Christians than I am. They attend service once a week, and the rest of the time they are bent upon getting all they can of pleasure and profit for themselves. Do you wonder that those who consider this spectacle come inevitably to the conclusion that either Christianity is at fault, is outworn, or else that it is presented in the wrong way ?"

The rector rose abruptly, walked to the entrance of the arbour, and stood staring out across the garden. Presently he turned and came back and stood over her.

" Since you ask me," he said slowly, " I do not wonder at it."

She raised her eyes swiftly.

"When you speak like that," she exclaimed with an enthusiasm that stirred him, despite the trouble of his mind, "I cannot think of you as a clergyman,—but as a man. Indeed," she added, in the surprise of her discovery, "I have never thought of you as a clergyman — even when I first saw you this morning. I could not account then for a sense of duality about you that puzzled me. Do you always preach as earnestly as that?"

"Why?"

"I felt as if you were throwing your whole soul into the effort—oh, I felt it distinctly. You made some of them, temporarily, a little uncomfortable, but they do not understand you, and you didn't change them. It seemed to me you realized this when Gordon Atterbury spoke to you. I tried to analyze the effect on myself — if it had been in the slightest degree possible for my reason to accept what you said you might, through sheer personality, have compelled me to reconsider. As it was, I found myself resisting you."

With his hands clasped behind him, he paced across the arbour and back again.

"Have you ever definitely and sincerely tried to put what the Church teaches into practice?" he asked.

"Orthodox Christianity? penance, asceticism, self-abnegation — repression — falling on my knees and seeking a forgiveness out of all proportion to the trespass, and filled with a sense of total depravity? If I did that I should lose *myself* — the only valuable thing I've got."

Hodder, who had resumed his pacing, glanced at her involuntarily, and fought an inclination to agree with her.

"I see no one upon whom I can rely but myself," she went on with the extraordinary energy she was able to summon at will, "and I am convinced that self-sacrifice — at least, indiscriminate, unreasoning self-sacrifice — is worse than useless, and to teach it is criminal ignorance. None of the so-called Christian virtues appeals to me: I hate humility. *You* haven't it. The only happiness I can see in the world lies in self-expression, and I certainly shouldn't find that in sewing garments for the poor.

The last thing that I could wish for would be immortality
as orthodox Christianity depicts it! And suppose I had
followed the advice of my Christian friends and remained
here, where they insisted my duty was, what would have
happened to me? In a senseless self-denial I should
gradually have withered into a meaningless old maid,
with no opinions of my own, and no more definite purpose
in life than to write checks for charities. Your Christianity commands that women shall stay at home, and
declares that they are not entitled to seek their own salvation, to have any place in affairs, or to meddle with
the realm of the intellect. Those forbidden gardens are
reserved for the lordly sex. St. Paul, you say, put us
in our proper place some twenty centuries ago, and we
are to remain there for all time."

He felt sweeping through him the reverse current of
hostility.

"And what I preach," he asked, "has tended to confirm you in such a mean conception of Christianity?"

Her eye travelled over the six feet of him — the kindling, reflecting eye of the artist; it rested for a moment
on the protesting locks of his hair, which apparently
could not be cut short enough to conform; on the hands,
which were strong and sinewy; on the wide, tolerant
mouth, with its rugged furrows, on the breadth and
height of the forehead. She lay for a moment, inert,
considering.

"What you preach — yes," she answered, bravely meeting his look. "What you *are* — no. You and your
religion are as far apart as the poles. Oh, this old argument, the *belief* that has been handed down to the man,
the *authority* with which he is clothed, and not the *man*
himself! How can one be a factor in life unless one
represents something which is the fruit of actual, personal
experience? Your authority is for the weak, the timid,
the credulous, — for those who do not dare to trust themselves, who run for shelter from the storms of life to a
papier-mâché fortress, made to look like rock. In order
to preach that logically you should be a white ascetic,

with a well-oiled manner, a downcast look lest you
stumble in your pride; lest by chance you might do
something original that sprang out of your own soul
instead of being an imitation of the saints. And if your
congregation took your doctrine literally, I can see a
whole army of white, meek Christians. But you are not
like that. Can't you see it for yourself?" she exclaimed.
" Can't you *feel* that you are an individual, a personality,
a force that might be put to great uses? That *will* be
because you are open-minded, because there is room in
you for growth and change?"

He strove with all his might to quell the inner conflagration which she had fanned into leaping flames.
Though he had listened before to doubt and criticism,
this woman, with her strange shifting moods of calm and
passion, with her bewildering faculty of changing from
passive to active resistance, her beauty (once manifest,
never to be forgotten), her unique individuality that now
attracted, now repelled, seemed for the moment the very
incarnation of the forces opposed to him and his religion.
Hodder, as he looked at her, had a flash of fierce resentment that now, of all times, she should suddenly have
flung herself across his path. For she was to be reckoned
with. Why did he not tell her she was an egoist? Why
didn't he speak out, defend his faith, denounce her views
as prejudiced and false?

" Have I made you angry?" he heard her say. " I am
sorry."

It was the hint of reproach in her tone to which the
man in him instantly responded. And what he saw now
was his portrait she had painted. The thought came to
him : was he indeed greater, more vital than the religion
he professed? God forbid! Did he ring true, and it
false?

She returned his gaze. And gradually, under her clear
olive skin, he saw the crimson colour mounting higher.
. . . She put forth her hand, simply, naturally, and
pressed his own, as though they had been friends for a
lifetime. . . .

CHAPTER X

I

THE annual scourge of summer had descended pitilessly upon the city once more, enervating, depressing, stagnating, and people moved languidly in the penetrating heat that steamed from the pores of the surrounding river bottoms.

The rector of St. John's realized that a crisis had come in his life, — a crisis he had tried to stave off in vain. And yet there was a period during which he pursued his shrunken duties as though nothing had happened to him ; as a man who has been struck in battle keeps on, loath to examine, to acknowledge the gravity of his wound ; fearing to, perhaps. Sometimes, as his mind went back to the merciless conflict of his past, his experience at the law school, it was the unchaining of that *other man* he dreaded, the man he believed himself to have finally subdued. But night and day he was haunted by the sorrowful and reproachful face of Truth.

Had he the courage, now, to submit the beliefs which had sustained him all these years to Truth's inexorable inspection? Did he dare to turn and open those books which she had inspired, — the new philosophies, the historical criticisms which he had neglected and condemned, which he had flattered himself he could do without, — and read of the fruit of Knowledge? Twice, thrice he had hesitated on the steps of the big library, and turned away with a wildly beating heart.

Day by day the storm increased, until from a cloud on the horizon it grew into a soul-shaking tempest. Pro-

foundly moved as he had been on that Sunday afternoon
in Eldon Parr's garden, he had resolutely resolved to
thrust the woman and the incident from his mind, to defer
the consideration of the questions she had raised — grave
though they were — to a calmer period. For now he was
unable to separate *her*, to eliminate the emotion — he was
forced to acknowledge — the thought of her aroused, from
the problems themselves. Who was she? At moments
he seemed to see her shining, accusing, as Truth herself,
and again as a Circe who had drawn him by subtle arts
from his wanderings, luring him to his death ; or, at other
times, as the mutinous daughter of revolt. But when he
felt, in memory, the warm touch of her hand, the old wild-
ness of his nature responded, he ceased to speculate or
care, and he longed only to crush and subdue her by the
brute power of the man in him. For good or bad, she had
woven her spell.

Here was the old, elemental, twofold contest, carnal and
spiritual, thoroughly revived ! . . .

He recalled, in his musings, the little theological school
surrounded by southern woods and fields, where he had
sometime walked under autumn foliage with the elderly
gentleman who had had such an influence on his life —
the dean. Mild-mannered and frail, patient in ordinary
converse, — a lion for the faith. He would have died for
it as cheerfully as any martyr in history. By the marvels of that faith Hodder had beheld, from his pew in the
chapel, the little man transformed. He knew young men,
their perplexities and temptations, and he dealt with them
personally, like a father. Hodder's doubts were stilled,
he had gained power of his temptations and peace for his
soul, and he had gone forth inspired by the reminder that
there was no student of whom the dean expected better
things. Where now were the thousands of which he had
dreamed, and which he was to have brought into the
Church? . . .

Now, he asked himself, was it the dean, or the dean's
theology through which his regeneration had come ?
Might not the inherent goodness of the dean be one

thing, and his theology quite another? Personality
again! He recalled one of the many things which Alison
Parr had branded on his memory, — "the belief, the
authority in which the man is clothed, and not the man!"
The dean's God had remained silent on the subject of
personality. Or, at the best, he had not encouraged it;
and there were — Hodder could not but perceive — certain
contradictions in his character, which were an anomalistic
blending of that of the jealous God of Moses and of the
God of Christ. There must be continuity — God could
not change. Therefore the God of infinite love must
retain the wrath which visited sins of the fathers on the
children, which demanded sacrifice, atonement, — an exact
propitiation for his anger against mankind. An innocent
life of sorrow and suffering!

And again, "You and your religion are as far apart as
the poles!" Had he, Hodder, outgrown the dean's religion, or had it ever been his own? Was there, after all,
such a thing as religion? Might it not be merely a fig-
ment of the fertile imagination of man? He did not
escape the terror of this thought when he paused to consider his labour of the past two years and the vanity of its
results. And little by little the feeling grew upon him,
such being the state of his mind, that he ought not to
continue, for the present at least, to conduct the services.
Should he resign, or go away for a while to some quiet
place before he made such a momentous decision? There
was no one to whom he could turn; no layman, and no
clergyman; not even the old bishop, whom he had more
than once mentally accused of being too broad and too
tolerant! No, he did not wish a clergyman's solution.
The significance of this thought flashed through him —
that the world itself was no longer seeking clergymen's
solutions. He must go off alone, and submit his faith to
the impartial test.

It was in a vigil of the night, when he lay in the hot
darkness, unable to sleep, that he came at length to this
resolve. And now that he had cut the knot he was too
just to blame Alison Parr for having pointed out — with

what often had seemed a pitiless cruelty — something of which he had had a constantly growing perception yet had continually sought to evade. And he reviewed, as the church bells recorded the silent hours, how, little by little, his confidence had crumbled before the shocks of the successive revelations — some of them so slight that they had passed unnoticed : comparisons, inevitably compelled; Dalton Street; the confessions of Eleanor Goodrich and Mrs. Constable ; Mr. Plimpton and his views of life — Eldon Parr ! Even the slamming of the carriage doors in Burton Street had had a significance !

Might it not prove that this woman had let fall into the turbid waters of his soul the drop that was to clear them forever? He would go away. He would not see her again.

Over the sleeping city, unapprehended, stole the dawn. He arose, but instead of falling on his knees he went to the window and lifted his face to the whitening sky. . . . Slowly out of the obscurity of the earth's shadow emerged the vague outlines of familiar things until they stood sharply material, in a silence as of death. A sparrow twittered, and suddenly the familiar, soot-grimed roofs were bathed in light, and by a touch made beautiful. . . .

Some hours later the city was wide awake. And Hodder, bathed and dressed, stood staring down from his study window into the street below, full now of young men and girls ; some with set faces, hurrying, intent, others romping and laughing as they dodged the trucks and trolley cars ; all on their way to the great shoe factory around the corner, the huge funnels of which were belching forth smoke into the morning air. The street emptied, a bell rang, a whistle blew, the hum of distant machinery began. . . .

II

Later that morning Hodder sat in his study. The shutters were closed, and the intensity of the tropical glare without was softened and diffused by the slanting

green slats. His eye wandered over the long and comfortable room which had been his sanctuary in the feverish
days of his ministry, resting affectionately on the hospitable chairs, the wide fireplace before which he had
been wont to settle himself on winter nights, and even on
the green matting — a cooling note in summer. And
there, in the low cases along the walls, were the rows of
his precious books, — his one hobby and extravagance.
He had grown to love the room. Would he ever come
back to it?

A step sour   in the hall, a knock, and the well-
known gaunt fo.   spectacled face of McCrae appeared
in the doorway.

"Ye wished to see me?" he asked.

"McCrae," said the rector, "I am going off for a
while."

His assistant regarded him a moment in silence. Although Hodder had no intention of explaining his reasons, he had a curious conviction that it were superfluous
to do so, that McCrae had guessed n.

"Why shouldn't ye? There's bu a handful left to
preach to in this weather."

"I wouldn't go, in this sudden way, if it were not —
imperative," Hodder added, trying to speak calmly.

"Why shouldn't ye?" McCrae repeated, almost fiercely.

Hodder smiled in spite of himself.

"There's no reason," he said, "except the added work
put on you without warning, and in this heat."

"Ye'll not need to worry," his assistant assured him,
"the heat's nothing to me." McCrae hesitated, and then
demanded abruptly, "Ye'll not be visiting?"

The question took Hodder by surprise.

"No," he answered quickly, and not quite steadily, and
hesitated in his turn, "I shan't be visiting."

"It's a rest ye need, I've been wanting to say it."
McCrae took a step forward, and for a moment it seemed
as though he were at last about to break the bonds of his
reserve. Perhaps he detected an instinctive shrinking on
the rector's part. At any rate, there was another instant

of silence, in which the two men faced each other across
the desk, and McCrae held out his hand. " Good luck to
ye," he said, as Hodder took it, " and don't have the parish
on your mind. Stay till ye're rested, and come back to
us."

He left the room abruptly. Hodder remained motionless, looking after him, and then, moved apparently by a
sudden impulse, started toward the door, — only to halt
and turn before he got to it. Almost he had opened his
lips to call his assistant back.   He could not do it — the
moment had come and fled when it might have been possible. Did this man hide, under his brusqueness and brevity
of speech, the fund of wisdom and the wider sympathy and
understanding he suspected ?   Hodder could have vouched
for it, and yet he had kept his own counsel. And he was
struck suddenly by the significance of the fact, often remarked, that McCrae in his brief and common-sense and
by no means enlivening sermons had never once referred
in any way to doctrine or dogma!

He spent half an hour in collecting and bestowing in
two large valises such articles as his simple needs would
demand, and then set out for a railroad office in the business portion of the city, where he bought his ticket and
berth. Then, after a moment of irresolution on the threshold of the place, he turned to the right, thrusting his way
through the sluggish crowds on Tower Street until he
came to the large bookstore where he had been wont to
spend, from time to time, some of his leisure moments.
A clerk recognized him, and was about to lead the way to
the rear, where the precious editions were kept, when
Hodder stopped him.

In casting about for a beginning in his venture over unknown seas, there had naturally come into his mind three
or four works which were anathema to the orthodox; one
of which, in seven volumes, went back to his seminary
days, and had been the subject of a ringing, denunciatory
sermon by the dean himself. Three of them were by
Germans of established reputations, another by a professor
of the University of Paris. The habit of years is strong.

And though he knew that many clergymen read these books, Hodder found it impossible to overcome a nervous sense of adventure,—nay (knowing his resolution), of apostasy, almost of clandestine guilt when he mentioned them. And it seemed to him that the face of the clerk betrayed surprise. One of the works was not in stock ; he would send the others that afternoon. Mr. Hodder would take them ? They made a formidable parcel, but a little handle was supplied and the rector hurried out, swinging himself on a Tower Street car.

It must not be thought that the whole of what is called modern criticism was new to Hodder. This would indeed be too much of a reflection on the open-mindedness of the seminary from which he had graduated. But he found himself, now, pondering a little cynically on that "open-mindedness"; on that concession — if it had been a concession — to the methods of science. There had been in truth a course of lectures on this subject ; but he saw now, very clearly, what a concerted effort had been put forward in the rest of the teaching to minimize and discredit it. Even the professor who gave the lectures had had the air of deploring them. Here it is, but on the whole one would better let it alone, — such was the inference. And he had let it alone, through all these years.

In the seminary, too, volumes by semi-learned clergymen had been thrust into his hands, efforts which Hodder recalled now, in spite of his mental state, with a smile. These invariably championed the doctrine of the virgin birth as the pillar on which the Incarnation depended. A favourite argument declared that although the Gospel texts in regard to it might be proven untrustworthy, the miraculous birth must have happened anyway ! And one of these clerical authors whom he had more recently read, actually had had the audacity to turn the weapons of the archenemy, science, back upon itself. The virgin birth was an established fact in nature, and had its place in the social economy of the bee. And did not parthenogenesis occur in the silk moth ?

In brief, the conclusion impressed upon him by his

seminary instruction was this : that historical criticism
had corrected some ideas and put some things in their
right place.   What these things were remained sufficiently
vague.   But whenever it attacked a cherished dogma it
was, on general principles, wrong.

Once again in his cool study, he cut the cord with a
trembling hand, and while he was eating the lunch his
housekeeper had prepared, dipped into one of the larger
volumes.   As he read again the critical disproofs he felt an
acute, almost physical pain, as though a vital part of him
were being cut away, as his mind dwelt upon those beautiful legends to which he had so often turned, and which
had seemed the very fountain of his faith.   Legends ! . . .

He closed the book.   The clock on the mantel struck
three; his train was to leave at five.   He rose and went
down into the silent church he had grown to love, seating
himself in one of the carved stalls of the choir, his eye
lingering in turn on each beautiful object: on the glowing
landscape in the window in memory of Eliza Parr, por-
traying the delectable country, with the bewildered yet en-
raptured faces of the pilgrims in the foreground; on the
graceful, shining lectern, the aspiring arches, the carved
marble altar behind the rail, and above it the painting of
the Christ on the cross.

The hours of greatest suffering are the empty hours.
Eloi, Eloi, lama sabachthani?   The hours when the mysterious sustaining and driving force is withdrawn, and a
lassitude and despair comes over us like that of a deserted
child: the hours when we feel we have reached the limit
of service, when our brief span of usefulness is done.
Had God brought him, John Hodder, to the height of the
powers of his manhood only to abandon him, to cast him
adrift on the face of the waters — led him to this great
parish, with all its opportunities, only that he might fail
and flee?

He sat staring at the face of the Man on the cross.   Did
he, in his overwrought state, imagine there an expression
he had never before remarked, or had the unknown artist
of the seventies actually risen above the mediocrity of the

figure in his portrayal of the features of the Christ? The
rector started, and stared again. There was no weakness
in the face, no meekness, no suggestion of the conception
of the sacrificed Lamb, no hint of a beatific vision of opening heavens — and yet no accusation, no despair. A
knowing — that were nearer — a knowing of all things
through the experiencing of all things, the suffering of all
things. For suffering without revelation were vain, indeed! A perfected wisdom that blended inevitably with
a transcendent love. Love and wisdom were one, then?
To reach comprehension through conquering experience
was to achieve the love that could exclaim, "they know
not what they do!"

Human or divine? Man or God? Hodder found himself inwardly repeating the words, the controversy which
had raged for nineteen hundred years, and not yet was
stilled. Perfection *is* divine. *Human!* Hodder repeated the word, as one groping on the theshold of a great
discovery. . . .

III

He was listening — he had for a long time been listening to a sound which had seemed only the natural accom-
paniment of the drama taking place in his soul, as though
some inspired organist were expressing in exquisite music
the undercurrent of his agony. Only gradually did he
become aware that it arose from the nave of the church,
and, turning, his eyes fell upon the bowed head and
shoulders of a woman kneeling in one of the pews. She
was sobbing.

His movement, he recalled afterward, did not come of a
conscious volition, as he rose and descended the chancel
steps and walked toward her; he stood for what seemed
a long time on the white marble of the aisle looking down
on her, his heart wrung by the violence of her grief, which
at moments swept through her like a tempest. She seemed
still young, but poverty had marked her with unmistakable signs. The white, blue-veined hands that clung to

the railing of the pew were thin; and the shirtwaist, though clean, was cheap and frayed. At last she rose from her knees and raised a tear-stained face to his, staring at him in a dumb bewilderment.

"Can I do anything for you?" he said gently, "I am the rector here."

She did not answer, but continued to stare uncomprehendingly. He sat down beside her in the pew.

"You are in trouble," he said. "Will you let me try to help you?"

A sob shook her — the beginning of a new paroxysm. He waited patiently until it was over. Suddenly she got rather wildly and unsteadily to her feet.

"I must go!" she cried. "Oh, God, what would I do if — if he wasn't there?"

Hodder rose too. She had thrust herself past him into the aisle, but if he had not taken her arm she would have fallen. Thus they went together to the door of the church, and out into the white, burning sunlight. In spite of her weakness she seemed actually to be leading him, impelled by a strange force and fled down the steps of the porch to the sidewalk. And there she paused, seeing him still beside her. Fortunately he had his hat in his hand.

"Where are you going?" she asked.

"To take you home," he replied firmly, "you ought not to go alone."

A look of something like terror came into her eyes.

"Oh, no!" she protested, with a vehemence that surprised him. "I am strong. Oh, thank you, sir, — but I can go alone. It's Dicky — my little boy. I've never left him so long. I had gone for the medicine and I saw the church. I used to go to church, sir, before we had our troubles — and I just went in. It suddenly came over me that God might help me — the doctor can do nothing."

"I will go with you," he said.

She ceased to resist, as one submitting to the fatality of a superior will.

The pavements that afternoon, as Hodder and the forlorn

L

woman left the cool porticoes of St. John's, were like the floor of a stone oven, and the work horses wore little bonnets over their heads. Keeping to the shady side, the rector and his companion crossed Tower Street with its trolley cars and its awninged stores, and came to that depressing district which had reproached him since the first Sunday of his ministry when he had traversed it with Eldon Parr. They passed the once prosperous houses, the corner saloons pandering to two vices, decked with the flamboyant signs of the breweries. The trees were dying along the asphalt and in the yards, the iron fences broken here and there, the copings stained with rust and soot. Hodder's thoughts might have been likened to the heated air that simmered above the bricks.

They were in Dalton Street! She seemed to have forgotten his presence, her pace quickened as she turned into a gate and flew up a flight of dirty stone steps, broken and sagging. Hodder took in, subconsciously, that the house was a dingy grey, of three stories and a Mansard roof, with a bay window on the yard side, and a fly-blown sign, "Rooms to Rent" hanging in one window. Across the street, on a lot that had once held a similar dignified residence, was the yellow brick building of the "Albert Hotel," and next door, on the east, a remodelled house of "apartments" with speaking tubes in the doorway.

The woman led him up another flight of steps to the open door of the house, through a hallway covered with a ragged carpet, where a dilapidated walnut hat-rack stood, up the stairs, threading a dark passage that led into a low-ceiled, stifling room at the very back. A stout, slatternly person in a wrapper rose as they entered, but the mother cast herself down beside the lounge where the child was. Hodder had a moment of fear that she was indeed too late, so still the boy lay, so pathetically wan was the little face and wasted the form under the cotton nightgown. The mother passed her hand across his forehead.

"Dicky!" she whispered fearfully, "Dicky!"

He opened his eyes and smiled at her, feebly.

The stout woman, who had been looking on with that intensity of sympathy of which the poor are capable, began waving gently the palm-leaf fan. She was German.

"He is so good, is Dicky. He smile at me when I fan him — once, twice. He complains not at all."

The mother took the fan from her hand.

"Thank you for staying with him, Mrs. Breitmann. I was gone longer than I expected." The fact that the child still lived, that she was again in his presence, the absorbing act of caring for him seemed to have calmed her.

"It is nothing, what I do," answered Mrs. Breitmann, and turned away reluctantly, the tears running on her cheeks. "When you go again, I come always, Mrs. Garvin. Ach!"

Her exclamation was caused by the sight of the tall figure and black coat of the rector, and as she left the room, Mrs. Garvin turned. And he noticed in her eyes the same expression of dread they had held when she had protested against his coming.

"Please don't think that I'm not thankful —" she faltered.

"I am not offering you charity," he said. "Can you not take from other human beings what you have accepted from this woman who has just left?"

"Oh, sir, it isn't that!" she cried, with a look of trust, of appeal that was new, "I would do anything — I will do anything. But my husband — he is so bitter against the church, against ministers! If he came home and found you here ——"

"I know — many people feel that way," he assented, "too many. But you cannot let a prejudice stand in the way of saving the boy's life, Mrs. Garvin."

"It is more than that. If you knew, sir ——"

"Whatever it is," he interrupted, a little sternly, "it must not interfere. I will talk to your husband."

She was silent, gazing at him now questioningly, yet with the dawning hope of one whose strength is all but gone, and who has found at last a stronger to lean upon.

The rector took the fan from her arrested hand and began to ply it.

"Listen, Mrs. Garvin. If you had come to the church half an hour later, I should have been leaving the city for a place far distant."

"You were going away? You stayed on my account?"

"I much prefer to stay, if I can be of any use, and I think I can. I am sure I can. What is the matter with the child?"

"I don't know, sir — he just lies there listless and gets thinner and thinner and weaker and weaker. Sometimes he feels sick, but not often. The doctor don't seem to know."

"What doctor have you?"

"His name is Welling. He's around the corner."

"Exactly," said the rector. "This is a case for Dr. Jarvis, who is the best child specialist in the city. He is a friend of mine, and I intend to send for him at once. And the boy must go to a hospital——"

"Oh, I couldn't, sir."

He had a poignant realization of the agony behind the cry. She breathed quickly through her parted lips, and from the yearning in her tired eyes — as she gazed at the poor little form — he averted his glance.

"Now, Mrs. Garvin, you must be sensible," he said. "This is no place for a sick child. And it is such a nice little hospital, the one I have in mind, and so many children get well and strong there," he added, cheerfully.

"*He* wouldn't hear of it." Hodder comprehended that she was referring to her husband. She added inconsequently: "If I let him go, and he never came back! Oh, I couldn't do it — I couldn't."

He saw that it was the part of wisdom not to press her, to give her time to become accustomed to the idea. Come back — to what? His eye wandered about the room, that bespoke the last shifts of poverty, for he knew that none but the desperate were driven to these Dalton Street houses, once the dwellings of the well-to-do, and all the more pitiful for the contrast.   The heated air reeked with the smell of stale cooking.   There was a gas stove at one side, a linoleum-covered table in the centre, littered with bottles, plates, and pitchers, a bed and chairs which had known better days, now obviously bruised and battered by many enforced movings.   In one corner was huddled a little group of toys.

He was suddenly and guiltily aware that the woman had followed his glance.

"We had them in Alder Street," she said.   "We might have been there yet, if we hadn't been foolish.   It's a pretty street, sir — perhaps you know it — you take the Fanshawe Avenue cars to Sherman Heights.   The air is like the country there, and all the houses are new, and Dicky had a yard to play in, and he used to be so healthy and happy in it. . . .   We were rich then, — not what *you'd* call rich," she added apologetically, "but we owned a little home with six rooms, and my husband had a good place as bookkeeper in a grocery house, and every year for ten years we put something by, and the boy came. We never knew how well off we were, until it was taken away from us, I guess.   And then Richard — he's my husband — put his savings into a company — he thought it was so safe, and we were to get eight per cent — and the company failed, and he fell sick and lost his place, and we had to sell the house, and since he got well again he's been going around trying for something else.   Oh, he's tried so hard, — every day, and all day long.   You wouldn't believe it, sir.   And he's so proud.   He got a job as porter, but he wasn't able to hold it — he wasn't strong enough. . . . That was in April.   It almost broke my heart to see him getting shabby — he used to look so tidy.   And folks don't want you when you're shabby." . . .

There sprang to Hodder's mind a sentence in a book he had recently read : "Our slums became filled with sick who need never have been sick ; with derelicts who need never have been abandoned." . . .

Suddenly, out of the suffocating stillness of the after-noon a woman's voice was heard singing a concert-hall air, accompanied by a piano played with vigour and abandon. And Hodder, following the sound, looked out across the grimy yard — to a window in the apartment house opposite.

"There's that girl again," said the mother, lifting her head. "She does sing nice, and play, poor thing! There was a time when I wouldn't have wanted to listen. But Dicky liked it so. . . . It's the very tune he loved. He don't seem to hear it now. He don't even ask for Mr. Bentley any more."

"Mr. Bentley?" the rector repeated. The name was somehow familiar to him.

The piano and the song ceased abruptly, with a bang.

"He lives up the street here a way — the kindest old gentleman you ever saw. He always has candy in his pockets for the children, and it's a sight to see them follow him up and down the sidewalk. He takes them to the Park in the cars on Saturday afternoons. That was all Dicky could think about at first — would he be well enough to go with Mr. Bentley by Saturday? And he was forever asking me to tell Mr. Bentley he was sick. I saw the old gentleman on the street to-day, and I almost went up to him. But I hadn't the courage."

The child moaned, stirred, and opened his eyes, gazing at them feverishly, yet without seeming comprehension. She bent over him, calling his name. . . . Hodder thrust the fan into her hand, and rose.

"I am going to telephone Dr. Jarvis," he said, "and then I shall come back, in order to be here when he arrives."

She looked up at him.

"Oh, thank you, sir, — I guess it's for the best ——"

Her voice died away, and the rector, seeking for the cause, saw that a man had entered the room. He walked up to the couch and stood for a moment staring moodily at the child, while the woman watched him, transfixed.

"Richard!" she said.

He paid no attention to her. She turned to Hodder. "This is my husband, sir. . . . Richard, I went into the church — just for a moment — I — I couldn't help it, and this gentleman — the minister — came home with me. He wanted to — he thought I was sick. And now he's going out to get the best doctor in the city — for Dicky."

The man turned suddenly and confronted the rector.

"Why don't you let him die, you and your church people?" he asked. "You've done your worst to kill him."

The woman put her hand fearfully, imploringly on the man's arm.

"Richard!" she whispered.

But as Hodder glanced from the derelict beside him a wave of comprehension passed through him that swept him clean of indignation, of resentment. And this man had been prosperous and happy!

"There is but one way to save the boy's life, Mr. Garvin," he said, "and that is to put him in charge of Dr. Jarvis."

The man made no reply, but went over to the window, staring out into the yard. There was something vaguely ominous in his attitude. The rector watched him a moment, and then turned to the mother.

"You must not lose hope," he told her.

She looked at him with terror-stricken eyes that sought to be grateful. He had picked up his hat from a corner of the littered table, and started to leave, when Garvin, by a sudden movement, planted himself in the doorway. Whether he had been drinking, or whether he were merely crazed by misfortune and the hopeless search in the heat for employment, and by lack of proper nourishment, Hodder could not say. There was a light in his eyes like that in a wounded animal's; and although he was thin and slight, he had the concentrated power of desperation.

"Say, what church do you come from?" he demanded.

"From St. John's," said the rector.

"Eldon Parr's church?"

Hodder started, in spite of himself, at the name.

"Mr. Parr is a member of the congregation."

"Come off! He owns it and runs it, the same as he does everything else in this town. Maybe you don't think

I read the Sunday papers.   Say, I was respectable once,
and had a good place. You wouldn't believe it, would
you?"

Hodder hesitated.   There was obviously no way to pass
the man except by using physical force.

"If you have anything to say to me, Mr. Garvin, I shall
be glad to talk to you later.   You must not stop me now,"
he said with a touch of severity.

"You'll listen to me, right here and now," cried Garvin.
"If you think I am going to let Eldon Parr's minister, or
any one else belonging to him, save that boy's life, you've
got another guess comin'.   That's all.   I'd rather have
him *die* — d'ye hear ?   I'd rather have him *die*."

The woman behind them whimpered. . . . The name
was ringing like a knell in Hodder's head — Eldon Parr!
Coming, as it had, like a curse from the lips of this wretched,
half-demented creature, it filled his soul with dismay.
And the accusation had in it the profound ring of truth.
He *was* Eldon Parr's minister, and it was Eldon Parr who
stood between him and his opportunity.

"Why do you speak of Mr. Parr ?" he asked, though
the question cost him a supreme effort.

"Why do I speak of him?   My God, because he ruined
me.   If it hadn't been for him, damn him, I'd have a home,
and health and happiness to-day, and the boy would be
well and strong instead of lying there with the life all but
gone out of him.   Eldon Parr did for me, and now he's
murdered my son — that's why I mention him."

In the sudden intensity of his feeling, Hodder seized
Garvin by the arms — arms that were little more than
skin and bone.   The man might be crazed, he might be
drunk : that he believed what he was saying there could
be no question.   He began to struggle violently, but the
rector was strong.

"Be still," he commanded.   And suddenly, overcome
less by the physical power than by the aspect of the clergyman, an expression of bewilderment came into his eyes,
and he was quiet.   Hodder dropped his arms.   "I do not
intend to go until I hear what you have to say.   It would

be useless, at any rate, since your child's life is at stake. Tell me how Mr. Parr has ruined you."

Garvin stared at him, half in suspicion, half in amazement.

"I guess you never knew of his ruining anybody, did you?" he demanded sullenly. "Well, I'll tell you all right, and you can go and tell *him*. He won't care much — he's used to it by this time, and he gets square with God by his churches and charities. Did you ever hear of a stock called Consolidated Tractions?"

Consolidated Tractions! In contrast to the sordid misery and degradation of this last refuge of the desperate Hodder saw the lofty, panelled smoking room at Francis Ferguson's, and was listening again to Wallis Plimpton's cynical amusement as to how he and Everett Constable and Eldon Parr himself had "got out" before the crash; "got out" with all the money of the wretch who now stood before him! His parishioners! his Christians! Oh God!

The man was speaking in his shrill voice.

"Well, I was a Traction sucker, all right, and I guess you wouldn't have to walk more than two blocks to find another in this neighbourhood. You think Eldon Parr's a big, noble man, don't you? You're proud to run his church, ain't you? You wouldn't believe there was a time when I thought he was a big man, when I was kind of proud to live in the same city with him. *She'll* tell you how I used to come home from the store and talk about him after supper, and hope that the kid there would grow up into a financier like Eldon Parr. The boys at the store talked about him: he sort of laid hold on our imaginations with the library he gave, and Elmwood Park, and the picture of the big organ in your church in the newspapers — and sometimes, Mary and me and the boy, in the baby carriage, on Sunday afternoons we used to walk around by his house, just to look at it. You couldn't have got me to believe that Eldon Parr would put his name to anything that wasn't straight.

"Then Consolidated Tractions came along, with Parr's name behind it. Everybody was talking about it, and how it was payin' eight per cent. from the start, and extra dividends and all, and what a marvel of finance it was.   Before the kid came, as soon as I married her, we began to save up for *him*. We didn't go to the theatres or nothing. Well, I put it all, five thousand dollars, into Consolidated. *She'll* tell you how we sat up half the night after we got the first dividend talking about how we'd send the kid to college, and after we went to bed we couldn't sleep.   It wasn't more than a year after that we began to hear things —and we couldn't sleep for sure, and the dividends stopped and the stock tumbled.   Even then I wouldn't believe it of him, that he'd take poor people's money that way when he had more than he knew what to do with.   I made up my mind if I went down to see him and told him about it, he'd make it right.   I asked the boss for an hour off, and headed for the Parr building—I've been tnere as much as fifty times since — but he don't bother with small fry.   The clerks laugh when they see me comin'. . . . I got sick worryin', and when I was strong enough to be around they'd filled my job at the grocery, and it wasn't long before we had to move out of our little home in Alder Street.   We've been movin' ever since," he cried, and tears of weakness were in his eyes, "until we've come to *this*, and we'll have to get out of here in another week. God knows where we'll go then."

Hodder shuddered.

"Then I found out how he done it—from a lawyer. The lawyer laughed at me, too.   Say, do you wonder I ain't got much use for your church people?   Parr got a corporation lawyer named Langmaid—he's another one of your millionnaire crooks—to fix it up and get around the law and keep him out of jail.   And then they had to settle with Tom Beatty for something like three hundred thousand.   You know who Beatty is—he owns this city —his saloon's around here on Elm Street.   All the crooks had to be squared.   Say," he demanded aggressively, "are Parr and Langmaid any better than Beatty, or any of the hold-up men Beatty covers?   There's a street-walker over there in those flats that's got a million times more chance to get to heaven — if there is any — than those financiers, as they call 'emselves! I ain't much on high finance, but I've got some respect for a second story man now — *he* takes some risks! I'll tell you what *they* did, they bought up the short car lines that didn't pay and sold 'em to *themselves* for fifty times as much as they were worth; and they got controlling interests in the big lines and leased 'em to themselves with dividends guaranteed as high as eighteen per cent. They capitalized the Consolidated for more millions than a little man like me can think of, and we handed 'em our money because we thought they were honest. We thought the men who listed the stock on the Exchange were honest. And when the crash came, they'd got away with the swag, like any common housebreakers. There were dummy directors, and a dummy president. Eldon Parr didn't have a share — sold out everything when she went over two hundred, but you bet he kept his stock in the leased lines, which guarantee more than they earn. He cleaned up five million, they say. . . . My money — the money that might give that boy fresh air, and good doctors. . . . Say, you believe in hell, don't you? You tell Eldon Parr to keep his charity, — he can't send any of it in here. And you'd better go back to that church of his and pray to keep his soul out of hell." . . .

His voice, which had risen even to a higher pitch, fell silent. And all at once, without warning, Garvin sank, or rather tumbled upon the bed, sobbing in a way that was terrible to see. The wife stole across the room, sat down beside him, and laid her hand on his shoulder. . . .

In spite of the intensity of his own anguish, Hodder was conscious of a curious detachment; and for months afterward particular smells, the sight of a gasoline stove, a certain popular tune gave him a sharp twinge of pain. The acid distilling in his soul etched the scene, the sounds, the odours forever in his memory: a stale hot wind from the alley rattled the shutter-slats, and blew the door to; the child stirred; and above the strident, irregular weeping rose again, in ironical contrast, the piano and the voice across the yard.   In that glimpse he had into the heart of life's terrible mystery he momentarily understood many things: he knew that behind the abandon of the woman's song was the same terror which reigned in the room in which he stood. . . .

There were voices in the passageway without, a woman saying in a German accent, "It is here, sir."

There was a knock at the door. . . .

CHAPTER XI

I

HODDER opened the door. In the dingy passageway he perceived a tall figure which immediately turned out to be that of an old gentleman. In spite of the heat, he wore a long coat and an old-fashioned, high collar, a black tie, under which was exposed a triangle of immaculate, pleated linen. In one hand he held a gold-headed stick, a large tall hat of which the silk nap was a little rubbed, a string sustaining a parcel, the brown paper wrapping of which was soaked : in the other, a manila bag containing lemons. His head was bent forward a little, the high dome of it was bald, but the white hair clustered thickly behind the temples. The face was clean-shaven, the cheeks touched with red, the nose high and dominating, distinctly philanthropic. And the blue eyes rested on the clergyman with a benevolence unfeigned.

"Good afternoon, sir," the old gentleman said; "I am told Mrs. Garvin lives here."

Before the rector could reply Mrs. Garvin herself stood between them.

"It's Mr. Bentley!" she exclaimed.

"I fear I'm intruding, ma'am," he said. "But some of Dicky's little friends have just informed me that he is ill, and I have taken the liberty of calling to inquire."

Mr. Bentley entered the room, — simple words to express that which was in some sort an event. He laid his parcels on the table, his hat and stick on a chair, and stood looking down in silence at the thin little form on the couch. Presently he turned.

157

"I'm afraid he's very ill, ma'am," he said gently.   "You have your own doctor, no doubt.   But if you will permit me, as a friend, to make a suggestion, we have in the city one of the best child specialists in the United States, who is never weary of curing these little ones, — Dr. Jarvis, — and I shal! be happy to ask him to come and see Dicky."

Mrs. Garvin glanced at Hodder, who came forward.

"I was just about to telephone for Dr. Jarvis, Mr. Bentley, when you arrived.   I am Mr. Hodder, of St. John's."

"How do you do, sir?"   The kindly eyes, alight with a gentle flame, rested upon the rugged figure of the rector. "I am glad that you, too, agree that Dr. Jarvis is advisable, Mr. Hodder."

There was a sound from the bed.   Garvin had got to his feet and was staring wildly, with reddened lids.

"Are you Horace Bentley?" he demanded.

"That is my name, sir," Mr. Bentley replied.   His expression of surprise was only momentary.   And in all his life Hodder had never beheld a greater contrast in human beings than between that gracious and courtly old man and the haggard, unkempt, unshaved, and starving outcast facing him.   Something like a film came over Garvin's eyes.

"He ruined you, too, twenty years back — Eldon Parr did for you, too.   Oh, I know his record, I've followed his trail — he got all the Grantham stock that would have made you a millionnaire!"

"Ah," replied Mr. Bentley, smiling to humour him, "that's something I have no wish to be, sir, — a millionnaire."   He met the frightened gaze of the wife.   "Good day, ma'am.   If you will allow me, I'll come to-morrow morning to learn what Dr. Jarvis will have had to say. Have courage, ma'am, have courage.   You may have faith in Dr. Jarvis."

The poor woman was incapable of speech.   Mr. Bentley picked up his hat and stick.

"I've taken the liberty of bringing Dicky a little ice and a few lemons."   His eyes rested again on the couch by the window. Then he turned to Garvin, who stood mutely, staring. "Good evening, sir," he said. " We must look for the best."

II

They went down the stairs of the shabby and battered house, stairs by the side of which holes had been knocked through the faded wall-paper — scars of frequent movings. The sound and smell of frying came out of the open door of what once had been the parlour, and on the front steps a little girl darted past them with a pitcher of beer. When they reached the sidewalk Mr. Bentley halted.

"If you were intending to telephone Dr. Jarvis, Mr. Hodder, there is a public station in the drug store just above here. I know that clergymen are busy persons, and I am passing it, if you are pressed for time."

"My only concern is to get Jarvis here," said the rector. " If I may go with you —— "

Once again in the hot sunlight, reaction had set in. Hodder was suddenly unstrung, and the kindly old gentleman beside him seemed for the instant the only fixture in a chaotic universe. It was not until later reflection that he realized Mr. Bentley might, by an intuitive sympathy, a depth of understanding, have divined something of his state, since the incidents which followed were to be accounted for on no other grounds. In such elemental moments the frail conventions are swept away : Mr. Bentley, whoever he might be, was no longer a stranger, and it seemed wholly natural to be walking with him up the street, to hear him saying, — not with perfunctory politeness, but in a tone that was itself an invitation, — " With pleasure, sir, we'll go together. And let us trust that the doctor will be at home."

Nor did Hodder stop to wonder, then, why Mr. Bentley should have sought in his conversation to dissipate something of the hideous blackness of a tragedy which must have moved him profoundly. How fortunate, he declared, that they should have arrived before it was too late ! For it was plain to be seen that these Garvins were good people who had been broken by adversity. . . . The boy had struck him particularly — a lovable, merry little fellow whose clothes, Mr. Bentley observed, were always neatly mended, betokening a mother with self-respect and character. He even spoke of Garvin: adversity, worry, the heat, constant brooding over a happier past and an uncertain future — was it surprising that the poor man's mind had become unhinged? They must make some plan for Garvin, said Mr. Bentley, get the man and his wife into the country for a while amongst kindly people. This might no doubt be arranged. . . .

"Here we are, sir."

The familiar smell of drugs, the sound of the trickling water in the soda fountain roused Hodder to reality, to action, and he hurried into the telephone booth, fumbled in the dog-eared book, got Dr. Jarvis's number and called it. An eternity seemed to elapse before he had a reply, heard his coin jangling in the box, recognized the voice of the great doctor's secretary. Yes, the doctor was in: would he speak to Mr. Hodder, of St. John's? . . . An interval, during which Hodder was suddenly struck with this designation of himself. Was he still of St. John's, then? An æon might have elapsed since he had walked down the white marble of its aisle toward the crouching figure in the pew. He was not that man, but another — and still Mr. Hodder, of St. John's. . . . Then he heard the specialist say, " Hello, Mr. Hodder, what can I do for you?" Heard his own voice in reply, explaining the case. Could the doctor find time? The doctor could: he was never too busy to attend to the poor, — though he did not say so: he would be there by half-past six. The rector hung up the receiver, opened the door of the booth and mopped his brow, for the heat was stifling.

"The doctor will go," he explained in answer to Mr. Bentley's inquiring look.

"Now, sir," said the old gentleman, when they were out of the store, " we have done all that we can for the time being. I do not live far from here. Perhaps you would

give me the pleasure of taking supper with me, if you have
no other engagement."

No other engagement! Not until then did Hodder remember his empty rooms in the parish house, and the
train which was to have borne him away from all this already speeding northward. He accepted gratefully, nor
did he pause to speculate upon the mystery by which the
stream of his life seemed so suddenly to have been diverted.
He had, indeed, no sense of mystery in the presence of
this splendidly sane, serene old man, any more than the
children who ran after him from the dingy yards and
passages, calling his name, clinging to the skirts of his
coat. These accepted him simply as an anomalous fact
in their universe, grinned at his pleasantries, and held up
grimy little hands for the kidney-shaped candy beans he
drew forth from his capacious pockets. In the intervals
he reminisced to the rector about the neighbourhood.

"It seems but a short while ago when the trees met
overhead — magnificent trees they were. The asphalt
and the soot killed them. And there were fruit trees in
that yard — " he pointed with his stick to a littered sun-
parched plot adjoining a battered mansion — "all pink and
white with blossoms in the spring. Mr. Hadley lived
there — one of our forgotten citizens. He is dead and
gone now and his family scattered. That other house,
where the boy lies, belonged to Mr. Villars, a relation of
the Atterbury family, and I can recall very well a little
girl with a pink sash and a white dress who used
to come running out to meet me with flowers in her
hands. Incredible as it may seem, she picked them in
that yard. I thought of her as I went in, how fresh
and happy she used to be, and what a different place
this was for children then. She must have some of her
own by this time."

The character of the street had changed to what might
be called shabby-genteel, and they stopped before a three-
story brick house — one of a row — that showed signs of
scrupulous care. The steps were newly scrubbed, the
woodwork neatly painted.

M

"This is where I live, sir," said Mr. Bentley, opening the door with a latchkey and leading the way into a high room on the right, darkened and cool, and filled with superb, old-fashioned rosewood furniture. It was fitted up as a library, with tall shelves reaching almost to the ceiling.

An old negro appeared, dressed in a swallow-tailed coat. His hair was as white as his master's, and his face creased with age.

"Sam," said Mr. Bentley, "I have brought home a gentleman for supper."

"Yassah, Misteh Ho'ace. I was jest agwine to open up de blin's."

He lifted the wire screens and flung back the shutters, beamed on the rector as he relieved him of his hat, and noiselessly retired. Curiosity, hitherto suppressed by more powerful feelings, awoke in Hodder speculations which ordinarily would have been aroused before: every object in the room bespoke gentility, was eloquent of a day when wealth was honoured and respected: photographs, daguerreotypes in old-fashioned frames bore evidence of friendships of the past, and over the marble mantel hung a portrait of a sweet-faced woman in the costume of the thirties, whose eyes reminded Hodder of Mr. Bentley's. Who was she?

Hodder wondered. Presently he found himself before a photograph on the wall beyond, at which he had been staring unconsciously.

"Ah, you recognize it," said Mr. Bentley.

"St. John's!"

"Yes," Mr. Bentley repeated, "St. John's." He smiled at Hodder's glance of bewilderment, and put his hand on the younger man's arm. "That picture was taken before you were born, sir, I venture to say — in 1869. I am very fond of it, for it gives the church in perspective, as you see. That was Mr. Gore's house" — he indicated a square, heavily corniced mansion — "where the hotel now stands, and that was his garden, next the church, where you see the trees above the wall."

The rector turned again and looked at his host, who was gazing at the picture thoughtfully.

"I ought to have remembered," he said. "I have seen your name in the church records, sir, and I have heard Mr. Waring speak of you."

"My dear Mr. Hodder, there is no reason why you should have known me. A great many years have passed since I was a parishioner of St. John's — a great many years."

"But it was you," the rector began, uncertainly, and suddenly spoke with conviction, "it was you who chose the architect, who did more than other men to make the church what it is."

"Whatever I may have done," replied Mr. Bentley, with simple dignity, "has brought its reward. To this day I have not ceased to derive pleasure from it, and often I go out of my way, through Burton Street, although the view is cramped. And sometimes," he added, with the hint of a twinkle in his eye, "I go in. This afternoon is not the first time I have seen you, Mr. Hodder."

"But — ?" said the rector. He stared at the other's face, and the question died on his lips.

"You wonder why I am no longer a parishioner. The time came when I could not afford to be." There was no hint of reproach in his voice, of bitterness. He spoke regretfully, indeed, but as one stating an incontrovertible fact. "I lost my fortune, I could not keep my pew, so I deeded it back to the church. My old friends, Mrs. Dimock and Asa Waring, and others, too, were very kind. But I could not accept their hospitality."

Hodder bowed his head in silence. What thundered indictment of the Church of Christ could have been as severe, as wholly condemning as these few words so dispassionately uttered by the man beside him?

The old darky entered, and announced supper.

Hodder had lost his way, yet a hand had been held out to him, and he seized it. With a sense of being led, psychically as well as physically, he followed Mr. Bentley

into a large bedroom where a high, four-posted bed lifted
a pleated canopy toward the ceiling.   And after he had
washed his hands they entered a dining-room looking out
upon a little yard in the rear, which had been transformed
into a garden.   Roses, morning glories, and nasturtiums
were growing against the walls; a hose lay coiled upon
the path; the bricks, baked during the day, were splashed
with water; the leaves and petals were wet, and the acrid
odour of moist earth, mingling with perfumes, penetrated
the room.   Hodder paused in the window.

"Sam keeps our flowers alive," he heard Mr. Bentley
say, "I don't know how."

"I scrubs 'em, sah," said Sam.   "Yassah, I washes 'em
like chilluns."

He found himself, at Mr. Bentley's request, asking
grace, the old darky with reverently bent head standing
behind his master; sitting down at a mahogany table that
reflected like a mirror the few pieces of old silver, to a
supper of beaten biscuits that burned one's fingers, of
broiled chicken and coffee, and sliced peaches and cream.
Mr. Bentley was talking of other days — not so long gone
by — when the great city had been a village, or scarcely
more.   The furniture, it seemed, had come from his own
house in what was called the Wilderness Road, not far
from the river banks, over the site of which limited trains
now rolled on their way eastward toward the northernmost
of the city's bridges.   He mentioned many names, some
remembered, some forgotten, — like his own; dwelt on
pleasures and customs gone by forever.

"A little while after I moved in here, I found that one
old man could not fill the whole of this house, so I let the
upper floors," he explained, smilingly.   "Some day I
must introduce you to my tenants, Mr. Hodder."

By degrees, as Hodder listened, he became calm.   Like
a child, he found himself distracted, talking, asking
questions: and the intervals grew longer between the recurrent surges of fear when the memory rose before him
of the events of the day, — of the woman, the child, and
the man: of Eldon Parr and this deed he had done;

hinting, as it did, of closed chambers of other deeds yet to be opened, of countless, hidden miseries still to be revealed: when he heard once more the tortured voice of the banker, and the question: "How would you like to live in this house — alone?" In contrast, now he beheld the peace in the face of the man whose worldly goods Eldon Parr had taken, and whom he had driven out of the church. Surely, this man had found a solution! . . . What was it? . . .

Hodder thought of the child, of the verdict of Dr. Jarvis, but he lingered on, loth to leave, — if the truth be told — *afraid* to leave; drawing strength from his host's calm, wondering as to the source of it, as to the life which was its expression; longing, yet not presuming, to question. The twilight deepened, and the old darky lit a lamp and led the way back to the library.

"Sam," said Mr. Bentley, "draw up the armchair for Mr. Hodder beside the window. It is cooler there."

"I ought to go," Hodder said. "I ought to see how the child is. Jarvis will have been there by this time, and there may be necessaries ——"

"Jarvis will have attended to that," Mr. Bentley replied. "Sit down, Mr. Hodder. I am not sure that, for the present, we have not done all in this case that is humanly possible."

"You mean," said the rector, "that they will accept nothing from me." It came from him, spontaneously, like a cry. He had not meant to say it. "I don't blame them. I don't blame them for losing their faith in God and man, in the Church. I ought to have seen it before, but I was blind, incredibly blind — until it struck me in the face. You saw it, sir, and you left a church from which the poor are thrust out, which refuses to heed the first precept of its Master."

"I saw it," answered Mr. Bentley, "but I could do nothing. Perhaps you can do — something."

"Ah!" Hodder exclaimed sharply, "why do you say that? The Church is paralyzed, chained. How can she reach these wretched people who are the victims of the ruthless individualism and greed of those who control her? You know — that man, Mr. Bentley." (Hodder could not bring himself to pronounce Eldon Parr's name.) "I had an affection for him, I pitied him, because he suffers ——"

"Yes," echoed Mr. Bentley, "he suffers."

Hodder was momentarily arrested by the sadness of his tone.

"But he doesn't know *why* he suffers — he cannot be made to see," the rector went on. "And he is making others suffer, — hideously, while he imagines himself a Christian. He *is* the Church to that miserable, hopeless wretch we saw to-day, and to hundreds of the same kind whom he has driven to desperation. And I — who am supposed to be the vicar of God — I am powerless. They have a contempt for me, a just contempt. They thrust me out of their doors, bid me to return and minister to their oppressors. You were right to leave, and I should have left long since."

He had not spoken with violence, or with a lack of control. He seemed rather to have regained a mastery of himself, and felt as a man from whom the shackles have been struck, proclaiming his freedom. Mr. Bentley's eyes lighted in involuntary response as he gazed at the figure and face before him. He pressed his hands together.

"If you will forgive a curiosity, Mr. Hodder, that is somewhat due to my interest in a church with which I have many precious associations, may I ask if this is a sudden determination on your part?"

"No," Hodder said. "I have known ever since I came here that something was wrong, but at first I couldn't see it, and after that I *wouldn't* see it. That is about what happened, as I look back on it.

"But the farther in I went," Hodder continued, "the more tangled and bewildered I became. I was hypnotized, I think," he added with a gesture, — "hypnotized, as a man is who never takes his eyes from a pattern. I wanted to get at this neighbourhood — Dalton Street — I mean, and finally I agreed to the establishment of a settlement house over here, to be paid for largely by Eldon Parr and Francis Ferguson. I couldn't see the folly of such an undertaking — the supreme irony of it, until — until it was pointed out to me." He hesitated; the remembrance of Alison Parr ran through him, a thread of pain. "And even then I tried to dodge the issue, I tried to make myself believe that good might flow out of evil; that the Church, which is supposed to be founded on the highest ideal ever presented to man, might compromise and be practical, that she might accept money which had been wrung from a trusting public by extortion, by thinly disguised thievery such as this Consolidated Tractions Company fraud, and do good with it! And at last I made up my mind to go away, to-day, to a quiet place where I might be alone, and reflect, when by a singular circumstance I was brought into contact with this man, Garvin. I see now, clearly enough, that if I had gone, I should never have come back."

"And you still intend to go?" Mr. Bentley asked.

Hodder leaned his elbow against the mantel. The lamplight had a curious effect on Mr. Bentley's face.

"What can I do?" he demanded. The question was not aimed directly at his host — it was in the nature of a renewed appeal to a tribunal which had been mute, but with which he now seemed vaguely aware of a certain contact. "Even supposing I could bring myself to accept the compromise — now that I see it clearly, that the end justifies the means — what good could I accomplish? You saw what happened this afternoon — the man would have driven me out if it hadn't been for you. This whole conception of charity is a crime against civilization — I had to have that pointed out to me, too, — this system of legalized or semi-legalized robbery and the distribution of largesse to the victims. The Church is doing wrong, is stultifying herself in encouraging it. She should set her face rigidly against it, stand for morality and justice and Christianity in *government*, not for pauperizing. It is her mission to enlighten these people, all people — to make them self-respecting, to give them some notion of the dignity of their souls and their rights before God and man."

"Aren't you yourself suggesting," said Mr. Bentley, "the course which will permit you to remain?"

Hodder was silent. The thought struck him with tremendous force. Had *he* suggested it? And how — why? Could it be done? Could *he* do it or begin it?

"We have met at last in a singular way," he heard Mr. Bentley going on, "in a way that has brushed aside the conventions, in a way — I am happy to say — that has enabled you to give me your confidence. And I am an old man, — that has made it easier. I saw this afternoon, Mr. Hodder, that you were troubled, although you tried to hide it."

"I knew that you saw it," Hodder said.

"Nor was it difficult for me to guess something of the cause of it. The same thing has troubled me."

"You?"

"Yes," Mr. Bentley answered. "I left St. John's, but the habits and affections of a lifetime are not easily severed. And some time before I left it I began to have visions of a future for it. There was a question, many years ago, as to whether a new St. John's should not be built in the West End, on a site convenient to the parishioners, and this removal I opposed. Mr. Waring stood by me. We foresaw the day when this district would be — what it is now — the precarious refuge of the unfortunate in the battle of life, of just such unhappy families as the Garvins, of miserable women who sell themselves to keep alive. I thought of St. John's, as you did, as an oasis in a desert of misery and vice. At that time I, too, believed in the system of charities which you have so well characterized as pauperizing."

"And now?"

Mr. Bentley smiled, as at a reminiscence.

"My eyes were opened," he replied, and in these simple words summed up and condemned it all. "They are craving bread, and we fling them stones. I came here. It was a house I owned, which I saved from the wreck, and as I look back upon what the world would call a misfortune, sir, I can see that it was a propitious event, for me. The street 'ran down,' as the saying goes. I grew gradually to know these people, my new neighbours, largely through their children, and I perceived many things I had not dreamed of — before then. I saw how the Church was hampered, fettered; I saw why they disliked and distrusted it."

"And yet you still believed that it had a mission?" Hodder interrupted. He had been listening with rapt attention.

"I still believed it," said Mr. Bentley. "My conception of that mission changed, grew, and yet it seemed further and further from fulfilment. And then you came to St. John's."

"I!" The cry was involuntary.

"You," Mr. Bentley repeated. "Sometimes," he added whimsically, "I go there, as I have told you. I saw you, I heard you preach. I talked to my friend Waring about you. I saw that *your* eyes were not opened, but I think I had a certain presentiment, for which I do not pretend to account, that they would be opened."

"You mean," said the rector, "that if I believe in the mission of the Church as I have partially stated it here tonight, I should stay and fight for it."

"Precisely," Mr. Bentley replied.

There was a note of enthusiasm, almost of militancy in the old gentleman's tone that surprised and agitated Hodder. He took a turn up and down the room before he answered.

"I ought to tell you that the view I expressed a moment ago is new to me. I had not thought of it before, and it is absolutely at variance with any previous ideas I have held. I can see that it must involve, if carried to its logical conclusion, a change in the conception of Christianity I have hitherto held."

He was too intent upon following up the thought to notice Mr. Bentley's expression of assent.

"And suppose," he asked, "I were unable to come to

any conclusion? I will be frank, Mr. Bentley, and confess to you that at present I cannot see my way. You have heard me preach — you know what my beliefs have been. They are shattered. And, while I feel that there is some definite connection between the view of the Church which I mentioned and her message to the individual, I do not perceive it clearly. I am not prepared at present to be the advocate of Christianity, because I do not know what Christianity is. I thought I knew.

"I shall have to begin all over again, as though I had never taken orders, submit to a thorough test, examine the evidence impartially. It is the only way. Of this much I am sure, that the Church as a whole has been engaged in a senseless conflict with science and progressive thought, that she has insisted upon the acceptance of facts which are in violation of reason and which have nothing to do with religion. She has taught them to me — made them, in fact, a *part* of me. I have clung to them as long as I can, and in throwing them over I don't know where I shall land."

His voice was measured, his words chosen, yet they expressed a withering indignation and contempt which were plainly the culmination of months of bewilderment — now replaced by a clear-cut determination.

"I do not blame any individual," he continued, "but the system by which clergymen are educated.

"I intend to stay here, now, without conducting any services, and find out for myself what the conditions are here in Dalton Street. You know those people, Mr. Bentley, you understand them, and I am going to ask you to help me. You have evidently solved the problem."

Mr. Bentley rose. And he laid a hand, which was not quite steady, on the rector's shoulder.

"Believe me, sir," he replied, "I appreciate something of what such a course must mean to you — a clergyman." He paused, and a look came upon his face, a look that might scarce have been called a smile — Hodder remembered it as a glow — reminiscent of many things. In it a life was summed up; in it understanding, beneficence, charity, sympathy, were all expressed, yet seemingly blended into one. "I do not know what my testimony may be worth to you, my friend, but I give it freely. I sometimes think I have been peculiarly fortunate. But I have lived a great many years, and the older I get and the more I see of human nature the firmer has grown my conviction of its essential nobility and goodness."

Hodder marvelled, and was silent.

"You will come here, often, — every day if you can. There are many men and women, friends of mine, whom I should like you to know, who would like to know you."

"I will, and thank you," Hodder answered. Words were inadequate for the occasion. . . .

CHAPTER XII

THE WOMAN OF THE SONG

On leaving Mr. Bentley, Hodder went slowly down Dalton Street, wondering that mere contact with another human being should have given him the resolution to turn his face once again toward the house whither he was bound. And this man had given him something more. It might hardly have been called faith ; a new courage to fare forth across the Unknown—that was it; hope, faint but revived.

Presently he stopped on the sidewalk, looked around him, and read a sign in glaring, electric letters, *Hotel Albert*. Despite the heat, the place was ablaze with lights. Men and women were passing, pausing — going in. A motor, with a liveried chauffeur whom he remembered having seen before, was standing in front of the Rath-skeller. The nightly carousal was beginning.

Hodder retraced his steps, crossed the street diagonally, came to the dilapidated gate he remembered so well, and looked up through the dusk at the house. If death had entered it, there was no sign : death must be a frequent visitor hereabouts. On the doorsteps he saw figures out-lined, slatternly women and men in shirtsleeves who rose in silence to make way for him, staring at him curiously. He plunged into the hot darkness of the hall, groped his way up the stairs and through the passage, and hesitated. A single gas jet burned low in the stagnant air, and after a moment he made out, by its dim light, a woman on her knees beside the couch, mechanically moving the tattered palm-leaf over the motionless little figure. The child was

still alive.   He drew a deep breath, and entered ; at the
sound of his step Mrs. Garvin suddenly started up.

"Richard ! " she cried, and then stood staring at the
rector.   " Have you seen my husband, sir ?   He went
away soon after you left."

Hodder, taken by surprise, replied that he had not.
Her tone, her gesture of anxiety he found vaguely disquieting.

" The doctor has been here ? " he asked.

" Yes," she answered absently.   " I don't know where
he can be — Richard.   He didn't even wait to see the
doctor.   And he thinks so much of Dicky, sir, he sits here
of an evening —— "

Hodder sat down beside her, and taking the palm-leaf
from her hand, began himself to fan the child.   Something
of her misgiving had communicated itself to him.

" Don't worry," he said.   " Remember that you have
been through a great deal, and it is natural that you should
be overwrought.   Your husband feels strongly.   I don't
blame him.   And the sight of me this afternoon upset
him.   He has gone out to walk."

"Richard is proud," she answered simply.   " He used
to say he'd rather die than take charity — and now he's
come to it.   And it's — that man, sir, who's got on his
brain, and changed him.   He wasn't always like this, but
now he can't seem to think of anything else.   He wakes
up in the night. . . .   And he used to have such a sweet
nature — you wouldn't have known him . . . and came
home so happy in the evenings in Alder Street, often with
a little fruit, or something he'd bought for us, and romp
with Dicky in the yard, and I'd stand and laugh at them.
Even after we'd lost our money, when he was sick that
time, he didn't feel this way.   It grew on him when he
couldn't get work, and then he began to cut things out of
the papers about Mr. Parr.   And I have sometimes thought
that *that's* kept him from getting work.   He talks about
it, and people don't know what to make of him.   They
don't know how hard he'd try if they'd give him something." . . .

"We shall find something," said the rector, striving to throw into his voice confidence and calm. He did not dare to look at her, but continued to move the fan.

The child stirred a little. Mrs. Garvin put out her hand.

"Yes, the doctor was here. He was very kind. Oh, sir," she exclaimed, "I hope you won't think us ungrateful — and that Mr. Bentley won't. Dr. Jarvis has hopes, sir, — he says — I forget the name he called it, what Dicky has. It's something uncommon. He says it was brought on by the heat, and want of food — good food. And he's coming himself in the morning to take him out to that hospital beyond the park — in an automobile, sir. I was just thinking what a pity it is Dicky wouldn't realize it. He's always wanted to ride in one." Suddenly her tears flowed, unheeded, and she clung to the little hand convulsively. "I don't know what I shall do without him, sir, I don't. . . . I've always had him . . . and when he's sick, among strangers." . . .

The rector rose to the occasion.

"Now, Mrs. Garvin," he said firmly, "you must remember that there is only one way to save the boy's life. It will be easy to get you a room near the hospital, where you can see him constantly."

"I know — I know, sir. But I couldn't leave his father, I couldn't leave Richard." She looked around distractedly. "Where is he?"

"He will come back presently," said the rector. "If not, I will look for him."

She did not reply, but continued to weep in silence. Suddenly, above the confused noises of the night, the loud notes of a piano broke, and the woman whose voice he had heard in the afternoon began once more with appalling vigour to sing. The child moaned.

Mrs. Garvin started up hysterically.

"I can't stand it — I can't stand her singing that now," she sobbed.

Thirty feet away, across the yard, Hodder saw the gleaming window from which the music came. He got to his feet. Another verse began, with more of the brazen emphasis of the concert-hall singer than ever. He glanced at the woman beside him, irresolutely.

" I'll speak to her," he said.

Mrs. Garvin did not appear to hear him, but flung herself down beside the lounge. As he seized his hat and left the room he had the idea of telephóning for a nurse, when he almost ran into some one in the upper hall, and recognized the stout German woman, Mrs. Breitmann.

" Mrs. Garvin " — he said, " she ought not to be left alone."

" I am just now going," said Mrs. Breitmann. " I stay with her until her husband come."

Such was the confidence with which, for some reason, she inspired him, that he left with an easier mind.

It was not until the rector had arrived at the vestibule of the apartment house next door that something of the difficulty and delicacy of the errand he had undertaken came home to him. Impulse had brought him thus far, but now he stood staring helplessly at a row of bells, speaking tubes, and cards. Which, for example, belonged to the lady whose soprano voice pervaded the neighbourhood ? He looked up and down the street, in the vain hope of finding a messenger. The song continued : he had promised to stop it. Hodder accused himself of cowardice.

To his horror, Hodder felt stealing over him, incredible though it seemed after the depths through which he had passed, a faint sense of fascination in the adventure. It was this that appalled him — this tenacity of the flesh, which no terrors seemed adequate to drive out. The sensation, faint as it was, unmanned him. There were still many unexplored corners in his soul.

He turned, once more contemplated the bells, and it was not until then he noticed that the door was ajar. He pushed it open, climbed the staircase, and stood in the doorway of what might be called a sitting room, his eyes fixed on a swaying back before an upright piano against the wall; his heart seemed to throb with the boisterous beat of the music. The woman's hair, in two long and heavy plaits falling below her waist, suddenly fascinated him. It was of the rarest of russet reds. She came abruptly to the end of the song.

"I beg your pardon——" he began.

She swung about with a start, her music dropping to the floor, and stared at him. Her tattered blue kimono fell away at her elbows, her full throat was bare, and a slipper she had kicked off lay on the floor beside her. He recoiled a little, breathing deeply. She stared at him.

"My God, how you scared me!" she exclaimed. Evidently a second glance brought to her a realization of his clerical costume. "Say, how did you get in here?"

"I beg your pardon," he said again, "but there is a very sick child in the house next door and I came to ask you if you would mind not playing any more to-night."

She did not reply at once, and her expression he found unsolvable. Much of it might be traced to a life which had contracted the habit of taking nothing on trust, a life which betrayed itself in unmistakable traces about the eyes. And Hodder perceived that the face, if the stamp of this expression could have been removed, was not unpleasing, although indulgence and recklessness were beginning to remould it.

"Quit stringin' me," she said.

For a moment he was at a loss. He gathered that she did not believe him, and crossed to the open window.

"If you will come here," he said, "I will show you the room where he lies. We hope to be able to take him to the hospital to-morrow." He paused a moment, and added: "He enjoyed your music very much when he was better."

The comment proved a touchstone.

"Say," she remarked, with a smile that revealed a set of surprisingly good teeth, "I *can* make the box talk when I get a-goin'. There's no stopping me this side of grand opera,—that's no fable. I'm not so bad for an enginoo, am I?"

Thus directly appealed to, in common courtesy he assented.

"No indeed," he said.

"That's right," she declared. "But the managers won't have it at any price. Those jays don't know anything, do they? They've only got a dream of what the public wants. You wouldn't believe it, but I've sung for 'em, and they threw me out. You *wouldn't* believe it, would you?"

"I must own," said the rector, "that I have never had any experience with managers."

She sat still considering him from the piano stool, her knees apart, her hands folded in her lap. Mockery came into her eyes.

"Say, what *did* you come in here for, honest injun?" she demanded.

He was aware of trying to speak sternly, and of failing. To save his life he could not, then, bring up before himself the scene in the little back room across the yard in its full terror and reality, reproduce his own feelings of only a few minutes ago which had impelled him hither. A month, a year might have elapsed. Every faculty was now centred on the woman in front of him, and on her life.

"Why do you doubt me?" he asked.

She continued to contemplate him. Her eyes were strange, baffling, smouldering, yellow-brown, shifting, — yet not shifty: eyes with a history. Her laugh proclaimed both effrontery and uneasiness.

"Don't get huffy," she said. "The kid's sick — that's on the level, is it? You didn't come 'round to see *me?*" The insinuation was in her voice as well as in her words. He did not resent it, but felt an odd thrill of commingled pity and — fear.

"I came for the reason I have given you," he replied; and added, more gently: "I know it is a good deal to ask, but you will be doing a great kindness. The mother is distracted. The child, as I told you, will be taken to the hospital in the morning."

She reached out a hand and closed the piano softly.

"I guess I can hold off for to-night," she said. "Sometimes things get kind of dull — you know, when there's

N

nothing doing, and this keeps me lively. How old is the kid?"

"About nine," he estimated.

"Say, I'm sorry." She spoke with a genuineness of feeling that surprised him. He went slowly, almost apologetically toward the door.

"Good night," he said, "and thank you."

Her look halted him.

"What's your hurry?" she demanded.

"I'm sorry," he said hastily, "but I must be going." He was, in truth, in a panic to leave.

"You're a minister, ain't you?"

"Yes," he said.

"I guess you don't think much of me, do you?" she demanded.

He halted abruptly, struck by the challenge, and he saw that this woman had spoken not for herself, but for an entire outlawed and desperate class. The fact that the words were mocking and brazen made no difference; it would have been odd had they not been so. With a shock of surprise he suddenly remembered that his inability to reach this class had been one of the causes of his despair! And now? With the realization, reaction set in, an overpowering feeling of weariness, a desire for rest — for sleep. The electric light beside the piano danced before his eyes, yet he heard within him a voice crying out to him to stay. Desperately tired though he was, he must not leave now. He walked slowly to the table, put his hat on it and sat down in a chair beside it.

"Why do you say that?" he asked.

"Oh, cut it out!" said the woman. "I'm on to you church folks." She laughed. "One of 'em came in here once, and wanted to pray. I made a monkey of him."

"I hope," said the rector, smiling a little, "that is not the reason why you wish me to stay."

She regarded him doubtfully.

"You're not the same sort," she announced at length.

"What sort was he?"

"He was easy, — old enough to know better — most of

the easy ones are. He marched in sanctimonious as you please, with his mouth full of salvation and Bible verses." She laughed again at the recollection.

" And after that," said the rector, " you felt that ministers were a lot of hypocrites."

"I never had much opinion of 'em," she admitted, " nor of church people, either," she added, with emphasis. " There's Ferguson, who has the department store, — he's 'way up in church circles. I saw him a couple of months ago, one Sunday morning, driving to that church on Burton Street, where all the rich folks go. I forget the name —— "

" St. John's," he supplied. He had got beyond surprise.

" St. John's — that's it. They tell me he gives a lot of money to it — money that he steals from the girls he hires. Oh, yes, he'll get to heaven — I don't think."

" How do you mean that he steals money from the girls ? "

"Say, you are innocent — ain't you ! Did you ever go down to that store? Do you know what a floorwalker is ? Did you ever see the cheap guys hanging around, and the young swells waiting to get a chance at the girls behind the counters? Why do you suppose so many of 'em take to the easy life ? I'll put you next — because Ferguson don't pay 'em enough to live on. That's why. He makes 'em sign a paper, when he hires 'em, that they live at home, that they've got some place to eat and sleep, and they sign it all right. That's to square up Ferguson's conscience. But say, if you think a girl can support herself in this city and dress on what he pays, you've got another guess comin'."

There rose up before him, unsummoned, the image of Nan Ferguson, in all her freshness and innocence, as she had stood beside him on the porch in Park Street. He was somewhat astonished to find himself defending his parishioner.

" May it not be true, in order to compete with other department stores, that Mr. Ferguson has to pay the same wages ? " he said.

She laughed.

"Forget it. I guess you know what Galt House is? That's where women like me can go when we get all played out and there's nothing left in the game — it's on River Street. Maybe you've been there."

Hodder nodded.

"Well," she continued, "Ferguson pays a lot of money to keep that going, and gets his name in the papers. He hands over to the hospitals where some of us die — and it's all advertised. He forks out to the church. Now, I put it to you, why don't he sink some of that money where it belongs — in living wages? Because there's nothing in it for him — that's why."

The rector looked at her in silence. He had not suspected her of so much intellect. He glanced about the apartment, at the cheap portière flung over the sofa; at the gaudy sofa cushions, two of which bore the names and colours of certain colleges. The gas log was almost hidden by dried palm leaves, a cigarette stump lay on the fender; on the mantel above were several photographs of men and at the other side an open door revealed a bedroom.

"This is a nice place, ain't it?" she observed. "I furnished it when I was on velvet — nothing was too good for me. Money's like champagne when you take the cork out, it won't keep. I was rich once. It was lively while it lasted," she added, with a sigh: "I've struck the down trail. I oughtn't, by rights, to be here fooling with you. There's nothing in it." She glanced at the clock. "I ought to get busy."

As the realization of her meaning came to him, he quivered.

"Is there no way but that?" he asked, in a low voice.

"Say, *you're* not a-goin' to preach, are you?"

"No," he answered, "God forbid! I was not asking the question of you."

She stared at him.

"Of who, then?"

He was silent.

"You've left me at the station. But on the level, you don't seem to know much, that's a fact. You don't think the man who owns these flats is in it for charity, do you? 'Single ladies,' like me, have to give up. And then there are other little grafts that wouldn't interest you. What church do you come from anyway?"

"You mentioned it a little while ago."

"St. John's!" She leaned back against the piano and laughed unrestrainedly. "That's a good one, to think how straight I've been talking to you."

"I'm much obliged to you," he said.

Again she gazed at him, now plainly perplexed.

"What are you giving me?"

"I mean what I say," he answered. "I am obliged to you for telling me things I didn't know. And I appreciate — your asking me to stay."

She was sitting upright now, her expression changed, her breath came more rapidly, her lips parted as she gazed at him.

"Do you know," she said, "I haven't had anybody speak to me like that for four years." Her voice betrayed excitement, and differed in tone, and she had cast off unconsciously the vulgarity of speech. At that moment she seemed reminiscent of what she must once have been; and he found himself going through an effort at reconstruction.

"Like what?" he asked.

"Like a woman," she answered vehemently.

"My name is John Hodder," he said, "and I live in the parish house, next door to the church. I should like to be your friend, if you will let me. If I can be of any help to you now, or at any other time, I shall feel happy. I promise not to preach," he added.

She got up abruptly, and went to the window. And when she turned to him again, it was with something of the old bravado.

"You'd better leave me alone, I'm no good," she said. "I'm much obliged to you, but I don't want any charity or probation houses in mine. And honest work's a thing of the past for me — even if I could get a job. Nobody would have me. But if they would, I couldn't work any more. I've got out of the hang of it." With a swift and decisive movement she crossed the room, opened a cabinet on the wall, revealing a bottle and glasses.

"So you're bent upon going — downhill?" he said.

"What can you do to stop it?" she retorted defiantly. "Give me religion — I guess you'd tell me. Religion's all right for those on top, but say, it would be a joke if I got it. There ain't any danger. But if I did, it wouldn't pay room-rent and board."

He sat mute. Once more the truth overwhelmed, the folly of his former optimism arose to mock him. What he beheld now, in its true aspect, was a disease of that civilization he had championed. . . .

She took the bottle from the cupboard and laid it on the table.

"What's the difference?" she demanded. "It's all over in a little while, anyway. I guess you'd tell me there was a hell. But if that's so, some of your church folks'll broil, too. I'll take my chance on it, if they will." She looked at him, half in defiance, half in friendliness, across the table. "Say, you mean all right, but you're only wastin' time here. You can't do me any good, I tell you, and I've got to get busy."

"May we not at least remain friends?" he asked, after a moment.

Her laugh was a little harsh.

"What kind of friendship would that be? You, a minister, and me a woman on the town?"

"If I can stand it, I should think you might."

"Well, I can't stand it," she answered.

He got up, and held out his hand. She stood seemingly irresolute, and then took it.

"Good night," he said.

"Good night," she repeated nonchalantly.

As he went out of the door she called after him:

"Don't be afraid I'll worry the kid!"

The stale odour of cigarette smoke with which the dim

corridor was charged intoxicated, threatened to overpower him. It seemed to be the reek of evil itself. A closing door had a sinister meaning. He hurried; obscurity reigned below, — the light in the lower hall being out; fumbled for the door-knob, and once in the street took a deep breath and mopped his brow; but he had not proceeded half a block before he hesitated, retraced his steps, reëntered the vestibule, and stooped to peer at the cards under the speaking tubes. Cheaply printed in large script, was the name of the tenant of the second floor rear, — MISS KATE MARCY. . . .

In crossing Tower Street he was frightened by the sharp clanging of a great electric car that roared past him, aflame with light. His brain had seemingly ceased to work, and he stumbled at the curb, for he was very tired. The events of the day no longer differentiated themselves in his mind but lay, a composite weight, upon his heart. At length he reached the silent parish house, climbed the stairs and searched in his pocket for the key of his rooms. The lock yielded, but while feeling for the switch he tripped and almost fell over an obstruction on the floor.

The flooding light revealed his travelling-bags, as he had piled them, packed and ready to go to the station.

CHAPTER XIII

WINTERBOURNE

I

HODDER fell asleep from sheer exhaustion, awaking during the night at occasional intervals to recall chimerical dreams in which the events of the day before were reflected, but caricatured and distorted. Alison Parr was talking to the woman in the flat, and both were changed, and yet he identified both : and on another occasion he saw a familiar figure surrounded by romping, ragged children — a figure which turned out to be Eldon Parr's !

Finally he was aroused by what seemed a summons from the unknown — the prolonged morning whistle of the shoe factory. For a while he lay as one benumbed, and the gradual realization that ensued might be likened to the straining of stiffened wounds. Little by little he reconstructed, until the process became unbearable, and then rose from his bed with one object in mind, — to go to Horace Bentley. At first he seized upon the excuse that Mr. Bentley would wish to hear the verdict of Dr. Jarvis, but immediately abandoned it as dishonest, acknowledging the true reason, that in all the world the presence of this one man alone might assuage in some degree the terror in his soul. For the first time in his life, since childhood, he knew a sense of utter dependence upon another human being. He felt no shame, would make no explanation for his early visit.

He turned up Tower, deliberately avoiding Dalton Street in its lower part, reached Mr. Bentley's door. The wrinkled, hospitable old darky actually seemed to radiate something of the personality with which he had so long been associated, and Hodder was conscious of a surge of relief, a return of confidence at sight of him. Yes, Mr. Bentley was at home, in the dining room. The rector said he would wait, and not disturb him.

" He done tole me to bring you out, sah, if you come," said Sam.

" He expects me?" exclaimed Hodder, with a shock of surprise.

" That's what he done tole me, sah, to ax you kindly for to step out when you come."

The sun was beginning to penetrate into the little back yard, where the flowers were still glistening with the drops of their morning bath; and Mr. Bentley sat by the window reading his newspaper, his spectacles on his nose, and a great grey cat rubbing herself against his legs. He rose with alacrity.

" Good morning, sir," he said, and his welcome implied that early morning visits were the most common and natural of occurrences. " Sam, a plate for Mr. Hodder. I was just hoping you would come and tell me what Dr. Jarvis had said about the case."

But Hodder was not deceived. He believed that Mr. Bentley understood perfectly why he had come, and the knowledge of the old gentleman's comprehension curiously added to his sense of refuge. He found himself seated once more at the mahogany table, permitting Sam to fill his cup with coffee.

" Jarvis has given a favourable report, and he is coming this morning himself, in an automobile, to take the boy out to the hospital."

" That is like Jarvis," was Mr. Bentley's comment. " We will go there, together, after breakfast, if convenient for you," he added.

" I hoped you would," replied the rector. " And I was going to ask you a favour. I have a check, given me by a young lady to use at my discretion, and it occurred to me that Garvin might be willing to accept some proposal from you." He thought of Nan Ferguson, and of the hope he had expressed of finding some one in Dalton Street.

"I have been considering the matter," Mr. Bentley said. "I have a friend who lives on the trolley line a little beyond the hospital, a widow. It is like the country there, you know, and I think Mrs. Bledsoe could be induced to take the Garvins. And then something can be arranged for him. I will find an opportunity to speak to him this morning."

Hodder sipped his coffee, and looked out at the morning-glories opening to the sun.

"Mrs. Garvin was alone last night. He had gone out shortly after we left, and had not waited for the doctor. She was greatly worried."

Hodder found himself discussing these matters on which, an hour before, he had feared to permit his mind to dwell. And presently, not without feeling, but in a manner eliminating all account of his personal emotions, he was relating that climactic episode of the woman at the piano. The old gentleman listened intently, and in silence.

"Yes," he said, when the rector had finished, "that is my observation. Most of them are driven to the life, and held in it, of course, by a remorseless civilization. Individuals may be culpable, Mr. Hodder — are culpable. But we cannot put the whole responsibility on individuals."

"No," Hodder assented, "I can see that now." He paused a moment, and as his mind dwelt upon the scene and he saw again the woman standing before him in bravado, the whole terrible meaning of her life and end flashed through him as one poignant sensation. Her dauntless determination to accept the consequence of her acts, her willingness to look her future in the face, cried out to him in challenge.

"She refused unconditionally," he said.

Mr. Bentley seemed to read his thought, divine his appeal.

"We must wait," he answered.

"Do you think ——?" Hodder began, and stopped abruptly.

"I remember another case, somewhat similar," said Mr.

Bentley. "This woman, too, had the spirit you describe — we could do nothing with her. We kept an eye on her, or rather Sally Grover did — *she* deserves credit — and finally an occasion presented itself."

"And the woman you speak of was — rehabilitated?" Hodder asked. He avoided the word "saved."

"Yes, sir. It was one of the fortunate cases. There are others which are not so fortunate."

Hodder nodded.

"We are beginning to recognize that we are dealing, in many instances, with a disease," Mr. Bentley went on. "I am far from saying that it cannot be cured, but sometimes we are forced to admit that the cure is not within our power, Mr. Hodder."

Two thoughts struck the rector simultaneously, the revelation of what might be called a modern enlightenment in one of Mr. Bentley's age, an indication of uninterrupted growth, of the sense of continued youth which had impressed him from the beginning; and, secondly, an intimation from the use of the plural pronoun we, of an association of workers (informal, undoubtedly) behind Mr. Bentley. While he was engaged in these speculations the door opened.

"Heah's Miss Sally, Marse Ho'ace," said Sam.

"Good morning, Sally," said Mr. Bentley, rising from the table with his customary courtesy, "I'm glad you came in. Let me introduce Mr. Hodder, of St. John's."

Miss Grover had capability written all over her. She was a young woman of thirty, slim to spareness, simply dressed in a shirtwaist and a dark blue skirt; alert, so distinctly American in type as to give a suggestion of the Indian. Her quick, deep-set eyes searched Hodder's face as she jerked his hand; but her greeting was cordial, and matter-of-fact. She stimulated curiosity.

"Well, Sally, what's the news?" Mr. Bentley asked.

"Gratz, the cabinet-maker, was on the rampage again, Mr. Bentley. His wife was here yesterday when I got home from work, and I went over with her. He was in a beastly state, and all the niggers and children in the neighbourhood, including his own, around the shop. Fusel oil, labelled whiskey," she explained, succinctly.

" What did you do ? "

" Took the bottle away from him," said Miss Grover. The simplicity of this method, Hodder thought, was undeniable. " Stayed there until he came to. Then I reckon I scared him some."

" How ? " Mr. Bentley smiled.

" I told him he'd have to see you. He'd rather serve three months than do that — said so. I reckon he would, too," she declared grimly. " He's better than he was last year, I think." She thrust her hand in the pocket of her skirt and produced some bills and silver, which she counted. " Here's three thirty-five from Sue Brady. I told her she hadn't any business bothering you, but she swears she'd spend it."

" That was wrong, Sally."

Miss Grover tossed her head.

" Oh, she knew I'd take it, well enough."

" I imagine she did," Mr. Bentley replied, and his eyes twinkled. He rose and led the way into the library, where he opened his desk, produced a ledger, and wrote down the amount in a fine hand.

" Susan Brady, three dollars and thirty-five cents. I'll put it in the savings bank to-day. That makes twenty-two dollars and forty cents for Sue. She's growing rich."

" Some man'll get it," said Sally.

" Sally," said Mr. Bentley, turning in his chair, " Mr. Hodder's been telling me about a rather unusual woman in that apartment house just above Fourteenth Street, on the south side of Dalton —— "

" I think I know her — by sight," Sally corrected herself. She appealed to Hodder. " Red hair, and lots of it — I suppose a man would call it auburn. She must have been something of a beauty, once."

The rector assented, in some astonishment.

" Couldn't do anything with her, could you ? I reckoned not. I've noticed her up and down Dalton Street at night."

Hodder was no longer deceived by her matter-of-fact tone.

"I'll tell you what, Mr. Hodder," she went on, energetically, "there's not a particle of use running after those people, and the sooner you find it out the less worry and trouble you give yourself."

"Mr. Hodder didn't run after her, Sally," said Mr. Bentley, in gentle reproof.

Hodder smiled.

"Well," said Miss Grover, "I've had my eye on her. She has a history — most of 'em have. But this one's out of the common. When they're brazen like that, and have had good looks, you can nearly always tell. You've got to wait for something to happen, and trust to luck to be on the spot, or near it. It's a toss-up, of course. One thing is sure, you can't make friends with that kind if they get a notion you're up to anything."

"Sally, you must remember — " Mr. Bentley began.

Her tone became modified. Mr. Bentley was apparently the only human of whom she stood in awe.

"All I meant was," she said, addressing the rector, "that you've got to run across 'em in some *natural* way."

"I understood perfectly, and I agree with you," Hodder replied. "I have come, quite recently, to the same conclusion myself."

She gave him a penetrating glance, and he had to admit, inwardly, that a certain satisfaction followed Miss Grover's approval.

"Mercy, I have to be going," she exclaimed, glancing at the black marble clock on the mantel. "We've got a lot of invoices to put through to-day. See you again, Mr. Hodder." She jerked his hand once more. "Good morning, Mr. Bentley."

"Good morning, Sally."

Mr. Bentley rose, and took his hat and gold-headed stick from the rack in the hall.

"You mustn't mind Sally," he said, when they had reached the sidewalk. "Sometimes her brusque manner is not understood. But she is a very extraordinary woman."

"I can see that," the rector assented quickly, and with a heartiness that dispelled all doubt of his liking for Miss Grover. Once more many questions rose to his lips, which he suppressed, since Mr. Bentley volunteered no information. Hodder became, in fact, so lost in speculation concerning Mr. Bentley's establishment as to forget the errand on which they were bound. And Sally Grover's words, apropos of the woman in the flat, seemed but an energetic driving home of the severe lessons of his recent experiences. And how blind he had been, he reflected, not to have seen the thing for himself! Not to have realized the essential artificiality of his former method of approach! And then it struck him that Sally Grover herself must have had a history.

Mr. Bentley, too, was preoccupied.

Presently, in the midst of these thoughts, Hodder's eyes were arrested by a crowd barring the sidewalk on the block ahead; no unusual sight in that neighbourhood, and yet one which aroused in him sensations of weakness and nausea. Thus were the hidden vice and suffering of these sinister places occasionally brought to light, exposed to the curious and morbid stares of those whose own turn might come on the morrow. It was only by degrees he comprehended that the people were gathered in front of the house to which they were bound. An ambulance was seen to drive away: it turned into the side street in front of them.

"A city ambulance!" the rector exclaimed.

Mr. Bentley did not reply.

The murmuring group which overflowed the uneven brick pavement to the asphalt was characteristic: women in calico, drudges, women in wrappers, with sleepy, awe-stricken faces; idlers, men and boys who had run out of the saloons, whose comments were more audible and caustic, and a fringe of children ceaselessly moving on the outskirts. The crowd parted at their approach, and they reached the gate, where a burly policeman, his helmet in his hand, was standing in the morning sunlight mop-

ping his face with a red handkerchief. He greeted Mr.
Bentley respectfully, by name, and made way for them to
pass in.

"What is the trouble, Ryan?" Mr. Bentley asked.

"Suicide, sir," the policeman replied. "Jumped off
the bridge this morning. A tug picked him up, but he
never came to — the strength wasn't in him. Sure it's all
wore out he was. There was a letter on him, with the
house number, so they knew where to fetch him. It's a
sad case, sir, with the woman in there, and the child gone
to the hospital not an hour ago."

"You mean Garvin?" Mr. Bentley demanded.

"It's him I mean, sir."

"We'd like to go in," said Mr. Bentley. "We came
to see them."

"You're welcome, sir, and the minister too. It's only
them I'm holdin' back," and the policeman shook his
stick at the people.

Mr. Bentley walked up the steps, and took off his hat
as he went through the battered doorway. Hodder
followed, with a sense of curious faces staring at them
from the thresholds as they passed; they reached the
upper passage, and the room, and paused: the shutters
were closed, the little couch where the child had been was
empty. On the bed lay a form — covered with a sheet,
and beside it a woman kneeling, shaken by sobs, ceaselessly calling a name. . . .

A stout figure, hitherto unperceived, rose from a corner
and came silently toward them — Mrs. Breitmann. She
beckoned to them, and they followed her into a room on
the same floor, where she told them what she knew, heedless of the tears coursing ceaselessly down her cheeks.

It seemed that Mrs. Garvin had had a premonition
which she had not wholly confided to the rector. She had
believed her husband never would come back; and early
in the morning, in spite of all that Mrs. Breitmann could
do, had insisted at intervals upon running downstairs
and scanning the street. At half past seven Dr. Jarvis
had come and himself carried down the child and

put him in the back of his automobile. The doctor had had a nurse with him, and had begged the mother to accompany them to the hospital, saying that he would send her back. But she would not be persuaded to leave the house. The doctor could not wait, and had finally gone off with little Dicky, leaving a powder with Mrs. Breitmann for the mother. Then she had become uncontrollable.

"Ach, it was terrible ! " said the kind woman. "She was crazy, yes — she was not in her mind. I make a little coffee, but she will not touch it. All those things about her home she would talk of, and how good he was, and how she lofed him more again than the child. . . . Und then the wheels in the street, and she makes a cry and runs to see — I cannot hold her. . . ."

"It would be well not to disturb her for a while," said Mr. Bentley, seating himself on one of the dilapidated chairs which formed a part of the German woman's meagre furniture. "I will remain here if you, Mr. Hodder, will make the necessary arrangements for the funeral. Have you any objections, sir ? "

"Not at all," replied the rector, and left the house, the occupants of which had already returned to the daily round of their lives: the rattle of dishes and the noise of voices were heard in the *ci devant* parlour, and on the steps he met the little waif with the pitcher of beer; in the street the boys who had gathered around the ambulance were playing baseball. Hodder glanced up, involuntarily, at the window of the woman he had visited the night before, but it was empty. He hurried along the littered sidewalks to the drug store, where he telephoned an undertaker; and then, as an afterthought, telephoned the hospital. The boy had arrived, and was seemingly no worse for the journey.

All this Hodder performed mechanically. Not until he was returning — not, indeed, until he entered the house did the whiff of its degrading, heated odours bring home to him the tragedy which it held, and he grasped the banister on the stairs. The thought that shook him now was of the cumulative misery of the city, of the world, of which this history on which he had stumbled was but one insignificant incident. But he went on into Mrs. Breitmann's room, and saw Mr. Bentley still seated where he had left him. The old gentleman looked up at him.

"Mrs. Breitmann and I are agreed, Mr. Hodder, that Mrs. Garvin ought not to remain in there. What do you think?"

"By all means, no," said the rector.

The German woman burst into a soliloquy of sympathy that became incoherent.

"She will not leave him, — *nein* — she will not come. . . ."

They went, the three of them, to the doorway of the death chamber and stood gazing at the huddled figure of the woman by the bedside. She had ceased to cry out: she was as one grown numb under torture; occasionally a convulsive shudder shook her. But when Mrs. Breitmann touched her, spoke to her, her grief awoke again in all its violence, and it was more by force than persuasion that she was finally removed. Mrs. Breitmann held one arm, Mr. Bentley another, and between them they fairly carried her out, for she was frail indeed.

As for Hodder, something held him back — some dread that he could not at once define. And while he groped for it, he stood staring at the man on the bed, for the hand of love had drawn back the sheet from the face. The battle was over of this poor weakling against the world; the torments of haunting fear and hate, of drink and despair had triumphed. The sight of the little group of toys brought up the image of the home in Alder Street as the wife had pictured it. Was it possible that this man, who had gone alone to the bridge in the night, had once been happy, content with life, grateful for it, possessed of a simple trust in his fellow-men — in Eldon Parr? Once more, unsummoned, came the memory of that evening of rain and thunder in the boy's room at the top of the great house in Park Street. He had pitied Eldon Parr then. Did he now?

o

He crossed the room, on tiptoe, as though he feared to
wake once more this poor wretch to his misery and hate.
Gently he covered again the face with the sheet.

Suddenly he knew the reason of his dread, — he had to
face the woman! He was a minister of Christ, it was his
duty to speak to her, as he had spoken to others in the
hour of sorrow and death, of the justice and goodness of
the God to whom she had prayed in the church. What
should he say, now? In an agony of spirit, he sat down
on the little couch beside the window and buried his face
in his hands. The sight of poor Garvin's white and wasted
features, the terrible contrast between this miserable tene-
ment and the palace with its unseen pictures and porcelains
and tapestries, brought home to him with indescribable
poignancy his own predicament. He was going to ask
this woman to be comforted by faith and trust in the God
of the man who had driven her husband to death! He
beheld Eldon Parr in his pew complacently worshipping
that God, who had rewarded him with riches and success
— beheld himself as another man in his white surplice
acquiescing in that God, preaching vainly. . . .

At last he got to his feet, went out of the room, reached
the doorway of that other room and looked in. Mr.
Bentley sat there ; and the woman, whose tears had ceased
to flow, was looking up into his face.

II

" *The office ensuing*," says the Book of Common Prayer,
meaning the Burial of the Dead, " *is not to be used for any
unbaptized adult, any who die excommunicate, or who have
laid violent hands on themselves.*"

Hodder had bought, with a part of Nan Ferguson's
money, a tiny plot in a remote corner of Winterbourne
Cemetery. And thither, the next morning, the body of
Richard Garvin was taken.

A few mourners had stolen into the house and up the
threadbare stairs into the miserable little back room, somehow dignified as it had never been before, and laid their gifts

upon the coffin. An odd and pitiful assortment they were — mourners and gifts: men and women whose only bond with the man in life had been the bond of misery; who had seen him as he had fared forth morning after morning in the hopeless search for work, and slunk home night after night bitter and dejected; many of whom had listened, jeeringly perhaps, to his grievance against the world, though it were in some sort their own. Death, for them, had ennobled him. The little girl whom Hodder had met with the pitcher of beer came tiptoeing with a wilted bunch of pansies, picked heaven knows where; stolen, maybe, from one of the gardens of the West End. Carnations, lilies of the valley, geraniums even — such were the offerings scattered loosely on the lid until a woman came with a mass of white roses that filled the room with their fragrance, — a woman with burnished red hair. Hodder started as he recognized her; her gaze was a strange mixture of effrontery and — something else; sorrow did not quite express it. The very lavishness of her gift brought to him irresistibly the reminder of another offering. . . . She was speaking.

" I don't blame him for what he done — I'd have done it, too, if I'd been him. But say, I felt kind of bad when I heard it, knowing about the kid, and all. I had to bring something —— "

Instinctively Hodder surmised that she was in doubt as to the acceptance of her flowers. He took them from her hand, and laid them at the foot of the coffin.

" Thank you," he said, simply.

She stared at him a moment with the perplexity she had shown at times on the night he visited her, and went out. . . .

Funerals, if they might be dignified by this name, were not infrequent occurrences in Dalton Street, and why this one should have been looked upon as of sufficient importance to collect a group of onlookers at the gate it is difficult to say. Perhaps it was because of the seeming interest in it of the higher powers — for suicide and consequent widows and orphans were not unknown there. This widow and this orphan were to be miraculously rescued, were to know Dalton Street no more. The rector of a fashionable church, of all beings, was the agent in the miracle. Thus the occasion was tinged with awe. As for Mr. Bentley, his was a familiar figure, and had been remarked in Dalton Street funerals before.

They started, the three mourners, on the long drive to the cemetery, through unfrequented streets lined with mediocre dwellings, interspersed with groceries and saloons — short cuts known only to hearse drivers : they traversed, for some distance, that very Wilderness road where Mr. Bentley's old-fashioned mansion once had stood on its long green slope, framed by ancient trees ; the Wilderness road, now paved with hot blocks of granite over which the carriage rattled ; spread with car tracks, bordered by heterogeneous buildings of all characters and descriptions, bakeries and breweries, slaughter houses and markets, tumble-down shanties, weedy corner lots and "refresh-ment-houses" that announced "Lager Beer, Wines and Liquors." At last they came to a region which was neither country nor city, where the road-houses were still in evidence, where the glass roofs of greenhouses caught the burning rays of the sun, where yards filled with marble blocks and half-finished tombstones appeared, and then they turned into the gates of Winterbourne.

Like the city itself, there was a fashionable district in Winterbourne : unlike the city, this district remained stationary. There was no soot here, and if there had been, the dead would not have minded it. They passed the Prestons and the Parrs ; the lots grew smaller, the tomb-stones less pretentious ; and finally they came to an open grave on a slope where the trees were still young, and where three men of the cemetery force lifted the coffin from the hearse — Richard Garvin's pallbearers.

John Hodder might not read the service, but there was none to tell him that the Gospel of John was not written for this man. He stood on the grass beside the grave, and a breeze from across the great river near by stirred the maple leaves above his head. "*I am the resurrection*

*and the life, saith the Lord ; he that believeth in me, though
he were dead, yet shall he live.*"   Nor was there any canon
to forbid the words of Paul : " *It is sown in corruption ; it
is raised in incorruption ; it is sown in dishonour ; it is raised
in glory ; it is sown in weakness ; it is raised in power ; it
is sown a natural body ; it is raised a spiritual body.*"

They laid the flowers on the fresh earth, even the white
roses, and then they drove back to the city.

CHAPTER XIV

A SATURDAY AFTERNOON

I

THE sight of a certain old gentleman as he walked along the shady side of Twenty-second Street about two o'clock on a broiling Saturday afternoon in midsummer was one not easily to be forgotten. A younger man, tall and vigorous, clad in a thin suit of blue serge, walked by his side. They were followed by a shouting troop of small boys who overran the pavements, and some of whom were armed with baseball bats. The big trolley car was hailed by a dozen dirty little hands.

Even the grumpy passengers were disarmed. The conductor took Mr. Bentley's bill deprecatingly, as much as to say that the newly organized Traction Company — just out of the receivers' hands — were the Moloch, not he, and rang off the fares under protest. And Mr. Bentley, as had been his custom for years, sat down and took off his hat, and smiled so benignly at those around him that they immediately began to talk to him. It was always irresistible, this desire to talk to Mr. Bentley. If you had left your office irritated and out of sorts, your nerves worn to an edge by the uninterrupted heat, you invariably got off at your corner feeling better. It was Phil Goodrich who had said that Horace Bentley had only to get on a Tower Street car to turn it into a church. And if he had chosen to establish that *dernier cri* of modern civilization where ladies go who have *welt-schmerz* without knowing why, — a sanitarium, he might have gained back again all the money he had lost in giving his Grantham stock to Eldon Parr.

Like the Pied Piper of Hamelin, he could have emptied Dalton Street of its children. In the first place, there was the irresistible inducement to any boy to ride several miles on a trolley without having this right challenged by the irate guardian of the vehicle, without being summarily requested to alight at twenty-five miles an hour: in the second place, there was the soda water and sweet biscuit partaken of after the baseball game in that pavilion, more imposing in one's eyes than the Taj Mahal. Mr. Bentley would willingly have taken all Dalton Street. He had his own *welt-schmerz*, though he did not go to a sanitarium to cure it; he was forced to set an age limit of ten, and then establish a high court of appeal; for there were boys whose biographies, if they are ever written, will be as hazy as those of certain world-wide celebrities who might be mentioned concerning the date and exact spot of the entrance of their heroes into the light. The solemn protestations, the tears, the recrimination even, brought pangs to the old gentleman's heart, for with all the will in the world he had been forced in the nature of things, to set a limit.

This limit had recently been increased by the unlooked-for appearance on these excursions of the tall man in the blue serge suit, whose knowledge of the national game and of other matters of vital import to youth was gratifying if sometimes disconcerting; who towered, an unruffled Gulliver, over their Lilliputian controversies, in which bats were waved and fists brought into play and language used on the meaning of which the Century dictionary is silent. On one former occasion, indeed, Mr. Bentley had found moral suasion, affection, and veneration of no avail, and had had to invoke the friendly aid of a park policeman to quell one of these incipient riots. To Mr. Bentley baseball was as a sealed book. The tall man's justice, not always worthy of the traditions of Solomon, had in it an element of force. To be lifted off the ground by strong arms at the moment you are about to dust the home plate with your adversary is humiliating, but effective. It gradually became apparent that a decision was a decision. And one Saturday this inexplicable person carried in his hand a

mysterious package which, when opened, revealed two pairs
of diminutive boxing gloves. They instantly became
popular.

By the time they had made the accidental and somewhat astounding discovery that he was a parson, they were
willing to overlook it; in view, perhaps, of his compensating accomplishments. Instead of advising them to turn
the other cheek, he taught them uppercuts, feints, and
jabs, and on the proof of this unexpected acquaintance
with a profession all of them openly admired, the last vestige of reserve disappeared. He was accepted without
qualifications.

II

Although the field to which they resorted was not in the
most frequented section of the park, pedestrians often
passed that way, and sometimes lingered. Thus, towards the
close of a certain Saturday in July, a young woman walked
out of the wood path and stood awhile gazing intently at
the active figure striding among the diminutive, darting
forms. Presently, with an amused expression, she turned
her head to discover Mr. Bentley, who sat on a green bench
under a tree, his hat and stick on the grass beside him.
She was unaware that he had been looking at her.

" Aren't they having a good time!" she said, and the
genuine thrill in her voice betrayed a rare and unmistakable pleasure.

" Ah," replied Mr. Bentley, smiling back at her, " you
like to see them, too. Most persons do. Children are
not meant for the city, my dear young lady, their natural
home is in the woods and fields, and these little fellows
are a proof of it. When they come out here, they run
wild. You perceive," he added with a twinkle, as an ex-
pletive of unquestionable vigour was hurled across the
diamond, "they are not always so polite as they might
be."

The young woman smiled again, but the look she gave
him was a puzzled one. And then, quite naturally, she

sank down on the grass, on the other side of Mr. Bentley's hat, watching the game for a while in silence.

"What a tyrant!" she exclaimed. Another uproar had been quelled, and two vigorously protesting runners sent back to their former bases.

"Oh, a benevolent tyrant," Mr. Bentley corrected her. "Mr. Hodder has the gift of managing boys, — he understands them. And they require a strong hand. His generation has had the training which mine lacked. In my day, at college, we worked off our surplus energy on the unfortunate professors, and we carried away chapel bells and fought with the townspeople."

It required some effort, she found, to imagine this benevolent looking old gentleman assaulting professors.

"Nowadays they play baseball and football, and box." He pointed to the boxing gloves on the grass. "Mr. Hodder has taught them to settle their differences in that way; it is much more sensible."

She picked off the white clover-tops.

"So that *is* Mr. Hodder, of St. John's," she said.

"Ah, you know him, then?"

"I've met him," she answered quietly. "Are these children connected with his church?"

"They are little waifs from Dalton Street and that vicinity," said Mr. Bentley. "Very few of them, I should imagine, have ever been inside of a church."

She seemed surprised.

"But — is it his habit to bring them out here?" The old gentleman beamed on her, perhaps with the hint of a smile at her curiosity.

"He has found time for it, this summer. It is very good of him."

She refrained from comment on this remark, falling into reflection, leaning back, with one hand outstretched, on the grass. The game went on vociferously, the shrill little voices piercing the silence of the summer afternoon. Mr. Bentley's eyes continued to rest on her.

"Tell me," he inquired, after a while, "are you not Alison Parr?"

She glanced up at him, startled.

" Yes."

" I thought so, although I have not seen you since you were a little girl. I knew your mother very well indeed, but it is too much to expect you to remember me, after all this time. No doubt you have forgotten my name. I am Mr. Bentley."

" Mr. Bentley ! " she cried, sitting upright and gazing at him. " How stupid of me not to have known you ! You *couldn't* have been any one else."

It was the old gentleman's turn to start. She rose impulsively and sat down on the bench beside him, and his hand trembled as he laid it in hers.

" Yes, my dear, I am still alive. But surely you cannot remember me, Alison ? "

The old look of almost stubborn honesty he recalled in the child came into her eyes.

" I do—and I don't," she said, perplexed. " It seemed to me as if I ought to have recognized you when I came up, and yet I hadn't the slightest notion who you were. I knew you were *somebody*."

He shook his head, but did not speak.

" But you have always been a *fact* in my existence — that is what I want to say," she went on. " It must be possible to remember a person and not recognize him, that is what I feel. I can remember you coming to our house in Ransome Street, and how I looked forward to your visits. And you used to have little candy beans in your pockets," she cried. " Have you now ? "

His eyes were a little dimmed as he reached, smilingly, into the skirts of a somewhat shiny but scrupulously brushed coat and produced a brightly colored handful. She took one, and put it in her mouth.

" Oh," she said, " how good they were ! Isn't it strange how a taste brings back events ? I can remember it all as if it were yesterday, and how I used to sit on your knee, and mother would tell me not to bother you."

" And now — you are grown," he said.

" Something more than grown," she smiled. " I was

thirty-one in May. Tell me," she asked, choosing another of the beans which he still absently held, " do you get them for *these?*" And she nodded toward the Dalton Street waifs.

" Yes," he said, " they are children, too."

" I can remember," she said, after a pause, " I can remember my mother speaking of you to me the year she died. I was almost grown, then. It was after we had moved up to Park Street, and her health had already begun to fail. That made an impression on me, but I have forgotten what she said — it was apropos of some recollection. No — it was a photograph — she was going over some old things." Alison ceased speaking abruptly, for the pain in Mr. Bentley's remarkable grey eyes had not escaped her. What was it about him? Why could she not recall ? Long-forgotten, shadowy episodes of the past tormented her, flitted provokingly through her mind — ungrasped : words dropped in her presence which had made their impression, but the gist of which was gone. Why had Mr. Bentley ceased coming to the house ? So strongly did she feel his presence now that the thought occurred to her, — perhaps her mother had not wished her to forget him !

" I did not suspect," she heard him saying, " that you would go out into the world and create the beautiful gardens of which I have heard. But you had no lack of spirit in those days, too."

" I was a most disagreeable child, perverse, — cantankerous — I can hear my mother saying it ! As for the gardens — they have given me something to do, they have kept me out of mischief. I suppose I ought to be thankful, but I still have the rebellious streak when I see what others have done, what others are doing, and I sometimes wonder what right I ever had to think that I might create something worth while."

He glanced at her quickly as she sat with bent head.

" Others put a higher value on what you have done."

"Oh, they don't know —" she exclaimed.

If something were revealed to him by her tone, he did not betray it, but went on cheerfully.

"You have been away a long time, Alison. It must interest you to come back, and see the changes in our Western civilization. We are moving very rapidly — in certain directions," he corrected himself.

She appraised his qualification.

"In certain directions, — yes. But they are little better in the East. I have scarcely been back," she added, "since I went to Paris to study. I have often thought I should like to return and stay awhile, only — I never seemed to get time. Now I am going over a garden for my father which was one of my first efforts, and which has always reproached me."

"And you do not mind the heat?" he asked. "Those who go East to live return to find our summers oppressive."

"Oh, I'm a salamander, I think," Alison laughed.

Thus they sat chatting, interrupted once or twice by urchins too small to join in the game, who came running to Mr. Bentley and stood staring at Alison as at a being beyond the borders of experience: and she would smile at them quite as shyly, — children being beyond her own. Her imagination was as keen, as unspoiled as a child's, and was stimulated by a sense of adventure, of the mystery which hung about this fine old gentleman who betrayed such sentiment for a mother whom she had loved and admired and still secretly mourned. Here, if there had been no other, was a compelling bond of sympathy. . . .

The shadows grew longer, the game broke up. And Hodder, surrounded by an argumentative group keeping pace with him, came toward them from the field; Alison watched him curiously as he turned this way and that to answer the insistent questions with which he was pelted, and once she saw him stride rapidly after a dodging delinquent and seize him by the collar amidst piercing yells of approval, and derision for the rebel.

"It's remarkable how he gets along with them," said Mr. Bentley, smiling at the scene. "Most of them have never known what discipline is."

The chorus approached. And Hodder, recognizing her,

dropped the collar he held. A young woman conversing with Mr. Bentley was no unusual sight, — he had made no speculations as to this one's identity. He left the boys, and drew near.

"You know Miss Parr, I believe," the old gentleman said.

Hodder took her hand. He had often tried to imagine his feelings if he should meet her again: what he should do and say, — what would be their footing. And now he had no time to prepare. . . .

"It is so strange," she said, with that note of wonder at life in her voice which he recalled so well, "that I should have come across Mr. Bentley here after so many years. How many years, Mr. Bentley?"

"Ah, my dear," he protested, "my measurements would not be yours."

"It is better for both of us not to say," Alison declared, laughingly.

"You knew Mr. Bentley?" asked Hodder, astonished.

"He was a very dear friend of my mother's, although I used to appropriate him when he came to our house. It was when we lived in Ransome Street, ages ago. But I don't think Mr. Bentley has grown a bit older."

"He is one of the few who have found the secret of youth," said the rector.

But the old gentleman had moved off into the path, — or perhaps it would be more accurate to say that he was carried off by the swarm which clustered around him, two smaller ones tugging at his hand, and all intent upon arriving at the soda-water pavilion near the entrance. They had followed him with their eyes, and they saw him turn around and smile at them, helplessly. Alison presented a perplexed face to Hodder.

"Does *he* bring them here, — or you?" she asked.

"I — " he hesitated. "Mr. Bentley has done this every Saturday afternoon for years," he said, "I am merely one of them."

She looked at him quickly. They had started to follow, in the cool path beneath the forest trees. Restraint fell upon them, brought about by the memory of the intimacy of their former meeting, further complicated on Hodder's part by his new attitude toward her father, and his finding her in the company, of all persons, of Mr. Bentley. Un-uttered queries pressed on the minds of both.

"Tell me about Mr. Bentley," she said.

Hodder hesitated.

"I scarcely know where to begin," he replied, yet smil-ing at the characteristic abruptness of her question. The modulations of her voice revealed again the searching, inquisitive spirit within her, and his responded to the intensity of the interest in Mr. Bentley.

"Begin anywhere."

"Anywhere?" he repeated, seeking to gain time.

"Yes — anywhere," she said impatiently.

"Well, he lives in Dalton Street, if you recall what kind of a place that is" (she nodded), "and he is known from one end of it to the other."

"I see what he *is* — he is the most extraordinary person I have ever known. Just to talk to him gives one such a queer feeling of — of dissatisfaction with one's self, and seeing him once more seems to have half revived in me a whole series of dead memories. And I have been trying to think, but it is all so tantalizing. There *is* some mystery about him," she insisted. "He disappeared suddenly, and my mother never mentioned him but once afterward, but other persons have spoken of him since — I forget who. He was so well known, and he used to go to St. John's."

"Yes, he used to go to St. John's."

"What happened to him — do you know? The reason he stopped coming to our house was some misunderstanding with my father, of course. I am positive my mother never changed her feelings toward him."

"I can only tell you what he has told me, which is all I know — authoritatively," Hodder replied. How could he say to her that her father had ruined Mr. Bentley? Indeed, with a woman of her fearlessness and honesty — and above all, her intuition, — he felt the cruelty of his position keenly. Hodder did not relish half truths; and he felt that, however scant his intercourse in the future might be with Alison Parr, he would have liked to have kept it on that basis of frankness in which it had begun. But the exact stage of disillusionment she had reached in regard to Eldon Parr was unknown to him, and he feared that a further revelation might possibly sever the already precarious tie between father and daughter.

He recounted, therefore, that Mr. Bentley had failed; and how he had before that given much of his estate away in charity, how he had been unable to keep his pew in St. John's, and had retired to the house in Dalton Street.

For some moments after he had finished Alison did not reply.

"What is his number in Dalton Street?" she asked.

Hodder informed her.

He could not read in her face whether she suspected that he could have told her more. And in spite of an inordinate, human joy in being again in her presence, his desire to hide from her that which had taken place within him, and the inability he felt to read his future, were instinctive: the more so because of the very spontaneity they had achieved at their first meeting. As a man, he shrank from confessing to her, however indirectly, the fact that she herself was so vital an element in his disillusionment. For the conversation in the garden had been the immediate cause of the inner ferment ending in his resolution to go away, and had directed him, by logical steps, to the encounter in the church with Mrs. Garvin. . . .

"You have not yet finished the garden?" he asked. "I imagined you back in the East by this time."

"Oh, I am procrastinating," she replied. "It is a fit of sheer laziness. I ought to be elsewhere, but I was born without a conscience. If I had one I should try to quiet it by reminding it that I am fulfilling a long-delayed promise — I am making a garden for Mrs. Larrabbee. You know her, of course, since she is a member of your congregation."

"Yes, I know her," he assented. And his mind was suddenly filled with vivid colour, — cobalt seas, and arsenic-

green spruces with purple cones, cardinal-striped awnings
that rattled in the salt breeze, and he saw once more the
panorama of the life which had passed from him and the
woman in the midst of it.   And his overwhelming thought
was of relief that he had somehow escaped.   In spite of
his unhappiness now, he would not have gone back.   He
realized for the first time that he had been nearer annihilation then than to-day.

"Grace isn't here to bother me with the ideas she has
picked up in Europe and catalogued," Alison continued.

"Catalogued!" Hodder exclaimed, struck by the per-
tinency of the word.

"Yes.   Did you ever know anybody who had succeeded half so well in piecing together and absorbing into
a harmonized whole all the divergent, artificial elements
that enter into the conventional world to-day?   Her character might be called a triumph of synthesis.   For she
has actually achieved an individuality — that is what
always surprises me when I think of her.   She has put
the puzzle picture together, she has become a person."

He remembered, with a start, that this was the exact
word Mrs. Larrabbee had used about Alison Parr.   If he
had searched the world, he could not have found a greater
contrast than that between these two women.   And when
she spoke again, he was to be further struck by her power
of logical insight.

"Grace wants me because she thinks I have become the
fashion — for the same reason that Charlotte Plimpton
wants me.   Only there is this difference — Grace will
know the exact value of what I shall have done.   Not
that she thinks me a Le Nôtre"— Alison laughed —   "What
I mean is, she sees behind, she sees *why* it is fashionable
to have a garden, since she has worked out the values of
that existence.   But there!" Alison added, with a pro-
vocative touch that did not escape him, "I am picking
your parishioners to pieces again."

"You have more right than I," he replied, "they have
been your friends since childhood."

"I thought you had gone away," she said.

"Why?" he demanded. Had she been to church again?

"My father told me before he left that you were to take a cruise with him on the yacht he has chartered."

"He wrote me from New York — I was unable to go," Hodder said slowly.

He felt her gaze upon him, but resolutely refused to meet it. . . . They walked on in silence until they came to the more open spaces near the edge of the Park, thronged that Saturday evening by crowds which had sought the city's breathing space. Perfect trees cast long, fantastic shadows across the lawns, fountains flung up rainbows from the midst of lakes; children of the tenements darted hither and thither, rolled and romped on the grass; family parties picnicked everywhere, and a very babel of tongues greeted the ear — the languages of Europe from Sweden to Italy.

Suddenly an exclamation from her aroused and thrilled him.

"Isn't it wonderful how happy they are, and with what simple pleasures they are satisfied! I often come over here on Saturdays and Sundays, just to talk to them."

"Talk to them!" he echoed stupidly. "In their own languages?"

"Oh, I know a little German and Italian, though I can't lay claim to Czech," she answered gayly. "Why are you so surprised that I should possess such modest accomplishments?"

"It's not the accomplishments." He hesitated.

"No. You are surprised that I should be interested in humanity." She stood facing him. "Well, I am," she said, half humorously, half defiantly. "I believe I am more interested in human beings than in anything else in the world — when they are natural, as these people are and when they will tell one their joys and their troubles and their opinions."

Enthusiasm, self-assertion, had as usual, transformed her, and he saw the colour glowing under her olive skin. Was she accusing him of a lack of frankness?

P

"And why," he asked, collecting himself, "did you think —— " he got no further.

"It's because you have an idea that I'm a selfish Epicurean, if that isn't tautology — because I'm interested in a form of art, the rest of the world can go hang. You have a prejudice against artists. I wish I really were one, but I'm not."

This speech contained so many surprises for him that he scarcely knew how to answer it.

"Give me a little time," he begged, "and perhaps I'll get over my prejudices. The worst of them, at any rate. You are helping me to do so." He tried to speak lightly, but his tone was more serious in the next sentence. "It seems to me personally that you *have* proved your concern for your fellow-creatures."

Her colour grew deeper, her manner changed.

"That gives me the opportunity to say something I have hoped to say, ever since I saw you. I hoped I should see you again."

"You are not going away soon?" he exclaimed.

The words were spoken before he grasped their significance.

"Not at once. I don't know how long I shall stay," she answered hurriedly, intent upon what was in her mind. "I have thought a great deal about what I said to you that afternoon, and I find it more than ever difficult to excuse myself. I shan't attempt to. I merely mean to ask you to forgive me."

"There is nothing to forgive," he assured her, under the influence of the feeling she had aroused.

"It's nice of you to say so, and to take it as you did — nicer than I can express. I am afraid I shall never learn to appreciate that there may be other points of view toward life than my own. And I should have realized and sympathized with the difficulties of your position, and that you were doing the best under the circumstances."

"No," he exclaimed, "don't say that! Your other instinct was the truer one, if indeed you *have* really changed it — I don't believe you have." He smiled at her again. "You didn't hurt my feelings, you did me a service. I told you so at the time, and I meant it. And, more than that, I understood."

"You understood —— ?"

"You were not criticizing me, you were — what shall I say? — merely trying to iron out some of the inconsistencies of life. Well, you helped me to iron out some of the inconsistencies of my own. I am profoundly grateful."

She gazed at him, puzzled. But he did not, he could not enlighten her. Some day she would discover what he meant.

"If so, I am glad," she said, in a low voice.

They were standing in the midst of the crowd that thronged around the pavilion. An urchin caught hold of the rector's coat.

"Here he is! Say, Mr. Hodder, ain't you going to have any sody?"

"Certainly we are," he replied, returning Alison's faint smile. . . . In the confusion that followed he caught a glimpse of her talking to Mr. Bentley; and later, after he had taken her hand, his eyes followed her figure wending its way in the evening light through the groups toward Park Street, and he saw above the tree-tops the red tiled roof of the great house in which she was living, alone.

CHAPTER XV

THE CRUCIBLE

I

For better or worse, John Hodder had flung his treasured beliefs into the crucible, and one by one he watched them crumble and consume away. None but his own soul knew what it cost him to make the test; and sometimes, in the early stages of it, he would cast down his book under the lamp and walk for hours in the night. Curiosity, and the despair of one who is lost impelled him to persist.

It had been said of him that he had a talent for the law, and he now discovered that his mind, once freed, weighed the evidence with a pitiless logic, paid its own tribute — despite the anguish of the heart — to the pioneers of truth whose trail it followed into the Unknown, who had held no Mystery more sacred than Truth itself, who had dared to venture into the nothingness between the whirling worlds.

He considered them, those whirling worlds, at night. Once they had been the candles of Jehovah, to light the path of his chosen nation, to herald the birth of his Son. And now? How many billions of blind, struggling creatures clung to them? Where now was this pin-point of humanity, in the midst of an appalling spectacle of a grinding, remorseless nature?

And that obscure Event on which he had staked his hopes? Was He, as John had written, the First Born of the Universe, the Word Incarnate of a system that defied time and space, the Logos of an outworn philosophy? Was that Universe conscious, as Berkeley had declared, or the blind monster of substance alone, or energy, as some modern scientists brutally and triumphantly maintained? Where was the Spirit that breathed in it of hope?

Such were some of the questions that thronged for solution. What was mind, what spirit? an attenuated vapour of the all-pervading substance?

He could not permit himself to dwell on these thoughts — madness lay that way. Madness, and a watching demon that whispered of substance, and sought to guide his wanderings in the night. Hodder clung to the shell of reality, to the tiny panorama of the visible and the finite, to the infinitesimal gropings that lay recorded before him on the printed page. Let him examine these first, let him discover — despite the price — what warrant the mind of man (the only light now vouchsafed to him in his darkness) gave him to speculate and to hope concerning the existence of a higher, truer Reality than that which now tossed and wounded him. It were better to know.

Scarcely had the body been lifted from the tree than the disputes commenced, the adulterations crept in. The spontaneity, the fire and zeal of the self-sacrificing itinerant preachers gave place to the paralyzing logic then pervading the Roman Empire, and which had sent its curse down the ages to the modern sermon; the geometrical rules of Euclid were made to solve the secrets of the universe. The simple faith of the cross which had inspired the martyr along the bloody way from Ephesus to the Circus at Rome was formalized by degrees into philosophy: the faith of future ages was settled by compromises, by manipulation, by bribery in Councils of the Church which resembled modern political conventions, and in which pagan Emperors did not hesitate to exert their influence over the metaphysical bishops of the factions. Recriminations, executions, murders — so the chronicles ran.

The prophet, the idealist disappeared, the priest with his rites and ceremonies and sacrifices, his power to save and damn, was once more in possession of the world,

The Son of Man was degraded into an infant in his mother's arms. An unhealthy, degenerating asceticism, drawn from pagan sources, began with the monks and anchorites of Egypt and culminated in the spectacle of Simeon's pillar. The mysteries of Eleusis, of Attis, Mithras, Magna Mater and Isis developed into Christian sacraments—the symbol became the thing itself. Baptism, the confession of the new life, following the customs of these cults, became *initiation ;* and from the same superstitious origins, the repellent materialistic belief that to eat of the flesh and drink of the blood of a god was to gain immortality : immortality of the body, of course.

Ah, when the superstitions of remote peoples, the fables and myths, were taken away; when the manufactured history and determinism of the Israelites from the fall of man to the coming of that Messiah, whom the Jews crucified because he failed to bring them their material Kingdom, were discredited; when the polemic and literal interpretations of evangelists had been rejected, and the pious frauds of tampering monks; when the ascetic Buddhism was removed; the cults and mysteries, the dogmas of an ancient naïve philosophy discarded; the crude science of a Ptolemy who conceived the earth as a flat terrestrial expanse and hell as a smoking pit beneath proved false; the revelation of a Holy City of jasper and gold and crystal, the hierarchy with its divine franchise to save and rule and conquer, — when all these and more were eliminated from Christianity, what was left?

Hodder surveyed the ruins. And his mind recalled that Sunday of rain in New York which had been the turning-point in his life, when he had listened to the preacher, when he had walked the streets unmindful of the wet, led on by visions, racked by fears. And the same terror returned to him now after all the years of respite, tenfold increased, of falling in the sight of man from the topmost tower.

What was to become of him, now that the very driving power of life was gone? Where would he go? to what

might he turn his hand, since all were vanity and illusion?
Careers meant nothing, had any indeed been possible to a
man forty, left staring at stark reality after the rainbow
had vanished.   Nineveh had mocked and conquered him
who had thought himself a conqueror.   Self flew back
and swung on its central pivot and took command.   *His*
future, *his* fate, what was to become of *him?*   Who else
now was to be considered?   And what was to restrain
him from reaching out his hand to pluck the fruit which
he desired? . . .

II

What control from the Unknown is this which now de-
presses and now releases the sensitive thing called the
soul of man, and sends it upward again until the green
light of hope shines through the surface water?   He
might have grown accustomed, Hodder thought, to the
obscurity of the deeps; in which, after a while, the sharp
agony of existence became dulled, the pressure benumbing.
He was conscious himself, at such times, of no inner re-
cuperation.   Something *drew* him up, and he would find
himself living again, at length to recognize the hand if
not to comprehend the power.

The hand was Horace Bentley's.

What was the source of that serenity which shone on
the face of his friend?   Was it the light of faith?   Faith
in — what?   Humanity, Mr. Bentley had told him on
that first evening when they had met: faith in a world
filled with cruelties, disillusionments, lies, and cheats!
On what Authority was it based?   Hodder never asked,
and no word of theology ever crossed Mr. Bentley's lips;
not by so much as a sign did he betray any knowledge he
may have had of the drama taking place in Hodder's soul;
no comment escaped him on the amazing anomalies of the
life the rector was leading, in the Church but not of it.

It was only by degrees Hodder came to understand that
no question would be asked, and the frequency of his visits
to Dalton Street increased.   He directed his steps thither,

sometimes hurriedly, as though pursued, as to a haven from a storm.   And a haven it was indeed !   At all hours of the day he came, and oftener in the night, in those first weeks, and if Mr. Bentley were not at home the very sight of the hospitable old darky brought surging up within him a sense of security, of relief; the library itself was filled with the peace of its owner.   How many others had brought their troubles here, had been lightened on the very threshold of this sanctuary !

Gradually Hodder began to realize something of their numbers.   Gradually, as he was drawn more and more into the network of the relationships of this extraordinary man, — nay, as he inevitably became a part of that network, — a period of bewilderment ensued.   He found himself involved, and quite naturally, in unpremeditated activities, running errands, forming human ties on a human basis.   No question was asked, no credentials demanded or rejected.   Who he was made no difference — he was a friend of Horace Bentley's.   He had less time to read, less time to think, to scan the veil of his future.

He had run through a score of volumes, critical, philosophical, scientific, absorbing their contents, eagerly anticipating their conclusions ; filled, once he had begun, with a mania to destroy, a savage determination to leave nothing, — to level all. . . .

And no , save for the less frequent relapsing moods, he had grown strangely unconcerned about his future, content to live in the presence of this man; to ignore completely the aspects of a life incomprehensible to the few, besides Mr. Bentley, who observed it.

What he now mostly felt was relief, if not a faint self-congratulation that he had had the courage to go through with it, to know the worst.   And he was conscious even, at times, of a faint reviving sense of freedom he had not known since the days at Bremerton.   If the old dogmas were false, why should he regret them ?   He, began to see that, once he had suspected their falsity, not to have investigated were to invite decay; and he pictured himself growing more unctuous, apologetic, plausible.   He had, at any rate, escaped the more despicable fate, and if he went to pieces now it would be as a man, looking the facts in the face, — not as a coward and a hypocrite.

Late one afternoon, when he dropped in at Mr. Bentley's house, he was informed by Sam that a lady was awaiting Mr. Bentley in the library. As Hodder opened the door he saw a tall, slim figure of a woman with her back toward him. She was looking at the photographs on the mantel.

It was Alison Parr!

He remembered now that she had asked for Mr. Bentley's number, but it had never occurred to him that he might one day find her here. And as she turned he surprised in her eyes a shyness he had never seen in them before. Thus they stood gazing at each other a moment before either spoke.

"Oh, I thought you were Mr. Bentley," she said.

"Have you been waiting long?" he asked.

"Three quarters of an hour, but I haven't minded it. This is such an interesting room, with its pictures and relics and books. It has a soothing effect, hasn't it? To come here is like stepping out of the turmoil of the modern world into a peaceful past."

He was struck by the felicity of her description.

"You have been here before?" he asked.

"Yes." She settled herself in the armchair; and Hodder, accepting the situation, took the seat beside her. "Of course I came, after I had found out who Mr. Bentley was. The opportunity to know him again was not to be missed."

"I can understand that," he assented.

"That is, if a child can even be said to know such a person as Mr. Bentley. Naturally, I didn't appreciate him in those days — children merely accept, without analyzing. And I have not yet been able to analyze, —I can only speculate and consider."

Her enthusiasm never failed to stir and excite Hodder. Nor would he have thought it possible that a new value could be added to Mr. Bentley in his eyes. Yet so it was.

He felt within him, as she spoke, the quickening of a stimulus.

"When I came in a little while ago," Alison continued, "I found a woman in black, with such a sweet, sad face. We began a conversation. She had been through a frightful experience. Her husband had committed suicide, her child had been on the point of death, and she says that she lies awake nights now thinking in terror of what might have happened to her if you and Mr. Bentley hadn't helped her. She's learning to be a stenographer. Do you remember her? — her name is Garvin."

"Did she say — anything more?" Hodder anxiously demanded.

"No," said Alison, surprised by his manner, "except that Mr. Bentley had found her a place to live, near the hospital, with a widow who was a friend of his. And that the child was well, and she could look life in the face again. Oh, it is terrible to think that people all around us are getting into such straits, and that we are so indifferent to it!"

Hodder did not speak at once. He was wondering, now that she had renewed her friendship with Mr. Bentley, whether certain revelations on her part were not inevitable. . . .

She was regarding him, and he was aware that her curiosity was aflame. Again he wondered whether it were curiosity or — interest.

"You did not tell me, when we met in the Park, that you were no longer at St. John's."

"Did Mr. Bentley tell you?"

"No. He merely said he saw a great deal of you. Martha Preston told me. She is still here, and goes to church occasionally. She was much surprised to learn that you were in the city."

"I am still living in the parish house," he said. "I am — taking my vacation."

"With Mr. Bentley?" Her eyes were still on his face.

"With Mr. Bentley," he replied.

He had spoken without bitterness. Although there

had indeed been bitterness in his soul, it passed away in the atmosphere of Mr. Bentley's house. The process now taking place in him was the same complication of negative and positive currents he had felt in her presence before. He was surprised to find that his old antipathy to agnosticism held over, in her case ; to discover, now, that he was by no means, as yet, in view of the existence of Horace Bentley, to go the full length of unbelief ! On the other hand, he saw that she had divined much of what had happened to him, and he felt radiating from her a sympathetic understanding which seemed almost a claim. She *had* a claim, although he could not have said of what it was constituted. Their personal relationship bore responsibilities. It suddenly came over him, in fact, that the two persons who in all the world were nearest him were herself and Mr. Bentley ! He responded, scarce knowing why he did so, to the positive current.

" With Mr. Bentley," he repeated, smiling, and meeting her eyes, " I have been learning something about the actual conditions of life in a modern city."

She bent a little toward him in one of those spontaneous movements that characterized her.

" Tell me — what *is* his life ? " she asked. " I have seen so little of it, and he has told me nothing himself. At first, in the Park, I saw only a kindly old gentleman, with a wonderful, restful personality, who had been a dear friend of my mother's. I didn't connect those boys with him. But since then — since I have been here twice, I have seen other things which make me wonder how far his influence extends." She paused.

" I, too, have wondered," said. the rector, thoughtfully. " When I met him, I supposed he were merely living in simple relationships with his neighbours here in Dalton Street, but by degrees I have discovered that his relationships are as wide as the city itself. And they have grown naturally — by radiation, as it were. One incident has led to another, one act of kindness to another, until now there seems literally no end to the men and women with whom he is in personal touch, who are ready to do anything in their power for him at any time. It is an institution, in fact, wholly unorganized, which in the final analysis is one man. And there is in it absolutely nothing of that element which has come to be known as charity."

Alison listened with parted lips.

"To give you an example," he went on, gradually becoming fired by his subject, by her absorption, "since you have mentioned Mrs. Garvin, I will tell you what happened in that case. It is typical of many. It was a question of taking care of this woman, who was worn out and crushed, until she should recover sufficiently to take care of herself. Mr. Bentley did not need any assistance from me to get the boy into the hospital — Dr. Jarvis worships him. But the mother ! I might possibly have got her into an institutional home — Mr. Bentley did better than that, far better. On the day of the funeral we went directly from the cemetery to the house of a widow who owns a little fruit farm beyond the Park. Her name is Bledsoe, and it is not an exaggeration to say that her house, small as it is, contains an endowed room always at Mr. Bentley's disposal.

"Mrs. Garvin is there now. She was received as a friend, as a guest — not as an inmate, a recipient of charity. I shall never forget how that woman ran out in the sun when she saw us coming, how proud she was to be able to do this thing, how she ushered us into the little parlour, that was all swept and polished, and how naturally and warmly she welcomed the other woman, dazed and exhausted, and took her hat and veil and almost carried her up the stairs. And later on I found out from Mrs. Grover, who lives here, Mrs. Bledsoe's history. Eight or nine years ago her husband was sent to prison for forgery, and she was left with four small children, on the verge of a fate too terrible to mention. She was brought to Mr. Bentley's attention, and he started her in life.

"And now Mrs. Garvin forms another link to that chain, which goes on growing. In a month she will be earning her own living as stenographer for a grain merchant whom Mr. Bentley set on his feet several years ago. One thing has led to the next. And I doubt if any neighbourhood could be mentioned, north or south or west, or even in the business portion of the city itself, where men and women are not to be found ready and eager to do anything in their power for him. Of course there have been exceptions, — what might be called failures in the ordinary terminology of charity, but there are not many."

When he had finished she sat quite still, musing over what he had told her, her eyes alight.

" Yes, it is wonderful," she said at length, in a low voice. " Oh, I *can* believe in that, making the world a better place to live in, making people happier. Of course every one cannot be like Mr. Bentley, but all may do their share in their own way. If only we could get rid of this senseless system of government that puts a premium on the acquisition of property! As it is, we have to depend on individual initiative. Even the good Mr. Bentley does is a drop in the ocean compared to what might be done if all this machinery which has been invented, if all these discoveries of science, by which the forces of an indifferent nature have been harnessed, could be turned to the service of all mankind. Think of how many Mrs. Garvins, of how many Dalton Streets there are in the world, how many stunted children working in factories or growing up into criminals in the slums ! I was reading a book just the other day on the effect of the lack of nutrition on character. We are breeding a million degenerate citizens by starving them, to say nothing of the effect of disease and bad air, of the constant fear of poverty that haunts the great majority of homes. There is no reason why that fear should not be removed, why the latest discoveries in medicine and science should not be at the disposal of all."

The genuineness of her passion was unmistakable. His whole being responded to it.

" Have you always felt like this ? " he asked.

" Like what ? "

" Indignant — that so many people were suffering."

His question threw her into reflection.

" Why, no," she answered, at length, " I never thought

— I see what you mean. Four or five years ago, when I was going to socialist lectures, my sense of all this — inequality, injustice was *intellectual*. I didn't get indignant over it, as I do now when I think of it."

" And why do you get indignant now ? "

" You mean," she asked, " that I have no right to be indignant, since I do nothing to attempt to better conditions ? "

" Not at all," Hodder disavowed. " Perhaps my question is too personal, but I didn't intend it to be. I was merely wondering whether any event or series of events had transformed a mere knowledge of these conditions into feeling."

" Oh ! " she exclaimed, but not in offence. Once more she relapsed into thought. And as he watched her, in silence, the colour that flowed and ebbed in her cheeks registered the coming and going of memories; of incidents in her life hidden from him, arousing in the man the torture of jealousy. But his faculties, keenly alert, grasped the entire field ; marked once more the empirical trait in her that he loved — her unflinching willingness to submit herself to an experiment.

" I suppose so," she replied at length, her thoughts naturally assuming speech. " Yes, I can see that it is so. Yet my experience has not been with these conditions with which Mr. Bentley, with which you have been brought in contact, but with the other side — with luxury. Oh, I am sick of luxury ! I love it, I am not at all sure that I could do without it, but I hate it, too, I rebel against it. You can't understand that."

" I think I can," he answered her.

" When I see the creatures it makes," she cried, " I hate it. My profession has brought me in such close contact with it that I rebelled at last, and came out here very suddenly, just to get away from it in the mass. To renew my youth, if I could. The gardens were only an excuse. I had come to a point where I wanted to be quiet, to be alone, to think, and I knew my father would be going away. So much of my girlhood was spent in that Park that I know every corner of it, and I — obeyed the impulse. I wanted to *test* it."

" Yes," he said, absorbed.

" I might have gone to the mountains or the sea, but some one would have come and found me, and I should have been bound again — on the wheel. I shouldn't have had the strength to resist. But here — have you ever felt," she demanded, " that you craved a particular *locality* at a certain time ? "

He followed her still.

" That is how I felt. These associations, that Park, the thought of my girlhood, of my mother, who understood me as no one else has since, assumed a certain value. New York became unbearable. It is just there, in the very centre of our modern civilization, that one sees the crudest passions. Oh, I have often wondered whether a man, however disillusioned, could see New York as a woman sees it when the glamour is gone. We are the natural prey of the conqueror still. We dream of independence —— "

She broke off abruptly.

This confession, with the sudden glimpse it gave him of the fires within her that would not die down, but burned now more fiercely than ever, sent the blood to his head. His face, his temples, were hot with the fierceness of his joy in his conviction that she had revealed herself to him. Why she had done so, he could not say. . . . This was the woman whom the world thought composed ; who had triumphed over its opposition, compelled it to bow before her ; who presented to it that self-possessed, unified personality by which he had been struck at their first meeting. Yet, paradoxically, the personality remained, — was more elusive than before. A thousand revelations, he felt, would not disclose it. He was no nearer to solving it now. . . . Yet the fires burned! She, too, like himself, was aflame and unsatisfied! She, too, had tasted success, and had revolted!

" But I don't get anywhere," she said wearily. " At times I feel this ferment, this anger that things are as they are, only to realize what helpless anger it is. Why not take the world as it appears and live and feel, instead of beating against the currents?"

"But isn't that inconsistent with what you said awhile ago as to a new civilization?" Hodder asked.

"Oh, that Utopia has no reality for me. I think it has, at moments, but it fades. And I don't pretend to be consistent. Mr. Bentley lives in a world of his own; I envy him with all my heart, I love and admire him, he cheers and soothes me when I am with him. But I can't see — whatever he sees. I am only aware of a remorseless universe grinding out its destinies. We Anglo-Saxons are fond of deceiving ourselves about life, of dressing it up in beautiful colours, of making believe that it actually contains happiness. All our fiction reflects this — that is why I never cared to read English or American novels. The Continental school, the Russians, the Frenchmen, refuse to be deluded. They are honest."

"Realism, naturalism," he mused, recalling a course in philosophy, "one would expect the Russian, in the conditions under which he lives, possessing an artistic temperament combined with a paralysis of the initiative and a sense of fate, to write in that way. And the Frenchmen, Rénan, Zola, and the others who have followed, are equally deterministic, but viewing the human body as a highly organized machine with which we may amuse ourselves by registering its sensations. These literatures are true in so far as they reflect the characteristics of the nations from which they spring. That is not to say that the philosophies of which they are the expressions are true. Nor is it to admit that such a literature is characteristic of the spirit of America, and can be applied without change to *our* life and atmosphere. We have yet, I believe, to develop our own literature, which will come gradually as we find ourselves."

"Find ourselves?" she repeated.

"Yes. Isn't that what we are trying to do? We are not determinists or fatalists, and to condemn us to such a philosophy would be to destroy us. We live on hope. In spite of our apparent materialism, we are idealists. And is it not possible to regard nature as governed by laws — remorseless, if you like the word — and yet believe, with Kant and Goethe, that there is an inner realm? You yourself struggle — you cling to ideals."

" Ideals ! " she echoed. " Ideals are useless unless one is able to see, to feel something beyond this ruthless mechanism by which we are surrounded and hemmed in, to have some perception of another scheme. Why struggle, unless we struggle for something definite? Oh, I don't mean heavenly rewards. Nothing could be more insipid and senseless than the orthodox view of the hereafter. I am talking about a scheme of life here and now."

" So am I," answered Hodder. " But may there not be a meaning in this very desire we have to struggle against the order of things as it appears to us ? "

" A meaning ? "

" A little while ago you spoke of your indignation at the inequalities and injustices of the world, and when I asked you if you had always felt this, you replied that this feeling had grown upon you. My question is this : whether that indignation would be present at all if it were not meant to be turned into action."

" You believe that an influence is at work, an influence that impels us against our reason ? "

" I should like to think so," he said. " Why should so many persons be experiencing such a feeling to-day, persons who, like yourself, are the beneficiaries of our present system of privilege ? Why should you, who have every reason to be satisfied, materially, with things as they are, be troubling yourself with thoughts of others who are less fortunate ? And why should we have the spectacle, to-day, of men and women all over this country in social work, in science and medicine and politics, striving to better conditions while most of them might be much more comfortable and luxurious letting well enough alone ? "

" But it's human to care," she objected.

" Ah — human ! " he said, and was silent. " What do we mean by human, unless it is the distinguishing mark

Q

of something within us that the natural world doesn't possess ? Unless it is the desire and willingness to strive for a larger interest than the *individual* interest, work and suffer for others ? And you spoke of making people happier. What do you mean by happiness ? Not merely the possession of material comforts, surely. I grant you that those who are overworked and underfed, who are burning with the consciousness of wrongs, who have no outlook ahead, are essentially hopeless and miserable. But by 'happiness' you mean something more than the complacency and contentment which clothing and food might bring, and the removal of the economic fear, — and even the restoration of self-respect."

" That their lives should be fuller ! " she exclaimed.

" That drudgery and despair should be replaced by interest and hope," he went on, " slavery by freedom. In other words, that the whole attitude toward life should be changed, that life should appear a bright thing rather than a dark thing, that labour should be *willing*, vicarious instead of forced and personal. Otherwise, any happiness worth having is out of the question."

She was listening now with parted lips, apparently unconscious of the fixity of her gaze.

" You mean it is a choice between that or nothing," she said, in a low voice. " That there is no use in lifting people out of the treadmill and removing the terror of poverty unless you can give them something more — than I have got."

" And something more — than I have got," — he was suddenly moved to reply. . . .

Presently, while the silence still held between them, the door opened and startled them into reality. Mr. Bentley came in.

The old gentleman gave no sign, as they rose to meet him, of a sense of tension in the atmosphere he had entered — yet each felt — somehow, that he *knew*. The tension was released. The same thought occurred to both as they beheld the peaceful welcome shining in his face, " Here is what we are seeking. Why try to define it ? "

"To think that I have been gossiping with Mrs. Meyer, while you were waiting for me!" he said. "She keeps the little florist's shop at the corner of Tower Street, and she gave me these. I little guessed what good use I should have for them, my dear."

He held out to her three fragrant, crimson roses that matched the responsive colour in her cheeks as she thanked him and pinned them on her gown. He regarded her an instant.

"But I'm sure Mr. Hodder has entertained you," Mr. Bentley turned, and laid his hand on the rector's shoulder.

"Most successfully," said Alison, cutting short his protest. And she smiled at Hodder, faintly.

Hodder, Bentley

CHAPTER XVI

AMID THE ENCIRCLING GLOOM

I

HODDER, in spite of a pressing invitation to remain for supper, had left them together. He turned his face westward, in the opposite direction from the parish house, still under the spell of that moment of communion which had lasted — he knew not how long, a moment of silent revelation to them both. She, too, was storm-tossed! She, too, who had fared forth so gallantly into life, had conquered only to be beaten down — to lose her way.

This discovery strained the very fibres of his being. So close he had been to her — so close that each had felt, simultaneously, complete comprehension of the other, comprehension that defied words, overbore disagreements. He knew that she had felt it. He walked on at first in a bewildered ecstasy, careless of aught else save that in a moment they two had reached out in the darkness and touched hands. Never had his experience known such communion, never had a woman meant what this woman meant, and yet he could not define that meaning. What need of religion, of faith in an unseen order when *this* existed? To have this woman in the midst of chaos would be enough!

Faith in an unseen order! As he walked, his mind returned to the argument by which he had sought to combat her doubts — and his own. Whence had the argument come? It was new to him — he had never formulated it before — that pity and longing and striving were a justification and a proof. Had she herself inspired, by some unknown psychological law, this first attempt of his to reform the universe, this theory which he had rather spoken than thought ? Or had it been the knowledge of her own longing, and his desire to assuage it ? As twilight fell, as his spirits ebbed, he could not apply it now — it meant nothing to him, evaded him, there was in it no solace. To regain his footing once more, to climb again without this woman whom he needed, and might not have ! Better to fall, to be engulfed. . . . The vision of her, tall and straight, with the roses on her breast, tortured him.

Thus ecstasy ebbed to despondency. He looked around him in the fading day, to find himself opposite the closed gates of the Botanical Gardens, in the southwestern portion of the city. . . . An hour later he had made his way back to Dalton Street with its sputtering blue lights and gliding figures, and paused for a moment on the far sidewalk to gaze at Mr. Bentley's gleaming windows. Should he go in ? Had that personality suddenly lost its power over him ? How strange that now he could see nothing glowing, nothing inspiring within that house, — only a kindly old man reading a newspaper !

He walked on, slowly, to feel stealing on him that desperate longing for adventure which he had known so well in his younger days. And he did not resist. The terror with which it had once inspired him was gone, or lingered only in the form of a delicious sense of uncertainty and anticipation. Anything might happen to him — anything would be grateful ; the thought of his study in the parish house was unbearable ; the Dalton Street which had mocked and repelled him suddenly became alluring with its champaigns of light and inviting stretches of darkness. In the block ahead, rising out of the night like a tower blazing with a hundred beacons, Hodder saw a hotel, heard the faint yet eager throbbing of music, beheld silhouetted figures flitting from automobiles and carriages across the white glare of the pavement, — figures of men and women.

He hastened his steps, the music grew louder and louder in his ears, he gained the ornamental posts crowned by their incandescent globes, made his way through the loiterers, descended the stone steps of the restaurant, and stood staring into it as at a blurred picture. The band crashed a popular two-step above the mingled voices and laughter. He sat down at a vacant table near the door, and presently became aware that a waiter had been for some time at his elbow.

"What will you have, sir?"

Then he remembered that he had not eaten, discovered that he was hungry, and ordered some sandwiches and beer. Still staring, the figures began to differentiate themselves, although they all appeared, somehow, in perpetual motion; hurrying, though seated. It was like gazing at a quivering cinematograph. Here and there ribbons of smoke curled upward, adding volume to the blue cloud that hung over the tables, which in turn was dissipated in spots by the industrious electric fans. Everywhere he looked he met the glances of women; even at the table next him, they were not so absorbed in their escorts as to be able to resist flinging him covert stares between the shrieks of laughter in which they intermittently indulged. The cumulative effect of all these faces was intoxicating, and for a long time he was unable to examine closely any one group. What he saw was a composite woman with flushed cheeks and soliciting eyes, becomingly gowned and hatted — to the masculine judgment. On the walls, heavily frescoed in the German style, he read, in Gothic letters:

"Wer liebt nicht Wein, Weib, und Gesang,
    Er bleibt ein Narr sein Leben lang."

The waiter brought the sandwiches and beer, yet he did not eat. In the middle distance certain figures began insistently to stand out, — figures of women sitting alone: wherever he looked he met a provoking gaze. One woman, a little farther away than the rest, seemed determinedly bent on getting a nod of recognition, and it was gradually borne in upon Hodder's consciousness that her features were familiar. In avoiding her eyes he studied the men at the next table, — or rather one of them, who loudly ordered the waiters about, who told brief anecdotes that were uproariously applauded; whose pudgy, bejewelled fingers were continually feeling for the bottle in the ice beside his chair, or nudging his companions with easy familiarity; whose little eyes, set in a heavy face, lighted now and again with a certain expression. . . . .

Suddenly Hodder pushed back his chair and got to his feet, overcome by a choking sensation like that of being asphyxiated by foul gases. He must get out at once, or faint. What he had seen in the man's eyes had aroused in him sheer terror, for it was the image of something in his own soul which had summarily gained supremacy and led him hither, unresisting, to its own abiding-place. In vain he groped to reconstruct the process by which that other spirit — which he would fain have believed his true spirit — had been drugged and deadened in its very flight. . . . He was aware, as he still stood uncertainly beside the table, of the white-aproned waiter looking at him, and of some one else, — the woman whose eyes had been fastened on him so persistently. She was close beside him, speaking to him.

" Seems to me we've met before."

He looked at her, at first uncomprehendingly, then with a dawning realization of her identity. Even her name came to him, unexpectedly, — Kate Marcy, — the woman in the flat !

" Ain't you going to invite me to have some supper ? " she whispered eagerly, furtively, as one accustomed to be rebuffed, yet bold in spite of it. " They'll throw me out if they think I'm accosting you."

How was it that, a moment ago, she had appeared to him mysterious, inviting ? At this range he could only see the paint on her cheeks, the shadows under her burning eyes, the shabby finery of her gown. Her wonderful bronze hair only made the contrast more pitiful. He acted automatically, drawing out for her the chair opposite his own, and sat down again.

" Say, but I'm hungry ! " she exclaimed, pulling off her gloves. She smiled at him, wanly, yet with a brazen coquettishness become habit.

" Hungry ! " he repeated idly.

" I guess you'd be, if you'd only had a fried egg and a cup of coffee to-day, and nothing last night."

He pushed over to her, hastily, with a kind of horror, the plate of sandwiches. She began eating them ravenously ; but presently paused, and thrust them back toward him. He shook his head.

" What's the matter with you ? " she demanded.

" Nothing," he replied.

" You ordered them, didn't you ? Ain't you eating anything ? "

" I'm not hungry," he said.

She continued eating awhile without comment. And he watched her as one fascinated, oblivious to his surroundings, in a turmoil of thought and emotion.

" I'm dry," she announced meaningly.

He hesitated a moment, and then gave her the bottle of beer. She made a wry face as she poured it out.

" Have they run out of champagne ? " she inquired.

This time he did not hesitate. The women of his acquaintance, at the dinner parties he attended, drank champagne. Why should he refuse it to this woman? A long-nosed, mediæval-looking waiter was hovering about, one of those bizarre, battered creatures who have long exhausted the surprises of life, presiding over this amazing situation with all the *sang froid* of a family butler. Hodder told him to bring champagne.

" What kind, sir ? " he asked, holding out a card.

" The best you have."

The woman stared at him in wonder.

" You're what an English Johnny I know would call a little bit of all right ! " she declared with enthusiastic approval.

" Since you are hungry," he went on, " suppose you have something more substantial than sandwiches. What would you like ? "

She did not answer at once. Amazement grew in her eyes, amazement and a kind of fear.

" Quit joshing ! " she implored him, and he found it dif-

ficult to cope with her style of conversation.   For a while
she gazed helplessly at the bill of fare.

"I guess you'll think it's funny," she said hesitatingly,
"but I feel just like a good beefsteak and potatoes.   Bring
a thick one, Walter."

The waiter sauntered off.

"Why should I think it strange?" Hodder asked.

"Well, if you knew how many evenings I've sat up
there in my room and thought what I'd order if I ever again
got hold of some rich guy who'd loosen up.   There ain't
any use trying to put up a bluff with you.   Nothing was
too good for me once, caviar, pâté de foie gras " (her pro-
nunciation is not to be imitated), "chicken casserole, peach
Melba, filet of beef with mushrooms, — I've had 'em all, and
I used to sit up and say I'd hand out an order like that.
You never do what you think you're going to do in this
life."

The truth of this remark struck him with a force she
did not suspect ; stung him, as it were, into a sense of reality.

"And now," she added pathetically, "all I want is a
beefsteak !   Don't that beat you?"

She appeared so genuinely surprised at this somewhat
contemptible trick fate had played her that Hodder smiled
in spite of himself.

"I didn't recognize you at first in that get-up," she
observed, looking at his blue serge suit.   "So you've
dropped the preacher business, have you?   You're wise,
all right."

"Why do you say that?" he asked.

"Didn't I tell you when you came 'round that time that
you weren't like the rest of 'em?   You're too human."

Once more the word, and on her lips, startled him.

"Some of the best men I have ever known, the broadest
and most understanding men, have been clergymen," he
found himself protesting.

"Well, they haven't dropped in on me.   The only one
I ever saw that measured up to something like that was
you, and now you've chucked it."

Had he, as she expressed the matter, "chucked it"? Her remark brought him reluctantly, fearfully, remorselessly — agitated and unprepared as he was — face to face with his future.

"You were too good for the job," she declared. "What is there in it? There ain't nobody converted these days that I can see, and what's the use of gettin' up and preachin' to a lot of sapheads that don't know what religion is? Sure they don't."

"Do you?" he asked.

"You've called my bluff." She laughed. "Say, do *you*? If there was anything in it you'd have kept on preachin' to that bunch and made some of 'em believe they was headed for hell; you'd have made one of 'em that owns the flat house I live in, who gets fancy rents out of us poor girls, give it up. That's a nice kind of business for a church member, ain't it?"

"Owns the house in which you live!"

"Sure." She smiled at him compassionately, pitying his innocence and ignorance. "Now I come to think of it, I guess he don't go to your church, — it's the big Baptist church on the boulevard. But what's the difference?"

"None," said Hodder, despondently.

She regarded him curiously.

"You remember when you dropped in that night, when the kid was sick?"

He nodded.

"Well, now you ain't in the business any more, I may as well tell you you kind of got in on me. I was sorry for you — honest, I was. I couldn't believe at first you was on the level, but it didn't take me long to see that they had gold-bricked you, too. I saw you weren't wise to what they were."

"You thought ——" he began and paused dumfounded.

"Why not?" she retorted. "It looked easy to me, — your line. How was I to know at first that they had you fooled? How was I to know you wasn't in the game?"

"The game?"

"Say, what else is it but a game? You must be on now,

ain't you? Why do they put up to keep the churches going? There ain't any coupons coming out of 'em. Maybe some of these millionnaires think they can play all the horses and win, — get into heaven and sell gold bricks on the side. But I guess most of 'em don't think about heaven. They just use the church for a front, and take in strangers in the back alley, — downtown."

Hodder was silent, overwhelmed by the brutal aptness of her figures. Nor did he take the trouble of a defence, of pointing out that hers was not the whole truth. What really mattered—he saw—was what she and those like her thought. Such minds were not to be disabused by argument; and indeed he had little inclination for it then.

"There's nothing in it."

By this expression he gathered she meant life. And some hidden impulse bade him smile at her.

" There is *this*," he answered.

She opened her mouth, closed it and stared at him, struck by his expression, striving uneasily to fathom hidden depths in his remark.

"I don't get on to you," she said lamely. "I didn't that other time. I never ran across anybody like you."

He tried to smile again.

"You mustn't mind me," he answered.

They fell into an oasis of silence, surrounded by mad music and laughter. Then came the long-nosed waiter carrying the beefsteak aloft, followed by a lad with a bucket of ice, from which protruded the green and gold neck of a bottle. The plates were put down, the beafsteak carved, the champagne opened and poured out with a flourish. The woman raised her glass.

"Here's how!" she said, with an attempt at gayety. And she drank to him. "It's funny how I ran across you again, ain't it?" She threw back her head and laughed.

He raised his glass, tasted the wine, and put it down again. A sheet of fire swept through him.

"What's the matter with it? Is it corked?" she demanded. "It goes to the right spot with me."

"It seems very good," he said, trying to smile, and turning to the food on his plate. The very idea of eating revolted him — and yet he made the attempt : he had a feeling, ill defined, that consequences of vital importance depended upon this attempt, on his natural acceptance of the situation. And, while he strove to reduce the contents of his plate, he racked his brain for some subject of conversation. The flamboyant walls of the room pressed in on every side ; comment of that which lay within their limits was impossible, — but he could not, somehow, get beyond them. Was there in the whole range of life one easy topic which they might share in common? Yet a bond existed between this woman and himself — a bond of which he now became aware, and which seemed strangely to grow stronger as the minutes passed and no words were spoken. Why was it that she, too, to whom speech came so easily, had fallen dumb? He began to long for some remark, however disconcerting. The tension increased.

She put down her knife and fork. Tears sprang into her eyes, — tears of anger, he thought.

"Say, it's no use trying to put up a bluff with me," she cried.

" Why do you say that?" he asked.

"You know what I mean, all right. What did you come in here for, anyway?"

"I don't know — I couldn't tell you," he answered.

The very honesty of his words seemed, for an instant, to disconcert her ; and she produced a torn lace handkerchief, which she thrust in her eyes.

" Why can't you leave me alone?" she demanded. "I'm all right."

If he did not at once reply, it was because of some inner change which had taken place in himself ; and he seemed to see things, suddenly, in their true proportions. He no longer feared a scene and its consequences. By virtue of something he had cast off or taken on, he was aware of a newly acquired mastery of the situation, and by a hidden and unconscious process he had managed to get at the real woman behind the paint : had beaten down, as it were without a siege, her defences. And he was incomparably awed by the sight of her quivering, frightened self.

Her weeping grew more violent. He saw the people at the next table turn and stare, heard the men laughing harshly. For the spectacle was evidently not an uncommon one here. She pushed away her unfinished glass, gathered up her velvet bag and rose abruptly.

"I guess I ain't hungry after all," she said, and started toward the door. He turned to the waiter, who regarded him unmoved, and asked for a check.

"I'll get it," he said.

Hodder drew out a ten-dollar bill, and told him to keep the change. The waiter looked at him. Some impulse moved him to remark, as he picked up the rector's hat :

"Don't let her put it over you, sir."

Hodder scarcely heard him. He hurried up the steps and gained the pavement, and somewhere in the black shadows beyond the arc-lights he saw her disappearing down the street. Careless of all comment he hastened on, overtook her, and they walked rapidly side by side. Now and again he heard a sob, but she said nothing. Thus they came to the house where the Garvins had lived, and passed it, and stopped in front of the dimly lighted vestibule of the flats next door. In drawing the key from her bag she dropped it : he picked it up and put it in the lock himself. She led the way without comment up the darkened stairs, and on the landing produced another key, opened the door of her rooms, fumbled for the electric button, and suddenly the place was flooded with light. He glanced in, and recoiled.

II

Oddly enough, the first thing he noticed in the confusion that reigned was the absence of the piano. Two chairs were overturned, and one of them was broken; a siphon of vichy lay on the floor beside a crushed glass and two or three of the cheap ornaments that had been swept

off the mantel and broken on the gaudy tiles of the
hearth. He glanced at the woman, who had ceased crying, and stood surveying the wreckage with the calmness,
the philosophic nonchalance of a class that comes to look
upon misfortune as inevitable.

"They didn't do a thing to this place, did they?" was
her comment. "There was two guys in here to-night
who got a notion they were funny."

Hodder had thought to have fathomed all the horrors of
her existence, but it was not until he looked into this room
that the bottomless depths of it were brought home to him.
Could it be possible that the civilization in which he lived
left any human being so defenceless as to be at the mercy
of the ghouls who had been here? The very stale odours
of the spilled whiskey seemed the material expression of the
essence of degraded souls; for a moment it overpowered
him. Then came the imperative need of action, and he
began to right one of the chairs. She darted forward.

"Cut it out!" she cried. "What business have you
got coming in here and straightening up? I was a fool
to bring you, anyway."

It was in her eyes that he read her meaning, and yet
could not credit it. He was abashed—ashamed; nay,
he could not define the feeling in his breast. He knew
that what he read was the true interpretation of her
speech, for in some manner—he guessed not how—she
had begun to idealize him, to feel that the touch of these
things defiled him.

"I believe I invited myself," he answered, with attempted cheerfulness. Then it struck him, in his predicament, that this was precisely what others had done!
"When you asked me a little while ago whether I had
left the Church, I let you think I had. I am still connected with St. John's, but I do not know how long I
shall continue to be."

She was on her knees with dustpan and whiskbroom,
cleaning up the fragments of glass on the stained carpet.
And she glanced up at him swiftly, diviningly.

"Say—you're in trouble yourself, ain't you?"

"'I GUESS I AIN'T HUNGRY AFTER ALL.'"

She got up impulsively, spilling some of the contents of the pan. A subtle change had come in her, and under the gallantly drooping feathers of her hat he caught her eye—the human eye that so marvellously reflects the phases of the human soul: the eye which so short a time before hardily and brazenly had flashed forth its invitation, now actually shone with fellowship and sympathy. And for a moment this look was more startling, more appalling than the other; he shrank from it, resented it even more. Was it true that they had something in common? And if so, was it sin or sorrow, or both?

"I might have known," she said, staring at him. In spite of his gesture of dissent, he saw that she was going over the events of the evening from her new point of view.

"I might have known, when we were sitting there in Harrod's, that you were up against it, too, but I couldn't think of anything but the way *I* was fixed. The agent's been here twice this week for the rent, and I was kind of desperate for a square meal."

Hodder took the dustpan from her hand, and flung its contents into the fireplace.

"Then we are both fortunate," he said, "to have met each other."

"I don't see where you come in," she told him.

He turned and smiled at her.

"Do you remember when I was here that evening about two months ago I said I should like to be your friend? Well, I meant it. And I have often hoped, since then, that some circumstance might bring us together again. You seemed to think that no friendship was possible between us, but I have tried to make myself believe that you said so because you didn't know me."

"Honest to God?" she asked. "Is that on the level?"

"I only ask for an opportunity to prove it," he replied, striving to speak naturally. He stooped and laid the dustpan on the hearth. "There! Now let's sit down."

She sank on the sofa, her breast rising and falling, her gaze dumbly fixed on him, as one under hypnosis. He took the rocker.

" I have wanted to tell you how grateful Mrs. Garvin—
the boy's mother — was for the roses you brought. She
doesn't know who sent them, but I intend to tell her, and
she will thank you herself. She is living out in the
country. And the boy—you would scarcely recognize
him."

"I couldn't play the piano for a week after—that
thing happened." She glanced at the space where the
instrument had stood.

"You taught yourself to play?" he asked.

"I had music lessons."

" Music lessons?"

"Not here—before I left home—up the State, in a
little country town, — Madison. It seems like a long
time ago, but it's only seven years in September. Mother
and father wanted all of us children to know a little more
than they did, and I guess they pinched a good deal to
give us a chance. I went a year to the high school, and
then I was all for coming to the city—I couldn't stand
Madison, there wasn't anything going on. Mother was
against it,—said I was too good-looking to leave home.
I wish I never had. You wouldn't believe I was good-
looking once, would you?"

She spoke dispassionately, not seeming to expect assent,
but Hodder glanced involuntarily at her wonderful crown
of hair. She had taken off her hat. He was thinking
of the typical crime of American parents, — and suddenly
it struck him that her speech had changed, that she had
dropped the suggestive slang of the surroundings in which
she now lived.

" I was a fool to come, but I couldn't see it then. All
I could think of was to get away to a place where something was happening. I wanted to get into Ferguson's—
everybody in Madison knew about Ferguson's, what a
grand store it was,—but I couldn't. And after a while
I got a place at the embroidery counter at Pratt's.
That's a department store, too, you know. It looked
fine, but it wasn't long before I fell wise to a few things."
(She relapsed into slang occasionally.) "Have you ever

tried to stand on your feet for nine hours, where you couldn't sit down for a minute ? Say, when Florry Kinsley and me —she was the girl I roomed with— would get home at night, often we'd just lie down and laugh and cry, we were so tired, and our feet hurt so. We were too used up sometimes to get up and cook supper on the little stove we had. And sitting around a back bedroom all evening was worse than Madison. We'd go out, tired as we were, and walk the streets."

He nodded, impressed by the fact that she did not seem to be appealing to his sympathy. Nor, indeed, did she appear—in thus picking up the threads of her past—to be consciously accounting for her present. She recognized no causation there.

"Say, did you ever get to a place where you just had to have something happen ? When you couldn't stand bein' lonely night after night, when you went out on the streets and saw everybody on the way to a good time but you ? We used to look in the newspapers for notices of the big balls, and we'd take the cars to the West End and stand outside the awnings watching the carriages driving up and the people coming in. And the same with the weddings. We got to know a good many of the swells by sight. There was Mrs. Larrabbee—" a certain awe crept into her voice — " and Miss Ferguson—she's sweet—and a lot more. Some of the girls used to copy their clothes and hats, but Florry and me tried to live honest. It was funny," she added irrelevantly, " but the more worn out we were at night, the more we'd want a little excitement, and we used to go to the dance-halls and keep going until we were ready to drop."

She laughed at the recollection.

" There was a floorwalker who never let me alone the whole time I was at Pratt's — he put me in mind of a pall-bearer. His name was Selkirk, and he had a family in Westerly, out on the Grade Suburban. . . . Some of the girls never came back at all, except to swagger in and buy expensive things, and tell us we were fools to work. And after a while I noticed Florry was getting discouraged.

R

We never had so much as a nickel left over on Saturdays, and they made us sign a paper, when they hired us, that we lived at home. It was their excuse for paying us six dollars a week. They do it at Ferguson's, too. They say they can get plenty of girls who do live at home. I made up my mind I'd go back to Madison, but I kept putting it off, and then father died, and I couldn't.

"And then, one day, Florry left. She took her things from the room when I was at the store, and I never saw her again. I got another roommate. I couldn't afford to pay for the room alone. You wouldn't believe I kept straight, would you?" she demanded, with a touch of her former defiance. "I had plenty of chances better than that floorwalker. But I knew I was good looking, and I thought if I could only hold out I might get married to some fellow who was well fixed. What's the matter?"

Hodder's exclamation had been involuntary, for in these last words she had unconsciously brought home to him the relentless predicament in the lives of these women. She had been saving herself — for what? A more advantageous sale!

"It's always been my luck," she went on reflectingly, "that when what I wanted to happen did happen, I never could take advantage of it. It was just like that to-night, when you handed me out the bill of fare, and I ordered beefsteak. And it was like that when — when *he* came along — I didn't do what I thought I was going to do. It's terrible to fall in love, isn't it? I mean the real thing. I've read in books that it only comes once, and I guess it's so."

Fortunately she seemed to expect no answer to this query. She was staring at the wall with unseeing eyes.

"I never thought of marrying him, from the first. He could have done anything with me — he was so good and generous — and it was him I was thinking about. That's love, isn't it? Maybe you don't believe a woman like me knows what love is. You've got a notion that goin' downhill, as I've been doing, kills it, haven't you? I wish to God it did — but it don't : the ache's there, and sometimes

f those bright, bitter cold winter days after a tha
the icicles are hanging everywhere. I went insi
walked up and down that long platform under th
roof. My, it was cold in there! I looked over a
gns, and made up my mind I'd go to Chicago.

meant to work, I never meant to spend the mone
o send it back. I'd put it aside — and then I'd g
ake a little. Say, it was easy not to work — and
t care what happened to me as long as I wasn't goin
him again. Well, I'm not trying to smooth it ove
pose there was something crooked about me fro
tart, but I just went clean to hell with that mone
when I heard he'd gone away, I came back here."
omething crooked!" The words rang in Hodder'
in his very soul. How was he or any man to esti
to unravel the justice from the injustice, to pass upo
merit of this woman's punishment? Here again, i
vitiated life, was only to be seen the remorseles
ing of law — cause and effect. Crooked! Had no
ree been crooked from the beginning — incapable o
straightened? She had herself naïvely confessed
Vas not the twist ingrained? And if so, where wa
alvation he had preached? There was good in he
— but what was "good"? ... He took no accoun
profound compassion.

at comfort could he give her, what hope could he
out that the twist, now gnarled and knotted, might
moved, that she might gain peace of soul and body
he "happiness" of which he had talked with Alison
? ... He raised his eyes, to discover that the
n's were fixed upon him, questioningly.

suppose I was a fool to tell you," she said, with a
of her old bitterness; "it can't do any good." Her
remark was startlingly astute. "You've found out
ourself, I guess, that all this talk about heaven and
nd repentance don't amount to anything. Hell
n't be any worse than I've been through, no matter
ot it is. And heaven!" She laughed, burst into
and quickly dried them. "You know the man I've

it comes in the daytime, and sometimes at night, and I
think I'll go crazy. When a woman like me is in love
there isn't anything more terrible on earth, I tell you. If
a girl's respectable and good it's bad enough, God knows,
if she can't have the man she wants; but when she's —
like me — it's hell. That's the only way I can describe it.
She feels there is nothing about her that's clean, that he
wouldn't despise. There's many a night I wished I could
have done what Garvin did, but I didn't have the nerve."

"Don't say that!" he commanded sharply.

"Why not? It's the best way out."

"I can see how one might believe it to be," he answered.
Indeed, it seemed that his vision had been infinitely ex-
tended, that he had suddenly come into possession of the
solution of all the bewildered, despairing gropings of the
human soul. Only awhile ago, for instance, the mood
of self-destruction had been beyond his imagination: to-
night he understood it, though he still looked upon it with
horror. And he saw that his understanding of her — or of
any human being — could never be of the intellect. He
had entered into one of those astounding yet simple relationships wherein truth, and truth alone, is possible.
He knew that such women lied, deceived themselves; he
could well conceive that the image of this first lover
might have become idealized in her vicissitudes; that the
memories of the creature-comforts, of first passion, might
have enhanced as the victim sank. It was not only because she did not attempt to palliate that he believed her.

"I remember the time I met him, — it was only four
years ago last spring, but it seems like a lifetime. It was
Decoration Day, and it was so beautiful I went out with
another girl to the Park, and we sat on the grass and
looked at the sky and wished we lived in the country.
He was in an automobile; I never did know exactly how
it happened, — we looked at each other, and he slowed up
and came back and asked us to take a ride. I had never
been in one of those things — but that wasn't why I went,
I guess. Well, the rest was easy. He lost his head, and
I was just as bad. You wouldn't believe me if I told you

how rich he was: it scared me when I found out about him, and he was so handsome and full of fun and spirits, and generous! I never knew anybody like him. Honest, I never expected he'd want to marry me. He didn't at first, — it was only after a while. I never asked him to, and when he began to talk about it I told him it would cut him off from his swell friends, and I knew his father might turn him loose. Oh, it wasn't the money! Well, he'd get mad all through, and say he never got along with the old man, and that his friends would have to take me, and he couldn't live without me. He said he would have me educated, and bought me books, and I tried to read them. I'd have done anything for him. He'd knocked around a good deal since he'd been to Harvard College, — he wasn't what you'd call a saint, but his heart was all right. And he changed, too, I could see it. He said he was going to make something out of himself.

"I didn't think it was possible to be so happy, but I had a feeling all along, inside of me, that it couldn't come off. I had a little flat in Rutger Street, over on the south side, and everything in the world I wanted. Well, one day, sure enough, the bell rang and I opened the door, and there stood a man with side whiskers staring at me, and staring until I was frightened to death. I never saw such eyes as he had. And all of a sudden I knew it was *his* father.

"'Is this Miss Marcy?'" he said.

"I couldn't say anything at all, but he handed me his card and smiled, I'll never forget how he smiled — and came right in and sat down. I'd heard of that man all my life, and how much money he'd made, and all that. Why, up in Madison folks used to talk about him — " she checked herself suddenly and stared at Hodder in consternation. "Maybe you know him!" she exclaimed. "I never thought!"

"Maybe I do," he assented wearily. In the past few moments suspicion had become conviction.

"Well — what difference does it make — now? It's all over, and I'm not going to bother him. I made up my

mind I wouldn't, on account of *him*, y
never fell that low — thank God!"

Hodder nodded. He could not
woman seemed to be living over agai
imagination.

"I just couldn't realize who it was s
me, but if I hadn't known it wouldn't l
ference. He could have done anything
and he knew how to get at me. He s
seen me, that he was sure I was a good
and loved his son, and that I wouldn't
boy when he had such a big future
wouldn't have thought, to look at the n
have been so gentle. I made a fool of
and told him I'd go away and never see
— that I'd always been against marryin
almost had tears in his eyes when he tha
I'd never regret it, and he pulled an e
pocket. I said I wouldn't take any m
back to him. I've always been sorry s
make him take it back — it never did ar
to me. But he had his way. He laid it
said he wouldn't feel right, and took r
just didn't care.

"Well, what do you think I did aft
went and played a piece on the piano, —
bear to hear that ragtime to this day. I
feel anything. And after a while I got u
envelope — it was full of crackly new hu
— thirty of 'em, and as I sat there starin
came on, like a toothache, in throbs, gett
time until I just couldn't stand it. I
sending the money back even then, but I
know how to do it, — and as I told you
care much. Then I remembered I'd pro
and I had to have some money for that
leave right off I wouldn't have the stre
hadn't even thought where to go: I cou
got dressed and went down to the depot

been talking about, that bought me off. I didn't intend
to tell you, but I see you can't help knowing — Eldon
Parr. I don't say he didn't do right from his way of
looking at things, — but say, it wasn't exactly Christian,
was it ? "

"No," he said, "it wasn't." He bowed his head, and
presently, when he raised it again, he caught something
in her look that puzzled and disturbed him — an element
of adoration.

"You're white through and through," she said, slowly
and distinctly.

And he knew not how to protest.

"I'll tell you something," she went on, as one who has
made a discovery. "I liked you the first time you came
in here — that night — when you wanted me to be friends;
well, there was something that seemed to make it impossible then. I felt it, if you didn't." She groped for
words. "I can't explain what it was, but now it's gone.
You're different. I think a lot more of you. Maybe it's
because of what you did at Harrod's, sitting down with
me and giving me supper when I was so hungry, and the
champagne. You weren't *ashamed* of me."

"Good God, why should I have been ! " he exclaimed.

"You ! Why shouldn't you ? " she cried fiercely.
"There's hardly a man in that place that wouldn't have
been. They all know me by sight — and some of 'em —
better. You didn't see 'em grinning when I came up to
you, but I did. My God — it's awful — it's awful ! . . . "
She burst into violent weeping, long deferred.

He took her hand in his, and did not speak, waiting for
the fit to spend itself. . . . And after a while the convulsive shudders that shook her gradually ceased.

"You must trust me," he said. "The first thing to-
morrow I'm going to make arrangements for you to get
out of these rooms. You can't stay here any longer."

"That's sure," she answered, trying to smile. "I'm
broke. I even owe the co — the policeman."

"The policeman ! "

"He has to turn it in to Tom Beatty and the politicians."

Beatty! Where had he heard the name? Suddenly it came to him that Beatty was the city boss, who had been eulogized by Mr. Plimpton!

"I have some good friends who will be glad to help you to get work — and until you do get work. You will have to fight — but we all have to fight. Will you try?"

"Sure, I'll try," she answered, in a low voice.

Her very tone of submission troubled him. And he had a feeling that, if he had demanded, she would have acquiesced in anything.

"We'll talk it over to-morrow," he went on, clinging to his note of optimism. "We'll find out what you can do easiest, to begin with."

"I might give music lessons," she suggested.

The remark increased his uneasiness, for he recognized in it a sure symptom of disease — a relapse into what might almost have been called levity, blindness to the supreme tragedy of her life which but a moment before had shaken and appalled her. He shook his head bravely:

"I'm afraid that wouldn't do — at first."

She rose and went into the other room, returning in a few moments with a work basket, from which she drew a soiled and unfinished piece of embroidery.

"There's a bureau cover I started when I was at Pratt's," she said, as she straightened it over her knees. "It's a copy of an expensive one. I never had the patience to finish it, but one of the salesladies there, who was an expert, told me it was pretty good. She taught me the stitch, and I had a notion at that time I might make a little money for dresses and the theatre. I was always clever with my hands."

"The very thing!" he said, with hopeful emphasis. "I'm sure I can get you plenty of it to do. And I'll come back in the morning."

He gave it back to her, and as she was folding it his glance fell on a photograph in the basket.

"I kept it, I don't know why," he heard her say; "I didn't have the heart to burn it."

He started, recovered himself, and rose.

"I'll go to see the agent the first thing to-morrow," he said. "And then — you'll be ready for me? You trust me?"

"I'd do anything for you," was her tremulous reply.

Her disquieting, submissive smile haunted him as he groped his way down the stairs to the street, and then the face in the photograph replaced it — the laughing eyes, the wilful, pleasure-loving mouth he had seen in the school and college pictures of Preston Parr.

CHAPTER XVII

RECONSTRUCTION

I

LIFE had indeed become complicated, paradoxical. He, John Hodder, a clergyman, rector of St. John's by virtue of not having resigned, had entered a restaurant of ill repute, had ordered champagne for an abandoned woman, and had no sense of sin when he awoke the next morning! The devil, in the language of orthodox theology, had led him there. He had fallen under the influence of the tempter of his youth, and all in him save the carnal had been blotted out.

More paradoxes! If the devil had not taken possession of him and led him there, it were more than probable that he could never have succeeded in any other way in getting on a footing of friendship with this woman, Kate Marcy. *Her* future, to be sure, *was* problematical. Here was no simple, sentimental case he might formerly have imagined, of trusting innocence betrayed, but a mixture of good and evil, selfishness and unselfishness. And she had, in spite of all, known the love which effaces self! Could the disintegration, in her case, be arrested?

Gradually Hodder was filled with a feeling which may be called amazement because, although his brain was no nearer to a solution than before, he was not despondent. For a month he had not permitted his mind to dwell on the riddle; yet this morning he felt stirring within him a new energy for which he could not account, a hope unconnected with any mental process! He felt in touch, once more, faintly but perceptibly, with something stable in the chaos. In bygone years he had not seen the chaos, but the illusion of an orderly world, a continual succession of

sunrises, *couleur de rose*, from the heights above Bremerton.
Now were the scales fallen from his eyes; now he saw the
evil, the injustice, the despair; felt, in truth, the weight
of the sorrow of it all, and yet that sorrow was unaccount-
ably transmuted, as by a chemical process, into something
which for the first time had a *meaning* — he could not say
what meaning. The sting of despair had somehow been
taken out of it, and it remained poignant!

Not on the obsession of the night before, when he had
walked down Dalton Street and beheld it transformed into
a realm of adventure, but upon his past life did he look
back now with horror, upon the even tenor of those days
and years in the bright places. His had been the highroad
of a fancied security, from which he had feared to stray,
to seek his God across the rough face of nature, from black,
forgotten cañons to the flying peaks in space. He had
feared *reality*. He had insisted upon gazing at the universe through the coloured glasses of an outworn theology,
instead of using his own eyes.

So he had left the highroad, the beaten way of salvation
many others had deserted, had flung off his spectacles, had
plunged into reality, to be scratched and battered, to lose
his way. Not until now had something of grim zest come
to him, of an instinct which was the first groping of a
vision, as to where his own path might lie. Through what
thickets and over what mountains he knew not as yet —
nor cared to know. He felt *resistance*, whereas on
the highroad he had felt none. On the highroad his
cry had gone unheeded and unheard, yet by holding
out his hand in the wilderness he had helped another,
bruised and bleeding, to her feet! Salvation! Let it be
what it might be, he would go on, stumbling and seeking,
through reality.

Even this last revelation, of Eldon Parr's agency
in another tragedy, seemed to have no further power
to affect him. . . . Nor could Hodder think of Alison
as in blood-relationship to the financier, or even to the
boy, whose open, pleasure-loving face he had seen in the
photograph.

II

A presage of autumn was in the air, and a fine, misty rain drifted in at his windows as he sat at his breakfast. He took deep breaths of the moisture, and it seemed to water and revive his parching soul. He found himself, to his surprise, surveying with equanimity the pile of books in the corner which had led him to the conviction of the emptiness of the universe — but the universe was no longer empty! It was cruel, but a warring force was at work in it which was not blind, but *directed*. He could not say why this was so, but he *knew* it, he *felt* it, sensed its energy within him as he set out for Dalton Street.

He was neither happy nor unhappy, but in equilibrium, walking with sure steps, and the anxiety in which he had fallen asleep the night before was gone: anxiety lest the woman should have fled, or changed her mind, or committed some act of desperation.

In Dalton Street a thin coat of yellow mud glistened on the asphalt, but even the dreariness of this neighbourhood seemed transient. He rang the bell of the flat, the door swung open, and in the hall above a woman awaited him. She was clad in black.

"You wouldn't know me, would you?" she inquired. "Say, I scarcely know myself. I used to wear this dress at Pratt's, with white collars and cuffs and — well, I just put it on again. I had it in the bottom of my trunk, and I guessed you'd like it."

"I didn't know you at first," he said, and the pleasure in his face was her reward.

The transformation, indeed, was more remarkable than he could have believed possible, for respectability itself would seem to have been regained by a costume, and the abundance of her remarkable hair was now repressed. The absence of paint made her cheeks strangely white, the hollows under the eyes darker. The eyes themselves alone betrayed the woman of yesterday; they still burned.

"Why," he exclaimed, looking around him, "you have been busy, haven't you?"

"I've been up since six," she told him proudly. The flat had been dismantled of its meagre furniture, the rug was rolled up and tied, and a trunk strapped with rope was in the middle of the floor. Her next remark brought home to him the full responsibility of his situation. She led him to the window, and pointed to a spot among the drenched weeds and rubbish in the yard next door. "Do you see that bottle? That's the first thing I did — flung it out there. It didn't break," she added significantly, "and there are three drinks in it yet."

Once more he confined his approval to his glance.

"Now you must come and have some breakfast," he said briskly. "If I had thought about it I should have waited to have it with you."

"I'm not hungry." In the light of his new knowledge, he connected her sudden dejection with the sight of the bottle.

"But you must eat. You're exhausted from all this work. And a cup of coffee will make all the difference in the world."

She yielded, pinning on her hat. And he led her, holding the umbrella over her, to a restaurant in Tower Street, where a man in a white cap and apron was baking cakes behind a plate-glass window. She drank the coffee, but in her excitement left the rest of the breakfast almost untasted.

"Say," she asked him once, "why are you doing this?"

"I don't know," he answered, "except that it gives me pleasure."

"Pleasure?"

"Yes. It makes me feel as if I were of some use."

She considered this.

"Well," she observed, revived by the coffee, "you're the queerest minister *I* ever saw."

When they had reached the pavement she asked him where they were going.

"To see a friend of mine, and a friend of yours," he told her. "He does not live far from here."

She was silent again, acquiescing. The rain had stopped, the sun was peeping out furtively through the clouds, the early loiterers in Dalton Street stared at them curiously. But Hodder was thinking of that house whither they were bound with a new gratitude, a new wonder that it should exist. Thus they came to the sheltered vestibule with its glistening white paint, its polished name plate and door-knob. The grinning, hospitable darky appeared in answer to the rector's ring.

"Good morning, Sam," he said; "is Mr. Bentley in?"

Sam ushered them ceremoniously into the library, and Kate Marcy gazed about her with awe, as at something absolutely foreign to her experience: the New Barrington Hotel, the latest pride of the city, recently erected at the corner of Tower and Jefferson and furnished in the French style, she might partially have understood. Had she been marvellously and suddenly transported and established there, existence might still have evinced a certain continuity. But this house! . . .

Mr. Bentley rose from the desk in the corner.

"Oh, it's you, Hodder," he said cheerfully, laying his hand on the rector's arm. "I was just thinking about you."

"This is Miss Marcy, Mr. Bentley," Hodder said.

Mr. Bentley took her hand and led her to a chair.

"Mr. Hodder knows how fond I am of young women," he said. "I have six of them upstairs, — so I am never lonely."

Mr. Bentley did not appear to notice that her lips quivered.

Hodder turned his eyes from her face. "Miss Marcy has been lonely," he explained, "and I thought we might get her a room near by, where she might see them often. She is going to do embroidery."

"Why, Sally will know of a room," Mr. Bentley replied. "Sam!" he called.

"Yessah — yes, Mistah Ho'ace." Sam appeared at the door.

"Ask Miss Sally to come down, if she's not busy."

Kate Marcy sat dumbly in her chair, her hands convulsively clasping its arms, her breast heaving stormily, her face becoming intense with the effort of repressing the wild emotion within her: emotion that threatened to strangle her if resisted, or to sweep her out like a tide and drown her in deep waters: emotion that had no one meaning, and yet summed up a life, — mysteriously and overwhelmingly aroused by the sight of a room, and of a kindly old gentleman who lived in it!

Mr. Bentley took the chair beside her.

"Why, I believe it's going to clear off, after all," he exclaimed. "Sam predicted it, before breakfast. He pretends to be able to tell by the flowers. After a while I must show you my flowers, Miss Marcy, and what Dalton Street can do by way of a garden — Mr. Hodder could hardly believe it, even when he saw it." Thus he went on, the tips of his fingers pressed together, his head bent forward in familiar attitude, his face lighted, speaking naturally of trivial things that seemed to suggest themselves; and careful, with exquisite tact that did not betray itself, to address both. A passing automobile startled her with the blast of its horn. "I'm afraid I shall never get accustomed to them," he lamented. "At first I used to be thankful there were no trolley cars on this street, but I believe the automobiles are worse."

A figure flitted through the hall and into the room, which Hodder recognized as Miss Grover's. She reminded him of a flying shuttle across the warp of Mr. Bentley's threads, weaving them together; swift, sure, yet never hurried or flustered. One glance at the speechless woman seemed to suffice her for a knowledge of the situation.

"Mr. Hodder has brought us a new friend and neighbour, Sally, — Miss Kate Marcy. She is to have a room near us, that we may see her often."

Hodder watched Miss Grover's procedure with a breathless interest.

"Why, Mrs. McQuillen has a room — across the street, you know, Mr. Bentley."

Sally perched herself on the edge of the armchair and laid her hand lightly on Kate Marcy's.

Even Sally Grover was powerless to prevent the inevitable, and the touch of her hand seemed the signal for the release of the pent-up forces. The worn body, the worn nerves, the weakened will gave way, and Kate Marcy burst into a paroxysm of weeping that gradually became automatic, convulsive, like a child's. There was no damming this torrent, once released. Kindness, disinterested friendship, was the one unbearable thing.

"We must bring her upstairs," said Sally Grover, quietly, "she's going to pieces."

Hodder helping, they fairly carried her up the flight, and laid her on Sally Grover's own bed.

That afternoon she was taken to Mrs. McQuillen's.

III

The fiends are not easily cheated. And during the nights and days that followed even Sally Grover, whose slight frame was tireless, whose stoicism was amazing, came out of the sick room with a white face and compressed lips. Tossing on the mattress, Kate Marcy enacted over again incident after incident of her past life, events natural to an existence which had been largely devoid of self-pity, but which now, clearly enough, tested the extreme limits of suffering. Once more, in her visions, she walked the streets, wearily measuring the dark, empty blocks, footsore, into the smaller hours of the night; slyly, insinuatingly, pathetically offering herself — all she possessed — to the hovering beasts of prey. And even these rejected her, with gibes, with obscene jests that sprang to her lips and brought a shudder to those who heard.

Sometimes they beheld flare up fitfully that mysterious thing called the human spirit, which all this crushing process had not served to extinguish. She seemed to be defending her rights, whatever these may have been! She expostulated with policemen. And once, when Hodder was present, she brought back vividly to his mind that first night he had seen her, when she had defied him and sent him away. In moments she lived over again the careless, reckless days when money and good looks had not been lacking, when rich food and wines had been plentiful. And there were other events which Sally Grover and the good-natured Irishwoman, Mrs. McQuillen, not holding the key, could but dimly comprehend. Education, environment, inheritance, character — what a jumble of causes! What Judge was to unravel them, and assign the exact amount of responsibility?

There were other terrible scenes when, more than semiconscious, she cried out piteously for drink, and cursed them for withholding it. And it was in the midst of one of these that an incident occurred which made a deep impression upon young Dr. Giddings, hesitating with his opiates, and assisting the indomitable Miss Grover to hold his patient. In the midst of the paroxysm Mr. Bentley entered and stood over her by the bedside, and suddenly her struggles ceased. At first she lay intensely still, staring at him with wide eyes of fear. He sat down and took her hand, and spoke to her, quietly and naturally, and her pupils relaxed. She fell into a sleep, still clinging to his fingers.

It was Sally who opposed the doctor's wish to send her to a hospital.

"If it's only a question of getting back her health, she'd better die," she declared. "We've got but one chance with her, Dr. Giddings, to keep her here. When she finds out she's been to a hospital, that will be the end of it with *her* kind. We'll never get hold of her again. I'll take care of Mrs. McQuillen."

Doctor Giddings was impressed by this wisdom.

"You think you *have* a chance, Miss Grover?" he asked. He had had a hospital experience.

Miss Grover was wont to express optimism in deeds rather than words.

"If I didn't think so, I'd ask you to put a little more in your hypodermic next time," she replied.

And the doctor went away, wondering. . . .

s

Drink! Convalescence brought little release for the watchers. The fiends would retire, pretending to have abandoned the field, only to swoop down again when least expected. There were periods of calm when it seemed as though a new and bewildered personality were emerging, amazed to find in life a kindly thing, gazing at the world as one new-born. And again, Mrs. McQuillen or Ella Finley might be seen running bareheaded across the street for Miss Grover. Physical force was needed, as the rector discovered on one occasion; physical force, and something more, a dauntlessness that kept Sally Grover in the room after the other women had fled in terror. Then remorse, despondency, another fear. . . .

As the weeks went by, the relapses certainly became fewer. *Something* was at work, as real in its effects as the sunlight, but invisible. Hodder felt it, and watched in suspense while it fought the beasts in this woman, rending her frame in anguish. The frame might succumb, the breath might leave it to moulder, but the struggle, he knew, would go until the beasts were conquered. Whence this knowledge?—for it *was* knowledge.

On the quieter days of her convalescence she seemed, indeed, more Madonna than Magdalen as she sat against the pillows, her red-gold hair lying in two heavy plaits across her shoulders, her cheeks pale; the inner, consuming fires that smouldered in her eyes died down. At such times her newly awakened innocence (if it might be called such;—pathetic innocence, in truth!) struck awe into Hodder; her wonder was matched by his own. Could there be another meaning in life than the pursuit of pleasure, than the weary effort to keep the body alive? Such was her query, unformulated. What animated these persons who had struggled over her so desperately,—Sally Grover, Mr. Bentley, and Hodder himself? Thus her opening mind. For she had a mind.

Mr. Bentley was the chief topic, and little by little he became exalted into a mystery of which she sought the explanation.

"I never knew anybody like him," she would exclaim.

" Why, I'd seen him on Dalton Street with the children following him, and I saw him again that day of the funeral. Some of the girls I knew used to laugh at him. We thought he was queer. And then, when you brought me to him that morning and he got up and treated me like a *lady*, I just couldn't stand it. I never felt so terrible in my life. I just wanted to die, right then and there. Something inside of me kept pressing and pressing, until I thought I *would* die. I knew what it was to hate myself, but I never hated myself as I have since then.

"He never says anything about God, and you don't, but when he comes in here he seems like God to me. He's so *peaceful*, — he makes me peaceful. I remember the minister in Madison, — he was a putty-faced man with indigestion, — and when he prayed he used to close his eyes and try to look pious, but he never fooled me. He never made me believe *he* knew anything about God. And don't think for a minute he'd have done what you and Miss Grover and Mr. Bentley did! He used to cross the street to get out of the way of drunken men — he wouldn't have one of them in his church. And I know of a girl he drove out of town because she had a baby and her sweetheart wouldn't marry her. He sent her to hell. Hell's *here* — isn't it ? "

These sudden remarks of hers surprised and troubled him. But they had another effect, a constructive effect. He was astonished, in going over such conversations afterwards, to discover that her questions and his efforts to answer them in other than theological terms were both illuminating and stimulating. Sayings in the Gospels leaped out in his mind, fired with new meanings ; so simple, once perceived, that he was amazed not to have seen them before. And then he was conscious of a palpitating joy which left in its wake a profound thankfulness. He made no attempt as yet to correlate these increments, these glimpses of truth into a system, but stored them preciously away.

He taxed his heart and intellect to answer her sensibly

and helpfully, and thus found himself avoiding the logic, the Greek philosophy, the outworn and meaningless phrases of speculation; found himself employing (with extraordinary effect upon them both) the simple words from which many of these theories had been derived. " He that hath seen me *hath* seen the Father." What she saw in Horace Bentley, he explained, *was* God. God wished us to know how to live, in order that we might find happiness, and therefore Christ taught us that the way to find happiness was to teach others how to live, — once we found out. Such was the meaning of Christ's Incarnation, to teach us how to live in order that we might find God and happiness. And Hodder translated for her the word Incarnation.

Now, he asked, how were we to recognize God, how might we know how he wished *us* to live, unless we saw him in human beings, in the souls into which he had entered? In Mr. Bentley's soul? Was this too deep?

She pondered, with flushed face.

" I never had it put to me like that," she said, presently. " I never could have known what you meant if I hadn't seen Mr. Bentley."

Here was a return flash, for him. Thus, teaching he taught. From this germ he was to evolve for himself the sublime truth that the world grows better, not through automatic, soul-saving machinery, but by Personality.

On another occasion she inquired about " original sin," a phrase which had stuck in her memory since the stormings of the Madison preacher. Here was a demand to try his mettle.

" It means," he replied after a moment, " that we are all apt to follow the selfish, animal instincts of our natures, to get all we can for ourselves without thinking of others, to seek animal pleasures. And we always suffer for it."

" Sure," she agreed. " That's what happened to me."

" And unless we see and know some one like Mr. Bentley," he went on, choosing his words, " or discover for ourselves what Christ was, and what he tried to tell us, we go on suffering, because we don't see any way out. We suffer because we feel that we are useless, that other persons are doing our work."

"That's what hell is!" She was very keen. "Hell's here," she repeated.

"Hell may *begin* here, and so may heaven," he answered.

"Why, *he's* in heaven now!" she exclaimed, "it's funny I never thought of it before." Of course she referred to Mr. Bentley.

Thus, by no accountable process of reasoning, he stumbled into the path which was to lead him to one of the widest and brightest of his vistas, the secret of eternity hidden in the Parable of the Talents! But it will not do to anticipate this matter. . . .

The divine in this woman of the streets regenerated by the divine in her fellow-creatures, was gasping like a new-born babe for breath. And with what anxiety they watched her! She grew strong again, went with Sally Grover and the other girls on Sunday excursions to the country, applied herself to her embroidery with restless zeal for days, only to have it drop from her nerveless fingers. But her thoughts were uncontrollable, she was drawn continually to the edge of that precipice which hung over the waters whence they had dragged her, never knowing when the vertigo would seize her. And once Sally Grover, on the alert for just such an occurrence, pursued her down Dalton Street and forced her back. . . .

Justice to Miss Grover cannot be done in these pages. It was she who bore the brunt of the fierce resentment of the reincarnated fiends when the other women shrank back in fear, and said nothing to Mr. Bentley or Hodder until the incident was past. It was terrible indeed to behold this woman revert — almost in the twinkling of an eye — to a vicious wretch crazed for drink, to feel that the struggle had to be fought all over again. Unable to awe Sally Grover's spirit, she would grow piteous.

"For God's sake let me go — I can't stand it. Let me go to hell — that's where I belong. What do you bother with me for? I've got a right." . . .

Once the doctor had to be called. He shook his head, but his eye met Miss Grover's, and he said nothing.

"I'll never be able to pull out, I haven't got the strength," she told Hodder, between sobs. "You ought to have left me be, that was where I belonged. I can't stand it, I tell you. If it wasn't for that woman watching me downstairs, and Sally Grover, I'd have had a drink before this. It ain't any use, I've got so I can't live without it—I don't want to live."

And then remorse, self-reproach, despair, —almost as terrible to contemplate. She swore she would never see Mr. Bentley again, she couldn't face him.

Yet they persisted, and gained ground. She did see Mr. Bentley, but what he said to her, or she to him, will never be known. She didn't speak of it. . . .

Little by little her interest was aroused, her pride in her work stimulated. None was more surprised than Hodder when Sally Grover informed him that the embroidery was really good; but it was thought best, for psychological reasons, to discard the old table-cover with its associations and begin a new one. On occasional evenings she brought her sewing over to Mr. Bentley's, while Sally read aloud to him and the young women in the library. Miss Grover's taste in fiction was romantic; her voice (save in the love passages, when she forgot herself) sing-song, but new and unsuspected realms were opened up for Kate Marcy, who would drop her work and gaze wide-eyed out of the window, into the darkness.

And it was Sally who must be given credit for the great experiment, although she took Mr. Bentley and Hodder into her confidence. On it they staked all. The day came, at last, when the new table-cover was finished. Miss Grover took it to the Woman's Exchange, actually sold it, and brought back the money and handed it to her with a smile, and left her alone.

An hour passed. At the end of it Kate Marcy came out of her room, crossed the street, and knocked at the door of Mr. Bentley's library. Hodder happened to be there.

"Come in," Mr. Bentley said.

She entered, breathless, pale. Her eyes, which had already lost much of the dissipated look, were alight with exaltation. Her face bore evidence of the severity of the hour of conflict, and she was perilously near to tears. She handed Mr. Bentley the money.

"What's this, Kate?" he asked, in his kindly way.

"It's what I earned, sir," she faltered. "Miss Grover sold the table-cover. I thought maybe you'd put it aside for me, like you do for the others."

"I'll take good care of it," he said.

"Oh, sir, I don't ever expect to repay you, and Miss Grover and Mr. Hodder——"

"Why, you are repaying us," he replied, cutting her short, "you are making us all very happy. And Sally tells me at the Exchange they like your work so well they are asking for more. I shouldn't have suspected," he added, with a humorous glance at the rector, "that Mr. Hodder knew so much about embroidery."

He rose, and put the money in his desk, — such was his genius for avoiding situations which threatened to become emotional.

"I've started another one," she told them, as she departed.

A few moments later Miss Grover appeared.

"Sally," said Mr. Bentley, "you're a wise woman. I believe I've made that remark before. You have managed that case wonderfully."

"There was a time," replied Miss Grover, thoughtfully, "when it looked pretty black. We've got a chance with her now, I think."

"I hope so. I begin to feel so," Mr. Bentley declared.

"If we succeed," Miss Grover went on, "it will be through the heart. And if we lose her again, it will be through the heart."

Hodder started at this proof of insight.

"You know her history, Mr. Hodder?" she asked.

"Yes," he said.

"Well, I don't. And I don't care to. But the way to

get at Kate Marcy, light as she is in some respects, is through her feelings. And she's somehow kept 'em alive. We've got to trust her, from now on — that's the only way. And that's what God does, anyhow."

This was one of Miss Grover's rare references to the Deity.

Turning over that phrase in his mind, Hodder went slowly back towards the parish house. God trusted individuals — even such as Kate Marcy. What did that mean? *Individual responsibility!* He repeated it. Was the world on that principle, then? It was as though a search-light were flung ahead of him and he saw, dimly, a new order — a new order in government and religion. And, as though spoken by a voice out of the past, there sounded in his ears the text of that sermon which had so deeply moved him, "I will arise and go to my Father."

The church was still open, and under the influence of the same strange excitement which had driven him to walk in the rain so long ago, he entered and went slowly up the marble aisle. Through the gathering gloom he saw the figure on the cross. And as he stood gazing at it, a message for which he had been waiting blazed up within him.

He would not leave the Church!

CHAPTER XVIII

THE RIDDLE OF CAUSATION

I

IN order to portray this crisis in the life of Kate Marcy, the outcome of which is still uncertain, other matters have been ignored.

How many persons besides John Hodder have seemed to read — in crucial periods — a meaning into incidents having all the outward appearance of accidents! What is it that leads us to a certain man or woman at a certain time, or to open a certain book? Order and design? or influence?

The night when he had stumbled into the café in Dalton Street might well have been termed the nadir of Hodder's experience. His faith had been blotted out, and with it had suddenly been extinguished all spiritual sense. The beast had taken possession. And then, when it was least expected, — nay, when despaired of, had come the glimmer of a light; distant, yet clear. He might have traced the course of his disillusionment, perhaps, but cause and effect were not discernible here.

They soon became so, and in the weeks that followed he grew to have the odd sense of a guiding hand on his shoulder, — such was his instinctive interpretation of it, rather than the materialistic one of things ordained. He might turn, in obedience to what seemed a whim, either to the right or left, only to recognize new blazes that led him on with surer step; and trivial accidents became events charged with meaning. He lived in continual wonder.

One broiling morning, for instance, he gathered up the last of the books whose contents he had a month before

265

so feverishly absorbed, and which had purged him of all fallacies. At first he had welcomed them with a fierce relief, sucked them dry, then looked upon them with loathing. Now he pressed them gratefully, almost tenderly, as he made his way along the shady side of the street towards the great library set in its little park.

He was reminded, as he passed from the blinding sunlight into the cool entrance hall, with its polished marble stairway and its statuary, that Eldon Parr's munificence had made the building possible : that some day Mr. Parr's bust would stand in that vestibule with that of Judge Henry Goodrich — Philip Goodrich's grandfather — and of other men who had served their city and their commonwealth.

Upstairs, at the desk, he was handing in the volumes to the young woman whose duty it was to receive them when he was hailed by a brisk little man in an alpaca coat, with a skin like brown parchment.

" Why, Mr. Hodder," he exclaimed cheerfully, with a trace of German accent, " I had an idea you were somewhere on the cool seas with our friend, Mr. Parr. He spoke, before he left, of inviting you."

It had been Eldon Parr, indeed, who had first brought Hodder to the library, shortly after the rector's advent, and Mr. Engel had accompanied them on a tour of inspection; the financier himself had enjoined the librarian to "take good care " of the clergyman. Mr. Waring, Mr. Atterbury, and Mr. Constable were likewise trustees. And since then, when talking to him, Hodder had had a feeling that Mr. Engel was not unconscious of the aura — if it may be called such — of his vestry.

Mr. Engel picked up one of the books as it lay on the counter, and as he read the title his face betrayed a slight surprise.

" Modern criticism ! " he exclaimed.

" You have found me out," the rector acknowledged, smiling.

" Come into my room, and have a chat," said the librarian, coaxingly.

It was a large chamber at the corner of the building, shaded by awnings, against which brushed the branches of an elm which had belonged to the original park. In the centre of the room was a massive oak desk, one whole side of which was piled high with new volumes.

"Look there," said the librarian, with a quick wave of his hand, "those are some which came in this week, and I had them put here to look over. Two-thirds of 'em on religion, or religious philosophy. Does that suggest anything to you clergymen?"

"Do many persons read them, Mr. Engel?" said the rector, at length.

"Read them!" cried Mr. Engel, quizzically. "We librarians are a sort of weather-vanes, if people only knew enough to consult us. We can hardly get a sufficient number of these new religious books — the good ones, I mean — to supply the demand. And the Lord knows what trash is devoured, from what the booksellers tell me. It reminds me of the days when this library was down on Fifth Street, years ago, and we couldn't supply enough Darwins and Huxleys and Spencers and popular science generally. That was an agnostic age. But now you'd be surprised to see the different kinds of men and women who come demanding books on religion — all sorts and conditions. They're beginning to miss it out of their lives; they want to *know*. If my opinion's worth anything, I should not hesitate to declare that we're on the threshold of a greater religious era than the world has ever seen."

Hodder thrust a book back into the pile, and turned abruptly, with a manner that surprised the librarian. No other clergyman to whom he had spoken on this subject had given evidence of this strong feeling, and the rector of St. John's was the last man from whom he would have expected it.

"Do you really think so?" Hodder demanded.

"Why, yes," said Mr. Engel, when he had recovered from his astonishment. "I'm sure of it. I think clergymen especially — if you will pardon me — are apt to forget that this is a reading age. That a great many people who used to get what instruction they had — ahem — from churches, for instance, now get it from books. I don't want to say anything to offend you, Mr. Hodder — "

" You couldn't," interrupted the rector. He was equally surprised at the discovery that he had misjudged Mr. Engel, and was drawn towards him now with a strong sympathy and curiosity.

" Well," replied Mr. Engel, " I'm glad to hear you say that." He restrained a gasp. Was this the orthodox Mr. Hodder of St. John's?

" Why," said Hodder, sitting down, " I've learned, as you have, by experience. Only my experience hasn't been so hopeful as yours — that is, if you regard yours as hopeful. It would be hypocritical of me not to acknowledge that the churches are losing ground, and that those who ought to be connected with them are not. I am ready to admit that the churches are at fault. But what you tell me of people reading these books gives me more courage than I have had for — for some time."

" Is it so ! " ejaculated the little man, relapsing into the German idiom of his youth.

" It is," answered the rector, with an emphasis not to be denied. " I wish you would give me your theory about this phenomenon, and speak frankly."

" But I thought — " the bewildered librarian began. " I saw you had been reading those books, but I thought — "

" Naturally you did," said Hodder, smiling. His personality, his ascendency, his poise, suddenly felt by the other, were still more confusing. " You thought me a narrow, complacent, fashionable priest who had no concern as to what happened outside the walls of his church, who stuck obstinately to dogmas and would give nothing else a hearing. Well, you were right."

" Ah, I didn't think all that," Mr. Engel protested, and his parchment skin actually performed the miracle of flushing. " I am not so stupid. And once, long ago, when I was young, I was going to be a minister myself."

" What prevented you ? " asked Hodder, interested.

"You want me to be frank — yes, well, I couldn't take the vows." The brown eyes of the quiet, humorous, self-contained and dried-up custodian of the city's reading flamed up. "I felt the call," he exclaimed. "You may not credit it to look at me now, Mr. Hodder. They said to me, 'here is what you must swear to believe before you can make men and women happier and more hopeful, rescue them from sin and misery!' You know what it was."

Hodder nodded.

"It was a crime. It had nothing to do with religion. I thought it over for a year — I couldn't. Oh, I have since been thankful. I can see now what would have happened to me — I should have had fatty degeneration of the soul."

The expression was not merely forcible, it was overwhelming. It brought up before Hodder's mind, with sickening reality, the fate he had himself escaped. *Fatty degeneration of the soul!*

The little man, seeing the expression on the rector's face, curbed his excitement, and feared he had gone too far.

"You will pardon me!" he said penitently, "I forget myself. I did not mean all clergymen."

"I have never heard it put so well," Hodder declared. "That is exactly what occurs in many cases."

"Yes, it is that," said Engel, still puzzled, but encouraged, eyeing the strong face of the other. "And they lament that the ministry hasn't more big men. Sometimes they get one with the doctrinal type of mind — a Newman — but how often? And even a Newman would be of little avail to-day. It is Eucken who says that the individual, once released from external authority, can never be turned back to it. And they have been released by the hundreds of thousands ever since Luther's time, are being freed by the hundreds of thousands to-day. Democracy, learning, science, are releasing them, and no man, no matter how great he may be, can stem that tide. The able men in the churches now — like your Phillips

Brooks, who died too soon — are beginning to see this.
They are those who developed after the vows of the
theological schools were behind them. Remove those
vows, and you will see the young men come. Young
men are idealists, Mr. Hodder, and they embrace other
professions where the mind is free, and which are not one
whit better paid than the ministry.

"And what is the result," he cried, "of the senseless
insistence on the letter instead of the spirit of the poetry
of religion?   Matthew Arnold was a thousand times right
when he inferred that Jesus Christ never spoke literally —
and yet he is still being taken literally by most churches,
and all the literal sayings which were put into his mouth
are maintained as Gospel truth!   What is the result of
proclaiming Christianity in terms of an ancient science and
theology which awaken no ..ckening response in the
minds and hearts of to-day?   *That!*" The librarian thrust
a yellow hand towards the pile of books. "The new wine
has burst the old skin and is running all over the world.
Ah, my friend, if you could only see, as I do, the yearning
for a satisfying religion which exists in this big city!
It is like a vacuum, and those books are rushing to supply
it. I little thought," he added dreamily, "when I renounced the ministry in so much sorrow that one day I
should have a church of my own. This library is my
church, and men and women of all creeds come here by
the thousands. But you must pardon me. I have been
carried away — I forgot myself."

"Mr. Engel," replied the rector, "I want you to regard
me as one of your parishioners."

The librarian looked at him mutely, and the practical,
desiccated little person seemed startlingly transformed into
a mediæval, German mystic.

"You are a great man, Mr. Hodder," he said. "I
might have guessed it."

It was one of the moments when protest would have
been trite, superfluous. And Hodder, in truth, felt something great swelling within him, something that was not
himself, and yet strangely was. But just what — in view

"'My God, how you scared me!'"

of his past strict orthodoxy and limited congregation —
Mr. Engel meant, he could not have said. Had the
librarian recognized, without confession on his part, the
change in him? divined his future intentions?

"It is curious that I should have met you this morning,
Mr. Engel," he said. "I expressed surprise when you
declared this was a religious age, because you corroborated
something I had felt, but of which I had no sufficient
proof. I felt that a great body of unsatisfied men and
women existed, but that I was powerless to get in touch
with them; I had discovered that truth, as you have so
ably pointed out, is disguised and distorted by ancient
dogmas; and that the old Authority, as you say, no longer
carries weight."

"Have you found the new one?" Mr. Engel demanded.

"I think I have," the rector answered calmly, "it lies in
personality. I do not know whether you will agree with
me that the Church at large has a future, and I will confess to you that there was a time when I thought she had
not. I see now that she has, once given to her ministers
that freedom to develop of which you speak. In spite of
the fact that truth has gradually been revealed to the
world by what may be called an Apostolic Succession of
Personalities, — Augustine, Dante, Francis of Assisi,
Luther, Shakespeare, Milton, and our own Lincoln and
Phillips Brooks, — to mention only a few, — the Church
as a whole has been blind to it. She has insisted upon
putting the individual in a strait-jacket, she has never
recognized that growth is the secret of life, that the
clothes of one man are binding on another."

"Ah, you are right — a thousand times right," cried
the librarian. "You have read Royce, perhaps, when he
says, 'This mortal shall put on individuality.'"

"No," said the rector, outwardly cool, but inwardly
excited by the coruscation of this magnificent paraphrase
    ul's sentence, by the extraordinary turn the conver-
sation had taken. "I am ashamed to own that I have
not followed the development of modern philosophy. The
books I have just returned, on historical criticism," he

went on, after a moment's hesitation, "infer what my attitude has been toward modern thought. We were made
acquainted with historical criticism in the theological seminary, but we were also taught to discount it. I *have* dis-
counted it, refrained from reading it,—until now. And
yet I have heard it discussed in conferences, glanced over
articles in the reviews. I had, you see, closed the door
of my mind. I was in a state where arguments make no
impression."

The librarian made a gesture of sympathetic assent,
which was also a tribute to the clergyman's frankness.

"You will perhaps wonder how I could have lived these
years in an atmosphere of modern thought and have remained uninfluenced. Well, I have recently been wondering—myself." Hodder smiled. "The name of Royce
is by no means unfamiliar to me, and he taught at Harvard when I was an undergraduate. But the prevailing
philosophy of that day among the students was naturalism.
I represent a revolt from it. At the seminary I imbibed
a certain amount of religious philosophy—but I did not
continue it, as thousands of my more liberal fellow-clergymen have done. My religion 'worked'—during the
time, at least, I remained in my first parish. I had
no interest in reconciling, for instance, the doctrine of
evolution with the argument for design. Since I have
been here in this city," he added, simply, "my days have
been filled with a continued perplexity—when I was not
too busy to think. Yes, there was an unacknowledged
element of fear in my attitude, though I comforted myself
with the notion that opinions, philosophical and scientific,
were in a state of flux."

"Yes, yes," said Mr. Engel, "I comprehend. But,
from the manner in which you spoke just now, I should
have inferred that you have been reading modern philosophy—that of the last twenty years. Ah, you have
something before you, Mr. Hodder. You will thank God,
with me, for that philosophy. It has turned the tide, set
the current running the other way. Philosophy is no
longer against religion, it is with it. And if you were to

ask me to name one of the greatest religious teachers of
our age, I should answer, William James. And there is
Royce, of whom I spoke, — one of our biggest men. The
dominant philosophies of our times have grown up since
Arnold wrote his 'Literature and Dogma,' and they are
in harmony with the quickening social spirit of the age,
which is a religious spirit — a Christian spirit, I call it.
Christianity is coming to its own. These philosophies,
which are not so far apart, are the flower of the thought
of the centuries, of modern science, of that most extraordinary of discoveries, modern psychology. And they
are far from excluding religion, from denying the essential of Christ's teachings. On the other hand, they grant
that the motive-power of the world is spiritual.

"And this," continued Mr. Engel, "brings me to
another aspect of authority. I wonder if it has struck
you? In mediæval times, when a bishop spoke *ex
cathedra*, his authority, so far as it carried weight, came
from two sources. First, the supposed divine charter of
the Church to save and damn. *That* authority is being
rapidly swept away. Second, he spoke with all the
weight of the then accepted science and philosophy. But
as soon as the new science began to lay hold on people's
minds, as — for instance — when Galileo discovered that
the earth moved instead of the sun (and the pope made
him take it back), that second authority began to crumble too. In the nineteenth century science had grown
so strong that the situation looked hopeless. Religion
had apparently irrevocably lost that warrant also, and
thinking men not spiritually inclined, since they had to
make a choice between science and religion, took science
as being the more honest, the more certain.

"And now what has happened? The new philosophies have restored your second Authority, and your first,
as you properly say, is replaced by the conception of Personality. Personality is nothing but the rehabilitation of
the prophet, the seer. Get him, as Hatch says, back into
your Church. The priests with their sacrifices and automatic rites, the logicians, have crowded him out. Why

T

do we read the Old Testament at all? Not for the laws of the Levites, not for the battles and hangings, but for the inspiration of the prophets. The authority of the prophet comes through personality, the source of which is in what Myers calls the infinite spiritual world — in God. It was Christ's own authority.

"And as for your other authority, your ordinary man, when he reads modern philosophy, says to himself, '*this* does not conflict with science!' But he gets no hint, when he goes to most churches, that there is, between the two, no real quarrel, and he turns away in despair. He may accept the pragmatism of James, the idealism of Royce, or even what is called neo realism. In any case, he gains the conviction that a force for good is at work in the world, and he has the incentive to become part of it. . . . But I have given you a sermon!"

"For which I can never be sufficiently grateful," said Hodder, with an earnestness not to be mistaken.

The little man's eyes rested admiringly, and not without emotion, on the salient features of the tall clergyman. And when he spoke again, it was in acknowledgment of the fact that he had read Hodder's purpose.

"You will have opposition, my friend. They will fight you — some persons we know. They do not wish — what you and I desire. But you will not surrender — I know ; . . . Mr. Engel broke off abruptly, and rang a bell on his desk. "I will make out for you a list. I hope you may come in again, often. We shall have other talks, — yes? I am always here."

Then it came to pass that Hodder carried back with him another armful of books. Those he had brought back were the Levellers of the False. These were the Builders of the True.

II

Hodder had known for many years that the writings of Josiah Royce and of William James had "been in the air," so to speak, and he had heard them mentioned at dinner parties by his more intellectual parishioners, such as Mrs. Constable and Martha Preston. Now he was able to smile at his former attitude toward these moderns, whose perusal he had deprecated as treason to the saints! And he remembered his horror on having listened to a fellow-clergyman discuss with calmness the plan of the " Varieties of Religious Experiences." A sacrilegious dissection of the lives of these very saints! The scientific process, the theories of modern psychology applied with *sang froid* to the workings of God in the human soul! Science he had regarded as the proclaimed enemy of religion, and in these days of the apotheosis of science not even sacred things were spared.

Now Hodder saw what the little librarian had meant by an authority restored. The impartial method of modern science had become so firmly established in the mind of mankind by education and reading that the ancient *unscientific* science of the Roman Empire, in which orthodox Christianity was clothed, no longer carried authority. In so far as modern science had discovered truth, religion had no quarrel with it. And if theology pretended to be the science of religion, surely it must submit to the test of the new science! The dogged clinging to the archaic speculations of apologists, saints, and schoolmen had brought religion to a low ebb indeed.

One of the most inspiring books he read was by an English clergyman of his own Church whom he had formerly looked upon as a heretic, with all that the word had once implied. It was a frank yet reverent study of the self-consciousness of Christ, submitting the life and teachings of Jesus to modern criticism and the scientific method. And the Saviour's divinity, rather than being lessened, was augmented. Hodder found it infinitely refreshing that the so-called articles of Christian belief, instead of being put first and their acceptance insisted upon, were made the climax of the investigation.

Religion, he began to perceive, was an *undertaking*, an attempt to find unity and harmony of the soul by adopt-

ing, *after mature thought*, a definite principle in life. If
harmony resulted, — if the principle *worked*, it was true.
Hodder kept an open mind, but he became a pragmatist
so far. Science, on the other hand, was in a sphere by
herself, and need have no conflict with religion ; science
was *not* an undertaking, but an impartial investigation by
close observation of facts in nature. Her object was to
discover truths by these methods alone. She had her
theories, indeed, but they must be submitted to rigorous
tests. This from a book by Professor Perry, an advocate
of the new realism.

On the other hand there were signs that modern
science, by infinitesimal degrees, might be aiding in the
solution of the Mystery. . . .

But religion, Hodder saw, was *trusting*. Not credulous,
silly trusting, but *thoughtful* trusting, accepting such
facts as were definitely known. Faith was trusting,
And faith without works was dead simply because there
could be no faith without works. There was no such
thing as belief that did not result in act.

A paragraph which made a profound impression on
Hodder at that time occurs in James's essay, "Is life
worth living ?"

"Now — what do I mean by 'trusting'? Is the word
to carry with it license to define in detail an invisible
world, and to authorize and excommunicate those whose
trust is different? . . . Our faculties of belief were not
given us to make orthodoxies and heresies withal; they
were given us to *live by*. And to trust our religions demands men first of all to live in the light of them, and to
act as if the invisible world which they suggest were real.
It is a fact of human nature that man can live and die by
the help of a sort of faith that goes without a single dogma
and definition."

Yet it was not these religious philosophies which had
saved him, though the stimulus of their current had started
his mind revolving like a motor. Their function, he
perceived now, was precisely to compel him to see what
had saved him, to reënforce it with the intellect, with the

reason, and enable him to save others.   The current set up,
— by a thousand suggestions of which he made notes, — a
personal construction, coördination, and he had the exhila-
ration of feeling, within him, a creative process all his
own.   Behold a mystery! a paradox! — one of many.
As his strength grew greater day by day, as his vision
grew clearer, he must exclaim with Paul : "Yet not I,
but the grace of God which was with me ! "

He, Hodder, was but an instrument transmitting power.
And yet — oh paradox! — the instrument continued to
improve, to grow stronger, to develop individuality and
personality day by day !   Life, present and hereafter, *was*
growth, development, the opportunity for service in a
Cause.   To cease growing was to die.

He perceived at last the form *all* religion takes is that
of consecration to a Cause, — one of God's many causes.
The meaning of life is to find one's Cause, to lose one's
self in it.   *His* was the liberation of the Word, — now
vouchsafed to him ; the freeing of the spark from under
the ashes.   The phrase was Alison's.   To help liberate
the Church, fan into flame the fire which was to consume the injustice, the tyranny, the selfishness of the
world, until the Garvins, the Kate Marcys, the stunted
children, and anæmic women were no longer possible.

It was Royce who, in one illuminating sentence, solved
for him the puzzle, pointed out whence his salvation had
come.   "*For your cause can only be revealed to you through
some presence that first teaches you to love the unity of the
spiritual life. . . .   You must find it in human shape.*"

Horace Bentley !

He, Hodder, had known this, but known it vaguely,
without sanction.   The light had shone for him even in
the darkness of that night in Dalton Street, when he
thought to have lost it forever.   And he had awakened
the next morning, safe, — safe yet bewildered, like a half
drowned man on warm sands in the sun.

"The will of the spiritual world, the divine will,
revealed in man."   What sublime thoughts, as old as the
Cross itself, yet continually and eternally new !

III

There was still another whose face was constantly before him, and the reflection of her distressed yet undaunted soul, — Alison Parr. The contemplation of her courage, of her determination to abide by nothing save the truth, had had a power over him that he might not estimate, and he loved her as a man loves a woman, for her imperfections. And he loved her body and her mind.

One morning, as he walked back from Mrs. Bledsoe's through an unfrequented, wooded path of the Park, he beheld her as he had summoned her in his visions. She was sitting motionless, gazing before her with clear eyes, as at the Fates. . . .

She started on suddenly perceiving him, but it was characteristic of her greeting that she seemed to feel no surprise at the accident which had brought them together.

"I am afraid," he said, smiling, "that I have broken in on some profound reflections."

She did not answer at once, but looked up at him, as he stood over her, with one of her strange, baffling gazes, in which there was the hint of a welcoming smile.

"Reflection seems to be a circular process with me," she answered. "I never get anywhere — like you."

"Like me!" he exclaimed, seating himself on the bench. Apparently their intercourse, so long as it should continue, was destined to be on the basis of intimacy in which it had begun. It was possible at once to be aware of her disturbing presence, and yet to feel at home in it.

"Like you, yes," she said, continuing to examine him. "You've changed remarkably."

In his agitation at this discovery of hers he again repeated her words.

"Why, you seem happier, you look happier. It isn't only that, I can't explain how you impress me. It struck me when you were talking to Mr. Bentley the other day. You seem to *see* something you didn't see when I first met you, that you didn't see the first time we were at Mr.

fixed — directed.
ᴜᴍᴇ sort — a momentous

"Yes," he replied, "you are right. It's more than remarkable that you should have guessed it."

She remained silent.

"I have decided," he found himself saying abruptly, "to continue in the Church."

Still she was silent, until he wondered whether she would answer him. He had often speculated to himself how she would take this decision, but he could make no surmise from her expression as she stared off into the wood. Presently she turned her head, slowly, and looked into his face. Still she did not speak.

"You are wondering how I can do it," he said.

"Yes," she acknowledged, in a low voice.

"I should like you to know — that is why I spoke of it. You have never asked me, and I have never told you that the convictions I formerly held I lost. And with them, for a while, went *everything*. At least so I believed."

"I knew it," she answered, "I could see that, too."

"When I argued with you, that afternoon, — the last time we talked together alone, — I was trying to convince myself, and you — " he hesitated, " — that there *was* something. The fact that you could not seem to feel it stimulated me."

He read in her eyes that she understood him. And he dared not, nor did he need to emphasize further his own intense desire that she should find a solution of her own.

"I wish you to know what I am telling you for two reasons," he went on. "It was you who spoke the words that led to the opening of my eyes to the situation into which I had been drifting for two years, who compelled me to look upon the inconsistencies and falsities which had gradually been borne in upon me. It was you, I think, who gave me the courage to face this situation squarely, since you possess that kind of courage yourself."

"Oh, no," she cried. "You would have done it anyway."

He paused a moment,

" For this reason, I owed it
you. I have realized, since that first meeting, that you
became my friend then, and that you spoke as a friend.
If you had not believed in my sincerity, you would not
have spoken. I wish you to know that I am fully aware
and grateful for the honour you did me, and that I
realize it is not always easy for you to speak so — to
any one."

She did not reply.

" There is another reason for my telling you now of
this decision of mine to remain a clergyman," he continued.
" It is because I value your respect and friendship, and I
hope you will believe that I would not take this course
unless I saw my way clear to do it with sincerity."

" One has only to look at you to see that you are
sincere," she said gently, with a thrill in her voice that
almost unmanned him. " I told you once that I should
never have forgiven myself if I had wrecked your life.
I meant it. I am very glad."

It was his turn to be silent.

" Just because *I* cannot see how it would be possible to
remain in the Church after one had been — emancipated,
so to speak," — she smiled at him, — "is no reason why
you may not have solved the problem."

Such was the superfine quality of her honesty. Yet
she trusted him! He was made giddy by a desire, which
he fought down, to justify himself before her. His eye
beheld her now as the goddess with the scales in her
hand, weighing and accepting with outward calm the
verdict of the balance. . . . Outward calm, but inner fire.

" It makes no difference," she pursued evenly, bent on
choosing her words, " that I cannot personally understand
your emancipation, that mine is different. I can only see
the preponderance of evil, of deception, of injustice — it
is *that* which shuts out everything else. And it's temper-
amental, I suppose. By looking at you, as I told you, I
can see that your emancipation is positive, while mine
remains negative. You have somehow regained a convic-

tion that the good is predominant, that there is some purpose in the universe."

He assented. Once more she relapsed into thought, while he sat contemplating her profile. She turned to him again with a tremulous smile.

"But isn't a conviction that the good is predominant, that there is a purpose in the universe, a long way from the positive assertions in the Creeds?" she asked. "I remember, when I went through what you would probably call disintegration, and which seemed to me enlightenment, that the Creeds were my first stumbling-blocks. It seemed wrong to repeat them."

"I am glad you spoke of this," he replied gravely. "I have arrived at many answers to that difficulty — which did not give me the trouble I had anticipated. In the first place, I am convinced that it was much more of a difficulty ten, twenty, thirty years ago than it is to-day. That which I formerly thought was a radical tendency towards atrophy, the drift of the liberal party in my own Church and others, as well as that which I looked upon with some abhorrence as the free-thinking speculation of many modern writers, I have now come to see is *recon-struction*. The results of this teaching of religion in modern terms are already becoming apparent, and some persons are already beginning to see that the Creeds express certain elemental truths in frankly archaic language. All this should be explained in the churches and the Sunday schools, — is, in fact, being explained in some, and also in books for popular reading by clergymen of my own Church, both here and in England. We have got past the critical age."

She followed him closely, but did not interrupt.

"I do not mean to say that the Creeds are not the sources of much misunderstanding, but in my opinion they do not constitute a sufficient excuse for any clergyman to abandon his Church on account of them. Indeed there are many who interpret them by modern thought — which is closer to the teachings of Christ than ancient thought — whose honesty cannot be questioned. Personally, I think that the Creeds either ought to be taken out of the service, or changed, or else there should be a note inserted in the service and catechism definitely permitting a liberal interpretation — which is exactly what so many clergymen, candidly, do now.

"When I was ordained a deacon, and then a priest, I took vows which would appear to be literally conflicting. Compelled to choose between these vows, I accept that as supreme which I made when I affirmed that I would teach nothing which I should be persuaded might not be concluded and affirmed by the Scripture. The Creeds were derived from the Scripture — not the Scripture from the Creeds. As an individual among a body of Christians I am powerless to change either the ordinal vows or the Creeds, I am obliged to wait for the consensus of opinion. But if, on the whole, I can satisfy my conscience in repeating the Creeds and reading the service, as other honest men are doing — if I am convinced that I have an obvious work to do in that Church, it would be cowardly for me to abandon that work."

Her eyes lighted up.

"I see what you mean," she said, "by staying in you can do many things that you could not do, you can help to bring about the change, by being frank. That is *your* point of view. You believe in the future of the Church."

"I believe in an universal, Christian organization," he replied.

"But while stronger men are honest," she objected, "are not your ancient vows and ancient Creeds continually making weaker men casuists?"

"Undoubtedly," he agreed vigorously, and thought involuntarily of Mr. Engel's phrase, fatty degeneration of the soul. "Yet I can see the signs, on all sides, of a gradual emancipation, of which I might be deemed an example." A smile came into his eyes, like the sun on a grey-green sea.

"Oh, you could never be a casuist!" she exclaimed, with a touch of vehemence. "You are much too positive. It is just *that* note, which is characteristic of so many clergymen, that note of smoothing-over and apology, which you lack. I could never feel it, even when you were orthodox. And now —— " words failed her as she inspected his ruggedness.

" And now," he took her up, to cover his emotion, " now I am not to be classified ! "

Still examining him, she reflected on this.

" Classified ? " Isn't it because you're so much of an individual that one fails to classify you ? You represent something new to my experience, something which seems almost a contradiction — an emancipated Church."

" You imagined me out of the Church, — but where ? " he demanded.

" That's just it," she wondered intimately, " where ? When I try, I can see no other place for you. Your place *is* in the pulpit."

He uttered a sharp exclamation, which she did not heed.

" I can't imagine you doing institutional work, as it is called, — you're not fitted for it, you'd be wasted in it. You gain by the historic setting of the Church, and yet it does not absorb you. Free to preach your convictions, unfettered, you will have a power over people that will be tremendous. You have a very strong personality."

She set his heart, his mind, to leaping by this unexpected confirmation on her part of his hopes, and yet the man in him was intent upon the woman. She had now the air of detached judgment, while he could not refrain from speculating anxiously on the effect of his future course on her and on their intimate relationship. He forbore from thinking, now, of the looming events which might thrust them apart, — put a physical distance between them, — his anxiety was concerned with the possible snapping of the thread of sympathy which had bound them. In this respect, he dreaded her own future as much as his own. What might *she* do ? For he felt, in her, a potential element of desperation ; a capacity to commit, at any moment, an irretrievable act.

" Once you have made your ideas your own," she mused, " you will have the power of convincing people."

" And yet — "

" And yet " — she seized his unfinished sentence, " you are not at all positive of convincing *me*. I'll give you the credit of forbearing to make proselytes." She smiled at him.

Thus she read him again.

"'If you call making proselytes a desire to communicate a view of life which gives satisfaction — " he began, in his serious way.

"Oh, I *want* to be convinced ! " she exclaimed, penitently, " I'd give anything to feel as you feel. There's something lacking in me, there must be, and I have only seen the disillusionizing side. You infer that the issue of the Creeds will crumble, — preach the new, and the old will fall away of itself. But what *is* the new ? How, practically, do you deal with the Creeds ? We have got off that subject."

" You wish to know ? " he asked.

" Yes — I wish to know."

" The test of any doctrine is whether it can be translated into life, whether it will make any difference to the individual who accepts it. The doctrines expressed in the Creeds must stand or fall by the test. Consider, for instance, the fundamental doctrine in the Creeds, that of the Trinity, which has been much scoffed at. A belief in God, you will admit, *has* an influence on conduct, and the Trinity defines the three chief aspects of the God in whom Christians believe. Of what use to quarrel with the word Person if God be conscious ? And the *character* of God has an influence on conduct. The ancients deemed him wrathful, jealous, arbitrary, and hence flung themselves before him and propitiated him. If the conscious God of the universe be good, he is spoken of as a Father. He is as once, in this belief, Father and Creator. And inasmuch as it is known that the divine qualities enter into man, and that one Man, Jesus, whose composite portrait — it is agreed — could not have been factitiously invented, was *filled* with them, we speak of God in man as the Son. And the Spirit of God that enters into the soul of man,

by a virgin birth, but in a manner acceptable to the educated and spiritually-minded, in terms of the philosophy of
the day. And yet how simply! 'In the beginning was
the Word, and the Word was with God, and the Word
was God.' I prefer John's explanation.

"It is historically true that, in the earlier days when the
Apostles' Creed was put forth, the phrase 'born of the
Virgin Mary' was inserted for the distinct purpose of laying stress on the humanity of Christ, and to controvert
the assertion of the Gnostic sect that he was not born at
all, but appeared in the world in some miraculous way.

"Thus to-day, by the aid of historical research, we are
enabled to regard the Creeds in the light of their usefulness to life.   The myth of the virgin birth probably arose
through the zeal of some of the writers of the Gospels to
prove that the prophecy of Isaiah predicted the advent of
the Jewish Messiah who should be born of a virgin.   Modern scholars are agreed that the word *Olmah* which Isaiah
uses does not mean virgin, but *young woman*.   There is
quite a different Hebrew word for 'virgin.'   The Jews,
at the time the Gospels were written, and before, had
forgotten their ancient Hebrew.   Knowing this mistake,
and how it arose, we may repeat the word Virgin Mary
in the sense used by many early Christians, as designat-
ing the young woman who was the mother of Christ.

"I might mention one or two other phrases, archaic
and obscure. 'The Resurrection of the Body' may refer
to the phenomenon of Christ's reappearance after death,
for which modern psychology may or may not account.
A little reflection, however, convinces one that the phenomenon did take place in *some manner*, or else, I think, we should
never have heard of Christ.   You will remember that the
Apostles fled after his death on the cross, believing what
he had told them was all only a dream.   They were human,
literal and cowardly, and they still needed some kind of
inner, energizing conviction that the individuality persisted after death, that the solution of human life was
victory over it, in order to gain the courage to go out and
preach the Gospel and face death themselves.   And it

was Paul who was chiefly instrumental in freeing the message from the narrow bounds of Palestine and sending it ringing down the ages to us. The miracle doesn't lie in *what Paul saw*, but in the whole man transformed, made incandescent, journeying tirelessly to the end of his days up and down the length and breadth of the empire, labouring, as he says, more abundantly than they all. It is idle to say that the thing which can transform a man's entire nature and life is not a reality."

She had listened, motionless, as under the spell of his words. Self-justification, as he proceeded, might easily have fused itself into a desire to convince her of the truth of his beliefs. But he was not deceived, he knew her well enough to understand, to feel the indomitable spirit of resistance in her. Swayed she could be, but she would not easily surrender.

" There is another phrase," she said after a moment, " which I have never heard explained, 'descended into hell.'"

"It was merely a matter of controverting those who declared Christ was taken from the cross before he died. In the childish science of the time, to say that one descended into hell was to affirm that he was actually dead, since the souls of the departed were supposed to go at once to hell. Hell and heaven were definite places. To say that Christ ascended to heaven and sat on the right hand of the Father is to declare one's faith that his responsible work in the spiritual realm continues."

"And the Atonement? doesn't that imply a sacrifice of propitiation?"

"Atonement may be pronounced At-one-ment," Hodder replied. "The old idea, illustrated by a reference to the sacrifice of the ancients, fails to convey the truth to modern minds. And moreover, as I have inferred, these matters had to be conveyed in symbols until mankind were prepared to grasp the underlying spiritual truths which Christ sought to convey. Orthodox Christianity has been so profoundly affected by the ancient Jewish religion that the conception of God as wrathful and jealous — a God wholly *outside* — has persisted to our times. The Atonement means union with the Spirit of the Universe through vicarious suffering, and experience teaches us that our own sufferings are of no account unless they be for a cause, for the furtherance of the design of the beneficent Spirit which is continually at work. Christ may be said to have died for humanity because he had to suffer death itself in order to reveal the complete meaning of life. You once spoke to me about the sense of sin — 'of being unable to feel it.'"

She glanced at him quickly, but did not speak.

"There is a theory concerning this," he continued, "which has undoubtedly helped many people, and which may be found in the writings of certain modern psychologists. It is that we have a conscious, or lower, *human* self, and a subconscious, or better self. This subconscious self stretches down, as it were, into the depths of the universe and taps the source of spiritual power. And it is through the subconscious self that every man is potentially divine. Potentially, because the conscious self has to reach out by an effort of the will to effect this union with the spiritual in the subconscious, and when it is effected, it comes from the response of the subconscious. Apparently from *without*, as a gift, and therefore, in theological language, it is called *grace*. This is what is meant by being 'born again,' the incarnation of the Spirit in the conscious, or human. The two selves are no longer divided, and the higher self assumes control, — takes the reins, so to speak.

"It is interesting, as a theory. And the fact that it has been seriously combated by writers who deny such a function of the subconscious does not at all affect the reality of the experience.

"Once we have had a vision of the true meaning of life a vision which stirs the energies of our being, what is called 'a sense of sin' inevitably follows. It is the discontent, the regret, in the light of a higher knowledge, for the lost opportunities, for a past life which has been uncontrolled by any unifying purpose, misspent in futile undertakings, wasted, perhaps, in follies and selfish caprices

U

which have not only harmed ourselves but others. Although we struggle, yet by habit, by self-indulgence, by lack of a sustained purpose, we have formed a character from which escape seems hopeless. And we realize that, in order to change ourselves, an actual regeneration of the will is necessary. For a while, perchance, we despair of this. The effort to get out of the rut we have made for ourselves seems of no avail. And it is not, indeed, until we arrive, gradually or otherwise, and through a proper interpretation of the life of Christ, at the *conviction* that we may *even now* become useful in the divine scheme that we have a sense of what is called 'the forgiveness of sins.' This *conviction*, this grace, this faith to embark on the experiment accomplishes of itself the revival of the will, the *rebirth* which we had thought impossible. We discover our task, high or humble, — our cause. We grow marvellously *at one* with God's purpose, and we feel that our will is acting in the same direction as his. And through our own atonement we see the meaning of that other Atonement which led Christ to the Cross. We see that our conviction, our grace, has come through him, and how he died for our sins."

"It's quite wonderful how logical and simple you make it, how thoroughly you have gone into it. You have solved it for yourself — and you will solve it for others — many others."

She rose, and he, too, got to his feet with a medley of feelings. The path along which they walked was already littered with green acorns. A gray squirrel darted ahead of them, gained a walnut and paused, quivering, halfway up the trunk, to gaze back at them. And the glance she presently gave him seemed to partake of the shyness of the wild thing.

"Thank you for explaining it to me," she said.

"I hope you don't think —— " he began.

"Oh, it isn't that!" she cried, with unmistakable reproach. "I asked you — I *made* you tell me. It hasn't seemed at all like — the confessional," she added, and smiled and blushed at the word. "You have put it so nicely, so naturally, and you have given me so much to think about. But it all depends — doesn't it? — upon whether one can *feel* the underlying truth of which you spoke in the first place; it rests upon a sense of the prevailing goodness of things. It seems to me cruel that what is called salvation, the solution of the problem of life, should depend upon an accidental discovery. We are all turned loose with our animal passions and instincts of self-preservation, by an indifferent Creator, in a wilderness, and left to find our way out as best we can. You answer that Christ showed us the way. There are elements in his teaching I cannot accept — perhaps because I have been given a wrong interpretation of them. I shall ask you more questions some day.

"But even then," she continued, "granted that Christ brought the complete solution, as you say, why should so many millions have lived and died, before and after his coming, who had suffered so, and who had never heard of him? That is the way my reason works, and I can't help it. I would help it if I could."

"Isn't it enough," he asked, "to know that a force is at work combating evil, — even if you are not yet convinced that it is a prevailing force? Can you not *trust* that it will be a prevailing force, if your sympathies are with it, without demanding a revelation of the entire scheme of the universe? Of what use is it to doubt the eternal justice?"

"Oh, use!" she cried, "I grant you its uselessness. Doubt seems an ingrained quality. I can't help being a fatalist."

"And yet you have taken your life in your own hands," he reminded her, gently.

"Only to be convinced of its futility," she replied.

Again, momentarily thrust back into himself, he wondered jealously once more what the disillusionments had been of that experience from before which she seemed, at times, ready to draw back a little the veil.

"A sense of futility is a sense of incompleteness," he said, "and generally precedes a sense of power."

" Ah, you have gained that! Yet it must always have been latent in you — you make one feel it. But now! " she exclaimed, as though the discovery had just dawned on her, "now you will need power, now you will have to fight as you have never fought in your life."

He found her enthusiasm as difficult to withstand as her stoicism.

" Yes, I shall have to fight," he admitted. Her partisanship was sweet.

" When you tell them what you have told me," she continued, as though working it out in her own mind, " they will never submit to it, if they can help it. My father will never submit to it. They will try to put you out, as a heretic, — won't they?"

" I have an idea that they will," he conceded, with a smile.

" And won't they succeed? Haven't they the power?"

" It depends, in the first place, on whether the bishop thinks me a heretic."

" Have you asked him?"

" No."

" But can't they make you resign?"

" They can deprive me of my salary."

She did not press this.

" You mustn't think me a martyr," he pleaded, in a lighter tone.

She paid no heed to this protest, but continued to regard him with a face lighted by enthusiasm.

" Oh, that's splendid of you! " she cried. " You are going to speak the truth as you see it, and let them do their worst. Of course, fundamentally, it isn't merely because they're orthodox that they won't like it, although they'll say so, and perhaps think so. It will be because — if you have really found the truth — they will instinctively fear its release. For it has a *social* bearing, too — hasn't it? — although you haven't explained that part of it."

" It has a distinct social bearing," he replied, amazed at the way her mind flew forward and grasped the entire issue, in spite of the fact that her honesty still refused to concede his premises. Such were the contradictions in her that he loved. And, though she did not suspect it, she had in her the Crusader's spirit. "I have always remembered what you once said, that many who believed themselves Christians had an instinctive feeling that there is a spark in Christianity which, if allowed to fly, would start a conflagration beyond their control. And that they had covered the spark with ashes. I, too," he added whimsically, "was buried under the ashes."

"And the spark," she demanded, "is not Socialism — their nightmare?"

"The spark is Christianity itself — but I am afraid they will not be able to distinguish it from Socialism. The central paradox in Christianity consists in the harmonizing of the individual and socialistic spirit, and this removes it as far from the present political doctrine of socialism as it is possible to be. Christianity, looked at from a certain viewpoint, — and I think the proper viewpoint, — is the most individualistic of religions, since its basic principle is the development of the individual into an autonomous being."

They stood facing each other on an open stretch of lawn. The place was deserted. Through the trees, in the near distance, the sightless front of the Ferguson mansion blazed under the September sun.

"Individualistic!" she repeated, as though dazed by the word applied to the religion she had discarded. "I can't understand. Do you think I ever *can* understand?" she asked him, simply.

"It seems to me you understand more than you are willing to give yourself credit for," he answered seriously. "You don't take into account your attitude."

"I see what you mean — a willingness to take the right road, if I can find it. I am not at all sure that I *want* to take it. But you must tell me more — more of what you have discovered. Will you?"

He just hesitated. She herself appeared to acknowledge no bar to their further intimacy — why should he?

"I will tell you all I know," he said.

Suddenly, as if by a transference of thought, she voiced what he had in mind.

"You are going to tell them the truth about themselves!" she exclaimed. "That they are not Christians!"

His silence was an admission.

"You must see," he told her, after the moment they had looked into each other's faces, "that this is the main reason why I must stay at St. John's, in the Church, if I conscientiously can."

"I see. The easier course would be to resign, to have scruples. And you believe there is a future for the Church."

"I believe it," he assented.

She still held his eyes.

"Yes, it *is* worth doing. If you see it that way it is more worth doing than anything else. Please don't think," she said, "that I don't appreciate why you have told me all this, why you have given me your reasons. I know it hasn't been easy. It's because you wish me to have faith in you for my *own* sake, not for yours. And I am grateful."

"And if that faith is justified, as you will help to justify it, that it may be transferred to a larger sphere," he answered.

She gave him her hand, but did not reply.

CHAPTER XIX

MR. GOODRICH BECOMES A PARTISAN

I

In these days of his preparation, she haunted him continually. In her he saw typified all those who possessed the divine discontent, the yearning unsatisfied, — the fatalists and the dreamers. And yet she seemed to have risen through instinct to share the fire of his vision of religion revealed to the countless ranks of strugglers as the hidden motive-power of the world, the impetus of scientist, statesman, artist, and philanthropist! They had stood together on the heights of the larger view, whence the whole of the battle-line lay disclosed.

At other and more poignant moments he saw her as waving him bravely on while he steamed out through towering seas to safety. The impression was that of smiling at her destiny. Had she fixed upon it? and did she linger now only that she might inspire him in his charge? She was capable, he knew, of taking calmly the irrevocable step, of accepting the decree as she read it. The thought tortured, the desire to save her from herself obsessed him; with true clairvoyance she had divined him aright when she had said that he wished her to have faith in him for her own sake. Could he save her in spite of herself? and how? He could not see her, except by chance. Was she waiting until he should have crossed the bar before she should pay some inexorable penalty of which he knew nothing?

Thus he speculated, suffered, was at once cast down and lifted up by the thought of her. To him, at least, she was one of those rare and dauntless women, the red

stars of history, by whom the Dantes and Leonardos are
fired to express the inexpressible, and common clay is
fused and made mad: one of those women who, the more
they reveal, become the more inscrutable.   Divinely inarticulate, he called her ; arousing the passion of the man,
yet stirring the sublimer efforts of the god.

What her feelings toward him, whether she loved him
as a woman loves a man he could not say, no man being a
judge in the supreme instance.   She beheld him emancipated, perhaps, from what she might have called the fetters of an orthodoxy for which she felt an instinctive
antagonism ; but whether, though proclaiming himself
free, the fact of his continuation in the ministry would
not of itself set up in her a reaction, he was unable to
predict.   Her antipathy to forms, he saw, was inherent.
Her interest — her fascinated absorption, it might be
called — in his struggle was spiritual, indeed, but it also
had mixed in it the individualistic zeal of the non-conform-
ist.   She resented the trammels of society, though she
suffered from her efforts to transcend them.   The course
he had determined upon appeared to her as a rebellion
not only against a cut-and-dried state of mind, but also
against vested privilege.   Yet she had in her, as she
confessed, the craving for what privilege brings in the
way of harmonious surroundings.   He loved her for her
contradictions.

Thus he was utterly unable to see what the future held
for him in the way of continued communion with her, to
evolve any satisfactory theory as to why she remained in
the city.   She had told him that the gardens were an excuse.   She had come, by her own intimation, to reflect,
to decide some momentous question.   Marriage ?   He
found this too agitating to dwell upon, summoning, as it
did, conjectures of the men she might have known ; and
it was perhaps natural, in view of her attitude, that he
could only think of such a decision on her part as surrender.

That he had caught and held her attention, although
by no conscious effort of his own, was clear to him.   But

had he not merely arrested her? Would she not presently disappear, leaving only in his life the scarlet thread
which she had woven into it for all time? Would he not
fail to change, permanently, the texture of hers?

Such were his hopes and fears concerning her, and they
were mingled inextricably with other hopes and fears
which had to do with the great venture of his life. He
dwelt in a realm of paradoxes, discovered that exaltation
was not incompatible with anxiety and dread. He had
no thought of wavering; he had achieved to an extent he
would not have believed possible the sense of consecration
which brings with it indifference to personal fortunes, and
the revelation of the inner world, and yet he shrank from
the wounds he was about to receive — and give. Outwardly controlled, he lived in the state of intense excitement of the leader waiting for the time to charge. . . .

II

The moment was at hand. September had waned, the
nights were cooling, his parishioners were returning from
the East. One of these was Eleanor Goodrich, whom he
met on a corner, tanned and revived from her long summer in Massachusetts. She had inherited the kindly
shrewdness of glance characteristic of gentlefolk, the
glance that seeks to penetrate externals in its concern for
the well-being of those whom it scrutinizes. And he was
subtly aware, though she greeted him cordially, that she
felt a change in him without being able to account
for it.

"I hear you have been here all summer," she said re-
proachfully. "Mother and father and all of us were
much disappointed that you did not come to us on the
Cape."

"I should have come, if it had been possible," he replied. "It seems to have done you a world of good."

"Oh, I!" She seemed slightly embarrassed, puzzled,
and did not look at him. "I am burned as disgracefully
as Evelyn. Phil came on for a month. He tells me he

hasn't seen you, but that isn't surprising, for he hasn't
been to church since June — and he's a vestryman now,
too."

She was in mourning for her father-in-law, who had
died in the spring. Phil Goodrich had taken his place.
Eleanor found the conversation, somehow, drifting out of
her control. It was not at all what she would have desired to say. Her colour heightened.

"I have not been conducting the services, but I resume
them next Sunday," said the rector. "I ought to tell
you," he went on, regarding her, "in view of the conversation we have had, that I have changed my mind concerning a great many things we have talked about — although I have not spoken of this as yet to any of the
members of the congregation."

She was speechless, and could only stare at him blankly.

"I mean," he continued, with a calmness that astonished
her afterwards, "that I have changed my whole conception as to the functions and future of the Church, that I
have come to your position, that we must make up our
minds for ourselves, and not have them made up for us.
And that we must examine into the truth of all statements, and be governed accordingly."

Her attitude was one of mingled admiration, concern,
and awe. And he saw that she had grasped something
of the complications which his course was likely to bring
about.

"But you are not going to leave us!" she managed to
exclaim.

"Not if it is possible to remain," he said, smiling.

"I am so glad." She was still overpowered by the disclosure. "It is good of you to tell me. Do you mind
my telling Phil?"

"Not at all," he assured her.

"Will you forgive me," she asked, after a slight pause
during which she had somewhat regained her composure,
"if I say that I always thought, or rather hoped you
would change? that your former beliefs seemed so — unlike you?"

He continued to smile at her as she stepped forward to take the car.

"I'll have to forgive you," he answered, "because you were right. . . ."

She was still in such a state of excitement when she arrived down town that she went direct to her husband's law office.

"I like this!" he exclaimed, as, unannounced, she opened the door of his sanctuary. "You might have caught me with one of those good-looking clients of mine."

"Oh, Phil!" she cried, "I've got such a piece of news, I couldn't resist coming to tell you. I met Mr. Hodder — and he's changed."

"Changed!" Phil repeated, looking up at her flushed face beside him. Instead of a law-book, he flung down a time table in which he had been investigating the trains to a quail shooting club in the southern part of the state. The transition to Mr. Hodder was, therefore, somewhat abrupt. "Why, Nell, to look at you, I thought it could be nothing else than my somewhat belated appointment to the United States Supreme Court. How has Hodder changed? I always thought him pretty decent."

"Don't laugh at me," she begged, "it's really serious — and no one knows it yet. He said I might tell you. Do you remember that talk we had at father's, when he first came, and we likened him to a modern Savonarola?"

"And George Bridges took the floor, and shocked mother and Lucy and Laureston," supplied Phil.

"I don't believe mother really was as much shocked as she appeared to be," said Eleanor. "At any rate, the thing that had struck us — you and me — was that Mr. Hodder looked as though he *could* say something helpful, if he only *would*. And then I went to see him afterwards, in the parish house — you remember? — after we had been reading modern criticism together, and he told me that the faith which had come down from the fathers was like an egg? It couldn't be chipped. I was awfully disappointed — and yet I couldn't help liking him, he was so nonest. And the theological books he gave me to read — which were so mediæval and absurd ! Well, he has come around to our point of view. He told me so himself."

"But what *is* our point of view, Nell?" her husband asked, with a smile. "Isn't it a good deal like Professor Bridges', only we're not quite so learned? We're just ordinary heathens, as far as I can make out. If Hodder has our point of view, he ought to go into the law or a trust company."

"Oh, Phil!" she protested, "and you're on the vestry! I do believe in Something, and so do you."

"*Something*," he observed, "is hardly a concrete and complete theology."

"Why do you make me laugh," she reproached him, "when the matter is so serious? What I'm trying to tell you is that I'm sure Mr. Hodder has worked it out. He's too sincere to remain in the Church and not have something constructive and satisfying. I've always said that he seemed to have a truth shut up inside of him which he could not communicate. Well, now he *looks* as though he were about to communicate it, as though he *had* discovered it. I suppose you think me silly, but you'll grant, whatever Mr. Hodder may be, *he* isn't silly. And women can feel these things. You know I'm not given to sentimentality, but I was never so impressed by the growth in any personality as I was this morning by his. He seems to have become himself, as I always imagined him. And, Phil, he was so fine ! He's absolutely incapable of posing, as you'll admit, and he stood right up and acknowledged that he'd been wrong in our argument. He hasn't had the services all summer, and when he resumes them next Sunday I gathered that he intends to make his new position clear."

Mr. Goodrich thrust his hands in his pockets and gave a low whistle.

"I guess I won't go shooting Saturday, after all," he declared. "I wouldn't miss Hodder's sermon for all the quail in Harrington County."

"It's high time you did go to church," remarked

Eleanor, contemplating, not without pride, her husband's close-cropped, pugnacious head.

"Your judgments *are* pretty sound, Nell. I'll do you that credit. And I've always owned up that Hodder would be a fighter if he ever got started. It's written all over him. What's more, I've a notion that some of our friends are already a little suspicious of him."

"You mean Mr. Parr?" she asked, anxiously.

"No, Wallis Plimpton."

"Oh!" she exclaimed, with disdain in her voice.

"Mr. Parr only got back yesterday, and Wallis told me that Hodder had refused to go on a yachting trip with him. Not only foolishness, but high treason." Phil smiled. "Plimpton's the weather-vane, the barometer of that crowd — he feels a disturbance long before it turns up — he's as sensitive as the stock market."

"He *is* the stock market," said Eleanor.

"It's been my opinion," Phil went on reflectively, "that they've all had just a trace of uneasiness about Hodder all along, an idea that Nelson Langmaid slipped up for the first time in his life when he got him to come. Oh, the feeling's been dormant, but it existed. And they've been just a little afraid that they couldn't handle him if the time ever came. He's not their type. When I saw Plimpton at the Country Club the other day he wondered, in that genial, off-hand manner of his, whether Hodder would continue to be satisfied with St. John's. Plimpton said he might be offered a missionary diocese. Oh, we'll have a fine old row."

"I believe," said Eleanor, "that *that's* the only thing that interests you."

"Well, it does please me," he admitted, "when I think of Gordon Atterbury and Everett Constable and a few others, — Eldon Parr, — who believe that religion ought to be kept archaic and innocuous, served in a form that won't bother anybody. By the way, Nell, do you remember the verse the Professor quoted about the Pharisees, and cleansing the outside of the cup and platter?"

"Yes," she answered, "why?"

"Well — Hodder didn't give you any intimation as to what he intended to do about that sort of thing, did he?"

"What sort of thing?"

"About the inside of Eldon Parr's cup, — so to speak. And the inside of Wallis Plimpton's cup, and Everett Constable's cup, and Ferguson's cup, and Langmaid's. Did it ever strike you that, in St. John's, we have the sublime spectacle of Eldon Parr, the Pharisee in chief, conducting the Church of Christ, who uttered that denunciation? That's what George Bridges meant. There's something rather ironical in such a situation, to say the least."

"I see," said Eleanor, thoughtfully.

"And what's more, it's typical," continued Phil, energetically, "the big Baptist church on the Boulevard is run by old Sedges, as canny a rascal as you could find in the state. The inside of *his* cup has never been touched, though he was once immersed in the Mississippi, they say, and swallowed a lot of water."

"Oh, Phil!"

"Hodder's been pretty intimate with Eldon Parr — that always puzzled me," Phil went on. "And yet I'm like you, I never doubted Hodder's honesty. I've always been curious to know what would happen when he found out the kind of thing Eldon Parr is doing every day in his life, making people stand and deliver in the interest of what he would call National Prosperity. Why, that fellow, Funk, they sent to the penitentiary the other day for breaking into the Addicks' house isn't a circumstance to Eldon Parr. He's robbed his tens of thousands, and goes on robbing them right along. By the way, Mr. Parr took most of Addicks' money before Funk got his silver."

"Phil, you have such a ridiculous way of putting things! But I suppose it's true."

"True! I should say it was! There was Mr. Bentley — that was mild. And there never was a hold-up of a western express that could compare to the Consolidated Tractions. Some of these big fellows have the same kind of

Congress!   And Mr. Plimpton was the more hurt since the happy suggestion was his own, and he had had no little difficulty in getting Mr. Beatty to agree to it.

Yet Mr. Plimpton's career in the ennobling rôle of peacemaker had, on the whole, been crowned with such success as to warrant his belief in the principle.   Mr. Parr, for instance,—in whose service, as in that of any other friend, Mr. Plimpton was always ready to act—had had misunderstandings with eminent fianciers, and sometimes with United States Senators.   Mr. Plimpton had made many trips to the Capitol at Washington, sometimes in company with Mr. Langmaid, sometimes not, and on one memorable occasion had come away smiling from an interview with the occupant of the White House himself.

Lest Mr. Plimpton's powers of premonition seem supernatural, it may be well to reveal the comparative simplicity of his methods.   Genius, analyzed, is often disappointing, —Mr. Plimpton's was selective and synthetic.   To illustrate in a particular case, he had met Mr. Parr in New York and had learned that the Reverend Mr. Hodder had not only declined to accompany the banker on a yachting trip, but had elected to remain in the city all summer, in his rooms in the parish house, while conducting no services.   Mr. Parr had thought this peculiar.   On his return home Mr. Plimpton had one day dropped in to see a Mr. Gaines, the real estate agent for some of his property. And Mr. Plimpton being hale-fellow-well-met, Mr. Gaines had warned him jestingly that he would better not let his parson know that he owned a half interest in a certain hotel in Dalton Street, which was leased at a profitable rate.

If Mr. Plimpton felt any uneasiness, he did not betray it.   And he managed to elicit from the agent, in an entirely casual and jovial manner, the fact that Mr. Hodder, a month or so before, had settled the rent of a woman for a Dalton Street flat, and had been curious to discover the name of the owner.   Mr. Gaines, whose business it was to recognize everybody, was sure of Mr. Hodder, although he had not worn clerical clothes.

x

Mr. Plimpton became very thoughtful when he had left the office. He visited Nelson Langmaid in the Parr Building. And the result of the conference was to cause Mr. Langmaid to recall, with a twinge of uneasiness, a certain autumn morning in a room beside Bremerton Lake when he had been faintly yet distinctly conscious of the admonitory whisperings of that sixth sense which had saved him on other occasions.

"Dash it!" he said to himself, after Mr. Plimpton had departed, and he stood in the window and gazed across at the flag on the roof of "Ferguson's." "It would serve me right for meddling in this parson business. Why did I take him away from Jerry Whitely, anyhow?"

It added to Nelson Langmaid's discomfort that he had a genuine affection, even an admiration for the parson in question. He might have known by looking at the man that he would wake up some day,—such was the burden of his lament. And there came to him, ironically out of the past, the very words of Mr. Parr's speech to the vestry after Dr. Gilman's death, that succinct list of qualifications for a new rector which he himself, Nelson Langmaid, had humorously and even more succinctly epitomized. Their "responsibility to the parish, to the city, and to God" had been to find a rector "neither too old nor too young, who would preach the faith as we received it, who was not sensational, and who did not mistake Socialism for Christianity." At the "Socialism" a certain sickly feeling possessed the lawyer, and he wiped beads of perspiration from his dome-like forehead.

He didn't pretend to be versed in theology — so he had declared — and at the memory of these words of his the epithet "ass," self applied, passed his lips. "You want a parson who will stick to his last, not too high or too low or too broad or too narrow, who has intellect without too much initiative . . . and will not get the church uncomfortably full of strangers and run you out of your pews." Thus he had capped the financier. Well, if they had caught a tartar, it served him, Nelson Langmaid, right. He recalled his talk with Gerald Whitely, and how his brother-in-law had lost his temper when they had got on the subject of personality. . . .

Perhaps Wallis Plimpton *could* do something. Langmaid's hopes of this were not high. It may have been that he had suspicions of what Mr. Plimpton would have called Hodder's "reasonableness." One thing was clear — that Mr. Plimpton was frightened. In the sanctuaries, the private confessionals of high finance (and Nelson Langmaid's office may be called so), the more primitive emotions are sometimes exhibited.

"I don't see what business it is of a clergyman, or of any one else, whether I own property in Dalton Street," Mr. Plimpton had said, as he sat on the edge of the lawyer's polished mahogany desk. "What does he expect us to do, — allow our real estate to remain unproductive merely for sentimental reasons? That's like a parson, most of 'em haven't got any more common sense than that. What right has he got to go nosing around Dalton Street? Why doesn't he stick to his church?"

"I thought you fellows were to build him a settlement house there," Langmaid observed.

"On the condition that he wouldn't turn socialist."

"You'd better have stipulated it in the bond," said the lawyer, who could not refrain, even at this solemn moment, from the temptation of playing upon Mr. Plimpton's apprehensions. "I'm afraid he'll make it his business, Wallis, to find out whether you own anything in Dalton Street. I'll bet he's got a list of Dalton Street property in his pocket right now."

Mr. Plimpton groaned.

"Thank God I don't own any of it!" said Langmaid.

"What the deuce does he intend to do?" the other demanded.

"Read it out in church," Langmaid suggested. "It wouldn't sound pretty, Wallis, to be advertised in the *Post* on Monday morning as owning that kind of a hotel."

"Oh, he's a gentleman," said Mr. Plimpton, "he wouldn't do anything as low as that!"

"But if he's become a socialist?" objected Langmaid.

"He wouldn't do it," his friend reiterated, none too confidently. "I shouldn't be surprised if he made me resign from the vestry and forced me to sell my interest. It nets me five thousand a year."

"What is the place?" Langmaid asked sympathetically, "Harrod's?"

Mr. Plimpton nodded.

"Not that I am a patron," the lawyer explained somewhat hastily. "But I've seen the building, going home. It looks to me as if it would burn down some day, Wallis."

"I wish it would," said Mr. Plimpton.

"If it's any comfort to you — to us," Langmaid went on, after a moment, "Eldon Parr owns the whole block above Thirteenth, on the south side — bought it three years ago. He thinks the business section will grow that way."

"I know," said Mr. Plimpton, and they looked at each other.

The name predominant in both minds had been mentioned.

"I wonder if Hodder really knows what he's up against." Mr. Plimpton sometimes took refuge in slang.

"Well, after all, we're not sure yet that he's 'up against' anything," replied Langmaid, who thought the time had come for comfort. "It may all be a false alarm. There's no reason, after all, why a Christian clergyman shouldn't rescue women in Dalton Street, and remain in the city to study the conditions of the neighbourhood where his settlement house is to be. And just because you or I would not be able to resist an invitation to go yachting with Eldon Parr, a man *might* be imagined who had that amount of moral courage."

"That's just it. Hodder seems to me, now I come to think of it, just the kind of John Brown type who wouldn't hesitate to get into a row with Eldon Parr if he thought it was right, and pull down any amount of disagreeable stuff about our ears."

"You're mixing your heroes, Wallis," said Langmaid.

"I can't help it. *You'd* catch it, too, Nelson. What in the name of sense possessed you to get such a man?"

This being a question the lawyer was unable to answer, the conversation came to another pause. And it was then that Mr. Plimpton's natural optimism reasserted itself.

"It isn't *done*, — the thing we're afraid of, that's all," he proclaimed, after a turn or two about the room. "Hodder's a gentleman, as I said, and if he feels as we suspect he does he'll resign like a gentleman and a Christian. I'll have a talk with him — oh, you can trust me! I've got an idea. Gordon Atterbury told me the other day there is a vacancy in a missionary diocese out west, and that Hodder's name had been mentioned, among others, to the bishops for the place. He'd make a rattling missionary bishop, you know, holding services in saloons and knocking men's heads together for profanity, and he boxes like a professional. Now, a word from Eldon Parr might turn the trick. Every parson wants to be a bishop."

Langmaid shook his head.

"You're getting out of your depths, my friend. The Church isn't Wall Street. And missionary bishops aren't chosen to make convenient vacancies."

"I don't mean anything crude," Mr. Plimpton protested. "But a word from the chief layman of a diocese like this, a man who never misses a General Convention, and does everything handsomely, might count, — particularly if they're already thinking of Hodder. The bishops would never suspect we wanted to get rid of him."

"Well," said Langmaid, "I advise you to go easy, all along the line."

"Oh, I'll go easy enough," Mr. Plimpton assented, smiling. "Do you remember how I pulled off old Senator Matthews when everybody swore he was dead set on voting for an investigation in the matter of those coal lands Mr. Parr got hold of in his state?"

"Matthews isn't Hodder, by a long shot," said Langmaid. "If you ask me my opinion, I'll tell you frankly that if Hodder has made up his mind to stay in St. John's a ton of dynamite and all the Eldon Parrs in the nation can't get him out."

"Can't the vestry make him resign?" asked Mr. Plimpton, uncomfortably.

"You'd better go home and study your canons, my friend. Nothing short of conviction for heresy can do it, if he doesn't want to go."

"You wouldn't exactly call him a heretic," Mr. Plimpton said ruefully.

"Would you know a heretic if you saw one?" demanded Langmaid.

"No, but my wife would, and Gordon Atterbury and Constable would, and Eldon Parr. But don't let's get nervous."

"Well, that's sensible at any rate," said Langmaid. . . .

So Mr. Plimpton had gone off optimistic, and felt even more so the next morning after he had had his breakfast in the pleasant dining room of the Gore Mansion, of which he was now master. As he looked out through the open window at the sunshine in the foliage of Waverley Place, the prospect of his being removed from that position of dignity and influence on the vestry of St. John's, which he had achieved, with others, after so much walking around the walls, seemed remote. And he reflected with satisfaction upon the fact that his wife, who was his prime minister, would be home from the East that day. Two heads were better than one, especially if one of the two were Charlotte Gore's. And Mr. Plimpton had often reflected upon the loss to the world, and the gain to himself, that she was a woman.

It would not be gallant to suggest that his swans were geese.

IV

The successful navigation of lower Tower Street, at noonday, required presence of mind on the part of the pedestrian. There were currents and counter-currents, eddies and backwaters, and at the corner of Vine a

veritable maelstrom through which two lines of electric
cars pushed their way, east and west, north and south,
with incessant clanging of bells ; followed by automobiles
with resounding horns, trucks and delivery wagons with
wheels reverberating on the granite.   A giant Irish policeman, who seemed in continual danger of a violent death,
and wholly indifferent to it, stood between the car tracks
and halted the rush from time to time, driving the people
like sheep from one side to the other.   Through the doors
of Ferguson's poured two conflicting streams of humanity,
and wistful groups of young women, on the way from
hasty lunches, blocked the pavements and stared at the
finery behind the plate-glass windows.

The rector, slowly making his way westward, permitted
himself to be thrust hither and thither, halted and shoved
on again as he studied the faces of the throng.   And
presently he found himself pocketed before one of the
exhibits of feminine interest, momentarily helpless, listening to the admiring and envious chorus of a bevy of
diminutive shop-girls on the merits of a Paris gown.   It
was at this moment that he perceived, pushing towards
him with an air of rescue, the figure of his vestryman,
Mr. Wallis Plimpton.

" Well, well, *well!* " he cried, as he seized Hodder by the
arm and pulled him towards the curb.   " What are you
doing here in the marts of trade ?   Come right along with
me to the Eyrie, and we'll have something to eat."

The Eyrie was a famous lunch club, of limited membership, at the top of the Parr Building, where financial
affairs of the first importance were discussed and settled.

Hodder explained that he had lunched at half-past
twelve.

" Well, step into my office a minute.   It does me good
to see you again, upon my word, and I can't let you get
by without a little pow-wow."

Mr. Plimpton's trust company, in Vine Street, resembled
a Greek temple.   Massive but graceful granite columns
adorned its front, while within it was partitioned off with
polished marble and ornamental grills.   In the rear,

guarded by the desks and flanked by the compartments of various subordinates, was the president's private sanctum, and into this holy of holies Mr. Plimpton led the way with the simple, unassuming genial air of the high priest of modern finance who understands men. The room was eloquent almost to affectation of the system and order of great business, inasmuch as it betrayed not the least sign of a workshop. On the dark oak desk were two leather-bound books and a polished telephone. The walls were panelled, there was a stone fireplace with andirons set, a deep carpet spread over the tessellated floor, and three leather-padded armchairs, one of which Mr. Plimpton hospitably drew forward for the rector. He then produced a box of cigars.

"You don't smoke, Mr. Hodder. I always forget. That's the way you manage to keep yourself in such good shape." He drew out a gold match box and seated himself with an air of gusto opposite his guest. "And you haven't had a vacation, they tell me."

"On the contrary," said the rector, "McCrae has taken the services all summer."

"But you've been in the city!" Mr. Plimpton exclaimed, puffing at his cigar.

"Yes, I've been in the city."

"Well, well, I'll bet you haven't been idle. Just between us, as friends, Mr. Hodder, I've often wondered if you didn't work too hard — there's such a thing as being too conscientious, you know. And I've an idea that the rest of the vestry think so. Mr. Parr, for instance. We know when we've got a good thing, and we don't want to wear you out. Oh, we can appreciate your point of view, and admire it. But a little relaxation — eh? It's too bad that you couldn't have seen your way to take that cruise — Mr. Parr was all cut up about it. I guess you're the only man among all of us fairly close to him, who really knows him well," said Mr. Plimpton, admiringly. "He thinks a great deal of you, Mr. Hodder. By the way, have you seen him since he got back?"

"No," Hodder answered."

"The trip did him good. I thought he was a little seedy in the spring — didn't you? Wonderful man! And when I think how he's slandered and abused it makes me hot. And he never says anything, never complains, lives up there all alone, and takes his medicine. That's real patriotism, according to my view. He could retire to-morrow — but he keeps on — why? Because he feels the weight of a tremendous responsibility on his shoulders, because he knows if it weren't for him and men like him upon whom the prosperity of this nation depends, we'd have famine and anarchy on our hands in no time. And look what he's done for the city, without ostentation, mind you! He never blows his own horn — never makes a speech. And for the Church! But I needn't tell *you*. When this settlement house and chapel are finished, they'll be coming out here from New York to get points. By the way, I meant to have written you. Have our revised plans come yet? We ought to break ground in November, oughtn't we?"

"I intend to lay my views on that matter before the vestry at the next meeting," the rector said.

"Well," declared Mr. Plimpton, after a scarcely perceptible pause, "I've no doubt they'll be worth listening to. If I were to make a guess," he continued, with a contemplative smile, blowing a thin stream of smoke towards the distant ceiling, "I should bet that you have spent your summer looking over the ground. I don't say that you have missed your vocation, Mr. Hodder, but I don't mind telling you that for a clergyman, for a man absorbed in spiritual matters, a man who can preach the sermons you preach, you've got more common-sense and business thoroughness than any one I have ever run across in your profession."

"Looking over the ground?" Hodder repeated, ignoring the compliment.

"Sure," said Mr. Plimpton, smiling more benignly than ever. "You mustn't be modest about it. Dalton Street. And when that settlement house is built, I'll guarantee it will be run on a business basis. No nonsense."

"What do you mean by nonsense?" Hodder asked. He did not make the question abrupt, and there was even the hint of a smile in his eyes, which Mr. Plimpton found the more disquieting.

"Why, that's only a form of speech. I mean you'll be practical, efficient, that you'll get hold of the people of that neighbourhood and make 'em see that the world isn't such a bad place after all, make 'em realize that we in St. John's want to help 'em out. That you won't make them more foolishly discontented than they are, and go preaching socialism to them."

"I have no intention of preaching socialism," said Hodder. But he laid a slight emphasis on the word which sent a cold shiver down Mr. Plimpton's spine, and made him wonder whether there might not be something worse than socialism.

"I knew you wouldn't," he declared, with all the heartiness he could throw into his voice. "I repeat, you're a practical, sensible man. I'll yield to none in my belief in the Church as a moral, uplifting, necessary spiritual force in our civilization, in my recognition of her high ideals, but we business men, Mr. Hodder, — as I am sure you must agree, — have got to live, I am sorry to say, on a lower plane. We've got to deal with the world as we find it, and do our little best to help things along. We can't take the Gospel literally, or we should all be ruined in a day, and swamp everybody else. You understand me?"

"I understand you," said the rector.

Mr. Plimpton's cigar had gone out. In spite of himself, he had slipped from the easy-going, casual tone into one that was becoming persuasive, apologetic, strenuous. Although the day was not particularly warm, he began to perspire a little; and he repeated the words over to himself, "I understand you." What the deuce *did* the rector know? He had somehow the air of knowing *everything*, — more than Mr. Plimpton did. And Mr. Plimpton was beginning to have the unusual and most disagreeable feeling of having been weighed in the balance and found wanting. He glanced at his guest, who sat quite still,

the head bent a trifle, the disturbing gray eyes fixed contemplatively on him — accusingly.   And yet the accusation did not seem personal with the clergyman, whose eyes
were apparently the medium, the channels of a greater, an
impersonal justice.   It was true that the man had
changed.   He was wholly baffling to Mr. Plimpton, whose
sense of alarm increased momentarily into an almost panicky feeling as he remembered what Langmaid had said.
Was this inscrutable rector of St. John's gazing, know-
ingly, at the half owner of Harrod's Hotel in Dalton Street,
who couldn't take the Gospel literally?   There was, evidently, no way to find out at once, and suspense would be
unbearable.   In vain he told himself that these thoughts
were nonsense, the discomfort persisted, and he had visions
of that career in which he had become one of the first citizens and the respected husband of Charlotte Gore crashing down about his ears.   Why?   Because a clergyman
should choose to be quixotic, fanatical?   He did not *look*
quixotic, fanatical, — Mr. Plimpton had to admit, — but a
good deal saner than he, Mr. Plimpton, must have appeared at that moment.   His throat was dry, and he
didn't even dare to make the attempt to relight his cigar.

"There's nothing like getting together — keeping in
touch with people, Mr. Hodder," he managed to say.
"I've been out of town a good deal this summer — putting
on a little flesh, I'm sorry to admit.   But I've been meaning to drop into the parish house and talk over those revised
plans with you.   I will drop in — in a day or two.   I'm
interested in the work, intensely interested, and so is Mrs.
Plimpton.   She'll help you.   I'm sorry you can't lunch
with me."

He had the air, now, of the man who finds himself dis-
agreeably and unexpectedly closeted with a lunatic; and
his language, although he sought to control it, became
even a trifle less coherent.

"You must make allowances for us business men, Mr.
Hodder.   I mean, of course, we're sometimes a little lax
in our duties — in the summer, that is.   Don't shoot the
pianist, he's doing his — ahem!   You know the story.

By the way, I hear great things of you ; I'm told it's on the cards that you're to be made a bishop."

"Oh," answered the rector, "there are better men mentioned than I."

"I want you to know this," said his vestryman, as he seized Hodder's hand, "much as we value you here, bitterly as we should hate to lose you, none of us, I am sure, would stand in the way of such a deserved advancement."

"Thank you, Mr. Plimpton," said the rector.

Mr. Plimpton watched the vigorous form striding through the great chamber until it disappeared. Then he seized his hat and made his way as rapidly as possible through the crowds to the Parr Building. At the entrance of the open-air roof garden of the Eyrie he ran into Nelson Langmaid.

"You're the very man I'm after," said Mr. Plimpton, breathlessly. "I stopped in your office, and they said you'd gone up."

"What's the matter, Wallis?" inquired the lawyer, tranquilly. "You look as if you'd lost a couple of bonds."

"I've just seen Hodder, and he *is* going to do it."

"Do what?"

"Sit down here, at this table in the corner, and I'll tell you."

For a practical man, it must be admitted that Mr. Plimpton had very little of the concrete to relate. And it appeared on cross-examination by Mr. Langmaid, — who ate his cold meat and salad with an exasperating and undiminished appetite — that the only definite thing the rector had said was that he didn't intend to preach socialism. This was reassuring.

"Reassuring!" exclaimed Mr. Plimpton, whose customary noonday hunger was lacking, "I wish you could have heard him say it!"

"The wicked," remarked the lawyer, "flee when no man pursueth. Don't shoot the pianist!" Langmaid set down his beer, and threw back his head and laughed. "If I were the Reverend Mr. Hodder, after such an exhibi·

tion as you gave, I should immediately have suspected the pianist of *something*, and I should have gone off by myself and racked my brains and tried to discover what it was. He's a clever man, and if he hasn't got a list of Dalton Street property now he'll have one by to-morrow, and the story of some of your transactions with Tom Beatty and the City Council."

"I believe you'd joke in the electric chair," said Mr. Plimpton, resentfully. "I'll tell you this, — and my experience backs me up, — if you can't get next to a man by a little plain talk, he isn't safe. I haven't got the market sense for nothing, and I'll give you this tip, Nelson, — it's time to stand from under. Didn't I warn you fellows that Bedloe Hubbell meant business long before he started in ? and this parson can give Hubbell cards and spades. Hodder can't see this thing as it is. He's been thinking, this summer. And a man of that kind is downright dangerous when he begins to think. He's found out things, and he's put two and two together, and he's the uncompromising type. He has a notion that the Gospel *can* be taken literally, and I could feel all the time I was talking to him he thought I was a crook."

" Perhaps he was right," observed the lawyer.

" That comes well from you," Mr. Plimpton retorted.

" Oh, I'm a crook, too," said Langmaid. "I discovered it some time ago. The difference between you and me, Wallis, is that I am willing to acknowledge it, and you're not. The whole business world, as we know it, is crooked, and if we don't cut other people's throats, they'll cut ours."

"And if we let go, what would happen to the country ? " his companion demanded.

Langmaid began to shake with silent laughter.

"Your solicitude about the country, Wallis, is touching. I was brought up to believe that patriotism had an element of sacrifice in it, but I can't see ours. And I can't imagine myself, somehow, as a Hercules bearing the burden of our Constitution. From Mr. Hodder's point of view, perhaps, — and I'm not sure it isn't the right one, —

the pianist *is* doing his damnedest, to the tune of — Dalton
Street.   We might as well look this thing in the face, my
friend.   You and I really don't believe in another world,
or we shouldn't be taking so much trouble to make this
one as we'd like to have it."

"I never expected to hear *you* talk this way," said Mr.
Plimpton.

"Well, it's somewhat of a surprise to me," the lawyer
admitted.

"And I don't think you put it fairly," his friend contended.   "I never can tell when you are serious, but this
is damned serious.   In business we have to deal with
crooks, who hold us up right and left, and if we stood
back you know as well as I do that everything would go
to pot.   And if we let the reformers have their way the
country would be bedlam.   We'd have anarchy and blood-
shed, revolution, and the people would be calling us, the
strong men, back in no time.   You can't change human
nature.   And *we* have a sense of responsibility — *we* support law and order and the Church, and found institutions, and give millions away in charity."

The big lawyer listened to this somewhat fervent defence of his order with an amused smile, nodding his head
slightly from side to side.

"If you don't believe in it," demanded Mr. Plimpton,
"why the deuce don't you drop it?"

"It's because of my loyalty," said Langmaid.   "I
wouldn't desert my pals.   I couldn't bear, Wallis, to see
you go to the guillotine without me."

Mr. Plimpton became unpleasantly silent.

"Well, you may think it's a joke," he resumed, after a
moment, "but there *will* be a guillotine if we don't look
out.   That confounded parson is getting ready to spring
something, and I'm going to give Mr. Parr a tip.   He'll
know how to handle him.   He doesn't talk much, but
I've got an idea, from one or two things he let drop, that
he's a little suspicious of a change in Hodder.   But he
ought to be warned."

"You're in no condition to talk to Mr. Parr, or to any

one else, except your wife, Wallis," Langmaid said. "You'd better go home, and let me see Mr. Parr. I'm responsible for Mr. Hodder, anyway."

"All right," Mr. Plimpton agreed, as though he had gained some shred of comfort from this thought. "I guess *you're* in worse than any of us."

CHAPTER XX

THE ARRAIGNMENT

I

Looking backward, Hodder perceived that he had really come to the momentous decision of remaining at St. John's in the twilight of an evening when, on returning home from seeing Kate Marcy at Mr. Bentley's he had entered the darkening church. It was then that his mission had appeared to him as a vision. Every day, afterward, his sense and knowledge of this mission had grown stronger.

To his mind, not the least of the trials it was to impose upon him, and one which would have to be dealt with shortly, was a necessary talk with his assistant, McCrae. If their relationship had from the beginning been unusual and unsatisfactory, adjectives would seem to defy what it had become during the summer. What *did* McCrae think of him? For Hodder had, it will be recalled, bidden his assistant good-by — and then had remained. At another brief interview, during which McCrae had betrayed no surprise, uttered no censure or comment, Hodder had announced his determination to remain in the city, and to take no part in the services. An announcement sufficiently astounding. During the months that followed, they had met, at rare intervals, exchanged casual greetings, and passed on. And yet Hodder had the feeling, more firmly planted than ever, that McCrae was awaiting, with an interest which might be called suspense, the culmination of the process going on within him.

Well, now that he had worked it out, now that he had reached his decision, it was incumbent upon him to tell his assistant what that decision was. Hodder shrank from it as from an ordeal. His affection for the man, his admiration for McCrae's faithful, untiring, and un-recognized services had deepened. He had a theory that McCrae really liked him — would even sympathize with his solution; yet he procrastinated. He was afraid to put his theory to the test. It was not that Hodder feared that his own solution was not the right one, but that McCrae might not find it so: he was intensely concerned that it should also be McCrae's solution, — the answer, if one liked, to McCrae's mute and eternal questionings. He wished to have it a fruition for McCrae as well as for himself; since theoretically, at least, he had pierced the hard crust of his assistant's exterior, and conceived him beneath to be all suppressed fire. In short, Hodder wished to go into battle side by side with McCrae. Therein lay his anxiety.

Another consideration troubled him — McCrae's family, dependent on a rather meagre salary. His assistant, in sustaining him in the struggle he meant to enter, would be making even a greater sacrifice than himself. For Hodder had no illusions, and knew that the odds against him were incalculable. Whatever, if defeated, his own future might be, McCrae's was still more problematical and tragic.

The situation, when it came, was even more difficult than Hodder had imagined it, since McCrae was not a man to oil the wheels of conversation. In silence he fol-lowed the rector up the stairs and into his study, in silence he took the seat at the opposite side of the table. And Hodder, as he hesitated over his opening, contem-plated in no little perplexity and travail the gaunt and non-committal face before him.

"McCrae," he began at length, "you must have thought my conduct this summer most peculiar. I wish to thank you, first of all, for the consideration you have shown me, and to tell you how deeply I appreciate your taking the entire burden of the work of the parish."

McCrae shook his head vigorously, but did not speak.

Y

"I owe it to you to give you some clew to what happened to me," the rector continued, "although I have an idea that you do not need much enlightenment on this matter. I have a feeling that you have somehow been aware of my discouragement during the past year or so, and of the causes of it. You yourself hold ideals concerning the Church which you have not confided to me. Of this I am sure. I came here to St. John's full of hope and confidence, gradually to lose both, gradually to realize that there was something wrong with me, that in spite of all my efforts I was unable to make any headway in the right direction. I became perplexed, dissatisfied — the results were so meagre, so out of proportion to the labour. And the very fact that those who may be called our chief parishioners had no complaint merely added to my uneasiness. *That* kind of success didn't satisfy me, and I venture to assume it didn't satisfy you."

Still McCrae made no sign.

"Finally I came to what may be termed a double conclusion. In the first place, I began to see more and more clearly that our modern civilization is at fault, to perceive how completely it is conducted on the materialistic theory of the survival of the fittest rather than that of the brotherhood of man, and that those who mainly support this church are, consciously or not, using it as a bulwark for the privilege they have gained at the expense of their fellow-citizens. And my second conclusion was that Christianity must contain some vital germ which I had somehow missed, and which I must find if I could, and preach and release it. That it was the release of this germ these people feared unconsciously. I say to you, at the risk of the accusation of conceit, that I believed myself to have a power in the pulpit if I could only discover the truth."

Hodder thought he detected, as he spoke these words, a certain relaxation of the tension.

"For a while, as the result of discouragement, of cowardice, I may say, of the tearing-down process of the theological structure — built of débris from many ruins — on which my conception of Christianity rested, I lost all faith. For many weeks I did not enter the church, as you yourself must know. Then, when I had given up all hope, through certain incidents and certain persons, a process of reconstruction began. In short, through no virtue which I can claim as my own, I believe I have arrived at the threshold of an understanding of Christianity as Our Lord taught it and lived it. And I intend to take the pulpit and begin to preach it.

"I am deeply concerned in regard to yourself, as to what effect my course may have on you. And I am not asking you to listen to me with a view that you should see your way clear to support me, McCrae, but rather that you should be fully apprised of my new belief and intentions. I owe this to you, for your loyal support in the past. I shall go over with you, later, if you care to listen, my whole position. It may be called the extreme Protestant position, and I use protestant, for want of a better word, to express what I believe is Paul's true as distinguished from the false of his two inconsistent theologies. It was this doctrine of Paul's of redemption by faith, of reacting grace by an inevitable spiritual law — of rebirth, if you will — that Luther and the Protestant reformers revived and recognized, rightly, as the vital element of Christ's teachings, although they did not succeed in separating it wholly from the dross which clung to it. It is the leaven which has changed governments, and which in the end, I am firmly convinced, will make true democracy inevitable. And those who oppose democracy inherently dread its workings.

"I do not know your views, but it is only fair to add at this time that I no longer believe in the external and imposed authority of the Church in the sense in which I formerly accepted it, nor in the virgin birth, nor in certain other dogmas in which I once acquiesced. Other clergymen of our communion have proclaimed, in speech and writing, their disbelief in these things. I have satisfied my conscience as they have, and I mean to make no secret of my change. I am convinced that not one man or woman in ten thousand to-day who has rejected Chris-

tianity ever knew what Christianity is. The science and
archaic philosophy in which Christianity has been swad-
dled and hampered is discredited, and the conclusion is
drawn that Christianity itself must be discredited."

"Ye're going to preach all this?" McCrae demanded,
almost fiercely.

"Yes," Hodder replied, still uncertain as to his assistant's attitude, "and more. I have fully reflected, and I
am willing to accept all the consequences. I understand
perfectly, McCrae, that the promulgation alone of the
liberal orthodoxy of which I have spoken will bring me
into conflict with the majority of the vestry and the congregation, and that the bishop will be appealed to. They
will say, in effect, that I have cheated them, that they
hired one man and that another has turned up, whom
they never would have hired. But that won't be the
whole story. If it were merely a question of doctrine, I
should resign. It's deeper than that, more sinister."
Hodder doubled up his hand, and laid it on the table.
"It's a matter," he said, looking into McCrae's eyes, "of
freeing this church from those who now hold it in chains.
And the two questions, I see clearly now, the doctrinal
and the economic, are so interwoven as to be inseparable.
My former, ancient presentation of Christianity left men
and women cold. It did not draw them into this church
and send them out again fired with the determination to
bring religion into everyday life, resolved to do their
part in the removal of the injustices and cruelties with
which we are surrounded, to bring Christianity into
government, where it belongs. Don't misunderstand me
— I'm not going to preach politics, but religion."

"I don't misunderstand ye," answered McCrae. He
leaned a little forward, staring at the rector from behind
his steel spectacles with a glance which had become
piercing.

"And I am going to discourage a charity which is a
mockery of Christianity," Hodder went on, "the spectacle
of which turns thousands of men and women in sickening
revolt against the Church of Christ to-day. I have dis-

covered, at last, how some of these persons have made their money, and are making it. And I am going to let them know, since they have repudiated God in their own souls, since they have denied the Christian principle of individual responsibility, that I, as the vicar of God, will not be a party to the transaction of using the Church as a means of doling out ill-gotten gains to the poor."

" Mr. Parr! " McCrae exclaimed.

" Yes," said the rector, slowly, and with a touch of sadness, " since you have mentioned him, Mr. Parr. But I need not say that this must go no farther. I am in possession of definite facts in regard to Mr. Parr which I shall present to him when he returns."

" Ye'll tell him to his face?"

" It is the only way."

McCrae had risen. A remarkable transformation had come over the man, — he was reminiscent, at that moment, of some Covenanter ancestor going into battle. And his voice shook with excitement.

" Ye may count on me, Mr. Hodder," he cried. " These many years I've waited, these many years I've seen what ye see now, but I was not the man. Aye, I've watched ye, since the day ye first set foot in this church. I knew what was going on inside of ye, because it was just that I felt myself. I hoped — I prayed ye might come to it."

The sight of this taciturn Scotchman, moved in this way, had an extraordinary effect on Hodder himself, and his own emotion was so inexpressibly stirred that he kept silence a moment to control it. This proof of the truth of his theory in regard to McCrae he found overwhelming.

" But you said nothing, McCrae," he began presently. " I felt all along that you knew what was wrong — if you had only spoken."

" I could not," said McCrae. " I give ye my word I tried, but I just could not. Many's the time I wanted to — but I said to myself, when I looked at you, ' wait, it will come, much better. than ye can say it.' And ye have made me see more than I saw, Mr. Hodder, — already ye have. Ye've got the whole thing in ye're eye, and I only had a part of it. It's because ye're the bigger man of the two."

" You thought I'd come to it ? " demanded Hodder, as though the full force of this insight had just struck him.

" Well," said McCrae, " I hoped. It seemed, to look at ye, ye'r true nature — what was by rights inside of ye. That's the best explaining I can do. And I call to mind that time ye spoke about not making the men in the classes Christians — that was what started me to thinking."

"And you asked me," returned the rector, "how welcome some of them would be in Mr. Parr's pew."

" Ah, it worried me," declared the assistant, with characteristic frankness, " to see how deep ye were getting in with *him*."

Hodder did not reply to this. He had himself risen, and stood looking at McCrae, filled with a new thought.

" There is one thing I should like to say to you — which is very difficult, McCrae, but I have no doubt you see the matter as clearly as I do. In making this fight, I have no one but myself to consider. I am a single man —— "

" Ye'll not need to go on," answered McCrae, with an odd mixture of sternness and gentleness in his voice. "I'll stand and fall with ye, Mr. Hodder. Before I ever thought of the Church I learned a trade, as a boy in Scotland. I'm not a bad carpenter. And if worse comes to worse, I've an idea I can make as much with my hands as I make in the ministry."

The smile they exchanged across the table sealed the compact between them.

II

The electric car which carried him to his appointment with the financier shot westward like a meteor through the night. And now that the hour was actually at hand, it seemed to Hodder that he was absurdly unprepared to meet it. New and formidable aspects, hitherto unthought of, rose in his mind, and the figure of Eldon Parr loomed to Brobdingnagian proportions as he approached it. In spite of his determination, the life-blood of his confidence ebbed, a sense of the power and might of the man who had now become his adversary increased; and that apprehension of the impact of the great banker's personality, the cutting edge with the vast achievements wedged in behind it, each adding weight and impetus to its momentum — the apprehension he had felt in less degree on the day of the first meeting, and which had almost immediately evaporated — surged up in him now. His fear was lest the charged atmosphere of the banker's presence might deflect his own hitherto clear perception of true worth. He dreaded, once in the midst of those disturbing currents, a bungling presentation of the cause which inspired him, and which he knew to be righteousness itself.

Suddenly his mood shifted, betraying still another weakness, and he saw Eldon Parr, suddenly, vividly — more vividly, indeed, than ever before — in the shades of the hell of his loneliness. And pity welled up, drowning the image of incarnate greed and selfishness and lust for wealth and power. The unique pathos of his former relationship with the man reasserted itself, and Hodder was conscious once more of the dependence which Eldon Parr had had on his friendship. During that friendship he, Hodder, had never lost the sense of being the stronger of the two, of being leaned upon: leaned upon by a man whom the world feared and hated, and whom he had been unable to regard with anything but compassion and the unquestionable affection which sprang from it. Appalled by this transition, he alighted from the car, and stood for a moment alone in the darkness gazing at the great white houses that rose above the dusky outline of shrubbery and trees.

At any rate, he wouldn't find that sense of dependence to-night. And it steeled him somewhat to think, as he resumed his steps, that he would meet now the other side, the hard side hitherto always turned away. Had he needed no other warning of this, the answer to his note asking for an appointment would have been enough, — a

brief and formal communication signed by the banker's
secretary. . . .

"Mr. Parr is engaged just at present, sir," said the
servant who opened the door. "Would you be good
enough to step into the library?"

Hardly had he entered the room when he heard a sound
behind him, and turned to confront Alison.   The thought
of her, too, had complicated infinitely his emotions concerning the interview before him, and the sight of her
now, of her mature beauty displayed in evening dress, of
her white throat gleaming whiter against the severe black
of her gown, made him literally speechless.   Never had
he accused her of boldness, and now least of all.   It was
the quality of her splendid courage that was borne in
upon him once more above the host of other feelings and
impressions, for he read in her eyes a knowledge of the
meaning of his visit.

They stood facing each other an appreciable moment.

"Mr. Langmaid is with him now," she said, in a low
voice.

"Yes," he answered.

Her eyes still rested on his face, questioningly, apprais-
ingly, as though she were seeking to estimate his prepared-
ness for the ordeal before him, his ability to go through
with it successfully, triumphantly.   And in her mention
of Langmaid he recognized that she had meant to sound a
note of warning.   She had intimated a consultation of the
captains, a council of war.   And yet he had never spoken
to her of this visit.   This proof of her partisanship, that
she had come to him at the crucial instant, overwhelmed
him.

"You know why I am here?" he managed to say.   It
had to do with the extent of her knowledge.

"Oh, why shouldn't I?" she cried, "after what you
have told me.   And could you think I didn't understand,
from the beginning, that it meant this?"

His agitation still hampered him.   He made a gesture
of assent.

"It was inevitable," he said.

"Yes, it was inevitable," she assented, and walked slowly to the mantel, resting her hand on it and bending her head. "I felt that you would not shirk it, and yet I realize how painful it must be to you."

"And to you," he replied quickly.

"Yes, and to me. I do not know what you know, specifically,— I have never sought to find out things, in detail. That would be horrid. But I understand — in general — I have understood for many years." She raised her head, and flashed him a glance that was between a quivering smile and tears. "And I know that you have certain specific information."

He could only wonder at her intuition.

"So far as I am concerned, it is not for the world," he answered.

"Oh, I appreciate that in you !" she exclaimed. "I wished you to know it. I wished you to know," she added, a little unsteadily, "how much I admire you for what you are doing. They are afraid of you — they will crush you if they can."

He did not reply.

"But you are going to speak the truth," she continued, her voice low and vibrating, "that is splendid ! It must have its effect, no matter what happens."

"Do you feel that ? " he asked, taking a step toward her.

"Yes. When I see you, I feel it, I think." . . .

Whatever answer he might have made to this was frustrated by the appearance of the figure of Nelson Langmaid in the doorway. He seemed to survey them benevolently through his spectacles.

"How are you, Hodder ? Well, Alison, I have to leave without seeing anything of you — you must induce your father not to bring his business home with him. Just a word," he added to the rector, "before you go up."

Hodder turned to Alison. "Good night," he said.

The gentle but unmistakable pressure of her hand he interpreted as the pinning on him of the badge of her faith. He was to go into battle wearing her colours. Their eyes met.

"Good night," she answered. . . .

In the hall the lawyer took his arm.

"What's the trouble, Hodder?" he asked, sympathet-ically.

Hodder, although on his guard, was somewhat taken aback by the directness of the onslaught.

"I'm afraid, Mr. Langmaid," the rector replied, "that it would take me longer to tell you than the time at your disposal."

"Dear me," said the lawyer, "this is too bad. Why didn't you come to me? I am a good friend of yours, Hodder, and there is an additional bond between us on my sister's account. She is extremely fond of you, you know. And I have a certain feeling of responsibility for you, — I brought you here."

"You have always been very kind, and I appreciate it," Hodder replied. "I should be sorry to cause you any worry or annoyance. But you must understand that I cannot share the responsibility of my acts with any one."

"A little advice from an old legal head is sometimes not out of place. Even Dr. Gilman used to consult me. I hope you will bear in mind how remarkably well you have been getting along at St. John's, and what a success you've made."

"Success!" echoed the rector.

Either Mr. Langmaid read nothing in his face, or was determined to read nothing.

"Assuredly," he answered, benignly. "You have man-aged to please everybody, Mr. Parr included, — and some of us are not easy to please. I thought I'd tell you this, as a friend, as your first friend in the parish. Your achievement has been all the more remarkable, following, as you did, Dr. Gilman. Now it would greatly distress me to see that state of things disturbed, both for your sake and others. I thought I would just give you a hint, as you are going to see Mr. Parr, that he is in rather a ner-vous state. These so-called political reformers have up-set the market and started a lot of legal complications —

gazed upon the undiscovered side, the dangerous side before which other men had quailed. Alison's words recurred to him, "they are afraid of you, they will crush you if they can." Eldon Parr betrayed, at any rate, no sign of fear. If his mental posture were further analyzed, it might be made out to contain an intimation that the rector, by some act, had forfeited the right to the unique privilege of the old relationship.

Well, the fact that the banker had, in some apparently occult manner, been warned, would make Hodder's task easier — or rather less difficult. His feelings were even more complicated than he had anticipated. The moments of suspense were trying to his nerves, and he had a shrewd notion that this making men wait was a favourite manœuvre of Eldon Parr's; nor had he underrated the benumbing force of that personality. It was evident that the financier intended him to open the battle, and he was — as he had expected — finding it difficult to marshal the regiments of his arguments. In vain he thought of the tragedy of Garvin. . . . The thing was more complicated. And behind this redoubtable and sinister Eldon Parr he saw, as it were, the wraith of that other who had once confessed the misery of his loneliness. . . .

At last the banker rang, sharply, the bell on his desk. A secretary entered, to whom he dictated a telegram which contained these words: "Langmaid has discovered a way out." It was to be sent to an address in Texas. Then he turned in his chair and crossed his knees, his hand fondling an ivory paper-cutter. He smiled a little.

"Well, Mr. Hodder," he said.

The rector, intensely on his guard, merely inclined his head in recognition that his turn had come.

"I was sorry," the banker continued, after a perceptible pause, "that you could not see your way clear to have come with me on the cruise."

"I must thank you again," Hodder answered, "but I felt — as I wrote you — that certain matters made it impossible for me to go."

that's why I'm here to-night.   Go easy with him,
you won't do anything foolish."

The lawyer accompanied this statement with a
this time he did not succeed in concealing his con

" That depends on one's point of view," Hodder re
with a smile.   " I do not know how you have c
suspect that I am going to disturb Mr. Parr, but
have to say to him is between him and me."

Langmaid took up his hat from the table, and sigh

" Drop in on me sometime," he said, " I'd like to ta
you."

Hodder heard a voice behind him, and turned.   A
vant was standing there.

" Mr. Parr is ready to see you, sir," he said.

The rector followed him up the stairs, to the room
the second floor, half office, half study, where the capitali
transacted his business when at home.

III

Eldon Parr was huddled over his desk reading a type-
written document; but he rose, and held out his hand,
which Hodder took.

" How are you, Mr. Hodder ? I'm sorry to have kept you
waiting, but matters of some legal importance have arisen
on which I was obliged to make a decision.   You're well,
I hope."   He shot a glance at the rector, and sat down
again, still holding the sheets.   " If you will excuse me a
moment longer, I'll finish this."

" Certainly," Hodder replied.

" Take a chair," said Mr. Parr, " you'll find the evening
paper beside you."

Hodder sat down, and the banker resumed his perusal
of the document, his eye running rapidly over the pages,
pausing once in a while to scratch out a word or to make
a note on the margin.   In the concentration of the man
on the task before him the rector read a design, an implication that the affairs of the Church were of a minor importance: sensed, indeed, the new attitude of hostility,

"I suppose you had your reasons, but I think you would have enjoyed the trip. I had a good, seaworthy boat — I chartered her from Mr. Lieber, the president of the Continental Zinc, you know. I went as far as Labrador. A wonderful coast, Mr. Hodder."

"It must be," agreed the rector. It was clear that Mr. Parr intended to throw upon him the onus of the first move. There was a silence, brief, indeed, but long enough for Hodder to feel more and more distinctly the granite hardness which the other had become, to experience a rising, reënforcing anger. He went forward, steadily but resolutely, on the crest of it. "I have remained in the city," he continued, "and I have had the opportunity to discover certain facts of which I have hitherto been ignorant, and which, in my opinion, profoundly affect the welfare of the church. It is of these I wished to speak to you."

Mr. Parr waited.

"It is not much of an exaggeration to say that ever since I came here I have been aware that St. John's, considering the long standing of the parish, the situation of the church in a thickly populated district, is not fulfilling its mission. But I have failed until now to perceive the causes of that inefficiency."

"Inefficiency?" The banker repeated the word.

"Inefficiency," said Hodder. "The reproach, the responsibility is largely mine, as the rector, the spiritual head of the parish. I believe I am right when I say that the reason for the decision, some twenty years ago, to leave the church where it is, instead of selling the property and building in the West End, was that it might minister to the poor in the neighbourhood, to bring religion and hope into their lives, and to exert its influence towards eradicating the vice and misery which surround it."

"But I thought you had agreed," said Mr. Parr, coldly, "that we were to provide for that in the new chapel and settlement house."

"For reasons which I hope to make plain to you, Mr.

Parr," Hodder replied, " those people can never be reached, as they ought to be reached, by building that settlement house. The principle is wrong, the day is past when such things can be done — *in that way.*" He laid an emphasis on these words. "It is good, I grant you, to care for the babies and children of the poor, it is good to get young women and men out of the dance-halls, to provide innocent amusement, distraction, instruction. But it is not enough. It leaves the great, transforming thing in the lives of these people untouched, and it will forever remain untouched so long as a sense of wrong, a continually deepening impression of an unchristian civilization upheld by the Church herself, exists. Such an undertaking as that settlement house — I see clearly now — is a palliation, a poultice applied to one of many sores, a compromise unworthy of the high mission of the Church. She should go to the root of the disease. It is her first business to make Christians, who, by amending their own lives, by going out individually and collectively into the life of the nation, will gradually remove these conditions."

Mr. Parr sat drumming on the table. Hodder met his look.

" So you, too, have come to it," he said.

" Have come to what ? "

" Socialism."

Hodder, in the state of clairvoyance in which he now surprisingly found himself, accurately summed up the value and meaning of the banker's sigh.

" Say, rather," he replied, " that I have come to Christianity. We shall never have what is called socialism until there is no longer any necessity for it, until men, of their own free will, are ready to renounce selfish, personal ambition and power and work for humanity, for the state."

Mr. Parr's gesture implied that he cared not by what name the thing was called, but he still appeared strangely, astonishingly calm; — Hodder, with all his faculties acute, apprehended that he was *dangerously* calm. The man who had formerly been his friend was now completely obliterated, and he had the feeling almost of being about to grapple, in mortal combat, with some unknown monster whose tactics and resources were infinite, whose victims had never escaped. The monster was *in* Eldon Parr — that is how it came to him. The wary, relentless demon was aroused. It behooved him, Hodder, to step carefully. . . .

"That is all very fine, Mr. Hodder, very altruistic, very Christian, I've no doubt — but the world doesn't work that way." (These were the words borne in on Hodder's consciousness.) "What drives the world is the motive furnished by the right of acquiring and holding property. If we had a division to-day, the able men would come out on top next year."

The rector shook his head. He remembered, at that moment, Horace Bentley.

"What drives the world is a far higher motive, Mr. Parr, the motive with which have been fired the great lights of history, the motive of renunciation and service which is transforming governments, which is gradually making the world a better place in which to live. And we are seeing men and women imbued with it, rising in ever increasing numbers on every side to-day."

"Service!" Eldon Parr had seized upon the word as it passed and held it. "What do you think my life has been? I suppose," he said, with a touch of intense bitterness, "that you, too, who six months ago seemed as reasonable a man as I ever met, have joined in the chorus of denunciators. It has become the fashion to-day, thanks to your socialists, reformers, and agitators, to decry a man because he is rich, to take it for granted that he is a thief and a scoundrel, that he has no sense of responsibility for his country and his fellow-men. The glory, the true democracy of this nation, lies in its equal opportunity for all. They take no account of that, of the fact that each has had the same chance as his fellows. No, but they cry out that the man who, by the sweat of his brow, has earned wealth ought to divide it up with the lazy and the self-indulgent and the shiftless.

" Take my case, for instance, — it is typical of thousands. I came to this city as a boy in my teens, with eight dollars in my pocket which I had earned on a farm. I swept the floor, cleaned the steps, moved boxes and ran errands in Gabriel Parker's store on Third Street. I was industrious, sober, willing to do anything. I fought, I tell you, every inch of my way. As soon as I saved a little money I learned to use every ounce of brain I possessed to hold on to it. I trusted a man once, and I had to begin all over again. And I discovered, once for all, if a man doesn't look out for himself, no one will.

" I don't pretend that I am any better than any one else, I have had to take life as I found it, and make the best of it. I conformed to the rules of the game; I soon had sense enough knocked into me to understand that the conditions were not of my making. But I'll say this for myself," Eldon Parr leaned forward over the blotter, " I had standards, and I stuck by them. I wanted to be a decent citizen, to bring up my children in the right way. I didn't squander my money, when I got it, on wine and women, I respected other men's wives, I supported the Church and the institutions of the city. I too — even I — had my ambitions, my ideals — and they were not entirely worldly ones. You would probably accuse me of wishing to acquire only the position of power which I hold. If you had accepted my invitation to go aboard the yacht this summer, it was my intention to unfold to you a scheme of charities which has long been forming in my mind, and which I think would be of no small benefit to the city where I have made my fortune. I merely mention this to prove to you that I am not unmindful, in spite of the circumstances of my own life, of the unfortunates whose mental equipment is not equal to my own."

By this " poor boy " argument which — if Hodder had known — Mr. Parr had used at banquets with telling effect, the banker seemed to regain perspective and equilibrium, to plant his feet once more on the rock of the justification of his life, and from which, by a somewhat extraordinary process he had not quite understood, he had been partially shaken off. As he had proceeded with his personal history, his manner had gradually become one of the finality of experience over theory, of the forbearance of the practical man with the visionary. Like most successful citizens of his type, he possessed in a high degree the faculty of creating sympathy, of compelling others to accept — temporarily, at least — his point of view. It was this faculty, Hodder perceived, which had heretofore laid an enchantment upon him, and it was not without a certain wonder that he now felt himself to be released from the spell.

The perceptions of the banker were as keen, and his sense of security was brief. Somehow, as he met the searching eye of the rector, he was unable to see the man as a visionary, but beheld — and, to do him justice — felt a twinge of respect for an adversary worthy of his steel. He, who was accustomed to prepare for clouds when they were mere specks on his horizon, paused even now to marvel why he had not dealt with this. Here was a man — a fanatic, if he liked — but still a man who positively did not fear him, to whom his wrath and power were as nothing! A new and startling and complicated sensation — but Eldon Parr was no coward. If he had, consciously or unconsciously, formerly looked upon the clergyman as a dependent, Hodder appeared to be one no more. The very ruggedness of the man had enhanced, expanded — as it were — until it filled the room. And Hodder had, with an audacity unparalleled in the banker's experience, arraigned by implication his whole life, managed to put him on the defensive.

"But if that be your experience," the rector said, "and it has become your philosophy, what is it in you that impels you to give these large sums for the public good?"

"I should suppose that you, as a clergyman, might understand that my motive is a Christian one."

Hodder sat very still, but a higher light came into his eyes.

"Mr. Parr," he replied, "I have been a friend of yours, and I am a friend still. And what I am going to tell you

z

is not only in the hope that others may benefit, but that
your own soul may be saved. I mean that literally — your
own soul. You are under the impression that you are a
Christian, but you are not and never have been one. And
you will not be one until your whole life is transformed,
until you become a different man. If you do not change,
it is my duty to warn you that the sorrow and suffering,
the uneasiness which you now know, and which drive
you on, in search of distraction, to adding useless sums of
money to your fortune — this suffering, I say, will become
intensified. You will die in the knowledge of it, and live
on after, in the knowledge of it."

In spite of himself, the financier drew back before
this unexpected blast, the very intensity of which had
struck a chill of terror in his inmost being. He had been
taken off his guard, — for he had supposed the day long past
— if it had ever existed — when a spiritual rebuke would
upset him ; the day long past when a minister *could* pronounce one with any force. That the Church should ever
again presume to take herself seriously had never occurred
to him. And yet — the man had denounced him in a moment of depression, of nervous irritation and exasperation
against a government which had begun to interfere with
the sacred liberty of its citizens, against political agitators
who had spurred that government on. The world was
mad. No element, it seemed, was now content to remain
in its proper place. His voice, as he answered, shook
with rage, — all the greater because the undaunted sternness by which it was confronted seemed to reduce it to
futility.

"Take care !" he cried, "take care ! You, nor any
other man, clergyman or no clergyman, have any right to
be the judge of my conduct."

"On the contrary," said Hodder, "if your conduct
affects the welfare, the progress, the reputation of the
church of which I am rector, I have the right. And I
intend to exercise it. It becomes my duty, however painful, to tell you, as a member of the Church, wherein you
have wronged the Church and wronged yourself."

He didn't raise his tone, and there was in it more of sorrow than of indignation.   The banker turned an ashen gray. . . .   A moment elapsed before he spoke, a transforming moment.   He suddenly became ice.

"Very well," he said.   "I can't pretend to account for these astounding views you have acquired — and I am using a mild term.   Let me say this" (he leaned forward a little, across the desk): "I demand that you be specific. I am a busy man, I have little time to waste, I have certain matters before me which must be attended to to-night. I warn you that I will not listen any longer to vague accusations."

It was Hodder's turn to marvel.   Did Eldon Parr, after all, have no sense of guilt?   Instantaneously, automatically, his own anger rose.

"You may be sure, Mr. Parr, that I should not be here unless I were prepared to be specific.   And what I am going to say to you I have reserved for your ear alone, in the hope that you will take it to heart, while it is not yet too late, and amend your life accordingly."

Eldon Parr shifted slightly.   His look became inscrutable, was riveted on the rector.

"I shall call your attention first to a man of whom you have probably never heard.   He is dead now — he threw himself into the river this summer, with a curse on his lips — I am afraid — a curse against you.   A few years ago he lived happily with his wife and child in a little house on the Grade Suburban, and he had several thousand dollars as a result of careful saving and systematic self-denial.

"Perhaps you have never thought of the responsibilities of a great name.   This man, like thousands of others in the city, idealized you.   He looked up to you as the soul of honour, as a self-made man who by his own unaided efforts — as you yourself have just pointed out — rose from a poor boy to a position of power and trust in the community.   He saw you a prominent layman in the Church of God.   He was dazzled by the brilliancy of your success, inspired by a civilization which gave such opportunities.   He recognized that he himself had not the brains for such an achievement, — his hope and love and ambition were centred in his boy."

At the word Eldon Parr's glance was suddenly dulled by pain. He tightened his lips.

"That boy was then of a happy, merry disposition, so the mother says, and every summer night as she cooked supper she used to hear him laughing as he romped in the yard with his father. When I first saw him this summer, it was two days before his father committed suicide. The child was lying, stifled with the heat, in the back room of one of those desolate lodging houses in Dalton Street, and his little body had almost wasted away.

"While I was there the father came in, and when he saw me he was filled with fury. He despised the Church, and St. John's above all churches, because *you* were of it; because you who had given so generously to it had wrecked his life. You had shattered his faith in humanity, his ideal. From a normal, contented man he had deteriorated into a monomaniac whom no one would hire, a physical and mental wreck who needed care and nursing. He said he hoped the boy would die.

"And what had happened? The man had bought, with all the money he had in the world, Consolidated Tractions. He had bought it solely because of his admiration for your ability, his faith in your name. It was inconceivable to him that a man of your standing, a public benefactor, a supporter of church and charities, would permit your name to be connected with any enterprise that was not sound and just. Thousands like Garvin lost all they had, while you are still a rich man. It is further asserted that you sold out all your stock at a high price, with the exception of that in the leased lines, which are guaranteed heavy dividends."

"Have you finished?" demanded Eldon Parr.

"Not quite, on this subject," replied the rector. "Two nights after that, the man threw himself in the river. His body was pulled out by men on a tugboat, and his worthless stock certificate was in his pocket. It is now in the possession of Mr. Horace Bentley. Thanks to

Mr. Bentley, the widow found a temporary home, and the child has almost recovered."

Hodder paused. His interest had suddenly become concentrated upon the banker's new demeanour, and he would not have thought it within the range of possibility that a man could listen to such a revelation concerning himself without the betrayal of some feeling. But so it was,— Eldon Parr had been coldly attentive, save for the one scarcely perceptible tremor when the boy was mentioned. His interrogatory gesture gave the very touch of perfection to this attitude, since it proclaimed him to have listened patiently to a charge so preposterous that a less reasonable man would have cut it short.

"And what leads you to suppose," he inquired, "that I am responsible in this matter? What leads you to infer that the Consolidated Tractions Company was not organized in good faith? Do you think that business men are always infallible? The street-car lines of this city were at sixes and sevens, fighting each other; money was being wasted by poor management. The idea behind the company was a public-spirited one, to give the citizens cheaper and better service, by a more modern equipment, by a wider system of transfer. It seems to me, Mr. Hodder, that you put yourself in a more quixotic position than the so-called reformers when you assume that the men who organize a company in good faith are personally responsible for every share of stock that is sold, and for the welfare of every individual who may buy the stock. We force no one to buy it. They do so at their own risk. I myself have thousands of dollars of worthless stock in my safe. I have never complained."

The full force of Hodder's indignation went into his reply.

"I am not talking about the imperfect code of human justice under which we live, Mr. Parr," he cried. "This is not a case in which a court of law may exonerate you, it is between you and your God. But I have taken the trouble to find out, from unquestioned sources, the truth about the Consolidated Tractions Company — I shall not

go into the details at length — they are doubtless familiar
to you. I know that the legal genius of Mr. Langmaid,
one of my vestry, made possible the organization of the
company, and thereby evaded the plain spirit of the law
of the state. I know that one branch line was bought
for two hundred and fifty thousand dollars, and capitalized for three millions, and that most of the others were
scandalously over-capitalized. I know that while the
coming transaction was still a secret, you and other
gentlemen connected with the matter bought up large
interests in other lines, which you proceeded to lease *to
yourselves* at guaranteed dividends which these lines do
not earn. I know that the first large dividend was paid
out of capital. And the stock which you sold to poor
Garvin was so hopelessly watered that it never could have
been anything but worthless. If, in spite of these facts,
you do not deem yourself responsible for the misery
which has been caused, if your conscience is now clear, it
is my duty to tell you that there is a higher bar of justice."

The intensity of the fire of the denunciation had, indeed, a momentary yet visible effect in the banker's
expression. Whatever the emotions thus lashed to self-
betrayal, anger, hatred, — fear, perhaps, Hodder could
not detect a trace of penitence; and he was aware, on
the part of the other, of a supreme, almost spasmodic
effort for self-control. The constitutional reluctance of
Eldon Parr to fight openly could not have been more
clearly demonstrated.

" Because you are a clergyman, Mr. Hodder," he began,
" because you are the rector of St. John's, I have allowed
you to say things to me which I would not have permitted
from any other man. I have tried to take into account
your point of view, which is naturally restricted, your par-
donable ignorance of what business men, who wish to do
their duty by Church and State, have to contend with.
When you came to this parish you seemed to have a sensible, a proportional view of things; you were content to
confine your activities to your own sphere, content not to
meddle with politics and business, which you could, at

first hand, know nothing about. The modern desire of clergymen to interfere in these matters has ruined the usefulness of many of them.

"I repeat, I have tried to be patient. I venture to hope, still, that this extraordinary change in you may not be permanent, but merely the result of a natural sympathy with the weak and unwise and unfortunate who are always to be found in a complex civilization. I can even conceive how such a discovery must have shocked you, temporarily aroused your indignation, as a clergyman, against the world as it is — and, I may add, as it has always been. My personal friendship for you, and my interest in your future welfare impel me to make a final appeal to you not to ruin a career which is full of promise."

The rector did not take advantage of the pause. A purely psychological curiosity hypnotized him to see how far the banker would go in his apparent generosity.

"I once heard you say, I believe, in a sermon, that the Christian religion is a leaven. It is the leaven that softens and ameliorates the hard conditions of life, that makes our relations with our fellow-men bearable. But life is a contest, it is war. It always has been, and always will be. Business is war, commerce is war, both among nations and individuals. You cannot get around it. If a man does not exterminate his rivals they will exterminate him. In other days churches were built and endowed with the spoils of war, and did not disdain the money. To-day they cheerfully accept the support and gifts of business men. I do not accuse them of hypocrisy. It is a recognition on their part that business men, in spite of hard facts, are not unmindful of the spiritual side of life, and are not deaf to the injunction to help others. And when, let me ask you, could you find in the world's history more splendid charities than are around us to-day? Institutions endowed for medical research, for the conquest of deadly diseases? libraries, hospitals, schools — men giving their fortunes for these things, the fruits of a life's work so laboriously acquired? Who can say that the modern capitalist is not liberal, is not a public benefactor?

"I dislike being personal, but you have forced it upon me. I dislike to refer to what I have already done in the matter of charities, but I hinted to you awhile ago of a project I have conceived and almost perfected of gifts on a much larger scale than I have ever attempted." The financier stared at him meaningly. "And I had you in mind as one of the three men whom I should consult, whom I should associate with myself in the matter. We cannot change human nature, but we can better conditions by wise giving. I do not refer now to the settlement house, which I am ready to help make and maintain as the best in the country, but I have in mind a system to be carried out with the consent and aid of the municipal government, of play-grounds, baths, parks, places of recreation, and hospitals, for the benefit of the people, which will put our city in the very forefront of progress. And I believe, as a practical man, I can convince you that the betterment which you and I so earnestly desire can be brought about in no other way. Agitation can only result in anarchy and misery for all."

Hodder's wrath, as he rose from his chair, was of the sort that appears incredibly to add to the physical stature, — the bewildering spiritual wrath which is rare indeed, and carries all before it.

"Don't tempt me, Mr. Parr!" he said. "Now that I know the truth, I tell you frankly I would face poverty and persecution rather than consent to your offer. And I warn you once more not to flatter yourself that existence ends here, that you will not be called to answer for every wrong act you have committed in accumulating your fortune, that what you call business is an affair of which God takes no account. What I say may seem foolishness to you, but I tell you, in the words of that Foolishness, that it will not profit you to gain the whole world and lose your own soul. You remind me that the Church in old time accepted gifts from the spoils of war, and I will add of rapine and murder. And the Church to-day, *to* repeat your own parallel, grows rich with money wrongfully got. Legally? Ah, yes, legally, perhaps. But that will not avail you. And the kind of church you speak of — to which I, to my shame, once consented — Our Lord repudiates. It is none of his. I warn you, Mr. Parr, in his Name, first to make your peace with your brothers before you presume to lay another gift on the altar."

During this withering condemnation of himself Eldon Parr sat motionless, his face grown livid, an expression on it that continued to haunt Hodder long afterwards. An expression, indeed, which made the banker almost unrecognizable.

"Go," he whispered, his hand trembling visibly as he pointed towards the door. "Go — I have had enough of this."

"Not until I have said one thing more," replied the rector, undaunted. "I have found the woman whose marriage with your son you prevented, whom you bought off and started on the road to hell without any sense of responsibility. You have made of her a prostitute and a drunkard. Whether she can be rescued or not is problematical. She, too, is in Mr. Bentley's care, a man upon whom you once showed no mercy. I leave Garvin, who has gone to his death, and Kate Marcy and Horace Bentley to your conscience, Mr. Parr. That they are representative of many others, I do not doubt. I tell you solemnly that the whole meaning of life is service to others, and I warn you, before it is too late, to repent and make amends. Gifts will not help you, and charities are of no avail."

At the reference to Kate Marcy Eldon Parr's hand dropped to his side. He seemed to have physical difficulty in speaking.

"Ah, you have found that woman!" He leaned an elbow on the desk, he seemed suddenly to have become weary, spent, old. And Hodder, as he watched him, perceived that his haggard look was directed towards a photograph in a silver frame on the table — a photograph of Preston Parr. At length he broke the silence.

"What would you have had me do?" he asked. "Permit my son to marry a woman of the streets, I suppose. That would have been Christianity, according to your notion. Come now, what would you have done, if your son had been in question?"

A wave of pity swept over the rector.

"Why," he said, "why did you have nothing but cruelty in your heart, and contempt for her? When you saw that she was willing, for the love of the son whom you loved, to give up all that life meant to her, how could you destroy her without a qualm? The crime you committed was that you refused to see God in that woman's soul, when he had revealed himself to you. You looked for wile, for cunning, for self-seeking, — and they were not there. Love had obliterated them. When you saw how meekly she obeyed you, and agreed to go away, why did you not have pity? If you had listened to your conscience, you would have known what to do.

"I do not say that you should not have opposed the marriage — then. Marriage is not to be lightly entered into. From the moment you went to see her you became responsible for her. You hurled her into the abyss, and she has come back to haunt you. You should have had her educated and cared for — she would have submitted to any plan you proposed. And if, after a sensible separation, you became satisfied as to her character and development, and your son still wished to marry her, you should have withdrawn your objections.

"As it is, and in consequence of your act, you have lost your son. He left you then, and you have no more control over him."

"Stop!" cried Eldon Parr, "for God's sake stop! I won't stand any more of this. I will not listen to criticism of my life, to strictures on my conduct from you or any other man." He reached for a book on the corner of his desk — a cheque book. "You'll want money for these people, I suppose," he added brutally. "I will give it, but it must be understood that I do not recognize any right of theirs to demand it."

"'YOU'LL WANT MONEY FOR THESE PEOPLE, I SUPPOSE,' HE ADDED
BRUTALLY."

For a moment Hodder did not trust himself to reply. He looked down across the desk at the financier, who was fumbling with the leaves.

"They do not demand it, Mr. Parr," he answered, gently. "And I have tried to make it plain to you that you have lost the right to give it. I expected to fail in this. I have failed."

"What do you mean?" Eldon Parr let the cheque book close.

"I mean what I said," the rector replied. "That if you would save your soul you must put an end, to-morrow, to the acquisition of money, and devote the rest of your life to an earnest and sincere attempt to make just restitution to those you have wronged. And you must ask the forgiveness of God for your sins. Until you do that, your charities are abominations in his sight. I will not trouble you any longer, except to say that I shall be ready to come to you at any time my presence may be of any help to you."

The banker did not speak. . . . With a single glance towards the library Hodder left the house, but paused for a moment outside to gaze back at it, as it loomed in the darkness against the stars.

CHAPTER XXI

ALISON GOES TO CHURCH

I

On the following Sunday morning the early light filtered into Alison's room, and she opened her strong eyes. Presently she sprang from her bed and drew back the curtains of the windows, gazing rapturously into the crystal day. The verdure of the Park was freshened to an incredible brilliancy by the dew, a thin white veil of mist was spread over the mirror of the waters, the trees flung long shadows across the turf.

A few minutes later she was out, thrilled by the silence, drawing in deep breaths of the morning air; lingering by still lakes catching the blue of the sky — a blue that left its stain upon the soul; as the sun mounted she wandered farther, losing herself in the wilderness of the forest.

At eight o'clock, when she returned, there were signs that the city had awakened. A mounted policeman trotted past her as she crossed a gravel drive, and on the tree-flecked stretches, which lately had been empty as Eden, human figures were scattered. A child, with a sailboat that languished for lack of wind, stared at her, first with fascination and wonder in his eyes, and then smiled at her tentatively. She returned the smile with a start.

Children had stared at her like that before now, and for the first time in her life she asked herself what the look might mean. She had never really been fond of them: she had never, indeed, been brought much in contact with them. But now, without warning, a sudden fierce yearning took possession of her: surprised and almost frightened, she stopped irresistibly and looked back at the thin little figure crouched beside the water, — to discover that his widened eyes were still upon her. Her own lingered on him shyly, and thus for a moment she hung in doubt whether to flee or stay, her heart throbbing as though she were on the brink of some unknown and momentous adventure. She took a timid step.

" What's your name ? " she asked.

The boy told her.

" What's yours ? " he ventured, still under the charm.

" Alison."

He had never heard of that name, and said so. They deplored the lack of wind. And presently, still mystified, but gathering courage, he asked her why she blushed, at which her colour deepened.

" I can't help it," she told him.

" I like it," the boy said.

Though the grass was still wet, she got down on her knees in her white skirt, the better to push the boat along the shore: once it drifted beyond their reach, and was only rescued by a fallen branch discovered with difficulty. The arrival of the boy's father, an anæmic-looking little man, put an end to their play. He deplored the condition of the lady's dress.

" It doesn't matter in the least," she assured him, and fled in a mood she did not attempt to analyze. Hurrying homeward, she regained her room, bathed, and at half past eight appeared in the big, formal dining-room, from which the glare of the morning light was carefully screened. Her father insisted on breakfasting here; and she found him now seated before the white table-cloth, reading a newspaper. He glanced up at her critically.

" So you've decided to honour me this morning," he said.

" I've been out in the Park," she replied, taking the chair opposite him. He resumed his reading, but presently, as she was pouring out the coffee, he lowered the paper again.

" What's the occasion to-day ? " he asked.

" The occasion ? " she repeated, without acknowledging that she had instantly grasped his implication.   His eyes were on her gown.

" You are not accustomed, as a rule, to pay much deference to Sunday."

" Doesn't the Bible say, somewhere," she inquired, " that the Sabbath was made for man ?   Perhaps that may be broadened after a while, to include woman."

" But you have never been an advocate, so far as I know, of women taking advantage of their opportunity by going to Church."

" What's the use," demanded Alison, " of the thousands of working women spending the best part of the day in the ordinary church, when their feet and hands and heads are aching ?   Unless some fire is kindled in their souls, it is hopeless for them to try to obtain any benefit from religion — so-called — as it is preached to them in most churches."

" Fire in their souls ! " exclaimed the banker.

" Yes.   If the churches offered those who might be leaders among their fellows a practical solution of exist-ence, kindled their self-respect, replaced a life of drudgery by one of inspiration — that would be worth while.   But you will never get such a condition as that unless your pulpits are filled by personalities, instead of puppets who are all cast in one mould, and who profess to be there by divine right."

" I am glad to see at least that you are taking an inter-est in religious matters," her father observed, meaningly.

Alison coloured.   But she retorted with spirit.

" That is true of a great many persons to-day who are thinking on the subject.   If Christianity is a solution of life, people are demanding of the churches that they shall perform their function, and show us how, and why, or else cease to encumber the world."

Eldon Parr folded up his newspaper.

" So you are going to Church this morning," he said.

" Yes.   At what time will you be ready ? "

"'What's your name?' she asked."

"At quarter to eleven. But if you are going to St. John's, you will have to start earlier. I'll order a car at half past ten."

"Where are *you* going?" She held her breath, unconsciously, for the answer.

"To Calvary," he replied coldly, as he rose to leave the room. "But I hesitate to ask you to come, — I am afraid you will not find a religion there that suits you."

For a moment she could not trust herself to speak. The secret which, ever since Friday evening, she had been burning to learn was disclosed. . . . Her father had broken with Mr. Hodder !

"Please don't order the motor for me," she said. "I'd rather go in the street cars."

She sat very still in the empty room, her face burning. Characteristically, her father had not once mentioned the rector of St. John's, yet had contrived to imply that her interest in Hodder was greater than her interest in religion. And she was forced to admit, with her customary honesty, that the implication was true.

The numbers who knew Alison Parr casually thought her cold. They admired a certain quality in her work, but they did not suspect that that quality was the incomplete expression of an innate idealism capable of being fanned into flame, — for she was subject to rare but ardent enthusiasms which kindled and transformed her incredibly in the eyes of the few to whom the process had been revealed. She had had even a longer list of suitors than any one guessed; men who — usually by accident — had touched the hidden spring, and suddenly beholding an unimagined woman, had consequently lost their heads. The mistake most of them had made (for subtlety in such affairs is not a masculine trait) was the failure to recognize and continue to present the quality in them which had awakened her. She had invariably discovered the feet of clay.

Thus disillusion had been her misfortune — perhaps it would be more accurate to say her fortune. She had built up, after each invasion, her defences more carefully

and solidly than before, only to be again astonished and
dismayed by the next onslaught, until at length the question had become insistent — the question of an alliance
for purposes of greater security.   She had returned to
her childhood home to consider it, frankly recognizing it
as a compromise, a fall. . . .

And here, in this sanctuary of her reflection, and out of
a quarter on which she had set no watch, out of a wilderness which she had believed to hold nothing save the
ruined splendours of the past, had come one who, like the
traditional figures of the wilderness, had attracted her by
his very uncouthness and latent power.   And the anomaly he presented in what might be called the vehemence
of his advocacy of an outworn orthodoxy, in his occupa-
tion of the pulpit of St. John's, had quickened at once her
curiosity and antagonism.   It had been her sudden discovery, or rather her instinctive suspicion of the inner
conflict in him which had set her standard fluttering in
response.   Once more (for the last time — something
whispered now) she had become the lady of the lists; she
sat on her walls watching, with beating heart and straining eyes, the closed helm of her champion, ready to fling
down the revived remnant of her faith as prize or forfeit.
She had staked all on the hope that he would not lower
his lance. . . .

Saturday had passed in suspense. . . . And now was
flooding in on her the certainty that he had not failed her ;
that he had, with a sublime indifference to a worldly
future and success, defied the powers.   With indifference,
too, to *her!*   She knew, of course, that he loved her.   A
man with less of greatness would have sought a middle
way. . . .

When, at half past ten, she fared forth into the sunlight, she was filled with anticipation, excitement, concern,
— feelings enhanced and not soothed by the pulsing
vibrations of the church bells in the softening air.   The
swift motion of the electric car was grateful. . . . But at
length the sight of familiar landmarks, old-fashioned
dwellings crowded in between the stores and factories of

lower Tower Street, brought back recollections of the days when she had come this way, other Sunday mornings, and in a more leisurely public vehicle, with her mother. Was it possible that she, Alison Parr, were going to church now? Her excitement deepened, and she found it difficult to bring herself to the realization that her destination *was* a church — the church of her childhood. At this moment she could only think of St. John's as the setting of the supreme drama.

When she alighted at the corner of Burton Street there was the well-remembered, shifting group on the pavement in front of the church porch. How many times, in the summer and winter, in fair weather and cloudy, in rain and sleet and snow had she approached that group, as she approached it now! Here were the people, still, in the midst of whom her earliest associations had been formed, changed, indeed, — but yet the same. No, the change was in her, and the very vastness of that change came as a shock. These had stood still, anchored to their traditions, while she — had she grown? or merely wandered? She had searched, at least, and *seen*. She had once accepted them — if indeed as a child it could have been said of her that she accepted anything ; she had been unable then, at any rate, to bring forward any comparisons.

Now she beheld them, collectively, in their complacent finery, as representing a force, a section of the army blocking the heads of the passes of the world's progress, resting on their arms, but ready at the least uneasy movement from below to man the breastworks, to fling down the traitor from above, to fight fiercely for the solidarity of their order. And Alison even believed herself to detect, by something indefinable in their attitudes as they stood momentarily conversing in lowered voices, an aroused suspicion, an uneasy anticipation. Her imagination went so far as to apprehend, as they greeted her unwonted appearance, that they read in it an addition to other vague and disturbing phenomena. Her colour was high.

" Why, my dear," said Mrs. Atterbury, "I thought you had gone back to New York long ago ! "

2 A

Beside his mother stood Gordon — more dried up, it seemed, than ever. Alison recalled him, as on this very spot, a thin, pale boy in short trousers, and Mrs. Atterbury a beautiful and controlled young matron associated with St. John's and with children's parties. She was wonderful yet, with her white hair and straight nose, her erect figure still slight. Alison knew that Mrs. Atterbury had never forgiven her for rejecting her son — or rather for being the kind of woman who could reject him.

" Surely you haven't been here all summer ? "

Alison admitted it, characteristically, without explanations.

" It seems so natural to see you here at the old church, after all these years," the lady went on, and Alison was aware that Mrs. Atterbury questioned — or rather was at a loss for the motives which had led such an apostate back to the fold. " We must thank Mr. Hodder, I suppose. He's very remarkable. I hear he is resuming the services to-day for the first time since June."

Alison was inclined to read a significance into Mrs. Atterbury's glance at her son, who was clearing his throat.

" But — where is Mr. Parr ? " he asked. " I understand he has come back from his cruise."

" Yes, he is back. I came without him — as you see."

She found a certain satisfaction in adding to the mystification, to the disquietude he betrayed by fidgeting more than usual.

" But — he always comes when he is in town. Business — I suppose — ahem ! "

" No," replied Alison, dropping her bomb with cruel precision, " he has gone to Calvary."

The agitation was instantaneous.

" To Calvary ! " exclaimed mother and son in one breath. " Why ? " It was Gordon who demanded. " A — a special occasion there — a bishop or something ? "

" I'm afraid you must ask him," she said.

She was delayed on the steps, first by Nan Ferguson, then by the Laureston Greys, and her news outdistanced her to the porch. Charlotte Plimpton, looking very red and solid, her eyes glittering with excitement, blocked her way.

"Alison!" she cried, in the slightly nasal voice that was a Gore inheritance, "I'm told your father's gone to Calvary! Has Mr. Hodder offended him? I heard rumours — Wallis seems to be afraid that something has happened."

"He hasn't said anything about it to me, Charlotte," said Alison, in quiet amusement, "but then he wouldn't, you know. I don't live here any longer, and he has no reason to think that I would be interested in church matters."

"But — why did *you* come?" Charlotte demanded, with Gore naïveté.

Alison smiled.

"You mean — what was my motive?"

Charlotte actually performed the miracle of getting redder. She was afraid of Alison — much more afraid since she had known of her vogue in the East. When Alison had put into execution the astounding folly (to the Gore mind) of rejecting the inheritance of millions to espouse a profession, it had been Charlotte Plimpton who led the chorus of ridicule and disapproval. But success, to the Charlotte Plimptons, is its own justification, and now her ambition (which had ramifications) was to have Alison "do" her a garden. Incidentally, the question had flashed through her mind as to how much Alison's good looks had helped towards her triumph in certain shining circles.

"Oh, of course I didn't mean that," she hastened to deny, although it was exactly what she had meant. Her curiosity unsatisfied — and not likely to be satisfied at once, she shifted abruptly to the other burning subject. "I was *so* glad when I learned you hadn't gone. Grace Larrabbee's garden is a *dream*, my dear. Wallis and I stopped there the other day and the caretaker showed it to us. Can't you make a plan for me, so that I may begin next spring? And there's something else I wanted to ask you. Wallis and I are going to New York the end of the month. Shall you be there?"

"I don't know," said Alison, cautiously.

"We want so much to see one or two of your gardens on Long Island, and especially the Sibleys', on the Hudson. I know it will be late in the season, — but don't you think you could take us, Alison? And I intend to give you a dinner. I'll write you a note. Here's Wallis."

"Well, well, *well*," said Mr. Plimpton, shaking Alison's hand. "Where's father? I hear he's gone to Calvary."

Alison made her escape. Inside the silent church, Eleanor Goodrich gave her a smile and a pressure of welcome. Beside her, standing behind the rear pew, were Asa Waring and — Mr. Bentley! Mr. Bentley returned to St. John's!

"*You* have come!" Alison whispered.

He understood her. He took her hand in his and looked down into her upturned face.

"Yes, my dear," he said, "and my girls have come — Sally Grover and the others, and some friends from Dalton Street and elsewhere."

The news, the sound of this old gentleman's voice and the touch of his hand suddenly filled her with a strange yet sober happiness. Asa Waring, though he had not overheard, smiled at her too, as in sympathy. His austere face was curiously illuminated, and she knew instinctively that in some way he shared her happiness. Mr. Bentley had come back! Yes, it was an augury. From childhood she had always admired Asa Waring, and now she felt a closer tie. . . .

She reached the pew, hesitated an instant, and slipped forward on her knees. Years had gone by since she had prayed, and even now she made no attempt to translate into words the intensity of her yearning — for what? Hodder's success, for one thing, — and by success she meant that he might pursue an unfaltering course. True to her temperament, she did not look for the downfall of the forces opposed to him. She beheld him persecuted, yet unyielding, and was thus lifted to an exaltation that amazed. . . . If he could do it, such a struggle must surely have an ultimate meaning ! Thus she found herself, trembling, on the borderland of faith. . . .

She arose, bewildered, her pulses beating. And presently glancing about, she took in that the church was fuller than she ever remembered having seen it, and the palpitating suspense she felt seemed to pervade, as it were, the very silence. With startling abruptness, the silence was broken by the tones of the great organ that rolled and reverberated among the arches ; distant voices took up the processional ; the white choir filed past, — first the treble voices of the boys, then the deeper notes of the men, — turned and mounted the chancel steps, and then she saw Hodder. Her pew being among the first, he passed very near her. Did he know she would be there ? The sternness of his profile told her nothing. He seemed at that moment removed, set apart, consecrated — this was the word that came to her, and yet she was keenly conscious of his presence.

Tingling, she found herself repeating, inwardly, two lines of the hymn :

> " Lay hold on life, and it shall be
> Thy joy and crown eternally."

" Lay hold on life ! "

The service began, — the well-remembered, beautiful appeal and prayers which she could still repeat, after a lapse of time, almost by heart; and their music and rhythm, the simple yet magnificent language in which they were clothed — her own language — awoke this morning a racial instinct strong in her, — she had not known how strong. Or was it something in Hodder's voice that seemed to illumine the ancient words with a new meaning ? Raising her eyes to the chancel she studied his head, and found in it still another expression of that race, the history of which had been one of protest, of development of its own character and personality. Her mind went back to her first talk with him, in the garden, and she saw how her intuition had recognized in him then the spirit of a people striving to assert itself. . . .

She stood with tightened lips, during the Apostles' Creed, listening to his voice as it rose, strong and unfaltering, above the murmur of the congregation. . . .

At last she saw him swiftly crossing the chancel, mounting the pulpit steps, and he towered above her, a dominant figure, his white surplice sharply outlined against the dark stone of the pillar. The hymn died away, the congregation sat down. There was a sound in the church, expectant, presaging, like the stirring of leaves at the first breath of wind, and then all was silent.

II

He had preached for an hour — longer, perhaps. Alison could not have said how long. She had lost all sense of time.

No sooner had the text been spoken, " Except a man be born again, he cannot see the Kingdom of God," than she seemed to catch a fleeting glimpse of an hitherto unimagined Personality. Hundreds of times she had heard those words, and they had been as meaningless to her as to Nicodemus. But now — now something was brought home to her of the magnificent certainty with which they must first have been spoken, of the tone and bearing and authority of him who had uttered them. Was Christ like that ? And could it be a Truth, after all, a truth only to be grasped by one who had experienced it ?

It was in vain that man had tried to evade this, the supreme revelation of Jesus Christ, had sought to substitute ceremonies and sacrifices for spiritual rebirth. It was in vain that the Church herself had, from time to time, been inclined to compromise. St. Paul, once the strict Pharisee who had laboured for the religion of works, himself had been reborn into the religion of the Spirit. It was Paul who had liberated that message of rebirth, which the world has been so long in grasping, from the narrow bounds of Palestine and sent it ringing down the ages to the democracies of the twentieth century.

And even Paul, though not consciously inconsistent, could not rid himself completely of that ancient, automatic conception of religion which the Master condemned, but had on occasions attempted fruitlessly to unite the new with the old. And thus, for a long time, Christianity had been wrongly conceived as *history*, beginning with what to Paul and the Jews was an historical event, the allegory of the Garden of Eden, the fall of Adam, and ending with the Jewish conception of the Atonement. This was a rationalistic and not a spiritual religion.

The miracle was not the *vision*, whatever its nature, which Saul beheld on the road to Damascus. The miracle was the *result* of that vision, the man *reborn*. Saul, the persecutor of Christians, become Paul, who spent the rest of his days, in spite of persecution and bodily infirmities, journeying tirelessly up and down the Roman Empire, preaching the risen Christ, and labouring more abundantly than they all! There was no miracle in the New Testament more wonderful than this.

The risen Christ! Let us not trouble ourselves about the psychological problems involved, problems which the first century interpreted in its own simple way. Modern science has taught us this much, at least, that we have by no means fathomed the limits even of a transcendent personality. If proofs of the Resurrection and Ascension were demanded, let them be *spiritual* proofs, and there could be none more convincing than the life of the transformed Saul, who had given to the modern, western world the message of salvation. . . .

That afternoon, as Alison sat motionless on a distant hillside of the Park, gazing across the tree-dotted, rolling country to the westward, she recalled the breathless silence in the church when he had reached this point and paused, looking down at the congregation. By the subtle transmission of thought, of feeling which is characteristic at dramatic moments of bodies of people, she knew that he had already contrived to stir them to the quick. It was not so much that these opening words might have been startling to the strictly orthodox, but the added fact that *Hodder* had uttered them. The sensation in the pews, as Alison interpreted it and exulted over it, was one of bewildered amazement that this *was* their rector, — the same man who had preached to them in June. Like Paul, of whom he spoke, he too was transformed, had come to his own, radiating a new power that seemed to shine in his face.

Still agitated, she considered that discourse now in her solitude, what it meant for him, for her, for the Church and civilization that a clergyman should have had the courage to preach it. He himself had seemed unconscious of any courage ; had never once — she recalled — been sensational. He had spoken simply, even in the intensest moments of denunciation. And she wondered now how he had managed, without stripping himself, without baring the intimate, sacred experiences of his own soul, to convey to them, so nobly, the change which had taken place in him. . . .

He began by referring to the hope with which he had come to St. John's, and the gradual realization that the church was a failure — a dismal failure when compared to the high ideal of her Master. By her fruits she should be known and judged. From the first he had contemplated, with a heavy heart, the sin and misery at their very gates. Not three blocks distant children were learning vice in the streets, little boys of seven and eight, underfed and anæmic, were driven out before dawn to sell newspapers, little girls thrust forth to haunt the saloons and beg, while their own children were warmed and fed. While their own daughters were guarded, young women in Dalton Street were forced to sell themselves into a life which meant slow torture, inevitable early death. Hopeless husbands and wives were cast up like driftwood by the cruel, resistless flood of modern civilization — the very civilization which yielded their wealth and luxury. The civilization which professed the Spirit of Christ, and yet was pitiless.

He confessed to them that for a long time he had been blind to the truth, had taken the inherited, unchristian view that the disease which caused vice and poverty might not be cured, though its ulcers might be alleviated. He had not, indeed, clearly perceived and recognized the disease. He had regarded Dalton Street in a very special sense as a reproach to St. John's, but now he saw that all such neighbourhoods were in reality a reproach to the *city*, *to the state*, *to the nation*. True Christianity and Democracy were identical, and the congregation of St. John's, as professed Christians and citizens, were doubly responsible, inasmuch as they not only made no protest or attempt to change a government which permitted the Dalton Streets to exist, but inasmuch also as, — directly or indirectly, — they derived a profit from conditions which were an abomination to God. It would be but an idle mockery for them to go and build a settlement house, if they did not first reform their lives.

Here there had been a decided stir among the pews. Hodder had not seemed to notice it.

When he, their rector, had gone to Dalton Street to invite the poor and wretched into God's Church, he was met by the scornful question : " Are the Christians of the churches any better than we ? Christians own the grim tenements in which we live, the saloons and brothels by which we are surrounded, which devour our children. Christians own the establishments which pay us starvation wages; profit by politics, and take toll from our very vice; evade the laws and reap millions, while we are sent to jail. Is their God a God who will lift us out of our misery and distress ? Are their churches for the poor ? Are not the very pews in which they sit as closed to us as their houses ? "

"I know thy works, that thou art neither cold nor hot. I would thou wert cold or hot."

One inevitable conclusion of such a revelation was that he had not preached to them the vital element of Christianity. And the very fact that his presentation of religion had left many indifferent or dissatisfied was proof

positive that he had dwelt upon non-essentials, laid emphasis upon the mistaken interpretations of past ages. There
were those within the Church who were content with
this, who — like the Pharisees of old — welcomed a religion which did not interfere with their complacency,
with their pursuit of pleasure and wealth, with their
special privileges; welcomed a Church which didn't raise
her voice against the manner of their lives — against the
order, the Golden Calf which they had set up, which did
not accuse them of deliberately retarding the coming of
the Kingdom of God.

Ah, that religion was not religion, for religion was a
spiritual, not a material affair. In *that* religion, vainly
designed by man as a compromise between God and
Mammon, there was none of the divine discontent of the
true religion of the Spirit, no need of the rebirth of the
soul. And those who held it might well demand, with
Nicodemus and the rulers of the earth, "How can these
things be?"

And there were others who still lingered in the Church,
perplexed and wistful, who had come to him and confessed that the so-called catholic acceptance of divine
truths, on which he had hitherto dwelt, meant nothing to
them. To these, in particular, he owed a special repa-
ration, and he took this occasion to announce a series of
Sunday evening sermons on the Creeds. So long as the
Creeds remained in the Prayer Book it was his duty to
interpret them in terms not only of modern thought, but
in harmony with the real significance of the Person and
message of Jesus Christ. Those who had come to him
questioning, he declared, were a thousand times right in
refusing to accept the interpretations of other men, the
consensus of opinion of more ignorant ages, expressed in
an ancient science and an archaic philosophy.

And what should be said of the vast and ever increasing
numbers of those not connected with the Church, who had
left it or were leaving it? and of the less fortunate to
whose bodily wants they had been ministering in the
parish house, for whom it had no spiritual message, and

who never entered its doors? The necessity of religion, of getting in touch with, of dependence on the Spirit of the Universe was inherent in man, and yet there were thousands — nay, millions in the nation to-day in whose hearts was an intense and unsatisfied yearning, who perceived no meaning in life, no Cause for which to work, who did not know what Christianity was, who had never known what it was, who wist not where to turn to find out. Education had brought many of them to discern, in the Church's teachings, an anachronistic medley of myths and legends, of theories of schoolmen and theologians, of surviving pagan superstitions which could not be translated into life. They saw, in Christianity, only the adulterations of the centuries. If any one needed a proof of the yearning people felt, let him go to the bookshops, or read in the publishers' lists to-day the announcements of books on religion. There was no supply where there was no demand.

Truth might no longer be identified with Tradition, and the day was past when councils and synods might determine it for all mankind. The era of forced acceptance of philosophical doctrines and dogmas was past, and that of freedom, of spiritual rebirth, of vicarious suffering, of willing sacrifice and service for a Cause was upon them. *That cause was Democracy.* Christ was uniquely the Son of God because he had lived and suffered and died in order to reveal to the world the meaning of this life and of the hereafter — the meaning not only for the individual, but for society as well. Nothing might be added to or subtracted from that message — it was complete.

True faith was simply trusting — trusting that Christ gave to the world the revelation of God's plan. And the Saviour himself had pointed out the proof: "If any man do his will, he shall know of the doctrine, whether it be of God, or whether I speak for myself." Christ had repeatedly rebuked those literal minds which had demanded material evidence: true faith spurned it, just as true friendship, true love between man and man, true trust scorned a written bond. To paraphrase St. James's words, faith without trust is dead — because faith without trust is impossible. God is a Spirit, only to be recognized in the Spirit, and every one of the Saviour's utterances were — not of the flesh, of the man — but of the Spirit within him. " He that hath seen me hath seen the Father ; " and " Why callest thou me good ? none is good save one, that is, God." The Spirit, the Universal Meaning of Life, incarnate in the human Jesus.

To be born again was to overcome our spiritual blindness, and then, and then only, we might behold the spirit shining in the soul of Christ. That proof had sufficed for Mark, had sufficed for the writer of the sublime Fourth Gospel, had sufficed for Paul. Let us lift this wondrous fact, once and for all, out of the ecclesiastical setting and incorporate it into our lives. Nor need the hearts of those who seek the Truth, who fear not to face it, be troubled if they be satisfied, from the Gospels, that the birth of Jesus was not miraculous. The physical never could prove the spiritual, which was the real and everlasting, which no discovery in science or history can take from us. The Godship of Christ rested upon no dogma, it was a conviction born into us with the new birth. And it becomes an integral part of our personality, our very being.

The secret, then, lay in a presentation of the divine message which would convince and transform and electrify those who heard it to *action* — a presentation of the message in terms which the age could grasp. That is what Paul had done, he had drawn his figures boldly from the customs of the life of his day, but a more or less intimate knowledge of these ancient customs were necessary before modern men and women could understand those figures and parallels. And the Church must awake to her opportunities, to her perception of the Cause. . . .

What, then, was the function, the mission of the Church Universal ? Once she had laid claim to temporal power, believed herself to be the sole agency of God on earth, had spoken *ex cathedra* on philosophy, history, theology, and science, had undertaken to confer eternal bliss and to damn forever. Her members, and even her priests, had gone from murder to mass and from mass to murder, and she had engaged in cruel wars and persecutions to curtail the liberties of mankind. Under that conception religion was a form of insurance of the soul. Perhaps a common, universal belief had been necessary in the dark ages before the sublime idea of education for the masses had come ; but the Church herself — through ignorance — had opposed the growth of education, had set her face sternly against the development of the individual, which Christ had taught, the privilege of man to use the faculties of the intellect which God had bestowed upon him. He himself, their rector, had advocated a catholic acceptance, though much modified from the mediæval acceptance, — one that professed to go behind it to an earlier age. Yes, he must admit with shame that he had been afraid to trust where God trusted, had feared to confide the working out of the ultimate Truth of the minds of the millions.

The Church had been monarchical in form, and some strove stubbornly and blindly to keep her monarchical. Democracy in government was outstripping her. Let them look around, to-day, and see what was happening in the United States of America. A great movement was going on to transfer actual participation in government from the few to the many, — a movement towards true Democracy, — and that was precisely what was about to happen in the Church. Her condition at present was one of uncertainty, transition — she feared to let go wholly of the old, she feared to embark upon the new. Just as the conservatives and politicians feared to give up the representative system, the convention, so was she afraid to abandon the synod, the council, and trust to man.

The light was coming slowly, the change, the rebirth of the Church by gradual evolution. By the grace of God those who had laid the foundations of the Church in which he stood, of all Protestantism, had built for the future. The racial instinct in them had asserted itself, had warned them that to suppress freedom in religion were to suppress it in life, to paralyze that individual initiative which was the secret of their advancement. . . .

The new Church Universal, then, would be the militant, aggressive body of the reborn, whose mission it was to send out into the life of the nation transformed men and women who would labour unremittingly for the Kingdom of God. Unity would come — but unity in freedom, true Catholicity. The truth would gradually pervade the masses — *be wrought out by them*. Even the great evolutionary forces of the age, such as economic necessity, were acting to drive divided Christianity into consolidation, and the starving churches of country villages were now beginning to combine. . . .

No man might venture to predict the details of the future organization of the united Church, although St. Paul himself had sketched it in broad outline : every worker, lay and clerical, labouring according to his gift, teachers, executives, ministers, visitors, missionaries, healers of sick and despondent souls. But the supreme function of the Church was to *inspire* — to inspire individuals to willing service for the cause, the Cause of Democracy, the fellowship of mankind. If she failed to inspire, the Church would wither and perish. And therefore she must revive again the race of inspirers, prophets, modern Apostles to whom this gift was given, going on their rounds, awaking cities and arousing whole country-sides.

But whence — it might be demanded by the cynical — were the prophets to come? Prophets could not be produced by training and education ; prophets must be born. *Reborn,* — that was the word. Let the Church have faith. Once her Cause were perceived, once her whole energy were directed towards its fulfilment, the prophets would arise, out of the East and out of the West, to stir mankind to higher effort, to denounce fearlessly the shortcomings and evils of the age. They had not failed in past ages, when the world had fallen into hopelessness, indifference, and darkness. And they would not fail now.

Prophets were personalities, and Phillips Brooks —
himself a prophet — had defined personality as a conscious
relationship with God. " All truth," he had said, " comes
to the world through personality." And down the ages
had come an Apostolic Succession of personalities, —
Paul, Augustine, Francis, Dante, Luther, Milton, — yes,
and Abraham Lincoln, and Phillips Brooks, whose Authority was that of the Spirit, whose light had so shone before
men that they had glorified the Father which was in
heaven ; the current of whose Power had so radiated, in
ever widening circles, as to make incandescent countless
other souls.

And which among them would declare that Abraham
Lincoln, like Stephen, had not seen his Master in the sky ?

The true prophet, the true apostle, then, was one inspired and directed by the Spirit, the laying on of hands
was but a symbol, — the symbol of the sublime truth that
one personality caught fire from another. Let the Church
hold fast to that symbol, as an acknowledgment, a reminder of a supreme mystery. Tradition had its value
when it did not deteriorate into superstition, into the
mechanical, automatic transmission characteristic of the
mediæval Church, for the very suggestion of which Peter
had rebuked Simon in Samaria. For it would be remembered that Simon had said: " Give me also this power,
that on whomsoever I lay hands, he may receive the Holy
Ghost."

The true successor to the Apostles must be an Apostle
himself. . . .

Jesus had seldom spoken literally, and the truths he
sought to impress upon the world had of necessity been
clothed in figures and symbols, — for spiritual truths might
be conveyed in no other way. The supreme proof of his
Godship, of his complete knowledge of the meaning of life
was to be found in his parables. To the literal, material
mind, for example, the parable of the talents was merely
an unintelligible case of injustice. . . . What was
meant by the talents ? They were *opportunities for service*.
Experience taught us that when we embraced one oppor-

tunity, one responsibility, the acceptance of it invariably led to another, and so the servant who had five talents, five opportunities, gained ten. The servant who had two gained two more. But the servant of whom only one little service was asked refused that, and was cast into outer darkness, to witness another performing the task which should have been his. Hell, here and hereafter, was the spectacle of wasted opportunity, and there is no suffering to compare to it.

The crime, the cardinal sin was with those who refused to serve, who shut their eyes to the ideal their Lord had held up, who strove to compromise with Jesus Christ himself, to twist and torture his message to suit their own notions as to how life should be led; to please God and Mammon at the same time, to bind Christ's Church for their comfort and selfish convenience. Of them it was written, that they shut up the Kingdom of Heaven against men; for they neither go in themselves, neither suffer them that are entering to go in. Were these any better than the people who had crucified the Lord for his idealism, and because he had not brought them the material Kingdom for which they longed?

That servant who had feared to act, who had hid his talent in the ground, who had said unto his lord, "I knew thee that thou art an hard man, reaping where thou hadst not sown," was the man without faith, the atheist who sees only cruelty and indifference in the order of things, who has no spiritual sight. But to the other servants it was said, "Thou hast been faithful over a few things, I will make thee ruler over many things. Enter thou into the joy of thy lord."

The meaning of life, then, was service, and by life our Lord did not mean mere human existence, which is only a part of life. The Kingdom of heaven is a *state*, and may begin here. And that which we saw around us was only one expression of that eternal life — a medium to work through, towards God. All was service, both here and hereafter, and he that had not discovered that the joy of service was the only happiness worth living for could have no conception of the Kingdom. To those who knew, there was no happiness like being able to say, "I have found my place in God's plan, *I am of use.*" Such was salvation. . . .

And in the parable of the Prodigal Son may be read the history of what are known as the Protestant nations. What happens logically when the individual is suddenly freed from the restraint of external authority occurred when Martin Luther released the vital spark of Christianity, which he got from Paul, and from Christ himself — the revelation of individual responsibility, that God the Spirit would dwell, by grace, in the individual soul. Ah, we had paid a terrible yet necessary price for freedom. We had wandered far from the Father, we had been reduced to the very husks of individualism, — become as swine. We beheld around us, to-day, selfishness, ruthless competition, as great contrasts between misery and luxury as in the days of the Roman Empire. But should we, for that reason, return to the leading-strings of authority? Could we if we would? A little thought ought to convince us that the liberation of the individual could not be revoked, that it had forever destroyed the power of authority to carry conviction. To go back to the Middle Ages would be to deteriorate and degenerate. No, we must go on. . . .

Luther's movement, in religion, had been the logical forerunner of democracy, of universal suffrage in government, the death-knell of that misinterpretation of Christianity as the bulwark of monarchy aud hierarchy had been sounded when he said, "*Ich kann nicht anders!*" The new Republic founded on the western continent had announced to the world the initiation of the transfer of Authority to the individual soul. God, the counterpart of the King, the ruler in a high heaven of a flat terrestrial expanse, outside of the world, was now become the Spirit of a million spheres, the indwelling spirit in man. Democracy and the religion of Jesus Christ both consisted in *trusting* the man — yes, and the woman — whom God trusts. Christianity was individualism carried beyond

2 B

philosophy into religion, and the Christian, the ideal citizen of the democracy, was free since he served not because he *had* to, but because he *desired* to of his own will, which, paradoxically, is God's will. God was in politics, to the confusion of politicians; God in government. And in some greater and higher sense than we had yet perceived, the saying *vox populi vox dei* was eternally true. He entered into the hearts of people and moved them, and so the world progressed. It was the function of the Church to make Christians, until — when the Kingdom of God should come — the blending should be complete. Then Church and State would be identical, since all the members of the one would be the citizens of the other. . . .

"I will arise and go to my father." Rebirth! A sense of responsibility, of consecration. So we had come painfully through our materialistic individualism, through our selfish Protestantism, to a glimpse of the true Protestantism — Democracy.

Our spiritual vision was glowing clearer. We were beginning to perceive that charity did not consist in dispensing largesse after making a fortune at the expense of one's fellow-men; that there was something still wrong in a government that permits it. It was gradually becoming plain to us, after two thousand years, that human bodies and souls rotting in tenements were more valuable than all the forests on all the hills; that government, Christian government, had something to do with these.

We should embody, in government, those sublime words of the Master, "Suffer little children to come unto me." And the government of the future would care for the little children. We were beginning to do it. Here, as elsewhere, Christianity and reason went hand in hand, for the child became the man who either preyed on humanity and filled the prisons and robbed his fellows, or else grew into a useful, healthy citizen. It was nothing less than sheer folly as well as inhuman cruelty to let the children sleep in crowded, hot rooms, reeking with diseases, and run wild throughout the long summer, learning vice in the city streets. And we still had slavery — economic slavery — yes, and the more horrible slavery of women and young girls in vice — as much a concern of government as the problem which had confronted it in 1861. . . . We were learning that there was something infinitely more sacred than property. . . .

And now Alison recalled, only to be thrilled again by an electric sensation she had never before experienced with such intensity, the look of inspiration on the preacher's face as he closed. The very mists of the future seemed to break before his importuning gaze, and his eyes seemed indeed to behold, against the whitening dawn of the spiritual age he predicted, the slender spires of a new Church sprung from the foundations of the old. A Church, truly catholic, tolerant, whose portals were wide in welcome of all mankind. The creative impulse, he had declared, was invariably religious, the highest art but the expression of the mute yearnings of a people, of a race. Thus had once arisen, all over Europe, those wonderful cathedrals which still cast their spell upon the world, and art to-day would respond — was responding — to the unutterable cravings of mankind, would strive once more to express in stone and glass and pigment what nations felt. Generation after generation would labour with unflagging zeal until the last sculptured fragment of the new Cathedral — the new Cathedral of Democracy — pointed upward toward the blue vault of heaven. Such was his vision — God the Spirit, through man reborn, carrying out his great Design. . . . .

CHAPTER XXII

"WHICH SAY TO THE SEERS, SEE NOT"

I

As Alison arose from her knees and made her way out of the pew, it was the expression on Charlotte Plimpton's face which brought her back once more to a sense of her surroundings; struck her, indeed, like a physical blow. The expression was a scandalized one. Mrs. Plimpton had moved towards her, as if to speak, but Alison hurried past, her exaltation suddenly shattered, replaced by a rising tide of resentment, of angry amazement against a materialism so solid as to remain unshaken by the words which had so uplifted her. Eddies were forming in the aisle as the people streamed slowly out of the church, and snatches of their conversation, in undertones, reached her ears.

"I should never have believed it!"

"Mr. Hodder, of all men. . . ."

"The bishop! . . ."

Outside the swinging doors, in the vestibule, the voices were raised a little, and she found her path blocked.

"It's incredible!" she heard Gordon Atterbury saying to little Everett Constable, who was listening gloomily. "Sheer Unitarianism, socialism, heresy."

His attention was forcibly arrested by Alison, in whose cheeks bright spots of colour burned. He stepped aside, involuntarily, apologetically, as though he had instinctively read in her attitude an unaccountable disdain. Everett Constable bowed uncertainly, for Alison scarcely noticed them.

"Ahem!" said Gordon, nervously, abandoning his

former companion and joining her, "I was just saying, it's incredible — "

She turned on him.

"It *is* incredible," she cried, "that persons who call themselves Christians cannot recognize their religion when they hear it preached."

He gave back before her, visibly, in an astonishment which would have been ludicrous but for her anger. He had never understood her — such had been for him her greatest fascination; — and now she was less comprehensible than ever. The time had been when he would cheerfully have given over his hope of salvation to have been able to stir her. He had never seen her stirred, and the sight of her even now in this condition was uncomfortably agitating. Of all things, an heretical sermon would appear to have accomplished this miracle !

"Christianity !" he stammered.

"Yes, Christianity." Her voice tingled. "I don't pretend to know much about it, but Mr. Hodder has at least made it plain that it is something more than dead dogmas, ceremonies, and superstitions."

He would have said something, but her one thought was to escape, to be alone. These friends of her childhood were at that moment so distasteful as to have become hateful. Some one laid a hand upon her arm.

"Can't we take you home, Alison ? I don't see your motor."

It was Mrs. Constable.

"No, thanks — I'm going to walk," Alison answered, — yet something in Mrs. Constable's face, in Mrs. Constable's voice, made her pause. Something new, something oddly sympathetic. Their eyes met, and Alison saw that the other woman's were tired, almost haggard — yet understanding.

"Mr. Hodder was right — a thousand times right, my dear," she said.

Alison could only stare at her, and the crimson in the bright spots of her cheeks spread over her face. Why had Mrs. Constable supposed that *she* would care to hear the sermon praised? But a second glance put her in possession of the extraordinary fact that Mrs. Constable herself was profoundly moved.

"I knew he would change," she went on, "I have seen for some time that he was too big a man not to change. But I had no conception that he would have such power, and such courage, as he has shown this morning. It is not only that he dared to tell us what we were — smaller men might have done that, and it is comparatively easy to denounce. But he has the vision to construct, he is a seer himself — he has really made me see what Christianity is. And as long as I live I shall never forget those closing sentences."

"And now?" asked Alison. "And now what will happen?"

Mrs. Constable changed colour. Her tact, on which she prided herself, had deserted her in a moment of un-looked-for emotion.

"Oh, I know that my father and the others will try to put him out — but can they?" Alison asked.

It was Mrs. Constable's turn to stare. The hand she suddenly and impulsively put forth trembled on Alison's wrist.

"I don't know, Alison — I'm afraid they can. It is too terrible to think about. . . . And they can't — they won't believe that many changes are coming, that this is but one of many signs. . . . Do come and see me."

Alison left her, marvelling at the passage between them, and that, of all persons in the congregation of St. John's, the lightning should have struck Mrs. Constable. . . . Turning to the right on Burton Street, she soon found herself walking rapidly westward through deserted streets lined by factories and warehouses, and silent in the Sabbath calm. . . . She thought of Hodder, she would have liked to go to him in that hour. . . .

In Park Street, luncheon was half over, and Nelson Langmaid was at the table with her father. The lawyer glanced at her curiously as she entered the room, and his usual word of banter, she thought, was rather lame. The two went on, for some time, discussing a railroad suit in Texas. And Alison, as she hurried through her meal, leaving the dishes almost untouched, scarcely heard them. Once, in her reverie, her thoughts reverted to another Sunday when Hodder had sat, an honoured guest, in the chair which Mr. Langmaid now occupied. . . .

It was not until they got up from the table that her father turned to her.

"Did you have a good sermon?" he asked.

It was the underlying note of challenge to which she responded.

"The only good sermon I have ever heard."

Their eyes met. Langmaid looked down at the tip of his cigar.

"Mr. Hodder," said Eldon Parr, "is to be congratulated."

II

Hodder, when the service was over, had sought the familiar recess in the robing-room, the words which he himself had spoken still ringing in his ears. And then he recalled the desperate prayer with which he had entered the pulpit, that it might be given him in that hour what to say: the vivid memories of the passions and miseries in Dalton Street, the sudden, hot response of indignation at the complacency confronting him. His voice had trembled with anger. . . . He remembered, as he had paused in his denunciation of these who had eyes and saw not, meeting the upturned look of Alison Parr, and his anger had turned to pity for their blindness — which once had been his own; and he had gone on and on, striving to interpret for them his new revelation of the message of the Saviour, to impress upon them the dreadful yet sublime meaning of life eternal. And it was in that moment the vision of the meaning of the evolution of his race, of the Prodigal turning to responsibility — of which he once had had a glimpse — had risen before his eyes in its completeness — the guiding hand of God in history! The Spirit in these complacent souls, as yet unstirred. . . .

So complete, now, was his forgetfulness of self, of his future, of the irrevocable consequences of the step he had taken, that it was only gradually he became aware that some one was standing near him, and with a start he recognized McCrae.

"There are some waiting to speak to ye," his assistant said.

"Oh!" Hodder exclaimed. He began, mechanically, to divest himself of his surplice. McCrae stood by.

"I'd like to say a word, first — if ye don't mind —" he began.

The rector looked at him quickly.

"I'd like just to thank ye for that sermon — I can say no more now," said McCrae; he turned away, and left the room abruptly.

This characteristic tribute from the inarticulate, loyal Scotchman left him tingling. . . . He made his way to the door and saw the people in the choir room, standing silently, in groups, looking toward him. Some one spoke to him, and he recognized Eleanor Goodrich.

"We couldn't help coming, Mr. Hodder — just to tell you how much we admire you. It was wonderful, what you said."

He grew hot with gratitude, with thankfulness that there were some who understood — and that this woman was among them, and her husband. . . . Phil Goodrich took him by the hand.

"I can understand that kind of religion," he said. "And, if necessary, I can fight for it. I have come to enlist."

"And I can understand it, too," added the sunburned Evelyn. "I hope you will let me help."

That was all they said, but Hodder understood. Eleanor Goodrich's eyes were dimmed as she smiled on her sister and her husband — a smile that bespoke the purest quality of pride. And it was then, as they made way for others, that the full value of their allegiance was borne in upon him, and he grasped the fact that the intangible barrier which had separated him from them had at last been broken down. His look followed the square shoulders and aggressive, close-cropped head of Phil Goodrich, the firm, athletic figure of Evelyn, who had represented to him an entire class of modern young women, vigorous, athletic, with a scorn of cant in which he secretly sympathized, hitherto frankly untouched by spiritual interests of any sort. She had, indeed, once bluntly told him that church meant nothing to her. . . .

In that little company gathered in the choir room were certain members of his congregation whom, had he taken thought, he would least have expected to see. There were Mr. and Mrs. Bradley, an elderly couple who had attended St. John's for thirty years ; and others of the same unpretentious element of his parish who were finding in modern life an increasingly difficult and bewildering problem. There was little Miss Tallant, an assiduous guild worker whom he had thought the most orthodox of persons; Miss Ramsay, who taught the children of the Italian mothers ; Mr. Caxton, the organist, a professed free-thinker, with whom Hodder had had many a futile argument ; and Martha Preston, who told him that he had made her think about religion seriously for the first time in her life.

And there were others, types equally diverse. Young men of the choir, and others whom he had never seen, who informed him shyly that they would come again, and bring their friends. . . .

And all the while, in the background, Hodder had been aware of a familiar face — Horace Bentley's. Beside him, when at length he drew near, was his friend Asa Waring — a strangely contrasted type. The uncompromising eyes of a born leader of men flashed from beneath the heavy white eyebrows, the button of the Legion of Honour gleaming in his well-kept coat seemed emblematic of the fire which in his youth had driven him forth to fight for the honour of his country — a fire still undimmed. It was he who spoke first.

"This is a day I never expected to see, Mr. Hodder," he said, "for it has brought back to this church the man to whom it owes its existence. Mr. Bentley did more, by his labour and generosity, his true Christianity, his charity and his wisdom, for St. John's than any other individual. It is you who have brought him back, and I wish personally to express my gratitude."

Mr. Bentley, in mild reproof, laid his hand upon the shoulder of his old friend.

"Ah, Asa," he protested, "you shouldn't say such things."

"Had it not been for Mr. Bentley," Hodder explained, "I should not be here to-day."

Asa Waring pierced the rector with his eye, appreciating the genuine feeling with which these words were spoken. And yet his look contained a question.

"Mr. Bentley," Hodder added, "has been my teacher this summer."

The old gentleman's hand trembled a little on the gold-headed stick.

"It is a matter of more pride to me than I can express, sir, that you are the rector of this church with which my most cherished memories are associated," he said. "But I cannot take any part of the credit you give me for the splendid vision which you have raised up before us to-day, for your inspired interpretation of history, of the meaning of our own times. You have moved me, you have given me more hope and courage than I have had for many a long year — and I thank you, Mr. Hodder. I am sure that God will prosper and guide you in what you have so nobly undertaken."

Mr. Bentley turned away, walking towards the end of the room. . . . Asa Waring broke the silence.

"I didn't know that you knew him, that you had seen what he is doing — what he has done in this city. I cannot trust myself, Mr. Hodder, to speak of Horace Bentley's life. . . . I feel too strongly on the subject. I have watched, year by year, this detestable spirit of greed, this lust for money and power creeping over our country

corrupting our people and institutions, and finally taint-
ing the Church itself. You have raised your voice
against it, and I respect and honour and thank you for it,
the more because you have done it without resorting to
sensation, and apparently with no thought of yourself.
And, incidentally, you have explained the Christian
religion to me as I have never had it explained in my life.

"I need not tell you you have made enemies — powerful ones. I can see that you are a man, and that you are
prepared for them. They will leave no stone unturned,
will neglect no means to put you out and disgrace you.
They will be about your ears to-morrow — this afternoon,
perhaps. I need not remind you that the outcome is
doubtful. But I came here to assure you of my friendship and support in all you hope to accomplish in making
the Church what it should be. In any event, what you
have done to-day will be productive of everlasting good."

In a corner still lingered the group which Mr. Bentley
had joined. And Hodder, as he made his way towards it,
recognized the faces of some of those who composed it.
Sally Grover was there, and the young women who lived
in Mr. Bentley's house, and others whose acquaintance he
had made during the summer. Mrs. Garvin had brought
little Dicky, incredibly changed from the wan little figure
he had first beheld in the stifling back room in Dalton
Street ; not yet robust, but freckled and tanned by the
country sun and wind. The child, whom he had seen
constantly in the interval, ran forward joyfully, and Hodder bent down to take his hand. . . .

These were his *friends*, emblematic of the new relationship in which he stood to mankind. And he owed them
to Horace Bentley! He wondered, as he greeted them,
whether they knew what their allegiance meant to him in
this hour. But it sufficed that they claimed him as their
own.

Behind them all stood Kate Marcy. And it struck him
for the first time, as he gazed at her earnestly, how her
appearance had changed. She gave him a frightened,
bewildered look, as though she were unable to identify

him now with the man she had known in the Dalton Street flat, in the restaurant. She was still struggling, groping, wondering, striving to accustom herself to the higher light of another world.

"I wanted to come," she faltered. "Sally Grover brought me. . . ."

Hodder went back with them to Dalton Street. His new ministry had begun. And on this, the first day of it, it was fitting that he should sit at the table of Horace Bentley, even as on that other Sunday, two years agone, he had gone to the home of the first layman of the diocese, Eldon Parr.

III

The peace of God passes understanding because sorrow and joy are mingled therein, sorrow and joy and striving. And thus the joy of emancipation may be accompanied by a heavy heart. The next morning, when Hodder entered his study, he sighed as his eye fell upon the unusual pile of letters on his desk, for their writers had once been his friends. The inevitable breach had come at last.

Most of the letters, as he had anticipated, were painful reading. And the silver paper-cutter with which he opened the first had been a Christmas present from Mrs. Burlingame, who had penned it, a lady of signal devotion to the church, who for many years had made it her task to supply and arrange the flowers on the altar. He had amazed and wounded her — she declared — inexpressibly, and she could no longer remain at St. John's — for the present, at least. A significant addition. He dropped the letter, and sat staring out of the window . . . presently arousing himself, setting himself resolutely to the task of reading the rest.

In the mood in which he found himself he did not stop to philosophize on the rigid yet sincere attitude of the orthodox. His affection for many of them curiously remained, though it was with some difficulty he strove to reconstruct a state of mind with which he had once

agreed. If Christianity were to sweep on, these few unbending but faithful ones must be sacrificed: such was
the law. . . . Many, while repudiating his new beliefs
— or unbeliefs! — added, to their regrets of the change in
him, protestations of a continued friendship, a conviction
of his sincerity. Others, like Mrs. Atterbury, were
frankly outraged and bitter. The contents of one lilac-
bordered envelope brought to his eyes a faint smile. Did
he know — asked the sender of this — could he know the
consternation he had caused in so many persons, including
herself? What was she to believe? And wouldn't he
lunch with her on Thursday?

Mrs. Ferguson's letter brought another smile — more
thoughtful. Her incoherent phrases had sprung from the
heart, and the picture rose before him of the stout but
frightened, good-natured lady who had never accustomed
herself to the enjoyment of wealth and luxury. Mr.
Ferguson was in such a state, and he must please not tell
her husband that she had written. Yet much in his sermon had struck her as so true. It seemed wrong to her to
have so much, and others so little! And he had made her
remember many things in her early life she had forgotten.
She hoped he would see Mr. Ferguson, and talk to
him. . . .

Then there was Mrs. Constable's short note, that troubled
and puzzled him. This, too, had in it an undercurrent of
fear, and the memory came to him of the harrowing afternoon he had once spent with her, when she would have
seemed to have predicted the very thing which had now
happened to him. And yet not that thing. He divined
instinctively that a maturer thought on the subject of his
sermon had brought on an uneasiness as the full consequences of this new teaching had dawned upon her —
consequences which she had not foreseen when she had
foretold the change. And he seemed to read between
the lines that the renunciation he demanded was too
great. . . . Would he not let her come and talk to
him? . . .

Miss Brewer, a lady of no inconsiderable property, was

among those who told him plainly that if he remained they would have to give up their pews. Three or four communications were even more threatening. Mr. Alpheus Gore, Mrs. Plimpton's brother, who at five and forty had managed to triple his share of the Gore inheritance, wrote that it would be his regretful duty to send to the bishop an Information on the subject of Mr. Hodder's sermon.

There were, indeed, a few letters which he laid, thankfully, in a pile by themselves. These were mostly from certain humble members of his parish who had not followed their impulses to go to him after the service, or from strangers who had chanced to drop into the church. Some were autobiographical, such as those of a trained nurse, a stenographer, a hardware clerk who had sat up late Sunday night to summarize what that sermon had meant to him, how a gray and hopeless existence had taken on a new colour. Next Sunday he would bring a friend who lived in the same boarding house. . . . Hodder read every word of these, and all were in the same strain: at last they could perceive a meaning to religion, an application of it to such plodding lives as theirs. . . .

One or two had not understood, but had been stirred, and were coming to talk to him. Another was filled with a venomous class hatred. . . .

The first intimation he had of the writer of another letter seemed from the senses rather than the intellect. A warm glow suffused him, mounted to his temples as he stared at the words, turned over the sheet, and read at the bottom the not very legible signature. The handwriting, by no means classic, became then and there indelibly photographed on his brain, and summed up for him the characteristics, the warring elements in Alison Parr. "All afternoon," she wrote, "I have been thinking of your sermon. It was to me very wonderful — it lifted me out of myself. And oh, I want so much to believe unreservedly what you expressed so finely, that religion *is* democracy, or the motive power behind democracy — the service of humanity by the reborn. I understand it *in-*

tellectually. I am willing to work for such a Cause, but there is something in me so hard that I wonder if it *can* dissolve. And then I am still unable to identify that Cause with the Church as at present constituted, with the dogmas and ceremonies that still exist. I am too thorough a radical to have your patience. And I am filled with rage — I can think of no milder word — on coming in contact with the living embodiments of that old creed, who hold its dogmas so precious. 'Which say to the seers, See not; and to the prophets, Prophesy not unto us right things, speak unto us smooth things, prophesy deceits.'

"You see, I have been reading Isaiah, and when I came to that paragraph it seemed so appropriate. *These people have always existed.* And will they not always continue to exist? I wish I could believe, wholly and unreservedly, that this class, always preponderant in the world, could be changed, diminished — done away with in a brighter future! I can, at least, sympathize with Isaiah's wrath.

"What you said of the longing, the yearning which exists to-day amongst the inarticulate millions moved me most — and of the place of art in religion, to express that yearning. Religion the motive power of art, and art, too, service. 'Consider the lilies of the field.' You have made it, at least, all-comprehensive, have given me a new point of view for which I can never be sufficiently grateful — and at a time when I needed it desperately. That you have dared to do what you have done has been and will be an inspiration, not only to myself, but to many others. This is a longer letter, I believe, than I have ever written in my life. But I wanted you to know."

He reread it twice, pondering over its phrases. "A new point of view . . . *at a time when I needed it desperately.*" It was not until then that he realized the full intensity of his desire for some expression from her since the moment he had caught sight of her in the church. But he had not been prepared for the unreserve, the impulsiveness with which she had actually written. Such was his agitation that he did not heed, at first, a knock on the door, which was repeated. He thrust the letter inside his coat as the janitor of the parish house appeared.

"There is a gentleman to see you, sir, in the office," he said.

Hodder went down the stairs. And he anticipated, from the light yet nervous pacing that he heard on the bare floor, that the visitor was none other than his vestryman, Mr. Gordon Atterbury. The sight of the gentleman's spruce figure confirmed the guess.

"Good morning, Mr. Atterbury," he said as he entered.

Mr. Atterbury stopped in his steps, as if he had heard a shot.

"Ah — good morning, Mr. Hodder. I stopped in on my way to the office."

"Sit down," said the rector.

Mr. Atterbury sat down, but with the air of a man who does so under protest, who had not intended to. He was visibly filled and almost quivering with an excitement which seemed to demand active expression, and which the tall clergyman's physical calm and self-possession seemed to augment. For a moment Mr. Atterbury stared at the rector as he sat behind his desk. Then he cleared his throat.

"I thought of writing to you, Mr. Hodder. My mother, I believe, has done so. But it seemed to me, on second thought, better to come to you direct."

The rector nodded, without venturing to remark on the wisdom of the course.

"It occurred to me," Mr. Atterbury went on, "that possibly some things I wish to discuss might — ahem — be dispelled in a conversation. That I might conceivably have misunderstood certain statements in your sermon of yesterday."

"I tried," said the rector, "to be as clear as possible."

"I thought you might not fully have realized the effect of what you said. I ought to tell you, I think, that as soon as I reached home I wrote out, as accurately as I could from memory, the gist of your remarks. And I must say frankly, although I try to put it mildly, that they appear to contradict and controvert the doctrines of the Church."

"Which doctrines?" Hodder asked.

Gordon Atterbury sputtered.

"Which doctrines?" he repeated. "Can it be possible that you misunderstand me? I might refer you to those which you yourself preached as late as last June, in a sermon which was one of the finest and most scholarly efforts I ever heard."

"It was on that day, Mr. Atterbury," replied the rector, with a touch of sadness in his voice, "I made the discovery that fine and scholarly efforts were not Christianity."

"What do you mean?" Mr. Atterbury demanded.

"I mean that they do not succeed in making Christians."

"And by that you imply that the members of your congregation, those who have been brought up and baptized and confirmed in this church, are not Christians?"

"I am sorry to say a great many of them are not," said the rector.

"In other words, you affirm that the sacrament of baptism is of no account."

"I affirm that baptism with water is not sufficient."

"I'm afraid that this is very grave," Mr. Hodder.

"I quite agree with you," replied the rector, looking straight at his vestryman.

"And I understood, — " the other went on, clearing his throat once more, "I think I have it correctly stated in my notes, but I wish to be quite clear, that you denied the doctrine of the virgin birth."

Hodder made a strong effort to control himself.

"What I have said I have said," he answered, "and I have said it in the hope that it might make some impression upon the lives of those to whom I spoke. You were one of them, Mr. Atterbury. And if I repeat and amplify my meaning now, it must be understood that I have no other object except that of putting you in the way of seeing that the religion of Christ is unique in that

2 c

it is dependent upon no doctrine or dogma, upon no external or material sign or proof or authority whatever. I am utterly indifferent to any action you may contemplate taking concerning me. Read your four Gospels carefully. If we do not arrive, through contemplation of our Lord's sojourn on this earth, of his triumph over death, of his message — which illuminates the meaning of our lives here — at that inner spiritual conversion of which he continually speaks, and which alone will give us charity, we are not Christians."

"But the doctrines of the Church, which we were taught from childhood to believe? The doctrines which you once professed, and of which you have now made such an unlooked-for repudiation!"

"Yes, I have changed," said the rector, gazing seriously at the twitching figure of his vestryman, "I was bound, body and soul, by those very doctrines." He roused himself. "But on what grounds do you declare, Mr. Atterbury," he demanded, somewhat sternly, "that this church is fettered by an ancient and dogmatic conception of Christianity? Where are you to find what are called the doctrines of the Church? What may be heresy in one diocese is not so in another, and I can refer to you volumes written by ministers of this Church, in good standing, whose published opinions are the same as those I expressed in my sermon of yesterday. The very cornerstone of the Church is freedom, but many have yet to discover this, and we have held in our Communion men of such divergent views as Dr. Pusey and Phillips Brooks. Mr. Newman, in his Tract Ninety, which was sincerely written, showed that the Thirty-nine Articles were capable of almost any theological interpretation. From what authoritative source are we to draw our doctrines? In the baptismal service the articles of belief are stated to be in the Apostles' Creed, but nowhere — in this Church — is it defined how their ancient language is to be interpreted. That is wisely left to the individual. Shall we interpret the Gospels by the Creeds, which in turn purport to be interpretations of the Gospels? Or shall we draw our conclusions as to what the Creeds may mean to us by pondering on the life of Christ, and striving to do his will? 'The letter killeth, but the Spirit maketh alive.'"

Hodder rose, and stood facing his visitor squarely. He spoke slowly, and the fact that he made no gesture gave all the more force to his words.

"Hereafter, Mr. Atterbury," he added, "so long as I am rector of this church, I am going to do my best to carry out the spirit of Christ's teaching — to make Christians. And there shall be no more compromise, so far as I can help it."

Gordon Atterbury had grown very pale. He, too, got to his feet.

"I — I cannot trust myself to discuss this matter with you any further, Mr. Hodder. I feel too deeply — too strongly on the subject. I do not pretend to account for this astonishing transformation in your opinions. Up to the present I have deemed St. John's fortunate — peculiarly fortunate, in having you for its rector. I am bound to say I think you have not considered, in this change of attitude on your part, those who have made St. John's what it is, who through long and familiar association are bound to it by a thousand ties, — those who, like myself, have what may be called a family interest in this church. My father and mother were married here, I was baptized here. I think I may go so far as to add, Mr. Hodder, that this is *our* church, the church which a certain group of people have built in which to worship God, as was their right. Nor do I believe we can be reproached with a lack of hospitality or charity. We maintain this parish house, with its clubs; and at no small inconvenience to ourselves we have permitted the church to remain in this district. There is no better church music in this city, and we have a beautiful service in the evening at which all pews are free. It is not unreasonable that we should have something to say concerning the doctrine to be preached here, that we should insist that that doctrine be in accordance with what we have always believed was the true doctrine, as received by this Church."

Up to this point Mr. Atterbury had had a feeling that he had not carried out with much distinction the programme which he had so carefully rehearsed on the way to the parish house. Hodder's poise had amazed and baffled him — he had expected to find the rector on the defensive. But now, burning anew with a sense of injustice, he had a sense at last of putting his case strongly.

The feeling of triumph, however, was short lived. Hodder did not reply at once. So many seconds, indeed, went by that Mr. Atterbury began once more to grow slightly nervous under the strange gaze to which he was subjected. And when the clergyman spoke there was no anger in his voice, but a quality — a feeling which was disturbing, and difficult to define.

" You are dealing now, Mr. Atterbury," he said, " with the things of Cæsar, not of God. This church belongs to God — not to you. But you have consecrated it to him. His truth, as Christ taught it, must not be preached to suit any man's convenience. When you were young you were not taught the truth — neither was I. It was mixed with adulterations which obscured and almost neutralized it. But I intend to face it now, and to preach it, and not the comfortable compromise which gives us the illusion that we are Christians because we subscribe to certain tenets, and permits us to neglect our Christian duties.

" And since you have spoken of charity, let me assure you that there is no such thing as charity without the transforming, personal touch. It isn't the bread or instruction or amusement we give people vicariously, but the *effect* of our gift — even if that gift be only a cup of cold water — in illuminating and changing their lives. And it will avail any church little to have a dozen settlement houses while her members acquiesce in a State which refuses to relieve her citizens from sickness and poverty. Charity bends down only to lift others up. And with all our works, our expenditure and toil, how many have *we* lifted up ? "

Gordon Atterbury's indignation got the better of him.

For he was the last man to behold with patience the shattering of his idols.

"I think you have cast an unwarranted reflection on those who have built and made this church what it is, Mr. Hodder," he exclaimed. "And that you will find there are in it many — a great many — earnest Christians who were greatly shocked by the words you spoke yesterday, who will not tolerate any interference with their faith. I feel it my duty to speak frankly, Mr Hodder, disagreeable though it be, in view of our former relations. I must tell you that I am not alone in the opinion that you should resign. It is the least you can do, in justice to us, in justice to yourself. There are other bodies — I cannot call them churches — which doubtless would welcome your liberal, and I must add atrophying, interpretation of Christianity. And I trust that reflection will convince you of the folly of pushing this matter to the extreme. We should greatly deplore the sensational spectacle of St. John's being involved in an ecclesiastical trial, the unpleasant notoriety into which it would bring a church hitherto untouched by that sort of thing. And I ought to tell you that I, among others, am about to send an Information to the bishop."

Gordon Atterbury hesitated a moment, but getting no reply save an inclination of the head, took up his hat.

"Ahem — I think that is all I have to say, Mr. Hodder. Good morning."

Even then Hodder did not answer, but rose and held open the door. As he made his exit under the strange scrutiny of the clergyman's gaze the little vestryman was plainly uncomfortable. He cleared his throat once more, halted, and then precipitately departed.

Hodder went to the window and thoughtfully watched the hurrying figure of Mr. Atterbury until it disappeared, almost skipping, around the corner. . . . The germ of truth, throughout the centuries, had lost nothing of its dynamic potentialities. If released and proclaimed it was still powerful enough to drive the world to insensate anger and opposition. . . .

As he stood there, lost in reflection, a shining automobile drew up at the curb, and from it descended a firm
lady in a tight-fitting suit whom he recognized as Mrs.
Wallis Plimpton. A moment later she had invaded the
office — for no less a word may be employed to express
her physical aggressiveness, the glowing health which she
radiated.

"Good morning, Mr. Hodder," she said, seating herself
in one of the straight-backed chairs. "I have been so
troubled since you preached that sermon yesterday, I could
scarcely sleep. And I made up my mind I'd come to you
the first thing this morning. Mr. Plimpton and I have
been discussing it. In fact, people are talking of nothing
else. We dined with the Laureston Greys last night,
and they, too, were full of it." Charlotte Plimpton looked
at him, and the flow of her words suddenly diminished.
And she added, a little lamely for her, "Spiritual matters
in these days are so difficult, aren't they?"

"Spiritual matters always were difficult, Mrs. Plimpton," he said.

"I suppose so," she assented hurriedly, with what was
intended for a smile. "But what I came to ask you is
this : what are we to teach our children?"

"Teach them the truth," the rector replied.

"One of the things which troubled me most was your
reference to modern criticism," she went on, recovering
her facility. "I was brought up to believe that the Bible
was true. The governess — Miss Standish, you know,
such a fine type of Englishwoman — reads the children
Bible stories every Sunday evening. They adore them,
and little Wallis can repeat them almost by heart — the
pillar of cloud by day, Daniel in the lions' den, and the
Wise Men from the East. If they aren't true, some one
ought to have told us before now."

A note of injury had crept into her voice.

"How do you feel about these things yourself?" Hodder inquired.

"How do I feel? Why, I have never thought about
them very much — they were there, in the Bible!"

" You were taught to believe them ? "

" Of course," she exclaimed, resenting what seemed a reflection on the Gore orthodoxy.

" Do they in any manner affect your conduct ? "

" My conduct ? " she repeated. " I don't know what you mean. I was brought up in the church, and Mr. Plimpton has always gone, and we are bringing up the children to go. Is that what you mean ? "

" No," Hodder answered, patiently, " that is not what I mean. I ask whether these stories in any way enter into your life, become part of you, and tend to make you a more useful woman ? "

" Well — I have never considered them in that way," she replied, a little perplexed.

" Do you believe in them yourself ? "

" Why — I don't know, — I've never thought. I don't suppose I do, absolutely — not in those I have mentioned."

" And you think it right to teach things to your children which you do not yourself believe ? "

" How am I to decide ? " she demanded.

" First by finding out yourself what you do believe," he replied, with a touch of severity.

" Mr. Hodder ! " she cried in a scandalized voice, " do you mean to say that I, who have been brought up in this church, do not know what Christianity is ? "

He looked at her and shook his head.

" You must begin by being honest with yourself," he went on, not heeding her shocked expression. " If you are really in earnest in this matter, I should be glad to help you all I can. But I warn you there is no achievement in the world more difficult than that of becoming a Christian. It means a conversion of your whole being — something which you cannot now even imagine. It means a consuming desire which, — I fear, — in consideration of your present mode of life, will be difficult to acquire."

" My present mode of life ! " she gasped.

" Precisely," said the rector. He was silent, regarding her. There was discernible not the slightest crack or crevice in the enamel of this woman's worldly armour.

For the moment her outraged feelings were forgotten. The man had fascinated her. To be told, in this authoritative manner, that she was wicked was a new and delightful experience. It brought back to her the real motive of her visit, which had in reality been inspired not only by the sermon of the day before, but by sheer curiosity.

"What would you have me do?" she demanded.

"Find yourself."

"Do you mean to say that I am not — myself?" she asked, now completely bewildered.

"I mean to say that you are nobody until you achieve conviction."

For Charlotte Plimpton, née Gore, to be told in her own city, by the rector of her own church that she was nobody was an event hitherto inconceivable! It was perhaps as extraordinary that she did not resent it. Curiosity still led her on.

"Conviction?" she repeated. "But I have conviction, Mr. Hodder. I believe in the doctrines of the Church."

"Belief!" he exclaimed, and checked himself strongly. "Conviction through feeling. Not until then will you find what you were put in the world for."

"But my husband — my children? I try to do my duty."

"You must get a larger conception of it," Hodder replied.

"I suppose you mean," she declared, "that I am to spend the rest of my life in charity."

"How you would spend the rest of your life would be revealed to you," said the rector.

It was the weariness in his tone that piqued her now, the intimation that he did not believe in her sincerity — had not believed in it from the first. The life-long vanity of a woman used to be treated with consideration, to be taken seriously, was aroused. This extraordinary man had refused to enter into the details which she inquisitively craved. Charlotte Plimpton rose.

"I shall not bother you any longer at present, Mr.

Hodder," she said sweetly. "I know you must have, this morning especially, a great deal to trouble you."

He met her scrutiny calmly.

"It is only the things we permit to trouble us that do so, Mrs. Plimpton," he replied. "My own troubles have arisen largely from a lack of faith on the part of those whom I feel it is my duty to influence."

It was then she delivered her parting shot, which she repeated, with much satisfaction, to her husband that evening. She had reached the door.

"Was there a special service at Calvary yesterday?" she asked innocently, turning back.

"Not that I know of."

"I wondered. Mr. Parr was there, I'm told — and he's never been known to desert St. John's except on the rarest occasions. But oh, Mr. Hodder, I must congratulate you on your influence with Alison. When she has been out here before *she* never used to come to church at all."

CHAPTER XXIII

THE CHOICE

I

PONDERING over Alison's note, he suddenly recalled and verified some phrases which had struck him that summer on reading Harnack's celebrated History of Dogma, and around these he framed his reply. " To act as if faith in eternal life and in the living Christ was the simplest thing in the world, or a dogma to which one has to submit, is *irreligious*. . . . It is Christian to pray that God would give the Spirit to make us strong to overcome *the feelings and the doubts of nature*. . . . Where this faith, obtained in this way, exists, it has always been supported by the conviction that the Man *lives* who brought life and immortality to light. To hold fast this faith is the goal of life, for only what we consciously strive for is in this matter our own. *What we think we possess is very soon lost*."

" *The feelings and the doubts of nature!* " The Divine Discontent, the striving against the doubt that every honest soul experiences and admits. Thus the contrast between her and these others who accepted and went their several ways was brought home to him.

He longed to talk to her, but his days were full. Yet the very thought of her helped to bear him up as his trials, his problems accumulated; nor would he at any time have exchanged them for the former false peace which had been bought (he perceived more and more clearly) at the price of compromise.

The worst of these trials, perhaps, was a conspicuous article in a newspaper containing a garbled account of his sermon and of the sensation it had produced amongst his fashionable parishioners. He had refused to see the reporter, but he had been made out a hero, a socialistic champion of the poor. The black headlines were nauseating; and beside them, in juxtaposition, were pen portraits of himself and of Eldon Parr. There were rumours that the banker had left the church until the recalcitrant rector should be driven out of it; the usual long list of Mr. Parr's benefactions was included, and certain veiled paragraphs concerning his financial operations. Mr Ferguson, Mr. Plimpton, Mr. Constable, did not escape,—although they, too, had refused to be interviewed. . . . The article brought to the parish house a bevy of reporters who had to be fought off, and another batch of letters, many of them from ministers, in approval or condemnation.

His fellow-clergymen called, some to express sympathy and encouragement, more of them to voice in person indignant and horrified protests. Dr. Annesley of Calvary — a counterpart of whose rubicund face might have been found in the Council of Trent or in mediæval fish-markets — pronounced his anathemas with his hands folded comfortably over his stomach, but eventually threw to the winds every vestige of his ecclesiastical dignity. . . .

Then there came a note from the old bishop, who was traveling. A kindly note, withal, if non-committal, — to the effect that he had received certain communications, but that his physician would not permit him to return for another ten days or so. He would then be glad to see Mr. Hodder and talk with him.

What would the bishop do? Hodder's relations with him had been more than friendly, but whether the bishop's views were sufficiently liberal to support him in the extreme stand he had taken he could not surmise. For it meant that the bishop, too, must enter into a conflict with the first layman of his diocese, of whose hospitality he had so often partaken, whose contributions had been on so lordly a scale. The bishop was in his seventieth year, and had hitherto successfully fought any attempt to supply him with an assistant, — coadjutor or suffragan.

At such times the fear grew upon Hodder that he might be recommended for trial, forced to abandon his fight to free the Church from the fetters that bound her: that the implacable hostility of his enemies would rob him of his opportunity.

Thus ties were broken, many hard things were said and brought to his ears. There were vacancies in the classes and guilds, absences that pained him, silences that wrung him. . . .

Of all the conversations he held, that with Mrs. Constable was perhaps the most illuminating and distressing. As on that other occasion, when he had gone to her, this visit was under the seal of confession, unknown to her husband. And Hodder had been taken aback, on seeing her enter his office, by the very tragedy in her face — the tragedy he had momentarily beheld once before. He drew up a chair for her, and when she had sat down she gazed at him some moments without speaking.

"I had to come," she said; "there are some things I feel I must ask you. For I have been very miserable since I heard you on Sunday."

He nodded gently.

"I knew that you would change your views — become broader, greater. You may remember that I predicted it."

"Yes," he said.

"I thought you would grow more liberal, less bigoted, if you will allow me to say so. But I didn't anticipate —" she hesitated, and looked up at him again.

"That I would take the extreme position I have taken," he assisted her.

"Oh, Mr. Hodder," she cried impulsively, "*was* it necessary to go so far? and all at once? I am here not only because I am miserable, but I am concerned on your account. You hurt me very much that day you came to me, but you made me your friend. And I wonder if you really understand the terrible, bitter feeling you have aroused, the powerful enemies you have made by speaking so — so unreservedly?"

"I was prepared for it," he answered. "Surely, Mrs. Constable, once I have arrived at what I believe to be the truth, you would not have me temporize?"

She gave him a wan smile.

"In one respect, at least, you have not changed," she told him. "I am afraid you are not the temporizing kind. But wasn't there, — mayn't there still be a way to deal with this fearful situation? You have made it very hard for us — for them. You have given them no loophole of escape. And there are many, like me, who do not wish to see your career ruined, Mr. Hodder."

"Would you prefer," he asked, "to see my soul destroyed? And your own?"

Her lips twitched.

"Isn't there any other way but that? Can't this transformation, which you say is necessary and vital, come gradually? You carried me away as I listened to you, — I was not myself when I came out of the church. But I have been thinking ever since. Consider my husband, Mr. Hodder," her voice faltered. "I shall not mince matters with you — I know you will not pretend to misunderstand me. I have never seen him so upset since — since that time Gertrude was married. He is in a most cruel position. I confessed to you once that Mr. Parr had made for us all the money we possess. Everett is fond of you, but if he espouses your cause, on the vestry, we shall be ruined."

Hodder was greatly moved.

"It is not *my* cause, Mrs. Constable," he said.

"Surely, Christianity is not so harsh and uncompromising as that! And do you quite do justice to — to some of these men? There was no one to tell them the wrongs they were committing — if they were indeed wrongs. Our civilization is far from perfect."

"The Church may have been remiss, mistaken," the rector replied. "But the Christianity she has taught, adulterated though it were, has never condoned the acts which have become commonplace in modern finance. There must have been a time, in the life of every one of these men, when they had to take that first step against which their consciences revolted, when they realized that fraud and taking advantage of the ignorant and weak were wrong. They have deliberately preferred gratification in this life to spiritual development — if indeed they believe in any future whatsoever. For ' whosoever will save his life shall lose it' is as true to-day as it ever was. They have had their choice — they still have it."

" I am to blame," she cried. " I drove my husband to it, I made him think of riches, it was I who cultivated Mr. Parr. And oh, I suppose I am justly punished. I have never been happy for one instant since that day."

He watched her, pityingly, as she wept. But presently she raised her face, wonderingly.

" You *do* believe in the future life after — after what you have been through?"

" I do," he answered simply.

" Yes — I am sure you do. It is *that*, what you are, convinces me you do. Even the remarkable and sensible explanation you gave of it when you interpreted the parable of the talents is not so powerful as the *impression* that you yourself believe after thinking it out for yourself — not accepting the old explanations. And then," she added, with a note as of surprise, " you are willing to sacrifice everything for it ! "

" And you?" he asked. " Cannot you, too, believe to that extent?"

" Everything?" she repeated. " It would mean — poverty. No — God help me — I cannot face it. I have become too hard. I cannot do without the world. And even if I could! Oh, you cannot know what you ask ! Everett, my husband — I must say it, you make me tell you everything — is not free. He is little better than a slave to Eldon Parr. I *hate* Eldon Parr," she added, with startling inconsequence.

" If I had only known what it would lead to when I made Everett what he is ! But I knew nothing of business, and I wanted money, position to satisfy my craving at the loss of — that other thing. And now I couldn't change my husband if I would. He hasn't the courage, he hasn't the vision. What there was of him, long ago, has been killed — and I killed it. He isn't — *anybody*, now."

She relapsed again into weeping.

"And then it might not mean only poverty — it might mean disgrace."

"Disgrace!" the rector involuntarily took up the word.

"There are some things he has done," she said in a low voice, "which he thought he was obliged to do — which Eldon Parr *made* him do."

"But Mr. Parr, too — ?" Hodder began.

"Oh, it was to shield Eldon Parr. They could never be traced to him. And if they ever came out, it would kill my husband. Tell me," she implored, "what can I do? What shall I do? You are responsible. You have made me more bitterly unhappy than ever."

"Are you willing," he asked, after a moment, "to make the supreme renunciation? to face poverty, and perhaps disgrace, to save your soul and others?"

"And — others?"

"Yes. Your sacrifice would not, could not be in vain. Otherwise I should be merely urging on you the individualism which you once advocated with me."

"Renunciation." She pronounced the word questioningly. "Can Christianity really mean that — renunciation of the world? Must we take it in the drastic sense of the Church of the early centuries — the Church of the Martyrs?"

"Christianity demands all of us, or nothing," he replied. "But the false interpretation of *renunciation* of the early Church has cast its blight on Christianity even to our day. Oriental asceticism, Stoicism, Philo and other influences distorted Christ's meaning. Renunciation does not mean asceticism, retirement from the world, a denial of life. And the early Christian, since he was not a citizen, since he took the view that this mortal existence was essentially bad and kept his eyes steadfastly fixed on another, was the victim at once of false philosophies and of the literal messianic prophecies of the Jews, which were taken over with Christianity. The earthly kingdom which was to come was to be the result of some kind of a cataclysm. Personally, I believe our Lord merely used the Messianic literature as a convenient framework for his spiritual Kingdom of heaven, and that the Gospels misinterpret his meaning on this point.

"Renunciation is not the withdrawal from, the denial of life, but the *fulfilment* of life, the submission to the divine will and guidance in order that our work may be shown us. Renunciation is the assumption, at once, of heavenly and earthly citizenship, of responsibility for ourselves and our fellow-men. It is the realization that the other world, the inner, spiritual world, is here, now, and that the soul may dwell in it before death, while the body and mind work for the coming of what may be called the collective kingdom. Life looked upon in that way is not bad, but good, — not meaningless, but luminous."

She had listened hungrily, her eyes fixed upon his face.

"And for me?" she questioned.

"For you," he answered, leaning forward and speaking with a conviction that shook her profoundly, "if you make the sacrifice of your present unhappiness, of your misery, all will be revealed. The labour which you have shirked, which is now hidden from you, will be disclosed, you will justify your existence by taking your place as an element of the community. You will be able to say of yourself, at last, 'I am of use.'"

"You mean — social work?"

The likeness of this to Mrs. Plimpton's question struck him. She had called it "charity." How far had they wandered in their teaching from the Revelation of the Master, since it was as new and incomprehensible to these so-called Christians as to Nicodemus himself!

"All Christian work is social, Mrs. Constable, but it is founded on love. 'Thou shalt love thy neighbour as thyself.' You hold your own soul precious, since it is the shrine of God. And for that reason you hold equally

precious your neighbour's soul.   Love comes first, as revelation, as imparted knowledge, as the divine gist of au-
tonomy — self-government.   And then one *cannot help
working*, socially, at the task for which we are made by
nature most efficient.   And in order to discover what
that task is, we must wait."

"Why did not some one tell me this, when I was
young?" she asked — not speaking to him.   "It seems
so simple."

"It *is* simple.   The difficult thing is to put it into
practice — the most difficult thing in the world.   Both
courage and faith are required, faith that is content to
trust as to the nature of the reward.   It is the wisdom
of foolishness.   Have you the courage?"

She pressed her hands together.

"Alone — perhaps I should have.   I don't know.   But
my husband!   I was able to influence him to his destruction, and now I am powerless.   Darkness has closed
around me.   He would not — he will not listen to me."

"You have tried?"

"I have attempted to talk to him, but the whole of my
life contradicts my words.   He cannot see me except as
the woman who drove him into making money.   Sometimes I think he hates me."

Hodder recalled, as his eyes rested on her compassionately, the sufferings of that other woman in Dalton
Street.

"Would you have me desert him — after all these
years?" she whispered.   "I often think he would be
happier, even now."

"I would have you do nothing save that which God
himself will reveal to you.   Go home, go into the church
and pray — pray for knowledge.   I think you will find
that you are held responsible for your husband.   Pray
that that which you have broken, you may mend again."

"Do you think there is a chance?"

Hodder made a gesture.

"God alone can judge as to the extent of his punish-
ments."

2 D

She got to her feet, wearily.

" I feel no hope — I feel no courage, but — I will try.
I see what you mean — that my punishment is my power-
lessness."

He bent his head.

" You are so strong — perhaps you can help me."

" I shall always be ready," he replied.

He escorted her down the steps to the dark blue
brougham with upstanding, chestnut horses which was
waiting at the curb. But Mrs. Constable turned to the
footman, who held open the door.

" You may stay here awhile," she said to him, and gave
Hodder her hand. . . .

She went into the church. . . .

II

Asa Waring and his son-in-law, Phil Goodrich, had
been to see Hodder on the subject of the approaching
vestry meeting, and both had gone away not a little astonished and impressed by the calmness with which the
rector looked forward to the conflict. Others of his
parishioners, some of whom were more discreet in their
expressions of sympathy, were no less surprised by his
attitude; and even his theological adversaries, such as
Gordon Atterbury, paid him a reluctant tribute. Thanks,
perhaps, to the newspaper comments as much as to any
other factor, in the minds of those of all shades of opinion in
the parish the issue had crystallized into a duel between
the rector and Eldon Parr. Bitterly as they resented the
glare of publicity into which St. John's had been dragged,
the first layman of the diocese was not beloved; and the
fairer-minded of Hodder's opponents, though appalled,
were forced to admit in their hearts that the methods by
which Mr. Parr had made his fortune and gained his ascendency would not bear scrutiny. . . . Some of them
were disturbed, indeed, by the discovery that there had
come about in them, by imperceptible degrees, in the last
few years a new and critical attitude towards the ways of

modern finance: most of them had an uncomfortable feeling that Hodder was somehow right, — a feeling which they sought to stifle when they reflected upon the consequences of facing it. For this would mean a disagreeable shaking up of their own lives. Few of them were in a position whence they might cast stones at Eldon Parr. . . .

What these did not grasp was the fact that that which they felt stirring within them was the new and spiritual product of the dawning twentieth century — the Social Conscience. They wished heartily that the new rector who had developed this disquieting personality would peacefully resign and leave them to the former, even tenor of their lives. They did not for one moment doubt the outcome of his struggle with Eldon Parr. The great banker was known to be relentless, his name was synonymous with victory. And yet, paradoxically, Hodder compelled their inner sympathy and admiration! . . .

Some of them, who did not attempt peremptorily to choke these processes, made the startling discovery that they were not, after all, so shocked by his doctrines as they had at first supposed. The trouble was that they could not continue to listen to him, as formerly, with comfort. . . . One thing was certain, that they had never expected to look forward to a vestry meeting with such breathless interest and anxiety. This clergyman had suddenly accomplished the surprising feat of reviving the Church as a burning, vital factor in the life of the community! He had discerned her enemy, and defied his power. . . .

As for Hodder, so absorbed had he been by his experiences, so wrung by the human contacts, the personal problems which he had sought to enter, that he had actually given no thought to the battle before him until the autumn afternoon, heavy with smoke, had settled down into darkness. The weather was damp and cold, and he sat musing on the ordeal now abruptly confronting him before his study fire when he heard a step behind him. He turned to recognize, by the glow of the embers, the heavy figure of Nelson Langmaid.

"I hope I'm not disturbing you, Hodder," he said. "The janitor said you were in, and your door is open."

"Not at all," replied the rector, rising. As he stood for a moment facing the lawyer, the thought of their friendship, and how it had begun in the little rectory overlooking the lake at Bremerton, was uppermost in his mind, — yes, and the memory of many friendly, literary discussions in the same room where they now stood, of pleasant dinners at Langmaid's house in the West End, when the two of them had often sat talking until late into the nights.

"I must seem very inhospitable," said Hodder. "I'll light the lamp — it's pleasanter than the electric light."

The added illumination at first revealed the lawyer in his familiar aspect, the broad shoulders, the big, reddish beard, the dome-like head, — the generous person that seemed to radiate scholarly benignity, peace, and good-will. But almost instantly the rector became aware of a new and troubled, puzzled glance from behind the round spectacles. . . .

"I thought I'd drop in a moment on my way up town — " he began. And the note of uncertainty in his voice, too, was new. Hodder drew towards the fire the big chair in which it had been Langmaid's wont to sit, and perhaps it was the sight of this operation that loosed the lawyer's tongue.

"Confound it, Hodder!" he exclaimed, "I like you — I always have liked you. And you've got a hundred times the ability of the average clergyman. Why in the world did you have to go and make all this trouble?"

By so characteristic a remark Hodder was both amused and moved. It revealed so perfectly the point of view and predicament of the lawyer, and it was also an expression of an affection which the rector cordially returned. . . . Before answering, he placed his visitor in the chair, and the deliberation of the act was a revelation of the unconscious poise of the clergyman. The spectacle of this self-command on the brink of such a crucial event as the vestry meeting had taken Langmaid aback more than he cared to show. He had lost the old sense of comradeship, of easy equality; and he had the odd feeling of dealing with a new man, at once familiar and unfamiliar, who had somehow lifted himself out of the everyday element in which they heretofore had met. The clergyman had contrived to step out of his, Langmaid's, experience: had actually set him — who all his life had known no difficulty in dealing with men — to groping for a medium of communication. . . .

Hodder sat down on the other side of the fireplace. He, too, seemed to be striving for a common footing.

"It was a question of proclaiming the truth when at last I came to see it, Langmaid. I could not help doing what I did. Matters of policy, of a false consideration for individuals could not enter into it. If this were not so, I should gladly admit that you had a just grievance, a peculiar right to demand why I had not remained the strictly orthodox person whom you induced to come here. You had every reason to congratulate yourself that you were getting what you doubtless would call a *safe* man."

"I'll admit I had a twinge of uneasiness after I came home," Langmaid confessed.

Hodder smiled at his frankness.

"But that disappeared."

"Yes, it disappeared. You seemed to suit 'em so perfectly. I'll own up, Hodder, that I was a little hurt that you did not come and talk to me just before you took the extraordinary — before you changed your opinions."

"Would it have done any good?" asked the rector, gently. "Would you have agreed with me any better than you do now? I am perfectly willing, if you wish, to discuss with you any views of mine which you may not indorse. And it would make me very happy, I assure you, if I could bring you to look upon the matter as I do."

This was a poser. And whether it were ingenuous, or had in it an element of the scriptural wisdom of the serpent, Langmaid could not have said. As a lawyer, he admired it.

"I wasn't in church, as usual,— I didn't hear the sermon," he replied. "And I never could make head or tail of theology — I always told you that. What I deplore, Hodder, is that you've contrived to make a hornets' nest out of the most peaceful and contented congregation in America. Couldn't you have managed to stick to religion instead of getting mixed up with socialism?"

"So you have been given the idea that my sermon was socialistic?" the rector said.

"Socialistic and heretical, it seems. Of course I'm not much of an authority on heresy, but they claim that you went out of your way to knock some of their most cherished and sacred beliefs in the head."

"But suppose I have come to the honest conclusion that in the first place these so-called cherished beliefs have no foundation in fact, and no influence on the lives of the persons who cherished them, no real connection with Christianity? What would you have me do, as a man? Continue to preach them for the sake of the lethargic peace of which you speak? leave the church paralyzed, as I found it?"

"Paralyzed! You've got the most influential people in the city."

Hodder regarded him for a while without replying.

"So has the Willesden Club," he said.

Langmaid laughed a little, uncomfortably.

"If Christianity, as one of the ancient popes is said to have remarked, were merely a profitable fable," the rector continued, "there might be something in your contention that St. John's, as a church, had reached the pinnacle of success. But let us ignore the spiritual side of this matter as non-vital, and consider it from the practical side. We have the most influential people in the city, but we have not their children. That does not promise well for the future. The children get more profit out of the country clubs. And then there is another question: is it going to continue to be profitable? Is it as profitable now as it was, say, twenty years ago?"

"You've got out of my depth," said Nelson Langmaid.

"I'll try to explain. As a man of affairs, I think you will admit, if you reflect, that the return of St. John's, considering the large amount of money invested, is scarcely worth considering. And I am surprised that as astute a man as Mr. Parr has not been able to see this long ago. If we clear all the cobwebs away, what is the real function of this church as at present constituted? Why this heavy expenditure to maintain religious services for a handful of people? Is it not, when we come down to facts, an increasingly futile effort to bring the influences of religion — of superstition, if you will — to bear on the so-called lower classes in order that they may remain contented with their lot, with that station and condition in the world where — it is argued — it has pleased God to call them? If that were not so, in my opinion there are very few of the privileged classes who would invest a dollar in the Church. And the proof of it is that the moment a clergyman raises his voice to proclaim the true message of Christianity they are up in arms with the cry of socialism. They have the sense to see that their privileges are immediately threatened.

"Looking at it from the financial side, it would be cheaper for them to close up their churches. It is a mere waste of time and money, because the influence on their less fortunate brethren in a worldly sense has dwindled to nothing. Few of the poor come near their churches in these days. The profitable fable is almost played out."

Hodder had spoken without bitterness, yet his irony was by no means lost on the lawyer. Langmaid, if the truth be told, found himself for the moment in the unusual predicament of being at a loss, for the rector had put forward with more or less precision the very cynical view which he himself had been clever enough to evolve.

"Haven't they the right," he asked, somewhat lamely, "to demand the kind of religion they pay for?"

"Provided you don't call it religion," said the rector.

Langmaid smiled in spite of himself.

"See here, Hodder," he said, "I've always confessed

frankly that I knew little or nothing about religion. I've come here this evening as your friend, without authority from anybody," he added significantly, "to see if this thing couldn't somehow be adjusted peaceably, for your sake as well as others'. Come, you must admit there's a grain of justice in the contention against you. When I went on to Bremerton to get you I had no real reason for supposing that these views would develop. I made a contract with you in all good faith."

"And I with you," answered the rector. "Perhaps you do not realize, Langmaid, what has been the chief factor in developing these views."

The lawyer was silent, from caution.

"I must be frank with you. It was the discovery that Mr. Parr and others of my chief parishioners were so far from being Christians as to indulge, while they supported the Church of Christ, in operations like that of the Consolidated Tractions Company, wronging their fellow-men and condemning them to misery and hate. And that you, as a lawyer, used your talents to make that operation possible."

"Hold on !" cried Langmaid, now plainly agitated. "You have no right — you can know nothing of that affair. You do not understand business."

"I'm afraid," replied the rector, sadly, "that I understand one side of it only too well."

"The Church has no right to meddle outside of her sphere, to dictate to politics and business."

"Her sphere," said Hodder, "is the world. If she does not change the world by sending out Christians into it, she would better close her doors."

"Well, I don't intend to quarrel with you, Hodder. I suppose it can't be helped that we look at these things differently, and I don't intend to enter into a defence of business. It would take too long, and it wouldn't help any." He got to his feet. "Whatever happens, it won't interfere with our personal friendship, even if you think me a highwayman and I think you a —— "

"A fanatic," Hodder supplied. He had risen, too, and

stood, with a smile on his face, gazing at the lawyer with an odd scrutiny.

"An idealist, I was going to say," Langmaid answered, returning the smile, "I'll admit that we need them in the world. It's only when one of them gets in the gear-box. . . ."

The rector laughed. And thus they stood, facing each other.

"Langmaid," Hodder asked, "don't you ever get tired and disgusted with the Juggernaut car?"

The big lawyer continued to smile, but a sheepish, almost boyish expression came over his face. He had not credited the clergyman with so much astuteness.

"Business, nowadays, is — business, Hodder. The Juggernaut car claims us all. It has become — if you will permit me to continue to put my similes into slang — the modern band wagon. And we lawyers have to get on it, or fall by the wayside."

Hodder stared into the fire.

"I appreciate your motive in coming here," he said, at length, "and I do you the justice of believing it was friendly, that the fact that you are, in a way, responsible for me to — to the congregation of St. John's did not enter into it. I realize that I have made matters particularly awkward for you. You have given them in me, and in good faith, something they didn't bargain for. You haven't said so, but you want me to resign. On the one hand, you don't care to see me tilting at the windmills, or, better, drawing down on my head the thunderbolts of your gods. On the other hand, you are just a little afraid for your gods. If the question in dispute were merely an academic one, I'd accommodate you at once. But I can't. I've thought it all out, and I have made up my mind that it is my clear duty to remain here and, if I am strong enough, wrest this church from the grip of Eldon Parr and the men whom he controls.

"I am speaking plainly, and I understand the situation thoroughly. You will probably tell me, as others have done, that no one has ever opposed Eldon Parr who has not been crushed. I go in with my eyes open, I am willing to be crushed, if necessary. You have come here to warn me, and I appreciate your motive. Now I am going to warn you, in all sincerity and friendship. I may be beaten, I may be driven out. But the victory will be mine nevertheless. Eldon Parr and the men who stand with him in the struggle will never recover from the blow I shall give them. I shall leave them crippled because I have the truth on my side, and the truth is irresistible. And they shall not be able to injure me permanently. And you, I regret deeply to say, will be hurt, too. I beg you, for no selfish reason, to consider again the part you intend to play in this affair."

Such was the conviction, such the unlooked-for fire with which the rector spoke that Langmaid was visibly shaken and taken aback in spite of himself.

"Do you mean," he demanded, when he had caught his breath, "that you intend to attack us publicly?"

"Is that the only punishment you can conceive of?" the rector asked. The reproach in his voice was in itself a denial.

"I beg your pardon, Hodder," said the lawyer, quickly. "And I am sure you honestly believe what you say, but——"

"In your heart you, too, believe it, Langmaid. The retribution has already begun. Nevertheless you will go on — for a while." He held out his hand, which Langmaid took mechanically. "I bear you no ill-will. I am sorry that you cannot yet see with sufficient clearness to save yourself."

Langmaid turned and picked up his hat and stick and left the room without another word. The bewildered, wistful look which had replaced the ordinarily benign and cheerful expression haunted Hodder long after the lawyer had gone. It was the look of a man who has somehow lost his consciousness of power.

CHAPTER XXIV

THE VESTRY MEETS

AT nine o'clock that evening Hodder stood alone in the arched vestry room, and the sight of the heavy Gothic chairs ranged about the long table brought up memories of comfortable, genial meetings prolonged by chat and banter. . . . The noise of feet, of subdued voices beside the coat room in the corridor, aroused him. All of the vestry would seem to have arrived at once.

He regarded them with a detached curiosity as they entered, reading them with a new insight. The trace of offhandedness in Mr. Plimpton's former cordiality was not lost upon him — an intimation that his star had set. Mr. Plimpton had seen many breaches healed — had healed many himself. But he had never been known as a champion of lost causes.

"Well, here we are, Mr. Hodder, on the stroke," he remarked. "As a vestry, I think we're entitled to the first prize for promptness. How about it, Everett?"

Everett Constable was silent.

"Good evening, Mr. Hodder," he said. He did not offer to shake hands, as Mr. Plimpton had done, but sat down at the far end of the table. He looked tired and worn; sick, the rector thought, and felt a sudden swelling of compassion for the pompous little man whose fibre was not as tough as that of these other *condottieri:* as Francis Ferguson's, for instance, although his soft hand and pink and white face framed in the black whiskers would seem to belie any fibre whatever.

Gordon Atterbury hemmed and hawed, — "Ah, Mr. Hodder," and seated himself beside Mr. Constable, in a chair designed to accommodate a portly bishop. Both of them started nervously as Asa Waring, holding his head high, as a man should who has kept his birthright, went directly to the rector.

"I'm glad to see you, Mr. Hodder," he said, and turning defiantly, surveyed the room. There was an awkward silence. Mr. Plimpton edged a little nearer. The decree might have gone forth for Mr. Hodder's destruction, but Asa Waring was a man whose displeasure was not to be lightly incurred.

"What's this I hear about your moving out of Hamilton Place, Mr. Waring? You'd better come up and take the Spaulding lot, in Waverley, across from us."

"I am an old man, Mr. Plimpton," Asa Waring replied. "I do not move as easily as some other people in these days."

Everett Constable produced his handkerchief and rubbed his nose violently. But Mr. Plimpton was apparently undaunted.

"I have always said," he observed, "that there was something very fine in your sticking to that neighbourhood after your friends had gone. Here's Phil!"

Phil Goodrich looked positively belligerent, and as he took his stand on the other side of Hodder his father-in-law smiled at him grimly. Mr. Goodrich took hold of the rector's arm.

"I missed one or two meetings last spring, Mr. Hodder," he said, "but I'm going to be on hand after this. My father, I believe, never missed a vestry meeting in his life. Perhaps that was because they used to hold most of 'em at his house."

"And serve port and cigars, I'm told," Mr. Plimpton put in.

"That was an inducement, Wallis, I'll admit," answered Phil. "But there are even greater inducements now."

In view of Phil Goodrich's well-known liking for a fight, this was too pointed to admit of a reply, but Mr. Plimpton was spared the attempt by the entrance of Nelson Langmaid. The lawyer, as he greeted them, seemed to be preoccupied, nor did he seek to relieve the

tension with his customary joke. A few moments of
silence followed, when Eldon Parr was seen to be standing in the doorway, surveying them.

"Good evening, gentlemen," he said coldly, and without more ado went to his customary chair, and sat down
in it. Immediately followed a scraping of other chairs.
There was a dominating quality about the man not to be
gainsaid.

The rector called the meeting to order. . . .

During the routine business none of the little asides
occurred which produce laughter. Every man in the
room was aware of the intensity of Eldon Parr's animosity,
and yet he betrayed it neither by voice, look, or gesture.
There was something uncanny in this self-control, this *sang
froid* with which he was wont to sit at boards waiting
unmoved for the time when he should draw his net about
his enemies, and strangle them without pity. It got on
Langmaid's nerves — hardened as he was to it. He had
seen many men in that net; some had struggled, some
had taken their annihilation stoically; honest merchants,
freebooters, and brigands. Most of them had gone out,
with their families, into that precarious border-land of
existence in which the to-morrows are ever dreaded.

Yet here, somehow, was a different case. Langmaid
found himself going back to the days when his mother
had taken him to church, and he could not bear to look at
Hodder. Since six o'clock that afternoon — had his companions but known it — he had passed through one of the
worst periods of his existence. . . .

After the regular business had been disposed of a brief
interval was allowed, for the sake of decency, to ensue.
That Eldon Parr would not lead the charge in person was
a foregone conclusion. Whom, then, would he put
forward? For obvious reasons, not Wallis Plimpton or
Langmaid, nor Francis Ferguson. Hodder found his
glance unconsciously fixed upon Everett Constable, who
moved nervously and slowly pushed back his chair. He
was called upon, in this hour and in the church his father
had helped to found, to make the supreme payment for

the years of financial prosperity. Although a little man, with his shoulders thrown back and his head high, he generally looked impressive when he spoke, and his fine features and clear-cut English contributed to the effect. But now his face was strained, and his voice seemed to lack command as he bowed and mentioned the rector's name. Eldon Parr sat back.

"Gentlemen," Mr. Constable began, "I feel it my duty to say something this evening, something that distresses me. Like some of you who are here present, I have been on this vestry for many years, and my father was on it before me. I was brought up under Dr. Gilman, of whom I need not speak. All here, except our present rector, knew him. This church, St. John's, has been a part — a large part — of my life. And anything that seems to touch its welfare, touches me.

"When Dr. Gilman died, after so many years of faithful service, we faced a grave problem, — that of obtaining a young man of ability, an active man who would be able to assume the responsibilities of a large and growing parish, and at the same time carry on its traditions, precious to us all: one who believed in and preached, I need scarcely add, the accepted doctrines of the Church, which we have been taught to think are sacred and necessary to salvation. And in the discovery of the Reverend Mr. Hodder, we had reason to congratulate ourselves and the parish. He was all that we had hoped for, and more. His sermons were at once a pleasure and an instruction.

"I wish to make it clear," he continued, "that in spite of the pain Mr. Hodder's words of last Sunday have given me, I respect and honour him still, and wish him every success. But, gentlemen, I think it is plain to all of you that he has changed his religious convictions. As to the causes through which that change has come about, I do not pretend to know. To say the least, the transition is a startling one, one for which some of us were totally unprepared. To speak restrainedly, it was a shock — a shock which I shall remember as long as I live.

"I need not go into the doctrinal question here, except to express my opinion that the fundamental facts of our religion were contradicted. And we have also to consider the effect of this preaching on coming generations for whom we are responsible. There are, no doubt, other fields for Mr. Hodder's usefulness. But I think it may safely be taken as a principle that this parish has the right to demand from the pulpit that orthodox teaching which suits it, and to which it has been accustomed. And I venture further to give it as my opinion — to put it mildly — that others have been as disturbed and shocked as I. I have seen many, talked with many, since Sunday. For these reasons, with much sorrow and regret, I venture to suggest to the vestry that Mr. Hodder resign as our rector. And I may add what I believe to be the feeling of all present, that we have nothing but good will for him, although we think we might have been informed of what he intended to do. And that in requesting him to resign we are acting for his own good as well as our own, and are thus avoiding a situation which threatens to become impossible, — one which would bring serious reflection on him and calamity on the church. We already, in certain articles in the newspapers, have had an indication of the intolerable notoriety we may expect, although I hold Mr. Hodder innocent in regard to those articles. I am sure he will have the good sense to see this situation as I see it, as the majority of the parish see it."

Mr. Constable sat down, breathing hard. He had not looked at the rector during the whole of his speech, nor at Eldon Parr. There was a heavy silence, and then Philip Goodrich rose, square, clean-cut, aggressive.

"I, too, gentlemen, have had life-long association with this church," he began deliberately. "And for Mr. Hodder's sake I am going to give you a little of my personal history, because I think it typical of thousands of men of my age all over this country. It was nobody's fault, perhaps, that I was taught that the Christian religion depended on a certain series of nature miracles and a chain of historical events, and when I went East to school I had more of this same sort of instruction. I have never, perhaps, been overburdened with intellect, but the time arrived nevertheless when I began to think for myself. Some of the older boys went once, I remember, to the rector of the school — a dear old man — and frankly stated our troubles. To use a modern expression, he 'stood pat' on everything. I do not say it was a consciously criminal act, — he probably saw no way out himself. At any rate, he made us all agnostics at one stroke.

"What I learned in college of science and history and philosophy merely confirmed me in my agnosticism. As a complete system for the making of atheists and materialists, I commend the education which I received. If there is any man here who believes religion to be an essential factor in life, I ask him to think of his children or grandchildren before he comes forward to the support of Mr. Constable.

"In that sermon which he preached last Sunday, Mr. Hodder, for the first time in my life, made Christianity intelligible to me. I want him to know it. And there are other men and women in that congregation who feel as I do. Gentlemen, there is nothing I would not give to have had Christianity put before me in that simple and inspiring way when I was a boy. And in my opinion St. John's is more fortunate to-day than it ever has been in its existence. Mr. Hodder should have an unanimous testimonial of appreciation from this vestry for his courage. And if the vote requesting him to resign prevails, I venture to predict that there is not a man on this vestry who will not live to regret it."

Phil Goodrich glared at Eldon Parr, who remained unmoved.

"Permit me to add," he said, "that this controversy, in other respects than doctrine, is more befitting to the Middle Ages than to the twentieth century, when this Church and other denominations are passing resolutions in their national conventions with a view to unity and freedom of belief."

Mr. Langmaid, Mr. Plimpton, and Mr. Constable sat still. Mr. Ferguson made no move. It was Gordon Atterbury who rushed into the breach, and proved that the extremists are allies of doubtful value.

He had, apparently, not been idle since Sunday, and was armed *cap-a-pie* with time-worn arguments that need not be set down. All of which went to show that Mr. Goodrich had not referred to the Middle Ages in vain. For Gordon Atterbury was a born schoolman. But he finished by declaring, at the end of twenty minutes (much as he regretted the necessity of saying it), that Mr. Hodder's continuance as rector would mean the ruin of the church in which all present took such a pride. That the great majority of its members would never submit to what was so plainly heresy.

It was then that Mr. Plimpton gathered courage to pour oil on the waters. There was nothing, in his opinion, — he remarked smilingly, in his function as peacemaker, — to warrant anything but the most friendly interchange of views. He was second to none in his regard for Mr. Hodder, in his admiration for a man who had the courage of his convictions. He had not the least doubt that Mr. Hodder did not desire to remain in the parish when it was so apparent that the doctrines which he now preached were not acceptable to most of those who supported the church. And he added (with sublime magnanimity) that he wished Mr. Hodder the success which he was sure he deserved, and gave him every assurance of his friendship.

Asa Waring was about to rise, when he perceived that Hodder himself was on his feet. And the eyes of every man, save one, were fixed on him irresistibly. The rector seemed unaware of it. It was Philip Goodrich who remarked to his father-in-law, as they walked home afterwards, of the sense he had had at that moment that there were just two men in the room, — Hodder and Eldon Parr. All the rest were ciphers; all had lost, momentarily, their feelings of partisanship and were conscious only of these two intense, radiating, opposing centres of force; and no man, oddly enough, could say which was the stronger. They seemingly met on equal terms. There could not be the slightest doubt that the rector did not mean to yield, and yet they might have been puzzled if they had asked themselves how they had read the fact in his face or manner. For he betrayed neither anger nor impatience.

No more did the financier reveal his own feelings. He still sat back in his chair, unmoved, in apparent contemplation. The posture was familiar to Langmaid. . . . Would he destroy, too, this clergyman? For the first time in his life, and as he looked at Hodder, the lawyer wondered. . . .

Hodder did not defend himself, made no apologies. Christianity was not a collection of doctrines, he reminded them, — but a mode of life. If anything were clear to him, it was that the present situation was not, with the majority of them, a matter of doctrines, but of unwillingness to accept the message and precept of Jesus Christ, and lead Christian lives. They had made use of the doctrines as a stalking-horse.

There was a stir at this, and Hodder paused a moment and glanced around the table. But no one interrupted.

He was fully aware of his rights, and he had no intention of resigning. To resign would be to abandon the work for which he was responsible, not to them, but to God. And he was perfectly willing — nay, eager to defend his Christianity before any ecclesiastical court, should the bishop decide that a court was necessary. The day of freedom, of a truer vision was at hand, the day of Christian unity on the vital truths, and no better proof of it could be brought forward than the change in him. In his ignorance and blindness he had hitherto permitted compromise, but he would no longer allow those who made only an outward pretence of being Christians to direct the spiritual affairs of St. John's, to say what should and what should not be preached. This was to continue to paralyze the usefulness of the church, to set at naught her mission, to alienate those who most had need of her, who hungered and thirsted after righteousness, and went away unsatisfied.

He had hardly resumed his seat when Everett Constable got up again. He remarked, somewhat unsteadily, that to prolong the controversy would be useless and painful to all concerned, and he infinitely regretted the necessity of putting his suggestion that the rector resign in the form of a resolution. . . . The vote was taken. Six men raised their hands in favour of his resignation — Nelson Langmaid among them : two, Asa Waring and Philip Goodrich, were against it. After announcing the result, Hodder rose.

"For the reason I have stated, gentlemen, I decline to resign," he said. " I stand upon my canonical rights."

Francis Ferguson arose, his voice actually trembling with anger. There is something uncanny in the passion of a man whose life has been ordered by the inexorable rules of commerce, who has been wont to decide all questions from the standpoint of dollars and cents. If one of his own wax models had suddenly become animated, the effect could not have been more startling.

In the course of this discussion, he declared, Mr. Hodder had seen fit to make grave and in his opinion unwarranted charges concerning the lives of some, if not all, of the gentlemen who sat here. It surprised him that these remarks had not been resented, but he praised a Christian forbearance on the part of his colleagues which he was unable to achieve. He had no doubt that their object had been to spare Mr. Hodder's feelings as much as possible, but Mr. Hodder had shown no disposition to spare their own. He had outraged them, Mr. Ferguson thought, — wantonly so. He had made these preposterous and unchristian charges an excuse for his determination to remain in a position where his usefulness had ceased.

No one, unfortunately, was perfect in this life, — not even Mr. Hodder. He, Francis Ferguson, was far from claiming to be so. But he believed that this arraignment of the men who stood highest in the city for decency, law, and order, who supported the Church, who revered its doctrines, who tried to live Christian lives, who gave their time and their money freely to it and to charities, — that this arraignment was an arrogant accusation and affront to be repudiated. He demanded that Mr. Hodder be definite. If he had any charges to make, let him make them here and now.

The consternation, the horror which succeeded such a stupid and unexpected tactical blunder on the part of the usually astute Mr. Ferguson were felt rather than visually discerned. The atmosphere might have been described as panicky. Asa Waring and Phil Goodrich smiled as Wallis Plimpton, after a moment's hush, scrambled to his feet, his face pale, his customary easiness and nonchalance now the result of an obvious effort. He, too, tried to smile, but swallowed instead as he remembered his property in Dalton Street. . . . Nelson Langmaid smiled, in spite of himself. . . . Mr. Plimpton implored his fellow-members not to bring personalities into the debate, and he was aware all the while of the curious, pitying expression of the rector. He breathed a sigh of relief at the opening words of Hodder, who followed him.

" Gentlemen," he said, " I have no intention of being personal, even by unanimous consent. But if Mr. Ferguson will come to me after this meeting I shall have not the least objection to discussing this matter with him in so far as he himself is concerned. I can only assure you now that I have not spoken without warrant."

There was, oddly enough, no acceptance of this offer by Mr. Ferguson. Another silence ensued, broken, at last, by a voice for which they had all been unconsciously waiting ; a voice which, though unemotional, cold, and matter-of-fact, was nevertheless commanding, and long accustomed to speak with an overwhelming authority. Eldon Parr did not rise.

" Mr. Hodder," he said, " in one respect seems to be under the delusion that we *are* still in the Middle Ages, instead of the twentieth century, since he assumes the right to meddle with the lives of his parishioners, to be the sole judge of their actions. That assumption will not be tolerated by free men. I, for one, gentlemen, do not propose to have a socialist for the rector of the church which I attend and support. And I maintain the privilege of an American citizen to set my own standards, within the law, and to be the sole arbitrar of those standards."

"Good!" muttered Gordon Atterbury. Langmaid moved uncomfortably.

"I shall not waste words," the financier continued. "There is in my mind no question that we are justified in demanding from our rector the Christian doctrines to which we have given our assent, and which are stated in the Creeds. That they shall be subject to the whims of the rector is beyond argument. I do not pretend to understand either, gentlemen, the nature of the extraordinary change that has taken place in the rector of St. John's. I am not well versed in psychology. I am incapable of flights myself. One effect of this change is an attitude on which reasonable considerations would seem to have no effect.

"Our resources, fortunately, are not yet at an end. It has been my hope, on account of my former friendship with Mr. Hodder, that an ecclesiastical trial might not be necessary. It now seems inevitable. In the meantime, since Mr. Hodder has seen fit to remain in spite of our protest, I do not intend to enter this church. I was prepared, gentlemen, as some of you no doubt know, to spend a considerable sum in adding to the beauty of St. John's and to the charitable activities of the parish. Mr. Hodder has not disapproved of my gifts in the past, but owing to his present scruples concerning my worthiness, I naturally hesitate to press the matter now." Mr. Parr indulged in the semblance of a smile. "I fear that he must take the responsibility of delaying this benefit, with the other responsibilities he has assumed."

His voice changed. It became sharper.

"In short, I propose to withhold all contributions for whatever purpose from this church while Mr. Hodder is rector, and I advise those of you who have voted for his resignation to do the same. In the meantime, I shall give my money to Calvary, and attend its services. And I shall offer further a resolution — which I am informed is within our right — to discontinue Mr. Hodder's salary."

There was that in the unparalleled audacity of Eldon Parr that compelled Hodder's unwilling admiration. He sat gazing at the financier during this speech, speculating curiously on the inner consciousness of the man who could utter it. Was it possible that he had no sense of guilt? Even so, he had shown a remarkable astuteness in relying on the conviction that he (Hodder) would not betray what he knew.

He was suddenly aware that Asa Waring was standing beside him.

"Gentlemen," said Mr. Waring, "I have listened to this discussion as long as I can bear it with patience. Had I been told of it, I should have thought it incredible that the methods of the money changers should be applied to the direction and control of the house of God. In my opinion there is but one word which is suitable for what has passed here to-night, and the word is persecution. Perhaps I have lived too long. I have lived to see honourable, upright men deprived of what was rightfully theirs, driven from their livelihood by the rapacity of those who strive to concentrate the wealth and power of the nation into their hands. I have seen this power gathering strength, stretching its arm little by little over the institutions I fought to preserve, and which I cherish: over our politics, over our government, yes, and even over our courts. I have seen it poisoning the business honour in which we formerly took such a pride, I have seen it reëstablishing a slavery more pernicious than that which millions died to efface. I have seen it compel a subservience which makes me ashamed, as an American, to witness."

His glance, a withering moral scorn, darted from under the grizzled eyebrows and alighted on one man after another, and none met it. Everett Constable coughed, Wallis Plimpton shifted his position, the others sat like stones. Asa Waring was giving vent at last to the pent-up feelings of many years.

"And now that power, which respects nothing, has crept into the sanctuary of the Church. Our rector recognizes it, I recognize it, — there is not a man here who, in his heart, misunderstands me. And when a man is found who has the courage to stand up against it, I honour him with all my soul, and a hope that was almost dead revives in me. For there is one force, and one force alone, able to overcome the power of which I speak, — the Spirit of Christ. And the mission of the Church is to disseminate that spirit. The Church is the champion on which we have to rely, or give up all hope of victory. The Church must train the recruits. And if the Church herself is betrayed into the hands of the enemy, the battle is lost.

"If Mr. Hodder is forced out of this church, it would be better to lock the doors. St. John's will be held up, and rightfully, to the scorn of the city. All the money in the world will not save her. Though crippled, she has survived one disgrace, when she would not give free shelter to the man who above all others expressed her true spirit, when she drove Horace Bentley from her doors after he had been deprived of the fortune which he was spending for his fellow-men. She will not survive another.

"I have no doubt Mr. Parr's motion to take from Mr. Hodder his living will go through. And still I urge him not to resign. I am not a rich man, even when such property as I have is compared to moderate fortunes of these days, but I would pay his salary willingly out of my own pocket rather than see him go. . . ."

"I call the attention of the Chairman," said Eldon Parr, after a certain interval in which no one had ventured to speak, "to the motion before the vestry relating to the discontinuance of Mr. Hodder's salary."

It was then that the unexpected happened. Gordon Atterbury redeemed himself. His respect for Mr. Waring, he said, made him hesitate to take issue with him.

He could speak for himself and for a number of people in the congregation when he reiterated his opinion that they were honestly shocked at what Mr. Hodder had preached, and that this was his sole motive in requesting Mr. Hodder to resign. He thought, under the circumstances, that this was a matter which might safely be left with the bishop. He would not vote to deprive Mr. Hodder of his salary.

The motion was carried by a vote of five to three. For Eldon Parr well knew that his will needed no re-enforcement by argument. And this much was to be said for him, that after he had entered a battle he never hesitated, never under any circumstances reconsidered the probable effect of his course.

As for the others, those who had supported him, they were cast in a less heroic mould. Even Francis Ferguson. As between the devil and the deep sea, he was compelled, with as good a grace as possible, to choose the devil. He was utterly unable to contemplate the disaster which might ensue if certain financial ties, which were thicker than cables, were snapped. But his affection for the devil was not increased by thus being led into a charge from which he would willingly have drawn back. Asa Waring might mean nothing to Eldon Parr, but he meant a great deal to Francis Ferguson, who had by no means forgotten his sensations of satisfaction when Mrs. Waring had made her first call in Park Street on Francis Ferguson's wife. He left the room in such a state of absent-mindedness as actually to pass Mr. Parr in the corridor without speaking to him.

The case of Wallis Plimpton was even worse. He had married the Gores, but he had sought to bind himself with hoops of steel to the Warings. He had always secretly admired that old Roman quality (which the Goodriches — their connections — shared) of holding fast to their course unmindful and rather scornful of influence which swayed their neighbours. The clan was sufficient unto itself, satisfied with a moderate prosperity and a continually increasing number of descendants. The name was unstained. Such are the strange incongruities in the hearts of men, that few realized the extent to which Wallis Plimpton had partaken of the general hero-worship of Phil Goodrich. He had assiduously cultivated his regard, at times discreetly boasted of it, and yet had never been sure of it. And now fate, in the form of his master, Eldon Parr, had ironically compelled him at one stroke to undo the work of years. As soon as the meeting broke up, he crossed the room.

"I can't tell you how much I regret this, Phil," he said. "Charlotte has very strong convictions, you know, and so have I. You can understand, I am sure, how certain articles of belief might be necessary to one person, and not to another."

"Yes," said Phil, "I can understand. We needn't mention the articles, Wallis." And he turned his back.

He never knew the pain he inflicted. Wallis Plimpton looked at the rector, who stood talking to Mr. Waring, and for the first time in his life recoiled from an overture. Something in the faces of both men warned him away.

Even Everett Constable, as they went home in the cars together, was brief with him, and passed no comments when Mr. Plimpton recovered sufficiently to elaborate on the justification of their act, and upon the extraordinary stand taken by Phil Goodrich and Mr. Waring.

"They might have told us what they were going to do." Everett Constable eyed him.

"Would it have made any difference, Plimpton?" he demanded.

After that they rode in silence, until they came to a certain West End corner, where they both decended. Little Mr. Constable's sensations were, if anything, less enviable, and he had not Mr. Plimpton's recuperative powers. He had sold that night, for a mess of pottage, the friendship and respect of three generations. And he had fought, for pay, against his own people.

And lastly, there was Langmaid, whose feelings almost defy analysis. He chose to walk through the still night the four miles that separated him from his home. And he went back over the years of his life until he found, in the rubbish of the past, a forgotten and tarnished jewel. The discovery pained him. For that jewel was the ideal he had carried away, as a youth, — from the old law school at the bottom of Hamilton Place, — a gift from no less a man than the great lawyer and public-spirited citizen, Judge Henry Goodrich — Philip Goodrich's grandfather, whose seated statue marked the entrance of the library. He, Nelson Langmaid, had gone forth from that school resolved to follow in the footsteps of that man, — but somehow he missed the path. Somehow the jewel had lost its fire. There had come a tempting offer, and a struggle — just one : a readjustment on the plea that the world had changed since the days of Judge Goodrich, whose uncompromising figure had begun to fade : an exciting discovery that he, Nelson Langmaid, possessed the gift of drawing up agreements which had the faculty of passing magically through the meshes of the Statutes. Affluence had followed, and fame, and even that high office which the Judge himself had held, the Presidency of the State Bar Association. In all that time, one remark, which he had tried to forget, had cut him to the quick. Bedloe Hubbell had said on the political platform that Langmaid got one hundred thousand dollars a year for keeping Eldon Parr out of jail.

Once he stopped in the street, his mind suddenly going back to the action of the financier at the vestry meeting. "Confound him!" he said aloud, "he has been a fool for once. I told him not to do it."

He stood at last in the ample vestibule of his house, singling out his latch-key, when suddenly the door opened, and his daughter Helen appeared.

"Oh, dad," she cried, "why are you so late? I've been watching for you. I know you've let Mr. Hodder stay."

She gazed at him with widened eyes.

"Don't tell me that you've made him resign. I can't — I won't believe it."

"He isn't going to resign, Helen," Langmaid replied, in an odd voice. "He — he refused to."

CHAPTER XXV

"RISE, CROWNED WITH LIGHT!"

I

THE Church of St. John's, after a peaceful existence of so many years, had suddenly become the stage on which rapid and bewildering dramas were played : the storm-centre of chaotic forces, hitherto unperceived, drawn from the atmosphere around her. For there had been more publicity, more advertising. "The Rector of St. John's will not talk"—such had been one headline: neither would the vestry talk. And yet, despite all this secrecy, the whole story of the suspension of Hodder's salary was in print, and an editorial (which was sent to him) from a popular and sensational journal, on "tainted money," in which Hodder was held up to the public as a martyr because he refused any longer to accept for the Church ill-gotten gains from Consolidated Tractions and the like.

This had opened again the floodgates of the mails, and it seemed as though every person who had a real or fancied grievance against Eldon Parr had written him. Nor did others of his congregation escape. The press of visitors at the parish house suddenly increased once more, men and women came to pour into his ears an appalling series of confessions; wrongs which, like Garvin's, had engendered bitter hatreds; woes, temptations, bewilderments. Hodder strove to keep his feet, sought wisdom to deal patiently with all, though at times he was tried to the uttermost. And he held steadfastly before his mind the great thing, that they *did* come. It was what he had longed for, prayed for, despaired of. He was no longer crying in the empty wilderness, but at last in touch — in

427

natural touch with life : with life in all its sorrow, its crudity and horror. He had contrived, by the grace of God, to make the connection for his church.

That church might have been likened to a ship sailing out of the snug harbour in which she had lain so long to range herself gallantly beside those whom she had formerly beheld, with complacent cowardice, fighting her fight : young men and women, enlisted under other banners than her own, doing their part in the battle of the twentieth century for humanity. Her rector was her captain. It was he who had cut her cables, quelled, for a time at least, her mutineers; and sought to hearten those of her little crew who wavered, who shrank back appalled as they realized something of the immensity of the conflict in which her destiny was to be wrought out.

To carry on the figure, Philip Goodrich might have been deemed her first officer. He, at least, was not appalled, but grimly conscious of the greatness of the task to which they had set their hands. The sudden transformation of conservative St. John's was no more amazing than that of the son of a family which had never been without influence in the community. But that influence had always been conservative. And Phil Goodrich had hitherto taken but a listless interest in the church of his fathers. Fortune had smiled upon him, trusts had come to him unsought. He had inherited the family talent for the law, the freedom to practise when and where he chose. His love of active sport had led him into many vacations, when he tramped through marsh and thicket after game, and at five and forty there was not an ounce of superfluous flesh on his hard body. In spite of his plain speaking, an overwhelming popularity at college had followed him to his native place, and no organization, sporting or serious, was formed in the city that the question was not asked, " What does Goodrich think about it ? "

His whole-souled enlistment in the cause of what was regarded as radical religion became, therefore, the subject of amazed comment in the many clubs he now neglected. The " squabble " in St. John's, as it was generally referred

to, had been aired in the press, but such was the magic
in a name made without conscious effort that Phil Goodrich's participation in the struggle had a palpably disarm-
ing effect : and there were not a few men who commonly
spent their Sunday mornings behind plate-glass windows,
surrounded by newspapers, as well as some in the athletic
club (whose contests Mr. Goodrich sometimes refereed),
who went to St. John's out of curiosity and who waited,
afterwards, for an interview with Phil or the rector.   The
remark of one of these was typical of others.   He had never
taken much stock in religion, but if Goodrich went in for
it he thought he'd go and look it over.

Scarcely a day passed that Phil did not drop in at the
parish house. . . .   And he set himself, with all the vigour
of an unsquandered manhood, to help Hodder to solve the
multitude of new problems by which they were beset. . . .

A free church was a magnificent ideal, but how was it
to be carried on without an Eldon Parr, a Ferguson, a
Constable, a Mrs. Larrabbee, or a Gore who would make
up the deficit at the end of the year?   Could weekly contributions, on the envelope system, be relied upon, provided the people continued to come and fill the pews of
absent and outraged parishioners?   The music was the
most expensive in the city, although Mr. Taylor, the
organist, had come to the rector and offered to cut his
salary in half, and to leave that in abeyance until the
finances could be adjusted.   And his example had been
followed by some of the high-paid men in the choir.
Others had offered to sing without pay.   And there were
the expenses of the parish house, an alarming sum now
Eldon Parr had withdrawn : the salaries of the assistants.
Hodder, who had saved a certain sum in past years, would
take nothing for the present. . . . Asa Waring and Phil
Goodrich borrowed on their own responsibility. . . .

II

Something of the overwhelming nature of the forces
Hodder had summoned was visibly apparent on that first

Sunday after what many had called his apostasy. Instead
of the orderly, sprucely-dressed groups of people which
were wont to linger in greetings before the doors of St.
John's, a motley crowd thronged the pavement and streamed
into the church, pressing up the aisles and invading the
sacred precincts where decorous parishioners had for so
many years knelt in comfort and seclusion. The familiar
figure of Gordon Atterbury was nowhere to be seen, and
the Atterbury pew was occupied by shopgirls in gaudy
hats. Eldon Parr's pew was filled, Everett Constable's,
Wallis Plimpton's; and the ushers who had hastily been
mustered were awestricken and powerless. Such a resistless invasion by the hordes of the unknown might well
have struck with terror some of those who hitherto had
had the courage to stand up loyally in the rector's support.
It had a distinct flavour of revolution: contained, for
some, a grim suggestion of a time when that vague, ir-
responsible, and restless monster, the mob, would rise in
its might and brutally and inexorably take possession of
all property.

Alison had met Eleanor Goodrich in Burton Street, and
as the two made their way into the crowded vestibule
they encountered Martha Preston, whose husband was
Alison's cousin, in the act of flight.

"You're not going in!" she exclaimed.

"Of course we are."

Mrs. Preston stared at Alison in amazement.

"I didn't know you were still here," she said, irrelevantly. "I'm pretty liberal, my dear, as you know, — but
this is more than I can stand. Look at them!" She drew
up her skirts as a woman brushed against her. "I believe
in the poor coming to church, and all that, but this is
mere vulgar curiosity, the result of all that odious advertising in the newspapers. My pew is filled with them.
If I had stayed, I should have fainted. I don't know
what to think of Mr. Hodder."

"Mr. Hodder is not to blame for the newspapers," replied Alison, warmly. She glanced around her at the
people pushing past, her eyes shining, her colour high,

and there was the ring of passion in her voice which had on Martha Preston a peculiarly disquieting effect. "I think it's splendid that they are here at all! I don't care what brought them."

Mrs. Preston stared again. She was a pretty, intelligent woman, at whose dinner table one was sure to hear the discussion of some "modern problem": she believed herself to be a socialist. Her eyes sought Eleanor Goodrich's, who stood by, alight with excitement.

"But surely you, Eleanor — you're not going in! You'll never be able to stand it, even if you find a seat. The few people we know who've come are leaving. I just saw the Allan Pendletons ——"

"Have you seen Phil?" Eleanor asked.

"Oh, yes, he's in there, and even he's helpless. And as I came out poor Mr. Bradley was jammed up against the wall. He seemed perfectly stunned. . . ."

At this moment they were thrust apart. Eleanor quivered as she was carried through the swinging doors into the church.

"I think you're right," she whispered to Alison, "it *is* splendid. There's something about it that takes hold of one, that carries one away. It makes me wonder how it can be guided — what will come of it?"

They caught sight of Phil pushing his way towards them, and his face bore the set look of belligerency which Eleanor knew so well, but he returned her smile. Alison's heart warmed towards him.

"What do you think of this?" he demanded. "Most of our respectable friends who dared to come have left in a towering rage — to institute lawsuits, probably. At any rate, strangers are not being made to wait until ten minutes after the service begins. That's one barbarous custom abolished."

"Strangers seem to have taken matters in their own hands for once." Eleanor smiled. "We've made up our minds to stay, Phil, even if we have to stand."

"That's the right spirit," declared her husband, glancing at Alison, who had remained silent, with approval and by no means a concealed surprise. "I think I know of a place where I can squeeze you in, near Professor Bridges and Sally, on the side aisle."

"Are George and Sally here?" Eleanor exclaimed.

"Mr. Hodder," said Phil, "is converting the heathen. You couldn't have kept George away. And it was George who made Sally stay!"

Presently they found themselves established between a rawboned young workingman who smelled strongly of soap, whose hair was plastered tightly against his forehead, and a young woman who leaned against the wall. The black in which she was dressed enhanced the whiteness and weariness of her face, and she sat gazing ahead of her, apparently unconscious of those who surrounded her, her hands tightly folded in her lap. In their immediate vicinity, indeed, might have been found all the variety of type seen in the ordinary street car. And in truth there were some who seemed scarcely to realize they were not in a public vehicle. An elaborately dressed· female in front of them, whose expansive hat brushed her neighbours, made audible comments to a stout man with a red neck which was set in a crease above his low collar.

"They tell me Eldon Parr's pew has a gold plate on it. I wish I knew which it was. It ain't *this* one, anyway, I'll bet."

"Say, they march in in this kind of a church, don't they?" some one said behind them.

Eleanor, with her lips tightly pressed, opened her prayer-book. Alison's lips were slightly parted as she gazed about her, across the aisle. Her experience of the Sunday before, deep and tense as it had been, seemed as nothing compared to this; the presence of all these people stimulated her inexpressibly, fired her; and she felt the blood pulsing through her body as she contrasted this gathering with the dignified, scattered congregation she had known. She scarcely recognized the church itself. . . . She speculated on the homes from which these had come, and the motives which had brought them.

For a second the perfume of the woman in front, mingling with other less definable odours, almost sickened her, evoking suggestions of tawdry, trivial, vulgar lives, fed on sensation and excitement; but the feeling was almost immediately swept away by a renewed sense of the bigness of the thing which she beheld, — of which, indeed, she was a part. And her thoughts turned more definitely to the man who had brought it all about. Could he control it, subdue it? Here was Opportunity suddenly upon him, like a huge, curving, ponderous wave. Could he ride it? or would it crush him remorselessly?

Sensitive, alert, quickened as she was, she began to be aware of other values: of the intense spiritual hunger in the eyes of the woman in black, the yearning of barren, hopeless existences. And here and there Alison's look fell upon more prosperous individuals whose expressions proclaimed incredulity, a certain cynical amusement at the spectacle: others seemed uneasy, as having got more than they had bargained for, deliberating whether to flee . . . and then, just as her suspense was becoming almost unbearable, the service began. . . .

How it had been accomplished, the thing she later felt, was beyond the range of intellectual analysis. Nor could she have told how much later, since the passage of time had gone unnoticed. Curiosities, doubts, passions, longings, antagonisms — all these seemed — as the most natural thing in the world — to have been fused into one common but ineffable emotion. Such, at least, was the impression to which Alison startlingly awoke. All the while she had been conscious of Hodder, from the moment she had heard his voice in the chancel; but somehow this consciousness of him had melted, imperceptibly, into that of the great congregation, once divided against itself, which had now achieved unity of soul.

The mystery as to how this had been effected was the more elusive when she considered the absence of all methods which might have been deemed revivalistic. Few of those around her evinced a familiarity with the historic service. And then occurred to her his explanation of personality as the medium by which all truth is

2 F

revealed, by which the current of religion, the motive
power in all history, is transmitted. Surely this was the
explanation, if it might be called one! That tingling
sense of a pervading spirit which was his, — and yet not
his. He was the incandescent medium, and yet, paradoxically, gained in identity and individuality and was
inseparable from the thing itself.

She could not see him. A pillar hid the chancel from
her view. . . .

The service, to which she had objected as archaic, became subordinate, spiritualized, dominated by the personality. Hodder had departed from the usual custom
by giving out the page of the psalter : and the verses, the
throbbing responses which arose from every corner of
the church, assumed a new significance, the vision of the
ancient seer revived. One verse he read resounded with
prophecy.

" Thou shalt deliver me from the strivings of the people:
and thou shalt make me the head of the heathen."

And the reply:

" A people whom I have not known shall serve me."

The workingman next to Alison had no prayer-book.
She thrust her own into his hand, and they read from it
together. . . .

When they came to the second hymn the woman in
front of her had wonderfully shed her vulgarity. Her
voice — a really good one — poured itself out :

> " See a long race thy spacious courts adorn,
>   See future sons, and daughters yet unborn,
>   In crowding ranks on every side arise,
>   Demanding life, impatient for the skies."

Once Alison would have been critical of the words.
She was beyond that, now. What did it matter, if the
essential Thing were present?

The sermon *was* a surprise. And those who had come
for excitement, for the sensation of hearing a denunciation of a class they envied and therefore hated, and nevertheless strove to imitate, were themselves rebuked. Were

not their standards the same? And if the standard were false, it followed inevitably that the life was false also.

Hodder fairly startled these out of their preconceived notions of Christianity. Let them shake out of their minds *everything* they had thought it to mean, church-going, acceptance of creed and dogma, contributive charity, withdrawal from the world, rites and ceremonies: it was none of these.

The motive in the world to-day was the acquisition of property; the motive of Christianity was absolutely and uncompromisingly opposed to this. Shock their practical sense as it might, Christianity looked forward with stead-fast faith to a time when the incentive to amass property would be done away with, since it was a source of evil and a curse to mankind. If they would be Christians, let them face that. Let them enter into life, into the struggles going on around them to-day against greed, corruption, slavery, poverty, vice and crime. Let them protest, let them fight, even as Jesus Christ had fought and pro-tested. For as sure as they sat there the day would come when they would be called to account, would be asked the question — what had they done to make the United States of America a better place to live in?

There were in the Apostolic writings and tradition mis-interpretations of life which had done much harm. Early Christianity had kept its eyes fixed on another world, and had ignored this: had overlooked the fact that every man and woman was put here to do a particular work. In the first epistle of Peter the advice was given, "submit your-selves to every ordinance of man for the Lord's sake." But Christ had preached democracy, responsibility, had foreseen a millennium, the fulfilment of his Kingdom, when all men, inspired by the Spirit, would make and keep in spirit the ordinances of God.

Before they could do God's work and man's work they must first be awakened, filled with *desire*. Desire was power. And he prayed that some of them, on this day, would receive that desire, that power which nothing could resist. The desire which would lead each and every one to the gates of the Inner World which was limitless and eternal, filled with dazzling light. . . .

Let them have faith then. Not credulity in a vague God they could not imagine, but faith in the Spirit of the Universe, humanity, in Jesus Christ who had been the complete human revelation of that Spirit, who had suffered and died that man might not live in ignorance of it. To doubt humanity, — such was the Great Refusal, the sin against the Holy Ghost, the repudiation of the only true God!

After a pause, he spoke simply of his hope for St. John's. If he remained here his ambition was that it would be the free temple of humanity, of Jesus Christ, supported not by a few, but by all, — each in accordance with his means. Of those who could afford nothing, nothing would be required. Perhaps this did not sound practical, nor would it be so if the transforming inspiration failed. He could only trust and try, hold up to them the vision of the Church as a community of willing workers for the Kingdom. . . .

III

After the service was over the people lingered in the church, standing in the pews and aisles, as though loath to leave. The woman with the perfume and the elaborate hat was heard to utter a succinct remark.

"Say, Charlie, I guess he's all right. I never had it put like that."

The thick-necked man's reply was inaudible.

Eleanor Goodrich was silent and a little pale as she pressed close to Alison. Her imagination had been stretched, as it were, and she was still held in awe by the vastness of what she had heard and seen. Vaster even than ever, — so it appeared now, — demanding greater sacrifices than she had dreamed of. She looked back upon the old as at receding shores. . . .

Alison, with absorbed fascination, watched the people; encountered, here and there, recognitions from men and women with whom she had once danced and dined in what now seemed a previous existence. Why had *they* come? and how had they received the message? She ran into a little man, a dealer in artists' supplies who once had sold her paints and brushes, who stared and bowed uncertainly. She surprised him by taking his hand.

"Did you like it?" she asked, impulsively.

"It's what I've been thinking for years, Miss Parr," he responded, "thinking and feeling. But I never knew it was Christianity. And I never thought—" he stopped and looked at her, alarmed.

"Oh," she said, "I believe in it, too—or try to."

She left him, mentally gasping. . . . Without, on the sidewalk, Eleanor Goodrich was engaged in conversation with a stockily built man, inclined to stoutness; he had a brown face and a clipped, bristly mustache. Alison paused involuntarily, and saw him start and hesitate as his clear, direct gaze met her own. . . .

Bedloe Hubbell was one of those who had once sought to marry her. She recalled him as an amiable and aimless boy; and after she had gone East she had received with incredulity and then with amusement the news of his venture into altruistic politics. It was his efficiency she had doubted, not his sincerity. Later tidings, contemptuous and eventually irritable utterances of her own father, together with accounts in the New York newspapers of his campaign, had convinced her in spite of herself that Bedloe Hubbell had actually shaken the seats of power. And somehow, as she now took him in, he looked it.

His transformation was one of the signs, one of the mysteries of the times. The ridicule and abuse of the press, the opposition and enmity of his childhood friends, had developed the man of force she now beheld, and who came forward to greet her.

"Alison!" he exclaimed. He had changed in one sense, and not in another. Her colour deepened as the sound of his voice brought back the lapsed memories of the old intimacy. For she had been kind to him, kinder than to any other; and the news of his marriage—to a woman from the Pacific coast — had actually induced in her certain longings and regrets. When the cards had reached her, New York and the excitement of the life into which she had been weakly, if somewhat unwittingly, drawn had already begun to pall.

"I'm so glad to see you," she told him. "I've heard — so many things. And I'm very much in sympathy with what you're doing."

They crossed the street, and walked away from the church together. She had surprised him, and made him uncomfortable.

"You've been away so long," he managed to say, "perhaps you do not realize——"

"Oh, yes, I do," she interrupted. "I am on the other side, on *your* side. I thought of writing you, when you so nearly won last autumn."

"*You* see it, too?" he exclaimed.

"Yes, I've changed, too. Not so much as you," she added, shyly. "I always had a certain sympathy, you know, with the Robin Hoods."

He laughed at her designation, both pleased and taken aback by her praise. . . . But he wondered if she knew the extent of his criticism of her father.

"That rector is a wonderful man," he broke out, irrelevantly. "I can't 'get over' him — I can't quite grasp the fact that he exists, that he has dared to do what he has done."

This brought her colour back, but she faced him bravely.

"You think he *is* wonderful, then?"

"Don't you?" he demanded.

She assented. "But I am curious to know why *you* do. Somehow, I never thought of you——"

"As religious," he supplied. "And you? If I remember rightly——"

"Yes," she interrupted, "I revolted, too. But Mr. Hodder puts it so — it makes one wonder."

"He has not only made me wonder," declared Bedloe Hubbell, emphatically, "I never knew what religion was until I heard this man last Sunday."

"Last Sunday!"

"Until then, I hadn't been inside of a church for fifteen years,— except to get married. My wife takes the children, occasionally, to a Presbyterian church near us."

"And why did you go then?" she asked.

"I am a little ashamed of my motive," he confessed. "There were rumours — I don't pretend to know how they got about—" he hesitated, once more aware of delicate ground. "Wallis Plimpton said something to a man who told me. I believe I went out of sheer curiosity to hear what Hodder would have to say. And then, I had been reading, wondering whether there were anything in Christianity, after all."

"Yes?" she said, careless now as to what cause he might attribute her eagerness. "And he gave you something?"

It was then she grasped the truth that this sudden renewed intimacy was the result of the impression Hodder had left upon the minds of both.

"He gave me *everything*," Bedloe Hubbell replied. "I am willing to acknowledge it freely. In his explanation of the parable of the Prodigal Son, he gave me the clew to our modern times. What was for me an inextricable puzzle has become clear as day. He has made me understand, at last, the force which stirred me, which goaded me until I was fairly compelled to embark in the movement which the majority of our citizens still continue to regard as quixotic. I did not identify that force with religion, then, and when I looked back on the first crazy campaign we embarked upon, with the whole city laughing at me and at the obscure and impractical personnel we had, there were moments when it seemed incomprehensible folly. I had nothing to gain, and everything to lose by such a venture. I was lazy and easy-going, as you know. I belonged to the privileged class, I had sufficient money to live in comparative luxury all my days, I had no grudge against these men whom I had known all my life."

"But it must have had *some* beginning," said Alison.

"I was urged to run for the city council, by these very men." Bedloe Hubbell smiled at the recollection. "They accuse me now of having indulged once in the same practice, for which I am condemning them. Our company did accept rebates, and we sought favours from the city government. I have confessed it freely on the platform. Even during my first few months in the council what may be called the old political practices seemed natural to me. But gradually the iniquity of it all began to dawn on me, and then I couldn't rest until I had done something towards stopping it.

"At length I began to see," he continued, "that education of the masses was to be our only preserver, that we should have to sink or swim by that. I began to see, dimly, that this was true for other movements going on to-day. Now comes Hodder with what I sincerely believe is the key. He compels men like me to recognize that our movements are not merely moral, but religious. Religion, as yet unidentified, is the force behind these portentous stirrings of politics in our country, from sea to sea. He aims, not to bring the Church into politics, but to make her the feeder of these movements. Men join them to-day from all motives, but the religious is the only one to which they may safely be trusted. He has rescued the jewel from the dustheap of tradition, and holds it up, shining, before our eyes."

Alison looked at her companion.

"That," she said, "is a very beautiful phrase."

Bedloe Hubbell smiled queerly.

"I don't know why I'm telling you all this. I can't usually talk about it. But the sight of that congregation this morning, mixed as it was, and the way he managed to weld it together——"

"Ah, you noticed that!" she exclaimed sharply.

"Noticed it!"

"I know. It was a question of feeling it."

There was a silence.

"Will he succeed?" she asked presently.

"Ah," said Bedloe Hubbell, "how is it possible to predict it? The forces against him are tremendous, and it is usually the pioneer who suffers. I agree absolutely with his definition of faith, I have it. And the work he has done already can never be undone. The time is ripe, and it is something that he has men like Phil Goodrich behind him, and Mr. Waring. I'm going to enlist, and from now on I intend to get every man and woman upon whom I have any influence whatever to go to that church. . . ."

A little later Alison, marvelling, left him.

CHAPTER XXVI

THE CURRENT OF LIFE

I

THE year when Hodder had gone east to Bremerton and Bar Harbor, he had read in the train a magazine article which had set fire to his imagination. It had to do with the lives of the men, the engineers who dared to deal with the wild and terrible power of the western hills, who harnessed and conquered roaring rivers, and sent the power hundreds of miles over the wilderness, by flimsy wires, to turn the wheels of industry and light the dark places of the cities. And, like all men who came into touch with elemental mysteries, they had their moments of pure ecstasy, gaining a tingling, intenser life from the contact with dynamic things ; and other moments when, in their struggle for mastery, they were buffeted about, scorched, and almost overwhelmed.

In these days the remembrance of that article came back to Hodder. It was as though he, too, were seeking to deflect and guide a force — the Force of forces. He, too, was buffeted, scorched, and bruised, at periods scarce given time to recover himself in the onward rush he himself had started, and which he sought to control. Problems arose which demanded the quick thinking of emergency. He, too, had his moments of reward, the reward of the man who is in touch with reality.

He lived, from day to day, in a bewildering succession of encouragements and trials, all unprecedented. If he remained at St. John's, an entire new organization would be necessary. . . . He did not as yet see it clearly ; and in the meantime, with his vestry alienated, awaiting the bishop's decision, he could make no definite plans, even if he had had the leisure. Wholesale desertions had occurred in the guilds and societies, the activities of which had almost ceased. Little Tomkinson, the second assistant, had resigned ; and McCrae, who worked harder than ever before, was already marked, Hodder knew, for dismissal if he himself were defeated.

And then there was the ever present question of money. It remained to be seen whether a system of voluntary offerings were practicable. For Hodder had made some inquiries into the so-called "free churches," only to discover that there were benefactors behind them, benefactors the Christianity of whose lives was often doubtful.

One morning he received in the mail the long-expected note from the bishop, making an appointment for the next day. Hodder, as he read it over again, smiled to himself. . . . He could gather nothing of the mind of the writer from the contents.

The piece of news which came to him on the same morning swept completely the contemplations of the approaching interview from his mind. Sally Grover stopped in at the parish house on her way to business.

"Kate Marcy's gone," she announced, in her abrupt fashion.

"Gone !" he exclaimed, and stared at her in dismay. "Gone where ?"

"That's just it," said Miss Grover. "I wish I knew. I reckon we'd got into the habit of trusting her too much, but it seemed the only way. She wasn't in her room last night, but Ella Finley didn't find it out until this morning, and she ran over scared to death, to tell us about it."

Involuntarily the rector reached for his hat.

"I've sent out word among our friends in Dalton Street," Sally continued. An earthquake could not have disturbed her outer, matter-of-fact calmness. But Hodder was not deceived : he knew that she was as profoundly grieved and discouraged as himself. "And I've got old Gratz, the cabinet-maker, on the job. If she's in Dalton Street, he'll find her."

"But what — ?" Hodder began.

Sally threw up her hands.

"You never can tell, with that kind. But it sticks in my mind she's done something foolish."

"Foolish?"

Sally twitched, nervously.

"Somehow I don't think it's a spree — but as I say, you can't tell. She's full of impulses. You remember how she frightened us once before, when she went off and stayed all night with the woman she used to know in the flat house, when she heard she was sick?"

Hodder nodded.

"You've inquired there?"

"That woman went to the hospital, you know. She may be with another one. If she is, Gratz ought to find her. . . . You know there was a time, Mr. Hodder, when I didn't have much hope that we'd pull her through. But we got hold of her through her feelings. She'd do anything for Mr. Bentley — she'd do anything for you, and the way she stuck to that embroidery was fine. I don't say she was cured, but whenever she'd feel one of those fits coming on she'd let us know about it, and we'd watch her. And I never saw one of that kind change so. Why, she must be almost as good looking now as she ever was."

"You don't think she has done anything — desperate?" asked Hodder, slowly.

Sally comprehended.

"Well — somehow I don't. She used to say if she ever got drunk again she'd never come back. But she didn't have any money — she's given Mr. Bentley every cent of it. And we didn't have any warning. She was as cheerful as could be yesterday morning, Mrs. McQuillen says."

"It might not do any harm to notify the police," replied Hodder, rising. "I'll go around to headquarters now."

He was glad of the excuse for action. He could not have sat still. And as he walked rapidly across Burton Street he realized with a pang how much his heart had been set on Kate Marcy's redemption. In spite of the fact that every moment of his time during the past fortnight had been absorbed by the cares, responsibilities, and trials thrust upon him, he reproached himself for not having gone oftener to Dalton Street. And yet, if Mr. Bentley and Sally Grover had been unable to foresee and prevent this, what could he have done?

At police headquarters he got no news. The chief received him deferentially, sympathetically, took down Kate Marcy's description, went so far as to remark, sagely, that too much mustn't be expected of these women, and said he would notify the rector if she were found. The chief knew and admired Mr. Bentley, and declared he was glad to meet Mr. Hodder. . . . Hodder left, too preoccupied to draw any significance from the nature of his welcome. He went at once to Mr. Bentley's.

The old gentleman was inclined to be hopeful, to take Sally Grover's view of the matter. He trusted, he said, Sally's instinct. And Hodder came away less uneasy, not a little comforted by a communion which never failed to fortify him, to make him marvel at the calmness of that world in which his friend lived, a calmness from which no vicarious sorrow was excluded. And before Hodder left, Mr. Bentley had drawn from him some account of the more recent complexities at the church. The very pressure of his hand seemed to impart courage.

" You won't stay and have dinner with me? "

The rector regretfully declined.

" I hear the bishop has returned," said Mr. Bentley, smiling.

Hodder was surprised. He had never heard Mr. Bentley speak of the bishop. Of course he must know him.

" I have my talk with him to-morrow."

Mr. Bentley said nothing, but pressed his hand again. . . .

On Tower Street, from the direction of the church, he beheld a young man and a young woman approaching him, absorbed in conversation. Even at a distance both seemed familiar, and presently he identified the lithe and dainty figure in the blue dress as that of the daughter of his vestryman, Francis Ferguson. Presently she turned her face, alight with animation, from her companion, and recognized him.

"It's Mr. Hodder!" she exclaimed, and was suddenly overtaken with a crimson shyness. The young man seemed equally embarrassed as they stood facing the rector.

"I'm afraid you don't remember me, Mr. Hodder," he said. "I met you at Mr. Ferguson's last spring."

Then it came to him. This was the young man who had made the *faux pas* which had caused Mrs. Ferguson so much consternation, and who had so manfully apologized afterwards. His puzzled expression relaxed into a smile, and he took the young man's hand.

"I was going to write to you," said Nan, as she looked up at the rector from under the wide brim of her hat. "Our engagement is to be announced Wednesday."

Hodder congratulated them. There was a brief silence, when Nan said tremulously:

"We're coming to St. John's!"

"I'm very glad," Hodder replied, gravely. It was one of those compensating moments, for him, when his tribulations vanished; and the tributes of the younger generation were those to which his heart most freely responded. But the situation, in view of the attitude of Francis Ferguson, was too delicate to be dwelt upon.

"I came to hear you last Sunday, Mr. Hodder," the young man volunteered, with that mixture of awkwardness and straightforwardness which often characterize his sex and age in referring to such matters. "And I had an idea of writing you, too, to tell you how much I liked what you said. But I know you must have had many letters. You've made me think."

He flushed, but met the rector's eye. Nan stood regarding him with pride.

"You've made *me* think, too," she added. "And we

intend to pitch in and help you, if we can be of any use."

He parted from them, wondering. And it was not until he had reached the parish house that it occurred to him that he was as yet unenlightened as to the young man's name. . . .

His second reflection brought back to his mind Kate Marcy, for it was with a portion of Nan Ferguson's generous check that her board had been paid. And he recalled the girl's hope, as she had given it to him, that he would find some one in Dalton Street to help. . . .

II

There might, to the mundane eye, have been an element of the ridiculous in the spectacle of the rector of St. John's counting his gains, since he had chosen — with every indication of insanity — to bring the pillars of his career crashing down on his own head. By no means the least, however, of the treasures flung into his lap was the tie which now bound him to the Philip Goodriches, which otherwise would never have been possible. And as he made his way thither on this particular evening, a renewed sense came upon him of his emancipation from the dreary, useless hours he had been wont to spend at other dinner tables. That existence appeared to him now as the glittering, feverish unreality of a nightmare filled with restless women and tired men who drank champagne, thus gradually achieving — by the time cigars were reached — an artificial vivacity. The caprice and superficiality of the one sex, the inability to dwell upon or even penetrate a serious subject, the blindness to what was going on around them; the materialism, the money standard of both, were nauseating in the retrospect.

How, indeed, had life once appeared so distorted to him, a professed servant of humanity, as to lead him in the name of duty into that galley?

Such was the burden of his thought when the homelike front of the Goodrich house greeted him in the darkness,

its unshrouded windows gleaming with friendly light.
As the door opened, the merry sound of children's
laughter floated down the stairs, and it seemed to Hodder
as though a curse had been lifted. . . . The lintel of
this house had been marked for salvation, the scourge had
passed it by: the scourge of social striving which lay like
a blight on a free people.

Within, the note of gentility, of that instinctive good
taste to which many greater mansions aspired in vain, was
sustained. The furniture, the pictures, the walls and
carpets were true expressions of the individuality of
master and mistress, of the unity of the life lived together;
and the rector smiled as he detected, in a corner of the
hall, a sturdy but diminutive hobby-horse — here the final,
harmonious touch.

There was the sound of a scuffle, treble shrieks of
ecstasy from above, and Eleanor Goodrich came out to
welcome him.

"It's Phil," she told him in laughing despair, "he
upsets all my discipline, and gets them so excited they
don't go to sleep for hours. . . ."

Seated in front of the fire in the drawing-room, he
found Alison Parr.

Her coolness, her radiancy, her complete acceptance
of the situation, all this and more he felt from the
moment he touched her hand and looked into her face.
And never had she so distinctly represented to him the
mysterious essence of fate. Why she should have made
the fourth at this intimate gathering, and whether or not
she was or had been an especial friend of Eleanor Goodrich he did not know. There was no explanation. . . .

A bowl of superb chrysanthemums occupied the centre
of the table. Eleanor lifted them off and placed them
on the sideboard.

"I've got used to looking at Phil," she explained, "and
craning is so painful."

The effect at first was to increase the intensity of the
intimacy. There was no reason — he told himself — why
Alison's self-possession should have been disturbed; and

as he glanced at her from time to time he perceived that it was not. So completely was she mistress of herself that presently he felt a certain faint resentment rising within him, — yet he asked himself why she should not have been. It was curious that his imagination would not rise, now, to a realization of that intercourse on which, at times, his fancy had dwelt with such vividness. The very interest, the eagerness with which she took part in their discussions seemed to him in the nature of an emphatic repudiation of any ties to him which might have been binding.

All this was only, on Hodder's part, to be aware of the startling discovery as to how strong his sense of possession had been, and how irrational, how unwarranted. For he had believed himself, as regarding her, to have made the supreme renunciation of his life. And the very fact that he had not consulted, could not consult her feelings and her attitude made that renunciation no less difficult. All effort, all attempt at achievement of the only woman for whom he had ever felt the sublime harmony of desire — the harmony of the mind and the flesh — was cut off.

To be here, facing her again in such close proximity, was at once a pleasure and a torture. And gradually he found himself yielding to the pleasure, to the illusion of permanency created by her presence. And, when all was said, he had as much to be grateful for as he could reasonably have wished; yes, and more. The bond (there *was* a bond, after all!) which united them was unbreakable. They had forged it together. The future would take care of itself.

The range of the conversation upon which they at length embarked was a tacit acknowledgment of a relationship which now united four persons who, six months before, would have believed themselves to have had nothing in common. And it was characteristic of the new interest that it transcended the limits of the parish of St. John's, touched upon the greater affairs to which that parish — if their protest prevailed — would now be dedicated. Not

2 ɢ

that the church was at once mentioned; but subtly implied as now enlisted, — and emancipated henceforth from
all ecclesiastical narrowness. . . . The amazing thing by
which Hodder was suddenly struck was the naturalness
with which Alison seemed to fit into the new scheme.
It was as though she intended to remain there, and had
abandoned all intention of returning to the life which
apparently she had once permanently and definitely
chosen. . . .

Bedloe Hubbell's campaign was another topic. And
Phil had observed, with the earnestness which marked his
more serious statements, that it wouldn't surprise him if
young Carter, Hubbell's candidate for mayor, overturned
that autumn the Beatty machine.

" Oh, do you think so! " Alison exclaimed with ex-
hilaration.

" They're frightened and out of breath," said Phil, " they
had no idea that Bedloe would stick after they had licked
him in three campaigns. Two years ago they tried to
buy him off by offering to send him to the Senate, and
Wallis Plimpton has never got through his head to this
day why he refused."

Mr. Plimpton's head, Eleanor declared dryly, was impervious to a certain kind of idea.

"I wonder if you know, Mr. Hodder, what an admirer
Mr. Hubbell is of yours? " Alison asked. " He is most
anxious to have a talk with you."

Hodder did not know.

" Well," said Phil, enthusiastically, to the rector, " that's
the best tribute you've had yet. I can't say that Bedloe
was a more unregenerate heathen than I was, but he was
pretty bad."

This led them, all save Hodder, into comments on the
character of the congregation the Sunday before, in the
midst of which the rector was called away to the telephone.
Sally Grover had promised to let him know whether or
not they had found Kate Marcy, and his face was grave
when he returned. . . . He was still preoccupied, an
hour later, when Alison arose to go.

"But your carriage isn't here," said Phil, going to the window.

"Oh, I preferred to walk," she told him, "it isn't far."

III

A blood-red October moon shed the fulness of its light on the silent houses, and the trees, still clinging to leaf, cast black shadows across the lawns and deserted streets. The very echoes of their footsteps on the pavement seemed to enhance the unreality of their surroundings. Some of the residences were already closed for the night, although the hour was not late, and the glow behind the blinds of the others was nullified by the radiancy from above. To Hodder, the sense of their isolation had never been more complete.

Alison, while repudiating the notion that an escort were needed in a neighbourhood of such propriety and peace, had not refused his offer to accompany her. And Hodder felt instinctively, as he took his place beside her, a sense of climax. This situation, like those of the past, was not of his own making. It was here, confronting him, and a certain inevitable intoxication at being once more alone with her prevented him from forming any policy with which to deal with it. He might either trust himself, or else he might not. And as she said, the distance was not great. But he could not help wondering, during those first moments of silence, whether she comprehended the strength of the temptation to which she subjected him. . . .

The night was warm. She wore a coat, which was open, and from time to time he caught the gleam of the moonlight on the knotted pearls at her throat. Over her head she had flung, mantilla-like, a black lace scarf, the effect of which was, in the soft luminosity encircling her, to add to the quality of mystery never exhausted. If by acquiescing in his company she had owned to a tie between them, the lace shawl falling over the coils of her dark hair and framing in its folds her face, had somehow made her once more a stranger. Nor was it until she presently looked up into his face with a smile that this impression was, if not at once wholly dissipated, at least contradicted.

Her question, indeed, *was* intimate.

" Why did you come with me? "

" Why? " he repeated, taken aback.

" Yes. I'm sure you have something you wish to do, something which particularly worries you."

" No," he answered, appraising her intuition of him, " there is nothing I can do, to-night. A young woman in whom Mr. Bentley is interested, in whom I am interested, has disappeared. But we have taken all the steps possible towards finding her."

" It was nothing — more serious, then? That, of course, is serious enough. Nothing, I mean, directly affecting your prospects of remaining — where you are? "

" No," he answered. He rejoiced fiercely that she should have asked him. The question was not bold, but a natural resumption of the old footing. " Not that I mean to imply," he added, returning her smile, " that those 'prospects' are in any way improved."

" Are they any worse? " she said.

" I see the bishop to-morrow. I have no idea what position he will take. But even if he should decide not to recommend me for trial many difficult problems still remain to be solved."

" I know. It's fine," she continued, after a moment, " the way you are going ahead as if there were no question of your not remaining, and getting all those people into the church and influencing them as you did when they had come for all sorts of reasons. Do you remember, the first time I met you, I told you I could not think of you as a clergyman. I cannot now — less than ever."

" What do you think of me as? " he asked.

" I don't know," she considered. " You are unlike any person I have ever known. It is curious that I cannot now even think of St. John's as a church. You have transformed it into something that seems new. I'm afraid I can't describe what I mean, but you have opened it up,

let in the fresh air, rid it of the musty and deadening
atmosphere which I have always associated with churches.
I wanted to see you, before I went away," she went on
steadily, "and when Eleanor mentioned that you were
coming to her house to-night, I asked her to invite me.
Do you think me shameless?"

The emphasis of his gesture was sufficient. He could
not trust himself to speak.

"Writing seemed so unsatisfactory, after what you had
done for me, and I never can express myself in writing.
I seem to congeal."

"After what I have done for you!" he exclaimed.
"What can I have done?"

"You have done more than you know," she answered,
in a low voice. "More, I think, than I know. How are
such things to be measured, put into words? You have
effected some change in me which defies analysis, a change
of attitude, — to attempt to dogmatize it would ruin it.
I prefer to leave it undefined — not even to call it an acquisition of faith. I *have* faith," she said, simply, "in
what *you* have become, and which has made you dare,
superbly, to cast everything away. . . . It is that, more
than anything you have said. What you are."

For the instant he lost control of himself.

"What *you* are," he replied. "Do you realize — can
you ever realize what your faith in me has been to me?"

She appeared to ignore this.

"I did not mean to say that you have not made many
things clear, which once were obscure, as I wrote you.
You have convinced me that true belief, for instance, is
the hardest thing in the world, the denial of practically all
these people, who profess to believe, represent. The majority of them insist that humanity is not to be trusted. . . ."

They had reached, in an incredibly brief time, the
corner of Park Street.

"When are you leaving?" he asked, in a voice that
sounded harsh in his own ears.

"Come!" she said gently, "I'm not going in yet, for
a while."

The Park lay before them, an empty garden filled with
checquered light and shadows under the moon. He followed her across the gravel, glistening with dew, past the
statue of the mute statesman with arm upraised, into
pastoral stretches — a delectable country which was theirs
alone. He did not take it in, save as one expression of
the breathing woman at his side. He was but partly conscious of a direction he had not chosen. His blood
throbbed violently, and a feeling of actual physical faint-
ness was upon him. He was being led, helplessly, all
volition gone, and the very idea of resistance became
chimerical. . . .

There was a seat under a tree, beside a still lake burnished by the moon. It seemed as though he could not
bear the current of her touch, and yet the thought of its
removal were less bearable . . . For she had put her
own hand out, not shyly, but with a movement so fraught
with grace, so natural that it was but the crowning
bestowal.

"Alison!" he cried, "I can't ask it of you. I have no
right."

"You're not asking it," she answered. "It is I who
am asking it."

"But I have no future — I may be an outcast to-morrow.
I have nothing to offer you." He spoke more firmly now,
more commandingly.

"Don't you see, dear, that it is just because your future
is obscure that I can do this? *You* never would have
done it, I know, — and I couldn't face that. Don't you
understand that *I* am demanding the great sacrifice?"

"Sacrifice!" he repeated. His fingers turned, and
closed convulsively on hers.

"Yes, sacrifice," she said gently. "Isn't it the braver
thing?"

Still he failed to catch her meaning.

"Braver," she explained, with her wonderful courage,
"braver if I love you, if I need you, if I cannot do without you."

He took her in his arms, crushing her to him in his

strength, in one ineffable brief moment finding her lips, inhaling the faint perfume of her smooth skin. Her lithe figure lay passively against him, in marvellous, unbelievable surrender.

"I see what you mean," he said, at length, "I should have been a coward. But I could not be sure that you loved me."

So near was her face that he could detect, even under the obscurity of the branches, a smile.

"And so I was reduced to this! I threw my pride to the winds," she whispered. "But I don't care. I was determined, selfishly, to take happiness."

"And to give it," he added, bending down to her. The supreme quality of its essence was still to be doubted, a bright star-dust which dazzled him, to evaporate before his waking eyes. And, try as he would, he could not realize to the full depth the joy of contact with a being whom, by discipline, he had trained his mind to look upon as the unattainable. They had spoken of the future, yet in these moments any consideration of it was blotted out. . . . It was only by degrees that he collected himself sufficiently to be able to return to it. . . . Alison took up the thread.

"Surely," she said, "sacrifice is useless unless it *means* something, unless it be a realization. It must be discriminating. And we should both of us have remained incomplete if we had not taken — this. You would always, I think, have been the one man for me, — but we should have lost touch." He felt her tremble. "And I needed you. I have needed you all my life — one in whom I might have absolute faith. *That* is my faith, of which I could not tell you a while ago. Is it — sacrilegious?"

She looked up at him. He shook his head, thinking of his own. It seemed the very distillation of the divine.

"All my life," she went on, "I have been waiting for the one who would risk everything. Oh, if you had faltered the least little bit, I don't know what I should have done. That would have destroyed what was left of me, put out, I think, the flickering fire that remained, instead of fanning it into flame. You cannot know how I watched you, how I prayed! I think it was prayer — I am sure it was. And it was because you did not falter, because you risked all, that you gained me. You have gained only what you yourself made, more than I ever was, more than I ever expected to be."

"Alison!" he remonstrated, "you mustn't say that."

She straightened up and gazed at him, taking one of his hands in her lithe fingers.

"Oh, but I must! It is the truth. I felt that you cared — women are surer in such matters than men. I must conceal nothing from you — nothing of my craftiness. Women *are* crafty, you know. And suppose you fail? Ah, I do not mean failure — you *cannot* fail, now. You have put yourself forever beyond failure. But what I mean is, suppose you were compelled to leave St. John's, and I came to you then as I have come now, and begged to take my place beside you? I was afraid to risk it. I was afraid you would not take me, even now, to-night. Do you realize how austere you are at times, how you have frightened me?"

"That I should ever have done that!" he said.

"When I looked at you in the pulpit you seemed so far from me, I could scarcely bear it. As if I had no share in you, as if you had already gone to a place beyond, where I could not go, where I never could. Oh, you will take me with you, now, — you won't leave me behind!"

To this cry every fibre of his soul responded. He had thought himself, in these minutes, to have known all feelings, all thrills, but now, as he gathered her to him again, he was to know still another, the most exquisite of all. That it was conferred upon him to give *this* woman protection, to shield and lift her, inspire her as she inspired him — this consciousness was the most exquisite of all, transcending all conception of the love of woman. And the very fulness of her was beyond him. A lifetime were insufficient to exhaust her. . . .

"I wanted to come to you *now*, John. I want to

share your failure, if it comes — all your failures. Because they will be *victories* — don't you see? I have never been able to achieve that kind of victory — real victory, by myself. I have always succumbed, taken the baser, the easier thing." Her cheek was wet. "I wasn't strong enough, by myself, and I never knew the stronger one. . . .

"See what my trust in you has been! I knew that you would not refuse me in spite of the fact that the world may misunderstand, may sneer at your taking me. I knew that you were big enough even for that, when you understood it, coming from me. I wanted to be with you, *now*, that we might fight it out together."

"What have I done to deserve so priceless a thing?" he asked.

She smiled at him again, her lip trembling.

"Oh, I'm not priceless, I'm only real, I'm only human — human and tired. You are so strong, you can't know how tired. Have you any idea why I came out here, this summer? It was because I was desperate — because I had almost decided to marry some one else."

She felt him start.

"I was afraid of it," he said.

"Were you? Did you think, did you wonder a little about me?" There was a vibrant note of triumph to which he reacted. She drew away from him a little. "Perhaps, when you know how sordid my life has been, you won't want me."

"Is that your faith, Alison?" he demanded. "God forbid! You have come to a man who also has confessions to make."

"Oh, I am glad. I want to know all of you — all, do you understand? That will bring us even closer together. And it was one thing I felt about you in the beginning, that day in the garden, that you had had much to conquer — more than most men. It was a part of your force and of your knowledge of life. You were not a sexless ascetic who preached a mere neutral goodness. Does that shock you?"

He smiled in turn.

" I went away from here, as I once told you, full of a high resolution not to trail the honour of my art — if I achieved art — in the dust. But I have not only trailed my art — I trailed myself. In New York I became contaminated, — the poison of the place, of the people with whom I came in contact, got into my blood. Little by little I yielded — I wanted so to succeed, to be able to confound all those who had doubted and ridiculed me ! I wasn't content to wait to deny myself for the ideal. Success was in the air. *That* was the poison, and I only began to realize it after it was too late.

" Please don't think I am asking pity — I feel that you *must* know. From the very first my success — which was really failure — began to come in the wrong way. As my father's daughter I could not be obscure. I was sought out, I was what was called picturesque, I suppose. The women petted me, although some of them hated me, and I had a fascination for a certain kind of men — the wrong kind. I began going to dinners, house parties, to recognize that advantages came that way. . . . It seemed quite natural. It was what many others of my profession tried to do, and they envied me my opportunities.

"I ought to say, in justice to myself, that I was not in the least cynical about it. I believed I was clinging to the ideal of art, and that all I wanted was a chance. And the people I went with had the same characteristics, only intensified, as those I had known here. Of course I was actually no better than the women who were striving frivolously to get away from themselves, and the men who were fighting to get money. Only I didn't know it.

" Well, my chance came at last. I had done several little things, when an elderly man who is tremendously rich, whose name you would recognize if I mentioned it, gave me an order. For weeks, nearly every day, he came to my studio for tea, to talk over the plans. I was really unsophisticated then — but I can see now — well, that the garden was a secondary consideration. . . . And the fact that I did it for *him* gave me a standing I should not otherwise have had. . . . Oh, it is sickening to look back upon, to think what an idiot I was in how little I saw. . . .

" That garden launched me, and I began to have more work than I could do. I was conscientious about it. I tried to make every garden better than the last. But I was a young woman, unconventionally living alone, and by degrees the handicap of my sex was brought home to me. I did not feel the pressure at first, and then — I am ashamed to say — it had in it an element of excitement, a sense of power. The poison was at work. I was amused. I thought I could carry it through, that the world had advanced sufficiently for a woman to do anything if she only had the courage. And I believed I possessed a true broadness of view, and could impress it, so far as I was concerned, on others. . . .

" As I look back upon it all, I believe my reputation for coldness saved me, yet it was that very reputation which increased the pressure, and sometimes I was fairly driven into a corner. It seemed to madden some men — and the disillusionments began to come. Of course it was my fault — I don't pretend to say it wasn't. There were many whom, instinctively, I was on my guard against, but some I thought really nice, whom I trusted, revealed a side I had not suspected. That was the terrible thing ! And yet I held to my ideal, tattered as it was. . . ."

Alison was silent a moment, still clinging to his hand, and when she spoke again it was with a tremor of agitation.

" It is hard to tell you this, but I wish you to know. At last I met a man, comparatively young, who was making his own way in New York, achieving a reputation as a lawyer. Shall I tell you that I fell in love with him ? He seemed to bring a new freshness into my life when I was beginning to feel the staleness of it. Not that I surrendered at once, but the reservations of which I was conscious at the first gradually disappeared — or rather I ignored them. He had charm, a magnificent self-confidence, but I think the liberality of the opinions he expressed, in regard to women, most appealed to me. I was weak on that side, and I have often wondered whether he knew it. I believed him incapable of a great refusal.

" He agreed, if I consented to marry him, that I should have my freedom — freedom to live in my own life and to carry on my profession. Fortunately, the engagement was never announced, never even suspected. One day he hinted that I should return to my father for a month or two before the wedding. . . . The manner in which he said it suddenly turned me cold. Oh," Alison exclaimed, " I was quite willing to go back, to pay my father a visit, as I had done nearly every year, but — how can I tell you? — he could not believe that I had definitely given up — my father's money. . . .

" I sat still and looked at him, I felt as if I were frozen, turned to stone. And after a long while, since I would not speak to him, he went out. . . . Three months later he came back and said that I had misunderstood him, that he couldn't live without me. I sent him away. . . . Only the other day he married Amy Grant, one of my friends. . . .

" Well, after that, I was tired — so tired ! Everything seemed to go out of life. It wasn't that I loved him any longer, — all had been crushed. But the illusion was gone, and I saw myself as I was. And for the first time in my life I felt defenceless, helpless. I wanted refuge. Did you ever hear of Jennings Howe ? "

" The architect ? "

Alison nodded. " Of course you must have — he is so well known. He has been a widower for several years. He liked my work, saw its defects, and was always frank about them, and I designed a good many gardens in connection with his houses. He himself is above all things an artist, and he fell into the habit of coming to my studio and giving me friendly advice, in the nicest way. He seemed to understand that I was going through some sort of a crisis. He called it ' too much society.' And then, without any warning, he asked me to marry him.

" That is why I came out here — to think it over. I didn't love him, and I told him so, but I respected him.

He never compromised in his art, and I have known him over and over to refuse houses because certain conditions were stipulated. To marry him was an acknowledgment of defeat. I realized that. But I had come to the extremity where I wanted peace — peace and protection. I wanted to put myself irrevocably beyond the old life, which simply could not have gone on, and I saw myself in the advancing years becoming tawdry and worn, losing little by little what I had gained at a price.

"So I came here — to reflect, to see, as it were, if I could find something left in me to take hold of, to build upon, to begin over again, perhaps, by going back to the old associations. I could think of no better place, and I knew that my father would be going away after a few weeks, and that I should be alone, yet with an atmosphere back of me, — my old atmosphere. That was why I went to church the first Sunday, in order to feel more definitely that atmosphere, to summon up more completely the image of my mother. More and more, as the years have passed, I have thought of her in moments of trouble. I have recovered her as I never had hoped to do in Mr. Bentley. Isn't it strange," she exclaimed wonderingly, "that he should have come into both our lives, with such an influence, at this time?

"And then I met you, talked to you that afternoon in the garden. Shall I make a complete confession? I wrote to Jennings Howe that very week that I could not marry him."

"You knew!" Hodder exclaimed. "You knew then?"

"Ah, I can't tell what I knew — or when. I knew, after I had seen you, that I couldn't marry him. Isn't that enough?"

He drew in his breath deeply.

"I should be less than a man if I refused to take you, Alison. And — no matter what happens, I can and will find some honest work to support you. But oh, my dear, when I think of it, the nobility and generosity of what you have done appalls me."

"No, no!" she protested, "you mustn't say that! I

needed you more than you need me. And haven't we both discovered the world, and renounced it? I can at least go so far as to say that, with all my heart. And isn't marriage truer and higher when man and wife start with difficulties and problems to solve together? It is that thought that brings me the greatest joy, that I may be able to help you. . . . Didn't you need me, just a little?"

"Now that I have you, I am unable to think of the emptiness which might have been. You came to me, like Beatrice, when I had lost my way in the darkness of the wood. And like Beatrice, you showed me the path, and hell and heaven."

"Oh, you would have found the path without me. I cannot claim that. I saw from the first that you were destined to find it. And, unlike Beatrice, I too was lost, and it was you who lifted me up. You mustn't idealize me." . . . She stood up. "Come!" she said. He too stood, gazing at her, and she lifted her hands to his shoulders. . . . They moved out from under the tree and walked for a while in silence across the dew-drenched grass, towards Park Street. The moon, which had ridden over a great space in the sky, hung red above the blackness of the forest to the west.

"Do you remember when we were here together, the day I met Mr. Bentley? And you never would have spoken!"

"How could I, Alison?" he asked.

"No, you couldn't. And yet — you would have let me go."

He put his arm in hers, and drew her towards him.

"I must talk to your father," he said, "some day — soon. I ought to tell him — of our intentions. We cannot go on like this."

"No," she agreed, "I realize it. And I cannot stay, much longer, in Park Street. I must go back to New York, until you send for me, dear. And there are things I must do. Do you know, even though I antagonize him so — my father, I mean — even though he suspects and bitterly resents my interest in you, my affection for you, and that I have lingered because of you, I believe, in his way, he has liked to have me here."

"I can understand it," Hodder said.

"It's because you are bigger than I, although he has quarrelled with you so bitterly. I don't know what definite wrongs he has done to other persons. I don't wish to know. I don't ask you to tell me what passed between you that night. Once you said that you had an affection for him — that he was lonely. He *is* lonely. In these last weeks, in spite of his anger, I can see that he suffers terribly. It is a tragedy, because he will never give in."

"It is a tragedy." Hodder's tone was agitated.

"I wonder if he realizes a little ——" she began, and paused. "Now that Preston has come home——"

"Your brother?" Hodder exclaimed.

"Yes. I forgot to tell you. I don't know why he came," she faltered. "I suppose he has got into some new trouble. He seems changed. I can't describe it now, but I will tell you about it. . . . It's the first time we've all three been together since my mother died, for Preston wasn't back from college when I went to Paris to study. . . ."

They stood together on the pavement before the massive house, fraught with so many and varied associations for Hodder. And as he looked up at it, his eye involuntarily rested upon the windows of the boy's room where Eldon Parr had made his confession. Alison startled him by pronouncing his name, which came with such unaccustomed sweetness from her lips.

"You will write me to-morrow," she said, "after you have seen the bishop?"

"Yes, at once. You mustn't let it worry you."

"I feel as if I had cast off that kind of worry forever. It is only — the other worries from which we do not escape, from which we do not wish to escape."

With a wonderful smile she had dropped his hands and gone in at the entrance, when a sound made them turn, the humming of a motor. And even as they looked it swung into Park Street.

"It's a taxicab!" she said. As she spoke it drew up almost beside them, instead of turning in at the driveway, the door opened, and a man alighted.

"Preston!" Alison exclaimed.

He started, turning from the driver, whom he was about to pay. As for Hodder, he was not only under-going a certain shock through the sudden contact, at such a moment, with Alison's brother: there was an additional shock that this *was* Alison's brother and Eldon Parr's son. Not that his appearance was shocking, although the well-clad, athletic figure was growing a trifle heavy, and the light from the side lamps of the car revealed dissipa-tion in a still handsome face. The effect was a subtler one, not to be analyzed, and due to a multitude of pre-conceptions.

Alison came forward.

"This is Mr. Hodder, Preston," she said simply.

For a moment Preston continued to stare at the rector without speaking. Suddenly he put out his hand.

"Mr. Hodder, of St. John's?" he demanded.

"Yes," answered Hodder. His surprise deepened to perplexity at the warmth of the handclasp that followed.

A smile that brought back vividly to Hodder the sunny expression of the schoolboy in the picture lightened the features of the man.

"I'm very glad to see you," he said, in a tone that left no doubt of its genuine quality.

"Thank you," Hodder replied, meeting his eye with kindness, yet with a scrutiny that sought to penetrate the secret of an unexpected cordiality. "I, too, have hoped to see you."

Alison, who stood by wondering, felt a meaning behind the rector's words. She pressed his hand as he bade her, once more, good night.

"Won't you take my taxicab?" asked Preston. "It is going down town anyway."

"I think I'd better stick to the street cars," Hodder

said. His refusal was not ungraceful, but firm. Preston did not insist.

In spite of the events of that evening, which he went over again and again as the midnight car carried him eastward, in spite of a new-born happiness the actuality of which was still difficult to grasp, Hodder was vaguely troubled when he thought of Preston Parr.

CHAPTER XXVII

RETRIBUTION

I

THE Bishop's House was a comfortable, double dwelling of a smooth, bright red brick and large, plate-glass windows, situated in a plot at the western end of Waverley Place. It had been bought by the Diocese in the nineties, and was representative of that transitional period in American architecture when the mansard roof had been repudiated, when as yet no definite types had emerged to take its place. The house had pointed gables, and a tiny and utterly useless porch that served only to darken the front door, made of heavy pieces of wood fantastically curved.

It was precisely ten o'clock in the morning when Hodder rang the bell and was shown into the ample study which he had entered on other and less vital occasions. He found difficulty in realizing that this pleasant room, lined with well-worn books and overlooking a back lawn where the clothes of the episcopal family hung in the yellow autumn sun, was to be his judgment seat, whence he might be committed to trial for heresy.

And this was the twentieth century! The full force of the preposterous fact smote him, and a consciousness of the distance he himself had travelled since the comparatively recent days of his own orthodoxy. And suddenly he was full again of a resentful impatience, not only that he should be called away from his labours, his cares, the strangers who were craving his help, to answer charges of such an absurd triviality, but that the performance of the great task to which he had set his hand, with God's help, should depend upon it. Would his enemies be permitted to drive him out thus easily ?

The old bishop came in, walking by the aid of a cane. He smiled at Hodder, who greeted him respectfully, and bidding him sit down, took a chair himself behind his writing table, from whence he gazed awhile earnestly and contemplatively at the rugged features and strong shoulders of the rector of St. John's. The effect of the look was that of a visual effort to harmonize the man with the deed he had done, the stir he had created in the city and the diocese; to readjust impressions.

A hint of humour crept into the bishop's blue eyes, which were watery, yet strong, with heavy creases in the corners. He indicated by a little gesture three bundles of envelopes, bound by rubber bands, on the corner of his blotter.

" Hodder," he said, " see what a lot of trouble you have made for me in my old age! All those are about you."

The rector's expression could not have been deemed stern, but it had met the bishop's look unflinchingly. Now it relaxed into a responding smile, which was not without seriousness.

" I am sorry, sir," Hodder answered, " to have caused you any worry or inconvenience."

" Perhaps," said the bishop, " I have had too much smooth sailing for a servant of Christ. Indeed, I have come to that conclusion."

Hodder did not reply. He was moved, even more by the bishop's manner and voice than his words. And the opening to their conversation was unexpected. The old man put on his spectacles, and drew from the top of one of the bundles a letter.

" This is from one of your vestrymen, Mr. Gordon Atterbury," he said, and proceeded to read it, slowly. When he had finished he laid it down.

" Is that, according to your recollection, Mr. Hodder, a fairly accurate summary of the sermon you gave when you resumed the pulpit at the end of the summer ? "

" Yes, sir," answered the rector, " it is surprisingly ac-

curate, with the exception of two or three inferences which
I shall explain at the proper moment."

"Mr. Atterbury is to be congratulated on his memory,"
the bishop observed a little dryly. "And he has saved
me the trouble of reading more. Now what are the in
ferences to which you object?"

Hodder stated them. "The most serious one," he
added, "is that which he draws from my attitude on the
virgin birth. Mr. Atterbury insists, like others who
cling to that dogma, that I have become what he vaguely
calls an Unitarian. He seems incapable of grasping my
meaning, that the only true God the age knows, the
world has ever known, is the God in Christ, is the Spirit
in Christ, and is there not by any material proof, but because we recognize it spiritually. And that doctrine and
dogma, ancient speculations as to how, definitely, that
spirit came to be in Christ, are fruitless and mischievous
to-day. Mr. Atterbury and others seem actually to resent my identification of our Lord's Spirit with the social
conscience as well as the individual conscience of our
time."

The bishop nodded.

"Hodder," he demanded abruptly, leaning forward over
his desk, "how did this thing happen?"

"You mean, sir——" There was, in the bishop's voice,
a note almost pathetic.

"I do not mean to ask you anything you may deem too
personal. And God forbid, as I look at you, as I have
known you, that I should doubt your sincerity. I am not
your inquisitor, but your bishop and your friend, and I
am asking for your confidence. Six months ago you were,
apparently, one of the most orthodox rectors in the diocese.
I recognize that you are not an impulsive, sensational
man, and I am all the more anxious to learn from your
own lips something of the influences, of the processes
which have changed you, which have been strong enough
to impel you to risk the position you have achieved."

By this unlooked-for appeal Hodder was not only disarmed, but smitten with self-reproach at the thought of

his former misjudgment and underestimation of the man
in whose presence he sat. And it came over him, not
only the extent to which, formerly, he had regarded the
bishop as too tolerant and easy-going, but the fact that he
had arrived here to-day prepared to find in his superior
anything but the attitude he was showing. Considering
the bishop's age, Hodder had been ready for a lack of
understanding of the step he had taken, even for querulous
reproaches and rebuke.

He had, therefore, to pull himself together, to adjust himself to the unexpected greatness of soul with which he was
being received before he began to sketch the misgivings
he had felt from the early days of his rectorship of St.
John's ; the helplessness and failure which by degrees had
come over him. He related how it had become apparent
to him that by far the greater part of his rich and fashionable congregation were Christians only in name, who kept
their religion in a small and impervious compartment
where it did not interfere with their lives. He pictured
the yearning and perplexity of those who had come to
him for help, who could not accept the old explanations,
and had gone away empty ; and he had not been able to
make Christians of the poor who attended the parish
house. Finally, trusting in the bishop's discretion, he
spoke of the revelations he had unearthed in Dalton Street,
and how these had completely destroyed his confidence in
the Christianity he had preached, and how he had put his
old faith to the test of unprejudiced modern criticism,
philosophy, and science. . . .

The bishop listened intently, his head bent, his eyes on
the rector.

"And you have come out — convinced ? " he asked
tremulously. " Yes, yes, I see you have. It is enough."

He relapsed into thought, his wrinkled hand lying idly
on the table.

" I need not tell you, my friend," he resumed at length,
" that a great deal of pressure has been brought to bear
upon me in this matter, more than I have ever before
experienced. You have mortally offended, among others,

the most powerful layman in the diocese, Mr. Parr, who complains that you have presumed to take him to task concerning his private affairs."

"I told him," answered Hodder, "that so long as he continued to live the life he leads, I could not accept his contributions to St. John's."

"I am an old man," said the bishop, "and whatever usefulness I have had is almost finished. But if I were young to-day, I should pray God for the courage and insight you have shown, and I am thankful to have lived long enough to have known you. It has, at least, been given me to realize that times have changed, that we are on the verge of a mighty future. I will be frank to say that ten years ago, if this had happened, I should have recommended you for trial. Now I can only wish you God-speed. I, too, can see the light, my friend. I can see, I think, though dimly, the beginnings of a blending of all sects, of all religions in the increasing vision of the truth revealed in Jesus Christ, stripped, as you say, of dogma, of fruitless attempts at rational explanation. In Japan and China, in India and Persia, as well as in Christian countries, it is coming, coming by some working of the Spirit the mystery of which is beyond us. And nations and men who even yet know nothing of the Gospels are showing a willingness to adopt what is Christ's, and the God of Christ."

Hodder was silent, from sheer inability to speak.

"If you had needed an advocate with me," the bishop continued, "you could not have had one to whose counsel I would more willingly have listened than that of Horace Bentley. He wrote asking to come and see me, but I went to him in Dalton Street the day I returned. And it gives me satisfaction, Mr. Hodder, to confess to you freely that he has taught me, by his life, more of true Christianity than I have learned in all my experience elsewhere."

"I had thought," exclaimed the rector, wonderingly, "that *I* owed him more than any other man."

"There are many who think that — hundreds, I should say," the bishop replied. . . . "Eldon Parr ruined him, drove him from the church. . . . It is strange how, outside of the church, his influence has silently and continuously grown until it has borne fruit in — this. Even now," he added after a pause, "the cautiousness, the dread of change which comes with old age might, I think, lead me to be afraid of it if I didn't perceive behind it the spirit of Horace Bentley."

It struck Hodder, suddenly, what an unconscious but real source of confidence this thought had likewise been to him. He spoke of it.

"It is not that I wouldn't trust you," the bishop went on. "I have watched you, I have talked to Asa Waring, I have read the newspapers. In spite of it all, you have kept your head, you have not compromised the dignity of the Church. But oh, my friend, I beg you to bear in mind that you are launched upon deep waters, that you have raised up many enemies — enemies of Christ — who seek to destroy you. You are still young. And the uncompromising experiment to which you are pledged, of freeing your church, of placing her in the position of power and influence in the community which is rightfully hers, is as yet untried. And no stone will be left unturned to discourage and overcome you. You have faith, — you have made me feel it as you sat here, — a faith which will save you from bitterness in personal defeat. You may not reap the victory, or even see it in your lifetime. But of this I am sure, that you will be able to say, with Paul, 'I have planted, Apollos watered, but God gave the increase.' Whatever happens, you may count upon my confidence and support. I can only wish that I were younger, that my arm were stronger, and that I had always perceived the truth as clearly as I see it now."

Hodder had risen involuntarily while these words were being spoken. They were indeed a benediction, and the intensity of his feeling warned him of the inadequacy of any reply. They were pronounced in sorrow, yet in hope, and they brought home to him, sharply, the nobility of the bishop's own sacrifice.

"And you, sir?" he asked.

"Ah," answered the bishop, "with this I shall have had my life. I am content. . . ."

"You will come to me again, Hodder, some other day," he said, after an interval, "that we may talk over the new problems. They are constructive, creative, and I am anxious to hear how you propose to meet them. For one thing, to find a new basis for the support of such a parish. I understand they have deprived you of your salary."

"I have enough to live on, for a year or so," replied the rector, quickly. "Perhaps more."

"I'm afraid," said the bishop, with a smile in his old eyes, "that you will need it, my friend. But who can say? You have strength, you have confidence, and God is with you."

II

Life, as Hodder now grasped it, was a rapidly whirling wheel which gave him no chance to catch up with the impressions and experiences through which it was dragging him. Here, for instance, were two far-reaching and momentous events, one crowding upon the other, and not an hour for reflection, realization, or adjustment! He had, indeed, after his return from the bishop's, snatched a few minutes to write Alison the unexpected result of that interview. But even as he wrote and rang for a messenger to carry the note to Park Street, he was conscious of an effort to seize upon and hold the fact that the woman he had so intensely desired was now his helpmate; and had, of her own free will, united herself with him. A strong sense of the dignity of their relationship alone prevented his calling her on the telephone — as it doubtless had prevented her. While she remained in her father's house, he could not. . . .

In the little room next to the office several persons were waiting to see him. But as he went downstairs he halted on the landing, his hand going to his forehead, a reflex movement significant of a final attempt to achieve the hitherto unattainable feat of imagining her as his wife. If he might only speak to her again — now, this morning! And yet he knew that he needed no confirmation. The reality was there, in the background; and though refusing to come forward to be touched, it had already grafted itself as an actual and vital part of his being, never to be eliminated.

Characteristically perfecting his own ideal, she had come to him in the hour when his horizon had been most obscure. And he experienced now an exultation, though solemn and sacred, that her faith had so far been rewarded in the tidings he now confided to the messenger. He was not, as yet, to be driven out from the task, to be deprived of the talent, the opportunity intrusted to him by his Lord — the emancipation of the parish of St. John's.

The first to greet him, when he entered his office, was one who, unknown to himself, had been fighting the battle of the God in Christ, and who now, thanks to John Hodder, had identified the Spirit as the transforming force. Bedloe Hubbell had come to offer his services to the Church. The tender was unqualified.

" I should even be willing, Mr. Hodder," he said with a smile, " to venture occasionally into a pulpit. You have not only changed my conception of religion, but you have made it for me something which I can now speak about naturally."

Hodder was struck by the suggestion.

" Ah, we shall need the laymen in the pulpits, Mr. Hubbell," he said quickly. " A great spiritual movement must be primarily a lay movement. And I promise you you shall not lack for opportunity."

III

At nine o'clock that evening, when a reprieve came, Hodder went out. Anxiety on the score of Kate Marcy, as well as a desire to see Mr. Bentley and tell him of the conversation with the bishop, directed his steps toward Dalton Street. And Hodder had, indeed, an intention of confiding to his friend, as one eminently entitled to it, the news of his engagement to Alison Parr.

Nothing, however, had been heard of Kate. She was not in Dalton Street, Mr. Bentley feared. The search of Gratz, the cabinet-maker, had been fruitless. And Sally Grover had even gone to see the woman in the hospital, whom Kate had befriended, in the hope of getting a possible clew. They sat close together before the fire in Mr. Bentley's comfortable library, debating upon the possibility of other methods of procedure, when a carriage was heard rattling over the pitted asphalt without. As it pulled up at the curb, a silence fell between them. The door-bell rang.

Hodder found himself sitting erect, rigidly attentive, listening to the muffled sound of a woman's voice in the entry. A few moments later came a knock at the library door, and Sam entered. The old darky was plainly frightened.

"It's Miss Kate, Marse Ho'ace, who you bin tryin' to fin'," he stammered.

Hodder sprang to his feet and made his way rapidly around the table, where he stood confronting the woman in the doorway. There she was, perceptibly swaying, as though the floor under her were rocked by an earthquake. Her handsome face was white as chalk, her pupils widened in terror. It was curious, at such an instant, that he should have taken in her costume, — yet it was part of the mystery. She wore a new, close-fitting, patently expensive suit of dark blue cloth and a small hat, which were literally transforming in their effect, demanding a palpable initial effort of identification.

He seized her by the arm.

"What is it?" he demanded.

"Oh, my God!" she cried. "He — he's out there — in the carriage."

She leaned heavily against the doorpost, shivering. . . . Hodder saw Sally Grover coming down the stairs.

"Take her," he said, and went out of the front door, which Sam had left open. Mr. Bentley was behind him.

The driver had descended from the box and was peering into the darkness of the vehicle when he heard them, and turned. At sight of the tall clergyman, an expression of relief came into his face.

" I don't like the looks of this, sir," he said. " I thought he was pretty bad when I went to fetch him——"

Hodder pushed past him and looked into the carriage. Leaning back, motionless, in the corner of the seat was the figure of a man. For a terrible moment of premonition, of enlightenment, the rector gazed at it.

" They sent for me from a family hotel in Ayers Street——" the driver was explaining. Mr. Bentley's voice interrupted him.

" He must be brought in, at once. Do you know where Dr. Latimer's office is, on Tower Street?" he asked the man. " Go there, and bring the doctor back with you as quickly as possible. If he is not in, get another physician."

Between them, the driver and Hodder got the burden out of the carriage and up the steps. The light from the hallway confirmed the rector's fear.

" It's Preston Parr," he said.

The next moment was too dreadful for surprise, but never had the sense of tragedy so pierced the innermost depths of Hodder's being as now, when Horace Bentley's calmness seemed to have forsaken him; and as he gazed down upon the features on the pillow, he wept. . . . Hodder turned away. Whatever memories those features evoked, memories of a past that still throbbed with life — these were too sacred for intrusion. The years of exile, of uncomplaining service to others in this sordid street and over the wide city had not yet sufficed to allay the pain, to heal the wound of youth. Nay, loyalty had kept it fresh — a loyalty that was the handmaid of faith. . . .

The rector softly left the room, only to be confronted with another harrowing scene in the library, where a frantic woman was struggling in Sally Grover's grasp. He went to her assistance. . . . Words of comfort, of entreaty were of no avail, — Kate Marcy did not seem to hear them. Hers, in contrast to that other, was the un-meaning grief, the overwhelming sense of injustice of the child; and with her regained physical strength the two had all they could do to restrain her.

"I will go to him," she sobbed, between her paroxysms, "you've got no right to keep me — he's mine . . . he came back to me — he's all I ever had. . . ."

So intent were they that they did not notice Mr. Bentley standing beside them until they heard his voice.

"What she says is true," he told them. "Her place is in there. Let her go."

Kate Marcy raised her head at the words, and looked at him — a strange, half-comprehending, half-credulous gaze. They released her, helped her towards the bedroom, and closed the door gently behind her. . . . The three sat in silence until the carriage was heard returning, and the doctor entered.

The examination was brief, and two words, laconically spoken, sufficed for an explanation — apoplexy, alcohol. The prostrate, quivering woman was left where they had found her.

Dr. Latimer was a friend of Mr. Bentley's, and betrayed no surprise at a situation which otherwise might have astonished him. It was only when he learned the dead man's name, and his parentage, that he looked up quickly from his note book.

"The matter can be arranged without a scandal," he said, after an instant. "Can you tell me something of the circumstances?"

It was Hodder who answered.

"Preston Parr had been in love with this woman, and separated from her. She was under Mr. Bentley's care when he found her again, I infer, by accident. From what the driver says, they were together in a hotel in Ayers Street, and he died after he had been put in a carriage. In her terror, she was bringing him to Mr. Bentley."

The doctor nodded.

"Poor woman!" he said unexpectedly. "Will you be good enough to let Mr. Parr know that I will see him at his house, to-night?" he added, as he took his departure.

IV

Sally Grover went out with the physician, and it was Mr. Bentley who answered the question in the rector's mind, which he hesitated to ask.

"Mr. Parr must come here," he said.

As the rector turned, mechanically, to pick up his hat, Mr. Bentley added:

"You will come back, Hodder?"

"Since you wish it, sir," the rector said.

Once in the street, he faced a predicament, but swiftly decided that the telephone was impossible under the circumstances, that there could be no decent procedure without going himself to Park Street. It was only a little after ten. The electric car which he caught seemed to lag, the stops were interminable. His thoughts flew hither and thither. Should he try first to see Alison? He was nearest to her now of all the world, and he could not suffer the thought of her having the news otherwise. Yes, he must tell her, since she knew nothing of the existence of Kate Marcy.

Having settled that, — though the thought of the blow she was to receive lay like a weight on his heart, — Mr. Bentley's reason for summoning Eldon Parr to Dalton Street came to him. That the feelings of Mr. Bentley towards the financier were those of Christian forgiveness was not for a moment to be doubted: but a meeting, particularly under such circumstances, could not but be painful indeed. It must be, it was, Hodder saw, for Kate Marcy's sake; yes, and for Eldon Parr's as well, that he be given this opportunity to deal with the woman whom he had driven away from his son, and ruined.

The moon, which had shed splendours over the world the night before, was obscured by a low-drifting mist as Hodder turned in between the ornamental lamps that marked the gateway of the Park Street mansion, and by some undiscerned thought-suggestion he pictured the heartbroken woman he had left beside the body of one who had been heir to all this magnificence. Useless now, stone and iron and glass, pictures and statuary. All the labour, all the care and cunning, all the stealthy planning to get ahead of others had been in vain! What indeed were left to Eldon Parr! It was he who needed pity, — not the woman who had sinned and had been absolved because of her great love; not the wayward, vice-driven boy who lay dead. The very horror of what Eldon Parr was now to suffer turned Hodder cold as he rang the bell and listened for the soft tread of the servant who would answer his summons.

The man who flung open the door knew him, and did not conceal his astonishment.

"Will you take my card to Miss Parr," the rector said, "if she has not retired, and tell her I have a message?"

"Miss Parr is still in the library, sir."

"Alone?"

"Yes, sir." The man preceded him, but before his name had been announced Alison was standing, her book in her hand, gazing at him with startled eyes, his name rising, a low cry, to her lips.

"John!"

He took the book from her, gently, and held her hands.

"Something has happened!" she said. "Tell me — I can bear it."

He saw instantly that her dread was for him, and it made his task the harder.

"It's your brother, Alison."

"Preston! What is it? He's done something——"

Hodder shook his head.

"He died — to-night. He is at Mr. Bentley's."

It was like her that she did not cry out, or even speak, but stood still, her hands tightening on his, her breast heaving. She was not, he knew, a woman who wept easily, and her eyes were dry. And he had it to be thankful for that it was given him to be with her, in this sacred relationship, at such a moment. But even now, such was the mystery that ever veiled her soul, he could not read her feelings, nor know what these might be towards the brother whose death he announced.

med never more out of place, yet pity *was* Hod-
minant feeling as he met the coldness, the relent-
of the glance. The thing that struck him, that
tarily kept closed his lips, was the awful, uncon-
timeliness of the man's entrance, and his unpre-
ness to meet the blow that was to crush him.

ay I ask, Mr. Hodder," he said, in an unemotional
v "what you are doing in this house?"

ll Hodder hesitated, an unwilling executioner.

ather," said Alison, "Mr. Hodder has come with a
mesae."

Ner, perhaps, had Eldon Parr given such complete
pre f his lack of spiritual intuition. The atmosphere,
ch y l with presage for him, gave him nothing.

d Hodder takes a strange way of delivering it," was
his t nment.

I h y took precedence over her natural directness.
Sh d her hand gently on his arm. And she had, at
tha stant, no thought of the long years he had neglected
her her brother.

" It's about — Preston," she said.

" Preston!" The name came sharply from Eldon
Par 's lips. "What about him? Speak, can't you?"

" died this evening," said Alison, simply.

I ler plainly heard the ticking of the clock on the
mai l . . . And the drama that occurred was the
mor orrible because it was hidden; played, as it were,
behi closed doors. For the spectators, there was only
the b nk wall, and the silence. Eldon Parr literally did
nothing, — made no gesture, uttered no cry. The death,
they knew, was taking place in his soul, yet the man stood
before them, naturally, for what seemed an interminable
time. . . .

" Where is he?" he asked.

"At Mr. Bentley's, in Dalton Street." It was Alison
who replied again.

Eve then he gave no sign that he read retribution in
he co cidence, betrayed no agitation at the mention of a
ame which, in such a connection, might well have struck

" I want to tell you, first, Alison, t⌐ said.

Her silence was eloquent. She looked ⌐ trustfully, in a way that made him wince. exact nature of her suffering, it was too d⌐ And yet she helped him, made it easier for ⌐ of her very trust, once given not to be wi⌐ gave him a paradoxical understanding of he⌐ beyond definition.

" You must know — you would have sometim⌐ that there was a woman he loved, whom he in⌐ marry — but she was separated from him. Sh⌐ what is called a bad woman, she was a working⌐ found her, this summer, and she told me the st⌐ she has been under the care of Mr. Bentley. She⌐ peared two or three days ago. Your brother m⌐ again, and he was stricken with apoplexy while wi⌐ this evening. She brought him to Mr. Bentley's h⌐

" My father — bought her and sent her away."

" You knew? "

" I heard a little about it at the time, by accident⌐ I have always remembered it. . . . I have always fe⌐ that something like this would happen."

Her sense of fatality, another impression she ga⌐ living in the deeper, instinctive currents of life, had⌐ been stronger upon him than now. . . . She re⌐ his hands.

" How strange," she said, "that the end should⌐ come at Mr. Bentley's! He loved my mother — sl⌐ the only woman he ever loved."

It came to Hodder as the completing touch⌐ revelation he had half glimpsed by the bedside.

"Ah," he could not help exclaiming, "that ⌐ much."

She had looked at him again, through sudden ⌐ though divining his reference to Mr. Bentley's gri⌐ a step make them turn. Eldon Parr had ent⌐ room. Never, not even in that last interview, ⌐ hardness seemed so concretely apparent as now.

the terror of judgment into his heart. They watched him while, with a firm step, he crossed the room and pressed a button in the wall, and waited.

"I want the closed automobile, at once," he said, when the servant came.

"I beg pardon, sir, but I think Gratton has gone to bed. He had no orders."

"Then wake him," said Eldon Parr, "instantly. And send for my secretary."

With a glance which he perceived Alison comprehended, Hodder made his way out of the room. He had from Eldon Parr, as he passed him, neither question, acknowledgment, nor recognition. Whatever the banker might have felt, or whether his body had now become a mere machine mechanically carrying on a life-long habit of action, the impression was one of the tremendousness of the man's consistency. A great effort was demanded to summon up the now almost unimaginable experience of his confidence; of the evening when, almost on that very spot, he had revealed to Hodder the one weakness of his life. And yet the effort was not to be, presently, without startling results. In the darkness of the street the picture suddenly grew distinct on the screen of the rector's mind, the face of the banker subtly drawn with pain as he had looked down on it in compassion; the voice with its undercurrent of agony:

"He never knew how much I cared — that what I was doing was all for him, building for him, that he might carry on my work."

V

So swift was the trolley that ten minutes had elapsed, after Hodder's arrival, before the purr of an engine and the shriek of a brake broke the stillness of upper Dalton Street and announced the stopping of a heavy motor before the door. The rector had found Mr. Bentley in the library, alone, seated with bent head in front of the fire, and had simply announced the intention of Eldon Parr to come. From the chair Hodder had unobtrusively chosen,

2 1

near the window, his eyes rested on the noble profile of his
friend.   What his thoughts were, Hodder could not surmise ; for he seemed again, marvellously, to have regained
the outward peace which was the symbol of banishment
from the inner man of all thought of self.

"I have prepared her for Mr. Parr's coming," he said to
Hodder at length.

And yet he had left her there ! Hodder recalled the
words Mr. Bentley had spoken, "It is her place."   Her
place, the fallen woman's, the place she had earned by a
great love and a great renunciation, of which no earthly
power might henceforth deprive her. . . .

Then came the motor, the ring at the door, the entrance
of Eldon Parr into the library.   He paused, a perceptible
moment, on the threshold as his look fell upon the man
whom he had deprived of home and fortune, — yes and of
the one woman in the world for them both.   Mr. Bentley
had risen, and stood facing him.   That shining, compassionate gaze should have been indeed a difficult one to
meet.   Vengeance was the Lord's, in truth !   What ordeal
that Horace Bentley in anger and retribution might have
devised could have equalled this !

And yet Eldon Parr did meet it — with an effort.   Hodder, from his corner, detected the effort, though it were
barely discernible, and would have passed a scrutiny less
rigid, — the first outward and visible sign of the lesion
within.   For a brief instant the banker's eyes encountered
Mr. Bentley's look with a flash of the old defiance, and
fell, and then swept the room.

"Will you come this way, Mr. Parr?"   Mr. Bentley said,
indicating the door of the bedroom.

Alison followed.   Her eyes, wet with unheeded tears,
had never left Mr. Bentley's face.   She put out her hand
to him. . . .

Eldon Parr had halted abruptly.   He knew from Alison
the circumstances in which his son had died, and how he
had been brought hither to this house, but the sight of the
woman beside the bed fanned into flame his fury against
a world which had cheated him, by such ignominious

means, of his dearest wish. He grew white with sudden passion.

"What is she doing here?" he demanded.

Kate Marcy, who had not seemed to hear his entrance, raised up to him a face from which all fear had fled, a face which, by its suggestive power, compelled him to realize the absolute despair clutching now at his own soul, and against which he was fighting wildly, hopelessly. It was lying in wait for him, with hideous patience, in the coming watches of the night. Perhaps he read in the face of this woman whom he had condemned to suffer all degradation, and over whom he was now powerless, something which would ultimately save her from the hell now yawning for him; a redeeming element in her grief of which she herself were not as yet conscious, a light shining in the darkness of her soul which in eternity would become luminous. And he saw no light — for him. *He* thrashed in darkness. . . . He had nothing, now, to give, no power longer to deprive. She had given all she possessed, the memorial of her kind which would outlast monuments.

It was Alison who crossed the room swiftly. She laid her hand protectingly on Kate Marcy's shoulder, and stooped, and kissed her. She turned to her father.

"It is her right," she said. "He belonged to her, — not to us. And we must take her home with us."

"No," answered Kate Marcy, "I don't want to go. I wouldn't live," she added with unexpected intensity, "with *him.*"

"You would live with me," said Alison.

"I don't want to live!" Kate Marcy got up from the chair with an energy they had not thought her to possess, a revival of the spirit which had upheld her when she had contended, singly, with a remorseless world. She addressed herself to Eldon Parr. "You took him from me, and I was a fool to let you. He might have saved me and saved himself. I listened to you when you told me lies as to how it would ruin him. . . . Well, I had him — you never did."

The sudden, intolerable sense of wrong done to her

love, the swift anger which followed it, the justness of her claim of him who now lay in the dignity of death clothed *her* — who in life had been crushed and blotted out — with a dignity not to be gainsaid. In this moment of final self-assertion she became the dominating person in the room, knew for once the birthright of human worth. They watched her in silence as she turned and gave one last, lingering look at the features of the dead, stretched out her hand towards them, but did not touch them . . . and then went slowly towards the door. Beside Alison she stopped.

"You are his sister?" she said.

"Yes."

She searched Alison's face, wistfully.

"I could have loved you."

"And can you not — still?"

Kate Marcy did not answer the question.

"It is because you understand," she said. "You're like those I've come to know — here. And you're like *him*. . . . I don't mean in looks. He, too, was good — and square." She spoke the words a little defiantly, as though challenging the verdict of the world. "And he wouldn't have been wild if he could have got going straight."

"I know," said Alison, in a low voice.

"Yes," said Kate Marcy, "you look as if you did. He thought a lot of you, he said he was only beginning to find out what you was. I'd like you to think as well of me as you can."

"I could not think better," Alison replied.

Kate Marcy shook her head.

"I got about as low as any woman ever got," she said. "Mr. Hodder will tell you. I want you to know that I wouldn't marry — your brother," she hesitated over the name. "He wanted me to — he was mad with me to-night, because I wouldn't — when *this* happened."

She snatched her hand free from Alison's, and fled out of the room, into the hallway. . . .

Eldon Parr had moved towards the bed, seemingly unaware of the words they had spoken. Perhaps, as he gazed upon the face, he remembered in his agony the sunny, smiling child who used to come hurrying down the steps in Ransome Street to meet him.

In the library Mr. Bentley and John Hodder, knowing nothing of her flight, heard the front door close on Kate Marcy forever. . . .

CHAPTER XXVIII

LIGHT

I

Two days after the funeral, which had taken place from Calvary, and not from St. John's, Hodder was no little astonished to receive a note from Eldon Parr's secretary requesting the rector to call in Park Street. In the same mail was a letter from Alison. "I have had," she wrote, "a talk with my father. The initiative was his. I should not have thought of speaking to him of my affairs so soon after Preston's death. It seems that he strongly suspected our engagement, which of course I at once acknowledged, telling him that it was your intention, at the proper time, to speak to him yourself.

"I was surprised when he said he would ask you to call. I confess that I have not an idea of what he intends to say to you, John, but I trust you absolutely, as always. You will find him, already, terribly changed. I cannot describe it — you will see for yourself. And it has all seemed to happen so suddenly. As I wrote you, he sat up both nights, with Preston — he could not be induced to leave the room. And after the first night he was different. He has hardly spoken a word, except when he sent for me this evening, and he eats nothing. . . . And yet, somehow, I do not think that this will be the end. I feel that he will go on living. . . .

"I did not realize how much he still hoped about Preston. And on Monday, when Preston so unexpectedly came home, he was happier than I have known him for years. It was strange and sad that he could not see, as I saw, that whatever will power my brother had had was gone. He

486

could not read it in the face of his own son, who was so quick to detect it in all others! And then came the tragedy. Oh, John, do you think we shall ever find that girl again? — I know you *are* trying — but we mustn't rest until we do. Do you think we ever shall? I shall never forgive myself for not following her out of the door, but I thought she had gone to you and Mr. Bentley."

Hodder laid the letter down, and took it up again. He knew that Alison felt, as he felt, that they never would find Kate Marcy. . . . He read on.

" My father wished to speak to me about the money. He has plans for much of it, it appears, even now. Oh, John, he will *never* understand. I want so much to see you, to talk to you — there are times when I am actually afraid to be alone, and without you. If it be weakness to confess that I need your reassurance, your strength and comfort constantly, then I am weak. I once thought I could stand alone, that I had solved all problems for myself, but I know now how foolish I was. I have been face to face with such dreadful, unimagined things, and in my ignorance I did not conceive that life held such terrors. And when I look at my father, the thought of immortality turns me faint. After you have come here this afternoon there can be no longer any reason why we should not meet, and all the world know it. I will go with you to Mr. Bentley's.

" Of course I need not tell you that I refused to inherit anything. But I believe I should have consented if I possibly could have done so. It seemed so *cruel* — I can think of no other word — to have to refuse at such a moment. Perhaps I have been cruel to him all my life — I don't know. As I look back upon everything, all our relations, I cannot see how I could have been different. He wouldn't let me. I still believe to have stayed with him would have been a foolish and useless sacrifice. . . . But he looked at me so queerly, as though he, too, had had a glimmering of what we might have been to each other after my mother died. Why is life so hard? And why are we always getting glimpses of things when it is too late? It is only honest to say that if I had it to do all over again, I should have left him as I did.

"It is hard to write you this, but he actually made the condition of my acceptance of the inheritance that I should not marry you. I really do not believe I convinced him that you wouldn't have me take the money under any circumstances. And the dreadful side of it all was that I had to make it plain to him — after what has happened — that my desire to marry you wasn't the main reason of my refusal. I had to tell him that even though you had not been in question, I couldn't have taken what he wished to give me, since it had not been honestly made. He asked me why I went on eating the food bought with such money, living under his roof? But I cannot, I will not leave him just yet. . . . It is two o'clock. I cannot write any more to-night. . . ."

II

The appointed time was at the November dusk, hurried forward nearly an hour by the falling panoply of smoke driven westward over the Park by the wet east wind. And the rector was conducted, with due ceremony, to the office upstairs which he had never again expected to enter, where that other memorable interview had taken place. The curtains were drawn. And if the green-shaded lamp — the only light in the room — had been arranged by a master of dramatic effect, it could not have better served the setting.

In spite of Alison's letter, Hodder was unprepared for the ravages a few days had made in the face of Eldon Parr. Not that he appeared older : the impression was less natural, more sinister. The skin had drawn sharply over the cheek-bones, and strangely the eyes both contradicted and harmonized with the transformation of the features. These, too, had changed. They were not dead and lustreless, but gleamed out of the shadowy caverns into which they had sunk, unyielding, indomitable in torment, — eyes of a spirit rebellious in the flames. . . .

This spirit somehow produced the sensation of its being

separated from the body, for the movement of the hand, inviting Hodder to seat himself, seemed almost automatic.

"I understand," said Eldon Parr, "that you wish to marry my daughter."

"It is true that I am to marry Alison," Hodder answered, "and that I intended, later on, to come to inform you of the fact."

He did not mention the death of Preston. Condolences, under the circumstances, were utterly out of the question.

"How do you propose to support her?" the banker demanded.

"She is of age, and independent of you. You will pardon me if I reply that this is a matter between ourselves," Hodder said.

"I had made up my mind that the day she married you I would not only disinherit her, but refuse absolutely to have anything to do with her."

"If you cannot perceive what she perceives, that you have already by your own life cut her off from you absolutely and that seeing her will not mend matters while you remain relentless, nothing I can say will convince you." Hodder did not speak rebukingly. The utter uselessness of it was never more apparent. The man was condemned beyond all present reprieve, at least.

"She left me," exclaimed Eldon Parr, bitterly.

"She left you, to save herself."

"We need not discuss that."

"I am far from wishing to discuss it," Hodder replied. "I do not know why you have asked me to come here, Mr. Parr. It is clear that your attitude has not changed since our last conversation. I tried to make it plain to you why the church could not accept your money. Your own daughter cannot accept it."

"There was a time," retorted the banker, "when you did not refuse to accept it."

"Yes," Hodder replied, "that is true." It came to him vividly then that it had been Alison herself who had cast the enlightening gleam which revealed his inconsistency. But he did not defend himself.

"I can see nothing in all this, Mr. Hodder, but a species of insanity," said Eldon Parr, and there crept into his tone both querulousness and intense exasperation. "In the first place, you insist upon marrying my daughter when neither she nor you have any dependable means of support. She never spared her criticisms of me, and you presume to condemn me, a man who, if he has neglected his children, has done so because he has spent too much of his time in serving his community and his country, and who has — if I have to say it myself — built up the prosperity which you and others are doing your best to tear down, and which can only result in the spread of misery. You profess to have a sympathy with the masses, but you do not know them as I do. They cannot control themselves, they require a strong hand. But I am not asking for your sympathy. I have been misunderstood all my life, I have become used to ingratitude, even from my children, and from the rector of the church for which I have done more than any other man."

Hodder stared at him in amazement.

"You really believe that!" he exclaimed.

"Believe it!" Eldon Parr repeated. "I have had my troubles, as heavy bereavements as a man can have. All of them, even this of my son's death, all the ingratitude and lack of sympathy I have experienced —" (he looked deliberately at Hodder) "have not prevented me, do not prevent me to-day from regarding my fortune as a trust. You have deprived St. John's, at least so long as you remain there, of some of its benefits, and the responsibility for that is on your own head. And I am now making arrangements to give to Calvary the settlement house which St. John's should have had."

The words were spoken with such an air of conviction, of unconscious plausibility, as it were, that it was impossible for Hodder to doubt the genuineness of the attitude they expressed. And yet it was more than his mind could grasp. . . . Horace Bentley, Richard Garvin, and the miserable woman of the streets whom he had driven to destroy herself had made absolutely no impression whatever! The gifts, the benefactions of Eldon Parr to his fellow-men would go on as before!

" You ask me why I sent for you," the banker went on. " It was primarily because I hoped to impress upon you the folly of marrying my daughter. And in spite of all the injury and injustice you have done me, I do not forget that you were once in a relationship to me which has been unique in my life. I trusted you, I admired you for your ability, for your faculty of getting on with men. At that time you were wise enough not to attempt to pass comment upon accidents in business affairs which are, if deplorable, inevitable."

Eldon Parr's voice gave a momentary sign of breaking.

" I will be frank with you. My son's death has led me, perhaps weakly, to make one more appeal. You have ruined your career by these chimerical, socialistic notions you have taken up, and which you mistake for Christianity. As a practical man I can tell you, positively, that St. John's will run downhill until you are bankrupt. The people who come to you now are in search of a new sensation, and when that grows stale they will fall away. Even if a respectable number remain in your congregation, after this excitement and publicity have died down, I have reason to know that it is impossible to support a large city church on contributions. It has been tried again and again, and failed. You have borrowed money for the Church's present needs. When that is gone I predict that you will find it difficult to get more."

This had every indication of being a threat, but Hodder, out of sheer curiosity, did not interrupt. And it was evident that the banker drew a wrong conclusion from his silence, which he may actually have taken for reluctant acquiescence. His tone grew more assertive.

" The Church, Mr. Hodder, cannot do without the substantial business men. I have told the bishop so, but he is failing so rapidly from old age that I might as well not have wasted my breath. He needs an assistant, a suffragan or coadjutor, and I intend to make it my affair to see that he gets one. When I remember him as he was ten years ago, I find it hard to believe that he is touched with these fancies. To be charitable, it is senile decay. He seems to forget what I have done for him, personally, — made up his salary, paid his expenses at different times, and no appeal for the diocese to me was ever in vain. But again, I will let that go.

"What I am getting at is this. You have made a mess of the affairs of St. John's, you have made a mess of your life. I am willing to give you the credit for sincerity. Some of my friends might not be. You want to marry my daughter, and she is apparently determined to marry you. If you are sensible and resign from St. John's now I will settle on Alison a sufficient sum to allow you both to live in comfort and decency the rest of your lives. I will not have it said of me that I permitted my daughter to become destitute."

After he had finished, the rector sat for so long a time that the banker nervously shifted in his chair. The clergyman's look had a cumulative quality, an intensity which seemed to increase as the silence continued. There was no anger in it, no fanaticism. On the contrary, the higher sanity of it was disturbing; and its extraordinary implication — gradually borne in upon Eldon Parr — was that he himself were not in his right mind. The words, when they came, were a confirmation of this inference.

"It is what I feared, Mr. Parr," he said. "You are as yet incapable of comprehending."

"What do you mean?" asked the banker, jerking his hand from the table.

The rector shook his head.

"If this great chastisement with which you have been visited has given you no hint of the true meaning of life, nothing I can say will avail. If you will not yet listen to the Spirit which is trying to make you comprehend, how then will you listen to me? How am I to open your eyes to the paradox of truth, that he who would save his life shall lose it, that it is easier for a camel to go through the eye of a needle, than for a rich man to enter into the Kingdom of God? If you will not believe him who said that, you will not believe me. I can only beg of you, strive to understand, that your heart may be softened, that your suffering soul may be released."

It is to be recorded, strangely, that Eldon Parr did not grow angry in his turn. The burning eyes looked out at Hodder curiously, as at a being upon whom the vials of wrath were somehow wasted, against whom the weapons of power were of no account. The fanatic had become a phenomenon which had momentarily stilled passion to arouse interest. . . . "Art thou a master of Israel, and knowest not these things?"

"Do you mean to say " — such was the question that sprang to Eldon Parr's lips — "that you take the Bible literally? What is your point of view? You speak about the salvation of souls, — I have heard that kind of talk all my life. And it is easy, I find, for men who have never known the responsibilities of wealth to criticize and advise. I regard indiscriminate giving as nothing less than a crime, and I have always tried to be painstaking and judicious. If I had taken the words you quoted at their face value, I should have no wealth to distribute to-day.

"I, too, Mr. Hodder, odd as it may seem to you, have had my dreams of doing my share of making this country the best place in the world to live in. It has pleased Providence to take away my son. He was not fitted to carry on my work, — that is the way with dreams. I was to have taught him to build up, and to give, as I have given. You think me embittered, hard, because I seek to do good, to interpret the Gospel in my own way. Before this year is out I shall have retired from all active business, and I intend to spend the rest of my life in giving away the money I have earned — all of it. I do not intend to spare myself, and giving will be harder than earning. I shall found institutions for research of disease, hospitals, playgrounds, libraries, and schools. And I shall make the university here one of the best in the country. What more, may I ask, would you have me do?"

"Ah," replied the rector, "it is not what I would have you do. It is not, indeed, a question of ' doing,' but of seeing."

"Of seeing?" the banker repeated. "As I say, of using judgment."

"Judgment, yes, but the judgment which has not yet dawned for you, the enlightenment which is the knowledge of God's will. Wordly wisdom is a rule of thumb many men may acquire, the other wisdom, the wisdom of the soul, is personal — the reward of revelation which springs from desire. You ask me what I think you should do. I will tell you — but you will not do it, you will be powerless to do it unless you see it for yourself, unless the time shall come when you are willing to give up everything you have held dear in life, — not your money, but your opinions, the very judgment and wisdom you value, until you have gained the faith which proclaims these worthless, until you are ready to receive the Kingdom of God as a little child. You are not ready, now. Your attitude, your very words, proclaim your blindness to all that has happened you, your determination to carry out, so far as it is left to you, your own will. You may die without seeing."

Crazy as it all sounded, a slight tremor shook Eldon Parr. There was something in the eyes, in the powerful features of the clergyman that kept him still, that made him listen with a fascination which — had he taken cognizance of it — was akin to fear. That this man believed it, that he would impress it upon others, nay, had already done so, the banker did not then doubt.

"You speak of giving," Hodder continued, "and you have nothing to give — nothing. You are poorer to-day than the humblest man who has seen God. But you have much, you have all to *restore*." Without raising his voice, the rector had contrived to put a mighty emphasis on the word. "You speak of the labour of giving, but if you seek your God and haply find him you will not rest night or day while you live until you have restored every dollar possible of that which you have wrongfully taken from others."

John Hodder rose and raised his arm in effective protest against the interruption Eldon Parr was about to make. He bore him down.

"I know what you are going to say, Mr. Parr, — that

it is not practical. That word 'practical' is the barrier
between you and your God. I tell you that God can make
anything practical. Your conscience, the spirit, tortures
you to-day, but you have not had enough torture, you still
think to escape easily, to keep the sympathy of a world
which despises you. You are afraid to do what God would
have you do. You have the opportunity, through grace,
by your example to leave the world better than you found
it, to do a thing of such magnitude as is given to few men,
to confess before all that your life has been blind and
wicked. That is what the Spirit is trying to teach you.
But you fear the ridicule of the other blind men, you have
not the faith to believe that many eyes would be opened
by your act. The very shame of such a confession, you
think, is not to be borne."

"Suppose I acknowledge, which I do not, your preposterous charge, how would you propose to do this
thing?"

"It is very simple," said the rector, "so far as the actual
method of procedure goes. You have only to establish a
board of men in whom you have confidence, — a court of
claims, so to speak, — to pass upon the validity of every
application, not from a business standpoint alone, but
from one of a broad justice and equity. And not only
that. I should have it an important part of the duties of
this board to discover for themselves other claimants who
may not, for various reasons, come forward. In the case
of the Consolidated Tractions, for instance, there are
doubtless many men like Garvin who invested their savings largely on the strength of your name. You cannot
bring him back to life, restore him to his family as he was
before you embittered him, but it would be a comparatively easy matter to return to his widow, with compound
interest, the sum which he invested."

"For the sake of argument," said Eldon Parr, "what
would you do with the innumerable impostors who would
overwhelm such a board with claims that they had bought
and sold stock at a loss? And that is only one case I
could mention."

"Would it be so dreadful a thing," asked Hodder, "to run the risk of making a few mistakes? It would not be business, you say. If you had the desire to do this, you would dismiss such an obsession from your brain, you would prefer to err on the side of justice and mercy. And no matter how able your board, in making restitution you could at best expect to mend only a fraction of the wrongs you have done."

"I shall waive, for the moment, my contention that the Consolidated Tractions Company, had it succeeded, would greatly have benefited the city. Even if it had been the iniquitous, piratical transaction you suggest, why should I assume the responsibility for all who were concerned in it?"

"If the grace were given you to do this, that question would answer itself," the rector replied. "The awful sense of responsibility, which you now lack, would overwhelm you."

"You have made me out a rascal and a charlatan," said Eldon Parr, "and I have listened patiently in my desire to be fair, to learn from your own lips whether there were anything in the extraordinary philosophy you have taken up, and which you are pleased to call Christianity. If you will permit me to be as frank as you have been, it appears to me as sheer nonsense and folly, and if it were put into practice the world would be reduced at once to chaos and anarchy."

"There is no danger, I am sorry to say, of its being put into practice at once," said Hodder, smiling sadly.

"I hope not," answered the banker, dryly. "Utopia is a dream in which those who do the rough work of the world cannot afford to indulge. And there is one more question. You will, no doubt, deride it as practical, but to my mind it is very much to the point. You condemn the business practices in which I have engaged all my life as utterly unchristian. If you are logical, you will admit that no man or woman who owns stock in a modern corporation is, according to your definition, Christian, and, to use your own phrase, can enter the Kingdom of God. I can tell you, as one who knows, that there is no corporation in this country which, in the struggle to maintain it self, is not forced to adopt the natural law of the survival of the fittest, which you condemn. Your own salary, while you had it, came from men who had made the money in corporations. Business is business, and admits of no sentimental considerations. If you can get around that fact, I will gladly bow to your genius. Should you succeed in reëstablishing St. John's on what you call a free basis — and in my opinion you will not — even then the money you would live on, and which supported the church, would be directly or indirectly derived from corporations."

" I do not propose to enter into an economic argument with you, Mr. Parr, but if you tell me that the flagrant practices indulged in by those who organized the Consolidated Tractions Company can be excused under any code of morals, any conception of Christianity, I tell you they cannot. What do we see to-day in your business world? Boards of directors, trusted by stockholders, betraying their trust, withholding information in order to profit thereby, buying and selling stock secretly; stock watering, selling to the public diluted values, — all kinds of iniquity and abuse of power which I need not go into. Do you mean to tell me, on the plea that business is business and hence a department by itself, that deception, cheating, and stealing are justified and necessary? The awakened conscience of the public is condemning you.

"The time is at hand, though neither you nor I may live to see it, when the public conscience itself is beginning to perceive this higher justice hidden from you. And you are attempting to mislead when you do not distinguish between the men who, for their own gain and power, mismanage such corporations as are mismanaged, and those who own stock and are misled.

" The public conscience of which I speak is the leaven of Christianity at work. And we must be content to work with it, to await its fulfilment, to realize that no one of us can change the world, but can only do his part in making it better. The least we can do is to refuse to indulge in practices which jeopardize our own souls, to

2 K

remain poor if we cannot make wealth honestly. Say what you will, the Christian government we are approaching will not recognize property, because it is gradually becoming clear that the holding of property delays the Kingdom at which you scoff, giving the man who owns it a power over the body of the man who does not. Property produces slavery, since it compels those who have none to work for those who have.

"The possession of property, or of sufficient property to give one individual an advantage over his fellows *is* inconsistent with Christianity. Hence it will be done away with, but only when enough have been emancipated to carry this into effect. Hence the saying of our Lord about the needle's eye — the danger to the soul of him who owns much property."

"And how about your Christian view of the world as a vale of tears?" Eldon Parr inquired.

"So long as humanity exists, there will always be tears," admitted the rector. "But it is a false Christianity which does not bid us work for our fellow-men, to relieve their suffering and make the world brighter. It is becoming clear that the way to do this effectively is through communities, coöperation, — through nations, and not individuals. And this, if you like, *is* practical, — so practical that the men like you, who have gained unexampled privilege, fear it more and more. The old Christian misconception, that the world is essentially a bad place, and which has served the ends of your privilege, is going by forever. And the motto of the citizens of the future will be the Christian motto, "I am my brother's keeper." The world is a good place because the Spirit is continually working in it, to make it better. And life is good, if only we take the right view of it, — the revealed view."

"What you say is all very fine," said Eldon Parr. "And I have heard it before, from the discontented, the socialists. But it does not take into account the one essential element, human nature."

"On the other hand, *your* scheme of life fails to reckon with the greater factor, divine nature," Hodder replied.

" When you have lived as long as I have, perhaps you
will think differently, Mr. Hodder." Eldon Parr's voice
had abruptly grown metallic, as though the full realization
had come over him of the severity of the clergyman's
arraignment; the audacity of the man who had ventured
to oppose him and momentarily defeated him, who had
won the allegiance of his own daughter, who had dared
condemn him as an evil-doer and give advice as to his
future course. He, Eldon Parr, who had been used to
settle the destinies of men! His anger was suddenly at
white heat; and his voice, which he strove to control, betrayed it.

" Since you have rejected my offer, which was made in
kindness, since you are bent on ruining my daughter's
life as well as your own, and she has disregarded my
wishes, I refuse to see either of you, no matter to what
straits you may come, as long as I live. That is understood. And she leaves this house to-day, never to enter
it again. It is useless to prolong this conversation, I
think."

" Quite useless, as I feared, Mr. Parr. Do you know
why Alison is willing to marry me? It is because the
strength has been given me to oppose you in the name of
humanity, and this in spite of the fact that her love for
you to-day is greater than it has ever been before. It is
a part of the heavy punishment you have inflicted on
yourself that you cannot believe in her purity. You insist on thinking that the time will come when she will
return to you for help. In senseless anger and pride you
are driving her away from you whom you will some day
need. And in that day, should God grant you a relenting
heart to make the sign, she will come to you, — but to
give comfort, not to receive it. And even as you have
threatened me, I will warn you, yet not in anger. Except
a man be born again, he cannot see the Kingdom of God,
nor understand the motives of those who would enter into
it. Seek and pray for repentance."

Infuriated though he was, before the commanding yet
compassionate bearing of the rector he remained speech-

less. And after a moment's pause, Hodder turned and left the room. . . .

III

When Hodder had reached the foot of the stairs, Alison came out to him. The mourning she wore made her seem even taller. In the face upturned to his, framed in the black veil and paler than he had known it, were traces of tears; in the eyes a sad, yet questioning and trustful smile. They gazed at each other an instant, before speaking, in the luminous ecstasy of perfect communion which shone for them, undimmed, in the surrounding gloom of tragedy. And thus, they felt, it would always shine. Of that tragedy of the world's sin and sorrow they would ever be conscious. Without darkness there could be no light.

"I knew," she said, reading his tidings, "it would be of no use. Tell me the worst."

"If you marry me, Alison, your father refuses to see you again. He insists that you leave the house."

"Then why did he wish to see you?"

"It was to make an appeal. He thinks, of course, that I have made a failure of life, and that if I marry you I shall drag you down to poverty and disgrace."

She raised her head, proudly.

"But he knows that it is I who insist upon marrying you! I explained it all to him — how I had asked you. Of course he did not understand. He thinks, I suppose, that it is simply an infatuation."

In spite of the solemnity of the moment, Hodder smiled down at her, touched by the confession.

"That, my dear, doesn't relieve me of responsibility. I am just as responsible as though I had spoken first, instead of you."

"But, John, you didn't —— ?" A sudden fear made her silent.

He took her hand and pressed it reassuringly.

"Give you up? No, Alison," he answered simply. "When you came to me, God put you in my keeping."

She clung to him suddenly, in a passion of relief.

"Oh, I never could give you up, I never would unless you yourself told me to. Then I would do it, — for you. But you won't ask me, now?"

He put his arm around her shoulders, and the strength of it seemed to calm her.

"No, dear. I would make the sacrifice, ask you to make it, if it would be of any good. As you say, he does not understand. And you couldn't go on living with him and loving me. That solution is impossible. We can only hope that the time will come when he will realize his need of you, and send for you."

"And did he not ask you anything more?"

Hodder hesitated. He had intended to spare her that. . . . Her divination startled him.

"I know, I know without your telling me. He offered you money, he consented to our marriage if you would give up St. John's. Oh, how could he!" she cried. "How could he so misjudge and insult you!"

"It is not me he misjudges, Alison, it is mankind, — it is God. That is his terrible misfortune." Hodder released her tenderly. "You must see him — you must tell him that when he needs you, you will come."

"I will see him now," she said. "You will wait for me?"

"Now?" he repeated, taken aback by her resolution, though it was characteristic.

"Yes, I will go as I am. I can send for my things. My father has given me no choice, no reprieve, — not that I wish one. I have you, dear. I will stay with Mr. Bentley to-night, and leave for New York to-morrow, to do what I have to do — and then you will be ready for me."

"Yes," he said, "I shall be ready."

He lingered in the well-remembered hall. . . . And when at last she came down again her eyes shone bravely through her tears, her look answered the question of his own. There was no need for speech. With not so much as a look behind she left, with him, her father's house.

Outside, the mist had become a drizzle, and as they went down the walk together beside the driveway she slipped her arm into his, pressing close to his side. Her intuition was perfect, the courage of her love sublime.

"I have you, dear," she whispered, "never in my life before have I been rich."

"Alison!"

It was all he could say, but the intensity of his mingled feeling went into the syllables of her name. An impulse made them pause and turn, and they stood looking back together at the great house which loomed the greater in the thickening darkness, its windows edged with glow. Never, as in this moment when the cold rain wet their faces, had the thought of its comfort and warmth and luxury struck him so vividly; yes, and of its terror and loneliness now, of the tortured spirit in it that found no rest.

"Oh, John," she cried, "if we only could!"

He understood her. Such was the perfect quality of their sympathy that she had voiced his thought. What were rain and cold, the inclemency of the elements to them? What the beauty and the warmth of those great, empty rooms to Eldon Parr? Out of the heaven of their happiness they looked down, helpless, into the horrors of the luxury of hell.

"It must be," he answered her, "in God's good time."

"Life is terrible!" she said. "Think of what he must have done to suffer so, to be condemned to *this!* And when I went to him, just now, he wouldn't even kiss me good-by. Oh, my dear, if I hadn't had you to take me, what should I have done? . . . It never was a home to me — to any of us. And as I look back now, all the troubles began when we moved into it. I can only think of it as a huge prison, all the more sinister for its cost-liness."

A prison! It had once been his own conceit. He drew her gently away, and they walked together along Park Street towards the distant arc-light at the corner which flung a gleaming band along the wet pavement.

"Perhaps it was because I was too young to know what trouble was when we lived in Ransome Street," she continued. "But I can remember now how sad my mother was at times — it almost seemed as though she had a premonition." Alison's voice caught. . . .

The car which came roaring through the darkness, and which stopped protestingly at their corner, was ablaze with electricity, almost filled with passengers. A young man with a bundle changed his place in order that they might sit together in one of the little benches bordering the aisle; opposite them was a laughing, clay-soiled group of labourers going home from work; in front, a young couple with a chubby child. He stood between his parents, facing about, gazing in unembarrassed wonder at the dark lady with the veil. Alison's smile seemed only to increase the solemnity of his adoration, and presently he attempted to climb over the barrier between them. Hodder caught him, and the mother turned in alarm, recapturing him.

"You mustn't bother the lady, Jimmy," she said, when she had thanked the rector. She had dimpled cheeks and sparkling blue eyes, but their expression changed as they fell on Alison's face, expressing something of the wonder of the child's.

"Oh, he isn't bothering me," Alison protested. "Do let him stand."

"He don't make up to everybody," explained the mother, and the manner of her speech was such a frank tribute that Alison flushed. There had been, too, in the look the quick sympathy for bereavement of the poor.

"Aren't they nice?" Alison leaned over and whispered to Hodder, when the woman had turned back. "One thing, at least, I shall never regret, — that I shall have to ride the rest of my life in the street cars. I love them. That is probably my only qualification, dear, for a clergyman's wife."

Hodder laughed. "It strikes me," he said, "as the supreme one."

They came at length to Mr. Bentley's door, flung open

in its usual wide hospitality by Sam. Whatever their fortunes, they would always be welcome here. . . . But it turned out, in answer to their question, that their friend was not at home.

"No, sah," said Sam, bowing and smiling benignantly, "but he done tole me to say, when you and Miss Alison come, hit was to make no diffunce, dat you bofe was to have supper heah. And I'se done cooked it — yassah. Will you kindly step into the liba'y, suh, and Miss Alison? Dar was a lady 'crost de city, Marse Ho'ace said — yassah."

"John," said Alison with a questioning smile, when they were alone before the fire, "I believe he went out on purpose, — don't you? — just that we might be here alone."

"He knew we were coming?"

"I wrote him."

"I think he might be convicted on the evidence," Hodder agreed. "But — ?" His question remained unasked.

Alison went up to him. He had watched her, absorbed and fascinated, as with her round arms gracefully lifted in front of the old mirror she had taken off her hat and veil ; smoothing, by a few deft touches, the dark crown of her hair. The unwonted intimacy of the moment, invoking as it did an endless reflection of other similar moments in their future life together, was in its effect overwhelming, bringing with it at last a conviction not to be denied. Her colour rose as she faced him, her lashes fell.

"Did you seriously think, dear, that we could have deceived Mr. Bentley? Then you are not as clever as I thought you. As soon as it happened I sent him a note — that very night. For I felt that he ought to be told first of all."

"And as usual," Hodder answered, "you were right."

Supper was but a continuation of that delicious sense of intimacy. And Sam, beaming in his starched shirt and swallow-tail, had an air of presiding over a banquet of state. And for that matter, none had ever gone away hungry from this table, either for meat or love. It was, indeed, a consecrated meal, — consecrated for being just there. Such was the tact which the old darky had acquired

from his master that he left the dishes on the shining mahogany board, and bowed himself out.

"When you wants me, Miss Alison, des ring de
bell."

She was seated, upright yet charmingly graceful, behind
the old English coffee service which had been Mr. Bentley's
mother's. And it was she who, by her wonderful self-possession, by the reassuring smile she gave him as she handed
him his cup, endowed it all with reality.

"It's strange," she said, "but it seems as though I had
been doing it all my life, instead of just beginning."

"And you do it as though you had," he declared.

"Which is a proof," she replied, "of the superior
adaptability of women."

He did not deny it. He would not then, in truth, have
disputed her wildest statement. . . . But presently, after
they had gone back into the library and were seated side
by side before the coals, they spoke again of serious things,
marvelling once more at a happiness which could be tinged
and yet unmarred by vicarious sorrow. Theirs was the
soberer, profounder happiness of gratitude and wonder,
too wise to exult, but which of itself is exalted; the
happiness which praises, and passes understanding.

"There are many things I want to say to you, John,"
she told him, once, "and they trouble me a little. It is
only because I am so utterly devoted to you that I wish you
to know me as I am. I have always had queer views, and
although much has happened to change me since I have
known and loved you, I am not quite sure how much those
views have changed. Love," she added, "plays such havoc
with one's opinions."

She returned his smile, but with knitted brows.

"It's really serious—you needn't laugh. And it's only
fair to you to let you know the kind of a wife you are
getting, before it is too late. For instance, I believe in
divorce, although I can't imagine it for us. One never
can, I suppose, in *this* condition—that's the trouble. I
have seen so many immoral marriages that I can't think
God intends people to live degraded. And I'm sick

and tired of the argument that an indissoluble marriage under all conditions is good for society. That a man or woman, the units of society, should violate the divine in themselves for the sake of society is absurd. They are merely setting an example to their children to do the same thing, which means that society in that respect will never get any better. In this love that has come to us we have achieved an ideal which I have never thought to reach. Oh, John, I'm sure you won't misunderstand me when I say that I would rather die than have to lower it."

"No," he answered, "I shall not misunderstand you."

"Even though it is so difficult to put into words what I mean. I don't feel that *we* really need the marriage service, since God has already joined us together. And it is not through our own wills, somehow, but through his. Divorce would not only be a crime against the spirit, it would be an impossibility while we feel as we do. But if love should cease, then God himself would have divorced us, punished us by taking away a priceless gift of which we were not worthy. He would have shut the gates of Eden in our faces because we had sinned against the Spirit. It would be quite as true to say ' whom God has put asunder no man may join together.' Am I hurting you ? "

Her hand was on the arm of his chair, and the act of laying his own on it was an assurance stronger than words. Alison sighed.

" Yes, I believed you would understand, even though I expressed myself badly, — that you would help me, that you have found a solution. I used to regard the marriage service as a compromise, as a lowering of the ideal, as something mechanical and rational put in the place of the spiritual ; that it was making the Church, and therefore God, conform to the human notion of what the welfare of society ought to be. And it is absurd to promise to love. We have no control over our affections. They are in God's hands, to grant or withdraw.

"And yet I am sure — this is new since I have known you — that if such a great love as ours be withdrawn it would be an unpardonable wrong for either of us to marry

again. That is what puzzles me — confounds the wisdom
I used to have, and which in my littleness and pride I
thought so sufficient. I didn't believe in God, but now I
feel him, through you, though I cannot define him. And
one of many reasons why I could not believe in Christ was
because I took it for granted that he taught, among other
things, a continuation of the marriage relation after love
had ceased to justify it."

Hodder did not immediately reply. Nor did Alison interrupt his silence, but sat with the stillness which at times
so marked her personality, her eyes trustfully fixed on him.
The current pulsing between them was unbroken. . . .
Hodder's own look, as he gazed into the grate, was that
of a seer.

"Yes," he said at length, "it is by the spirit and not the
letter of our Lord's teaching that we are guided. The
Spirit which we draw from the Gospels. And everything
written down there that does not harmonize with it is the
mistaken interpretation of men. Once the Spirit possesses
us truly, we are no longer troubled and confused by texts.

"The alpha and omega of Christ's message is rebirth
into the knowledge of that Spirit, and hence submission
to its guidance. And that is what Paul meant when he
said that it freed us from the law. You are right, Alison,
when you declare it to be a violation of the Spirit for a
man and woman to live together when love does not exist.
Christ shows us that laws were made for those who are
not reborn. Laws are the rules of society, to be followed
by those who have not found the inner guidance, who live
and die in the flesh. But the path which those who live
under the control of the Spirit are to take is opened up to
them as they journey. If all men and women were reborn
we should have the paradox, which only the reborn can
understand, of what is best for the individual being best
for society, because under the will of the Spirit none can
transgress upon the rights and happiness of others. The
Spirit would make the laws and rules superfluous.

"And the great crime of the Church, for which she is
paying so heavy an expiation, is that her faith wavered,

and she forsook the Spirit and resumed the law her Master had condemned. She no longer insisted on that which Christ proclaimed as imperative, rebirth. She became, as you say, a mechanical organization, substituting, as the Jews had done, hard and fast rules for inspiration. She abandoned the Communion of Saints, sold her birthright for a mess of pottage, for worldly, temporal power when she declared that inspiration had ceased with the Apostles, when she failed to see that inspiration is *personal*, and comes through rebirth. For the sake of increasing her membership, of dominating the affairs of men, she has permitted millions who lived in the law and the flesh, who persisted in forcing men to live by the conventions and customs Christ repudiated, and so stultify themselves, to act in Christ's name. The unpardonable sin against the Spirit is to doubt its workings, to maintain that society will be ruined if it be substituted for the rules and regulations supposed to make for the material comforts of the nations, but which in reality suppress and enslave the weak.

"Nevertheless in spite of the Church, marvellously *through* the Church the germ of our Lord's message has come down to us, and the age in which we live is beginning to realize its purport, to condemn the Church for her subservient rationalism.

"Let us apply the rule of the Spirit to marriage. If we examine the ideal we shall see clearly that the marriage-service is but a symbol. Like baptism, it is a worthless and meaningless rite unless the man and the woman have been born again into the Spirit, released from the law. If they are still, as St. Paul would say, in the flesh, let them have, if they wish, a civil permit to live together, for the Spirit can have nothing to do with such an union. True to herself, the Church symbolizes the union of *her members*, the reborn. She has nothing to do with laws and conventions which are supposedly for the good of society, nor is any union accomplished if those whom she supposedly joins are not reborn. If they are, the Church can neither make it or dissolve it, but merely confirm and acknowledge the work of the Spirit. And every work of the Spirit is a sacrament. Not baptism and communion and marriage only, but every act of life."

"Oh, John," she exclaimed, her eyes lighting, "I can believe that! How beautiful a thought! I see now what is meant when it is said that man shall not live by bread alone, but by every word that proceedeth out of the mouth of God. That is the hourly guidance which is independent of the law. And how terrible to think that all the spiritual beauty of such a religion should have been hardened into chapter and verse and regulation. You have put into language what I think of Mr. Bentley,— that *his* acts are sacraments. . . . It is so simple when you explain it this way. And yet I can see why it was said, too, that we must become as children to understand it."

"The difficult thing," replied Hodder, gravely, "is to retain it, to hold it after we have understood it — even after we have experienced it. To continue to live in the Spirit demands all our effort, all our courage and patience and faith. We cannot, as you say, promise to love for life. But the marriage service, interpreted, means that we will use all our human endeavour, with the help of the Spirit, to remain in what may be called the reborn state, since it is by the Spirit alone that true marriage is sanctified. When the Spirit is withdrawn, man and woman are indeed divorced.

"The words 'a sense of duty' belong to moral philosophy and not to religion. Love annuls them. I do not mean to decry them, but the reborn are lifted far above them by the subversion of the will by which our will is submitted to God's. It is so we develop, and become, as it were, God. And hence those who are not married in the Spirit are not spiritually man and wife. No consecration has taken place, Church or no Church. If rebirth occurs later, to either or both, the individual conscience — which is the Spirit, must decide whether, as regards each other, they are bound or free, and we must stand or fall by that. Men object that this is opening the door to individualism. What they fail to see is that the door *is* open, wide, to-day, and can never again be closed: that the law of the naturally born is losing its power, that the worn-out authority of the Church is being set at naught because that authority was devised by man to keep in check those who were not reborn. The only check to material individualism is *spiritual* individualism, and the reborn man or woman *cannot* act to the detriment of his fellow-creatures."

In her turn she was silent, still gazing at him, her breath coming deeply, for she was greatly moved.

"Yes," she said simply, "I can see now why divorce between us would be a sacrilege. I *felt* it, John, but I couldn't reason it out. It is the consecration of the Spirit that justifies the union of the flesh. For the Spirit, in that sense, does not deny the flesh."

"That would be to deny life," Hodder replied.

"I see. Why was it all so hidden!" The exclamation was not addressed to him — she was staring pensively into the fire. But presently, with a swift movement, she turned to him.

"You will preach this, John, — all of it!"

It was not a question, but the cry of a new and wider vision of his task. Her face was transfigured. And her voice, low and vibrating, expressed no doubts. "Oh, I am proud of you! And if they put you out and persecute you I shall always be proud, I shall never know why it was given me to have this, and to live. Do you remember saying to me once that faith comes to us in some human form we love? You are my faith. And faith in you is my faith in humanity, and faith in God."

Ere he could speak of his own faith in her, in mankind, by grace of which he had been lifted from the abyss, there came a knock at the door. And even as they answered it a deeper knowledge filtered into their hearts.

Horace Bentley stood before them. And the light from his face, that shone down upon them, was their benediction.

AFTERWORD

ALTHOUGH these pages have been published serially, it is with a feeling of reluctance that I send them out into the world, for better or worse, between the covers of a book. They have been written with reverence, and the reading of the proofs has brought back to me vividly the long winters in which I pondered over the matter they contain, and wrote and rewrote the chapters.

I had not thought to add anything to them by way of an afterword. Nothing could be farther from my mind than to pose as a theologian; and, were it not for one or two of the letters I have received, I should have supposed that no reader could have thought of making the accusation that I presumed to speak for any one except myself. In a book of this kind, the setting forth of a personal view of religion is not only unavoidable, but necessary; since, if I wrote sincerely, Mr. Hodder's solution must coincide with my own — *so far as I have been able to work one out*. Such as it is, it represents many years of experience and reflection. And I can only crave the leniency of any trained theologian who may happen to peruse it.

No one realizes, perhaps, the incompleteness of the religious interpretations here presented more keenly than I. More significant, more vital elements of the truth are the rewards of a mind which searches and craves, especially in these days when the fruit of so many able minds lies on the shelves of library and bookshop. Since the last chapter was written, many suggestions have come to me which I should like to have the time to develop for this volume. But the nature of these elements is positive, — I can think of nothing I should care to subtract.

Here, then, so far as what may be called religious doc-

trine is concerned, is merely a personal solution. We are
in an age when the truth is being worked out through
many minds, a process which seems to me both Christian
and Democratic. Yet a gentleman has so far misunderstood this that he has already accused me, in a newspaper,
of committing all the heresies condemned by the Council
of Chalcedon, — and more !

I have no doubt that he is right. My consolation must
be that I have as company — in some of my heresies, at
least — a goodly array of gentlemen who wear the cloth
of the orthodox churches whose doctrines he accuses me
of denying. The published writings of these clergymen are accessible to all. The same critic declares that my
interpretations are without "authority." This depends,
of course, on one's view of "authority." But his accusation
is true equally against many men who — if my observation
be correct — are doing an incalculable service for religion
by giving to the world their own personal solutions, in-
terpreting Christianity in terms of modern thought. No
doubt these, too, are offending the champions of the
Council of Chalcedon.

And does the gentleman, may I ask, ever read the pages
of the Hibbert Journal?

Finally, I have to meet a more serious charge, that Mr.
Hodder remains in the Church because of "the dread
of parting with the old, strong anchorage, the fear of
anathema and criticism, the thought of sorrowing and dis-
approving friends." Or perhaps he infers that it is I
who keep Mr. Hodder in the Church for these personal
reasons. Alas, the concern of society is now for those
upon whom the Church has lost her hold, who are seeking
for a solution they can accept. And the danger to-day
is not from the side of heresy. The rector of St. John's,
as a result of his struggle, gained what I believe to be a
higher and surer faith than that which he formerly held,
and in addition to this the realization of the presence of a
condition which was paralyzing the Church's influence.

One thing I had hoped to make clear, that if Mr.
Hodder had left the Church under these circumstances, he

would have made the Great Refusal. The situation which he faced demanded something of the sublime courage of his Master.

Lastly, may I be permitted to add that it is far from my intention to reflect upon any particular denomination. The instance which I have taken is perhaps a pronounced rather than a particular case of the problem to which I have referred, and which is causing the gravest concern to thoughtful clergymen and laymen of all denominations.

WINSTON CHURCHILL.

SANTA BARBARA, CALIFORNIA,
March 31, 1913.